Timber

Northwest Reprints

Northwest Reprints
Series Editor: Robert J. Frank

Other titles in the series:

Nehalem Tillamook Tales
  told by Clara Pearson
  collected by Elizabeth Jacobs
  Introduction by Jarold Ramsey

Oregon Detour
  by Nard Jones
  Introduction by George Venn

The Viewless Winds
  by Murray Morgan
  Introduction by Harold Simonson

Tall Tales from Rogue River
  The Yarns of Hathaway Jones
  Edited by Stephen Dow Beckham

The Land is Bright
  by Archie Binns
  Introduction by Ann Ronald

Beyond the Garden Gate
  by Sophus K. Winter
  Introduction by Barbara Meldrum

Happy Valley
  by Anne Shannon Monroe
  Introduction by Karen Blair

Botanical Exploration of the Trans-Mississippi West
  by Susan Delano McKelvey
  Introduction by Stephen Dow Beckham

Timber

Roderick Haig-Brown

Introduction by Glen A. Love

**Oregon State University Press
Corvallis, Oregon**

The paper in this book meets the guidelines for permanence and durability of the Committee on Production Guidelines for Book Longevity of the Council on Library Resources and the minimum requirements of the American National Standard for Permanence of Paper for Printed Library Materials Z39.48-1984.

Library of Congress Cataloging-in-Publication Data

Haig-Brown, Roderick Langmere, 1908-1976.
  Timber / Roderick Haig-Brown ; introduction by Glen A. Love.
    p. ; cm. -- (Northwest reprints)
    Includes bibliographical references (p.).
    ISBN 0-87071-514-3 (alk. paper). -- ISBN 0-87071-515-1 (pbk. alk. paper)
    1. Forest products industry--Northwest, Pacific--Fiction. 2. Trade-unions--Loggers--Northwest, Pacific--Fiction. 3. Loggers--Northwest, Pacific--Fiction. I. Title. II. Series.
    PR9199.3.H29T55 1993
    813'.52--dc20   93-6737
                                                    CIP

Introduction © 1993 Glen A. Love
 All rights reserved
Printed in the United States of America

PREFACE

but there were things
That covered what a man was, and set him apart
From others, things by which others knew him. The place
Where he lived, the horse he rode, his relatives, his wife,
His voice, complexion, beard, politics, religion or lack of it,
And so on. With time, these things fall away
Or dwindle into shadows: river sand blowing away
From some long-buried old structure of bleached boards
That appears a vague shadow through the sand-haze,
   and then stands clear,
Naked, angular, itself.
        from "Trial and Error," H.L. Davis

People new to a region are especially interested in what things might set them apart from others. In works by Northwest writers, we get to know about the place where we live, about each other, about our history and culture, and about our flora and fauna. And with time, some things about ourselves start to come into focus out of the shadows of our history.

To give readers an opportunity to look into the place where Northwesterners live, the Oregon State University Press is making available again many books that are out of print. The Northwest Reprints Series will reissue a range of books, both fiction and nonfiction. Books will be selected for different reasons: some for their literary merit, some for their historical significance, some for provocative concerns, and some for these and other reasons together. Foremost, however, will be the book's potential to interest a range of readers who are curious about the region's voice and complexion. The Northwest Reprints Series will make works of well-known and lesser-known writers available for all.

RJF

*Roderick Haig-Brown
1927*

Introduction

To many readers of nature writing and angling literature, mention of author Roderick Haig-Brown of Campbell River, British Columbia, conjures images of a master of the wilds, a Prospero of the rivers, lakes, and forests of his Vancouver Island homeland. I can recall, as a boy in the years during and after World War II, my first encounter with a Haig-Brown book. It was called *A River Never Sleeps*, and it stirred in me, a city kid from the low-rent environs of Seattle with few opportunities for wilderness retreats, a deepfelt response to the woods and waters of the Pacific Northwest.

For the first time, I felt the strong pull of adventurous life in my country's wilderness. I loved to fish, but was usually limited to nearby urban Green Lake, or to the creeks north of Seattle within bicycle range. *A River Never Sleeps* seemed to open up dramatic possibilities. More than that, I got from Haig-Brown's writing a sense of a tradition, a code of behavior—originating, I realize now, in the English sporting tradition of the fields and streams of the author's youth—which offered me a guide to right conduct in nature. With no family or community models of my own to follow in such matters, I fastened lovingly upon this sage from the North. A Canadian, to be sure, but we always assumed in Seattle that Canadians were "just like us." And here was one, only 300 miles, as the gull flies, from my home who lived a life such as I dreamed of, and who wrote with such beauty and grace about the wild Northwest country that it made me ache with desire to be a part of it all.

Later, with more Haig-Brown books under my belt, like *Return to the River, Fisherman's Spring,* and *Fisherman's Winter,* I gave up forever fishing with worms. I followed the Thoreau of angling into the priestly mysteries of fishing the artificial fly. With Haig-Brown as guide and mentor, I began to think about the necessity for conserving our Northwest resources, for releasing fish unharmed instead of killing them, for considering the future and helping to check the headlong assault upon the Northwest environment by the forces of greed and "development."

My admiration for Roderick Haig-Brown and his work even led me, as a teenager, to inveigle my mother and step-father into a car trip north to Vancouver Island and Campbell River. I argued that it was beautiful country, and so it was, but my secret motivation was to track the shadowy Nimrod of the North to his Campbell River home. I knew where he lived from his wonderful description of it and his family in *Measure of the Year.* Once there, I planned to present myself for his inspection and approval. Maybe he would even offer to take me fishing in the mythical river that ran by his door. Maybe!

After coaxing my parents across to Vancouver Island and ever-north, we at last reached the town of Campbell River. Here, sadly, youthful embarrassment and a sense of inadequacy settled upon me. My resolve to meet the Great Spirit withered within. Instead, I poked unhappily about the village and waterfront while my parents wondered rather pointedly why the hell we had driven all the way up there. I remember that we confronted our frustrations with one another—as we often did in those days—with a fierce game of three-handed pinochle that night in our rented tourist-cabin. The next morning we started back to Seattle. End of pilgrimage.

Though I know now that it is best to leave writers alone to write, rather than pester them with unwanted attention, I'm very sorry not to have met Roderick Haig-Brown. Especially after hearing from one of my colleagues that he once had happened to bumble along the Campbell River, right through the Master's place, without even knowing who he was, and was nevertheless warmly received! There is no justice. I regret not having the memory of what I imagine would have been his firm handshake and his friendly but measuring glance. I continue to search his many books for such evidence of him as I was never to find in person. In contacting two of his children, Valerie and Alan, upon whom I have relied for some of the biographical and bibliographical details in what follows, I have had a kind of second chance, a surrogate completion of a youthful wish. I am grateful to them for that, as well as for the information which they have provided.

*   *   *

Roderick Haig-Brown was born in Lancing, Sussex, England, in 1908 and raised in Dorset, in the country of Thomas Hardy. His father, a teacher, outdoorsman, and writer, served in the army during World War I, and was killed in 1918 in the last big German offensive. His mother, an understanding woman, saw that her young son grew up with a chance to find himself, despite the pressures of a well-meaning but large and imposing family, on both her own and her husband's side, whose members had strong ideas as to what was best for a fatherless boy. Rebellious in school, young Haig-Brown was expelled from the notable Charterhouse School, where his paternal grandfather had been headmaster.

In 1926, at age eighteen and anxious to explore a new country, he came to the Pacific Northwest where, with an entry into the woods provided by a relative, he went to work as a scaler and timber surveyor in a logging camp near Mt. Vernon, in the state of Washington. He worked there for a short while, until his U. S. visa expired. Attracted by the nearby wild country of Canada, he moved north to another logging operation in the remote Nimpkish River country of upper Vancouver Island. After each of his hard days in the woods, he kept a diary and worked on articles applying the traditions and lore of English field and stream, which he had learned from his father and his uncles back in England, to the rugged wilderness country of the Nimpkish. The articles he sent back to English sporting magazines, where they were often accepted. He returned to England in 1930 and 1931, where his first book, *Silver: The Life Story of an Atlantic Salmon*, was published in 1931. Living in London, struggling for a start as a writer, he found himself homesick for the Pacific Coast:

> *It was by no means a dull time, as I scratched for an uncertain living with newspapers and magazines, scrambled through love affairs, published my first book, and wrote a good part of the second one. But the rivers were tame and tiny, there were no mountains, not even a rock bluff; there were no mauve and purple twilights with trolling lines cutting the*

*rippled water. The people were set in their ways
and their places, unchanging, and I, though native-
born, was a stranger.
I think I knew then that I was Canadian, that I might
go elsewhere but my heart would settle for nowhere else. There was nothing I wanted to write of
except Canada, the part of Canada I knew, and
nothing that I wanted to know so much more of*
(*Writings and Reflections* (hereinafter abbreviated
as *Writings*), "Coastscape" [1973],15-16).

He returned to Vancouver Island in 1932, committed to spending his life as a writer in the Pacific
Northwest. He married Ann Elmore of Seattle in 1934
and they went to live on the banks of Campbell River,
eventually settling in the house, "Above Tide," where
they raised four children and where Haig-Brown
wrote the books which have made his name known,
including *The Western Angler* (1939), *Return to the
River* (1941), *A River Never Sleeps* (1946), *Measure of
the Year* (1950), and *Fisherman's Spring* (1951).
During World War II he served in the Canadian Army.
He also was the local judge of the provincial court in
Campbell River for over thirty years. In his later life,
until his death in 1976, he was a leading advocate for
conservation in British Columbia. His final writings,
including *The Living Land* (1961), *Fisherman's Fall*
(1964), *The Salmon* (1974), *Bright Waters, Bright Fish*
(1980), and the posthumous collections *The Master
and His Fish* (1981), and *Writings and Reflections*
(1982), are evidence of his increasing concern for the
future of his country.

The author of 28 books, recipient of many
honors for his work, Roderick Haig-Brown is not well-

known as a writer of fiction. Though he wrote two novels for adults, *Timber* (1942) and *On the Highest Hill* (1949), and several highly regarded books of fiction for younger readers, he is best remembered as a writer of books about nature, especially fly-fishing. For all his early success as a nature writer, though, Haig-Brown saw the novel as an important and necessary step in his development as a writer. For, as he often said, he was a writer who happened to fish, not a fisherman who happened to write. Writing a successful novel was a challenge which he faced with some eagerness and anticipation as he approached the middle stage of his career. As he looked back upon his early writings in 1939, just before he wrote *Timber*, he said,

> *My first book was published in 1931, and I have called myself a writer ever since. I like the practice of the profession as well as I had liked the idea of it and I have always taken the job seriously—perhaps too seriously for my own financial good. But now, after four books and ten years of self-training, I feel that I am ready to produce what I have always wanted to—good solid fiction about human beings. The way to this has been through the things I knew and felt fit to handle—birds, fish, animals, and the open country of British Columbia. My upbringing did at least make me a good fly-fisherman, a keen and accurate observer, and an admirer of decent writing. If I have broken away far enough to find a sympathetic understanding of people, I have also followed the original direction to the point of becoming a tolerably good amateur biologist* (*Writings*, "If Armageddon's On" [1939], 94).

*   *   *

No one today, I think, would entitle a novel *Timber*, unless it were perhaps subsidized by a trade association of mill-owners. But in the time when Haig-Brown was conceiving his first long work of fiction, the word "timber" encompassed several meanings and associations that were favorable to him and his audience, and that he believed he could handle successfully in a novel. As he was to define the word in a glossary of logging terms at the end of the book,

> *"Timber!" is the traditional warning cry of fallers from coast to coast. Without the exclamation point the statement is somewhat calmer, but rather more comprehensive. Timber is the logger's word for standing trees, the untouched resource. Finally it is the word of the sawmill men for their most spectacular product—the great squared "timbers" cut for bridge and other construction purposes. I believe a Washington mill once squared out a Douglas fir timber 6 feet by 6 feet and 175 feet long* (Timber, 409).

The timber industry seemed to Haig-Brown, as he thought about it, an inevitable choice for his first novel. First of all, he knew the woods well from his early experiences in the logging camps. He had been a part of all phases of the work—cruising, surveying, falling, bucking, scaling, rigging, working in the mills—and his son Alan recalls that men who had worked with his father in the woods, men perhaps not familiar with his literary reputation, later remembered him above everything else as "a good logger." As Roderick Haig-Brown himself recalled his early days in the logging camps, "My friends were realists to a man; they begged me to tell the truth, all the truth, not as poets and writers and film directors see it, but as they themselves saw it—the daily truth of hard work and danger, of great trees falling and great machines thundering, of molly hogans and buckle guys and long-splices" (*Writings*, "The Writer in Isolation" [1959], 60).

Second, in writing *Timber* he would be working with the kinds of characters that he felt he knew well, while he honed his skills in dealing with people in his writing. On this point, Haig-Brown was sensitive to the criticism that his literary talents lay in description, in recreating natural settings and action, rather than in creating believable characters. He was determined to remedy this. A novel about loggers offered him ample opportunity to use his powers of description, while it also allowed him to concentrate upon the lives of people he liked and understood.

Third, he believed that no one had as yet discovered the logger as serious literary material. The North American logger had come into being in the forest of the Northeast nearly three hundred years earlier. Loggers had followed the westward movement of empire in ensuing centuries, cutting their way through the big woods of the Penobscot in Maine, through the white pine forests of the Great Lakes country, to the mountains of the Pacific Northwest, covered with apparently endless forest of Douglas-fir, "thick as hair on the back of a dog," as an old logger ballad put it. And yet, the logger had not been the subject of books. He appears occasionally, to be sure, but in a lesser role, as for example Billy Kirby, the indefatigable chopper who lays the woods low in

James Fenimore Cooper's *The Pioneers* (1823), or as a formidable force, but less interesting than the Indian, in Thoreau's *The Maine Woods* (1864), or as the pair of shadowy bums who undercut the narrator's pleasure at his own wood-splitting in Robert Frost's "Two Tramps in Mud Time" (1936). In folklore, the logger had been given popular currency by the Paul Bunyan stories, later appropriated for literary purposes by Northwesterner James Stevens in his *Paul Bunyan* (1925) and *The Saginaw Paul Bunyan* (1932).

Lamenting the absence of serious interest in the logger in print, Stewart Holbrook begins his book on the American lumberjack,

> *There has been a plenty of books about pioneers in the United States. Explorers have been the subject of much fact and fiction; so have the trappers, traders, and missionaries to the Red Men. Enough to fill a large library has been written about cowboys, Indian fighters, railroad builders, and the men and women of the covered wagon. If there has been a serious book about the American logger it has escaped my notice, and I have been looking for a long time* (Holy Old Mackinaw, ix).

When Holbrook wrote this in 1938, the American logger had indeed been ignored in serious literature, with the exception of such books by James Stevens as *Brawnyman* (1926) and *Homer in the Sagebrush* (1928). The complaint has been most memorably answered in more recent times by Ken Kesey's *Sometimes a Great Notion* (1964). The same absence of books on the Canadian logger, up to the time of *Timber*, could be cited, though one little-known but admirable exception should be mentioned,

M. Allerdale Grainger's *Woodsmen of the West* (1908), an excellent autobiographical account of life in the early logging camps north of Vancouver.

When *Timber* appeared in 1942, Holbrook wrote an appreciative review of it, concluding that writers of fiction about the woods, with the exception of Haig-Brown and Stevens, had romanticized it to the point

Haig-Brown, 1927

of absurdity. *Timber*, Holbrook claimed, was "written by a man who not only knows loggers at first hand, having been one, but who has been scrupulously careful to keep his characters and his scene always in character. . . . His donkey-punchers and chokermen and buckers and punks are authentic, convincing. Their everyday talk has the ring of the bunkhouse, the high-lead side, and of the 'skidroad' of the town" ("Stewart Holbrook Reviews 'Timber'"). That all of this would appeal to readers, most of whom would be from the towns and not the woods, must have been something of a gamble for a writer like Haig-Brown, but one that he was eager to take.

A fourth reason why Haig-Brown wanted to write a novel about life and work in the woods was that the struggle over unionization of loggers was a matter of great interest to him. And this struggle linked his subject to the sweeping radical social movements of the time, deepened by the effects of the Great Depression of the 1930s and explored in such powerful novels of radical class conflict as John Steinbeck's *In Dubious Battle* (1936) and *The Grapes of Wrath* (1939). At the time that he was writing *Timber*, Haig-Brown assessed his own political predispositions:

> *I suppose no young Canadian or American writer, starting to learn his job in the thirties, could possibly avoid getting a good shot of radicalism. I was resistant for a while—training and family background again—but now my conservative friends call me a good scarlet radical. My radical friends call me a good solid conservative. . . . [T]hough I am pro-labour, and would jump to the bright side of the barricades as soon as they were*

erected, I think I can claim to have a tolerably open mind (*Writings*, "If Armageddon's On" [1939], 94-95).

His pro-labor inclination is seen in the author's notes for *Timber*, in which he says, "Very baldly, my story is of a logger who, with a logger's typical independence, fights shy of unionism and is eventually killed by an accident in the woods which proper unionism could have prevented" ("RLHB Collection"). In writing the novel, the notion of a single main character seems to have twisted in his hands, and he gives us two principal loggers instead of one. Johnny Holt and Alec (Slim) Crawford share the proletarian thrust of the story. Johnny is the less reflective of the two, a consummately skilled loader of logs, quick on his feet ("catty," as his fellow-loggers would say), and proud of his skills, getting a kick out of being fast and good at his work. With Johnny, the job was "'so goddamned easy he doesn't know he's doing it,'" as the more thoughtful Alec says of him (16). But as the story opens, Johnny's young helper has just been killed in an accident, trying to emulate the catlike Johnny. As Alec Crawford warns the men,

> *"It's just a racket. . . . And you guys fall for it. You keep on falling for it and making money for the companies. If you're hellish good you get by and make wages for yourself. f you're not you try to keep up and get killed trying, or else get fired because you can't make it"* (16-17).

To Alec's reasoned arguments for unionization, Johnny hotly replies, "'And we'd have a bunch of foreign bastards telling us what to do. . . .'"(18).

Through the friendship of these two men, Haig-Brown is able to explore the typicalities of the logger's life, the daily work of the camps, the release from work and tedium experienced in the visits to town, and the slow realization of the advantages of unionization, realization made slower by the casual ethnic and racial prejudices of the men. On the owners' side we see the suppression of the union movement through the infamous blacklist. In addition, Haig-Brown gives the novel his own kind of distinctiveness in his depiction of nature, both as restorative, as seen in Johnny and Alec's wilderness retreats, and as stage for proper management and stewardship for the forests in the future.

Haig-Brown's compelling interest in the natural is interestingly extended into the emotional and sexual lives of his characters in this novel. The relationship between Johnny and his wife Julie, and the triangular associations between them and Alec, is given a vibrancy and fullness which seems linked to the sensuous physicality and beauty of the natural world, upon which the author has centered his interest in his earlier writings. The women in the novel, especially Julie, but even such minor characters as her more worldly friend Dolly, who is physically attracted to Alec, but who leaves him for a more secure relationship, are uniquely drawn. They are not only emotionally strong, but are often intellectually superior, in the face of male stubbornness and anger.

As an experiment, in part, to develop its creator's novelistic skills, *Timber* shows uneven achievement. The novel's people are less powerfully rendered than those of a Thomas Hardy, a Frederick Philip Grove, or a John Steinbeck. But they are believable in their everyday realism, they are part of a world drawn with convincing detail and solidity, and they are fictionally somewhat unique in the author's suggestive depiction of their buried sensual lives. The novel's structure is effectively bracketed by the inquests into logging deaths which open and close the book. But the dramatic value of the novel's climax does not seem fully realized, and there are other points at which artistic emphasis may be swallowed by the counterforce toward understatement. Still, Haig-Brown had proved that he could be a novelist. Indeed, he was to produce in his second, and last, novel, *On the Highest Hill* (1949), a work which was to strike a note of originality for which even *Timber* leaves us unprepared.

*   *   *

The struggle between working class loggers and wealthy mill owners depicted in Haig-Brown's *Timber* was a central issue in the 1930s and 1940s. In the 1990s, the conflict in the forests is being waged over the fate of the last stands of old-growth trees. But we can read in *Timber*'s pages, as well as in the literary and public career of its author, something of how we got from there to here. The call of "Timber!" no longers rings unambiguously in our minds with the old romance of collective progress and individual conquest. Indeed, there is a kind of Melvillean puzzle involved in the cutting down of great trees. "Lo, how the mighty are fallen," say the Scriptures. Joe Ben, the ebullient Fundamentalist logger in Ken Kesey's 1964 novel, *Sometimes A Great Notion*, reminds his mates that a logger invariably stops whatever he is doing to watch a tree fall, no matter how many times he has seen trees fall, or how far away he is. Why? An unlikely philosopher, Joe Ben, or Joby, as he is called, finds in the call "Timber!" and the crash to earth of a forest giant a perverse and hell-driven wish to fell the Tree of Righteousness. "'*People are hot to see the righteous felled..* . . . I mean that people just *naturally* sinners at heart got to chop down the righteous to keep from *feeling* like sinners'" (436-39).

An economic determinist would relate it all to inexorable systems of profit and exploitation. An ecological view might find in our laying the forest low another manifestation of our narrow anthropocentrism. We cut down the magnificent old-growth forests because we *could*. Not just for greed and profits but from the arrogance of our humanism. The environmental heritage of the cut-and-run period of logging is the realization that we are less noble than that which we have destroyed. Which takes us back to Joby again.

I don't think that Haig-Brown came so far as this in his lifetime toward a belief in an Earth-First environmentalism, any more than he did toward Joby's Fundamentalism. But it seems clear that the decent, rational humanist Haig-Brown expected the same decency and rationality with respect to the forests to prevail in others who followed him. He did not wholly anticipate the swift triumph of the acquisitive mentality in the years following the publication of *Timber*. Haig-Brown, nevertheless, did his best, in his own civilized and reasonable way, to turn aside the industrial juggernaut, which has since felled the ancient forests of British Columbia, and the rest of the world, at breakneck pace. He wrote no more novels about the bang and grab days of the woods. His experiment in adult fiction ended with his next novel, *On the Highest Hill,* which was, significantly, to turn inward with a main character whose life became increasingly a rejection of the sort of communal issues and solutions posited in *Timber.*

As Haig-Brown recalled the period after *Timber* was written, he says, "I turned more and more to factual and even semi-didactic writing about wildlife and environment" (*Writings,* "The Drama of Our Environment" [1970], 215-16). These efforts may be found in the records of conservation groups and public battles, and in such published works as *The Living Land* (1961) and *Writings and Reflections* (1982). He was not sanguine about the outcome in these later years, but he fought the good fight. As he said,

> *It is in the history of civilizations that conservationists are always defeated, boomers always win, and the civilizations always die. I think there has never been, in any state, a conservationist government, because there has never yet been a people with sufficient humility to take conservation seriously* (*Above Tide,* 118-19).

As his daughter Valerie Haig-Brown recalls his advice to a friend, "'You won't win, but you gotta fight 'em'" ("Roderick Haig-Brown," 18). He clearly recognized, long before most of the rest of us, that it was time for a new conservation ethic. With loomings of environmental crisis all around us, with no place left to run to, we may now be reaching the point at which we can take conservation seriously. If so, this change will be marked by a reversal of the spirit of aggressive individualism and exploitation of the public resources which characterizes the time of *Timber*.

*　　　*　　　*

There is one more aspect of *Timber*, an achievement perhaps unanticipated and unintended, which seems to me to bear mentioning. It has to do with the regional significance of the book, particularly as it relates to the larger importance of the author's work. Roderick Haig-Brown was raised in the south of England, in Thomas Hardy country. His maternal grandfather was a friend of Hardy's. Indeed, in 1886, the year Hardy published the fictional *The Mayor of Casterbridge*, Haig-Brown's grandfather became, for the second time, the mayor of Dorchester, the town upon which the fictional Casterbridge was based. The youthful Roderick entered into his diary for April 6, 1924, "Went to see Thomas Hardy with Grandfather. Had quite a good day for Sunday" (*Writings*, "Hardy's Dorset" [1957], 39, 41). Hardy served Haig-Brown later as a reminder of the fecundity of associations between people and the land. This rich relationship, Haig-Brown felt, characterized the England of his birth:

When I lived in Dorset, I went often to fish for salmon below Bindon Mill, near Wool. To get there I crossed Wool Bridge, where the ghostly coach of the D'Urbervilles is said to pass. And I looked unfailingly, with a sense of pity and sadness, toward Wellbridge House, where Tess spent her

> *fearful bridal night. . . . For Thomas Hardy nursed his own grey and gentle spirit, conceived in the land, upon the land. And he spread its richness abroad for people everywhere to feel and know"* (*Writings*, 47).

Haig-Brown reflects upon Hardy's country, and England, as a land so steeped in its history of associations between people and land that we in "new lands" like Canada and the United States, cannot realize its richness. "For the writer, for the novelist especially, there is more to understand, more to use in the thousand square miles of Dorset than in the three hundred and fifty thousand square miles of my home province" (*Writings*, 44). It was the same complaint about the thinness of the New World scene that Nathaniel Hawthorne had voiced a hundred years earlier in his preface to *The Marble Faun*. Haig-Brown went on to note that

> *The people of my country, except for the Indians, whose memories and traditions we have destroyed, came here yesterday and many of them will be gone tomorrow with no more trace than a few mouldering boards under the second growth. The country has little time to mould them and they have little time for it, unless to build a dam or cut down a forest before they run for the cities* (*Writings*, 45).

Yet at the same time that Haig-Brown decries the insignificance of the human connections to this new country, he has, like Hawthorne, committed himself to it, and, as a writer, to creating it anew. *Timber*, of course, depicts the exploitative period which Haig-Brown describes above. The forests are there to be cut; the loggers to do their work and move on. But as the novel itself presages at its conclusion a more settled future for the surviving characters, so does the history of the region itself reveal a human movement toward some sort of tenuous relationship with the land. Now, the rush toward exploitation seems to have reached a checkpoint, a moment of awareness. Like it or not, there is nowhere else for us to go. We are in this place, and we must remain here. The magnificent old-growth forests which are the setting for Haig-Brown's novel, are, in the half-century since its publication, nearly gone. Different stories are being written today, in the second growth and the clearcuts.

But the yield of human values was begun with Haig-Brown, who, like Willa Cather and her fictional writer-hero, Jim Burden, in *My Àntonia*, came young into a new country. '"*Primus ego in patriam mecum . . . deducam Musas,*'" Jim quotes from Virgil : "'for I shall be the first, if I live, to bring the Muse into my country'" (171). Though Haig-Brown addresses his filial piety to the storied landscapes and ivied walls of his boyhood Dorset, he serves his own readers by bringing the Muse west into new country. He renews the cycle of human connection to the land by putting down new roots, beginning the pattern of meaningful human presence—the pattern we call art—by which this land, too, has begun to be significant to its inhabitants.

Because Haig-Brown wrote of it so well, the Campbell River is something more than the stream by which he lived and fished and worked. And the Nimpkish is more than a wandering blue line on a map of northern Vancouver Island. These places, and a hundred more, are rendered real and important to us by the writer's art, which has lodged them in our minds by the same process which has graced Hardy's Dorset, or Hawthorne's New England. As the first writer in a new country, Roderick Haig-Brown has served it perhaps better than he knew, spreading its life abroad for people everywhere to feel and know.

Glen A. Love

Works Cited

Cather, Willa. *My Àntonia*. Boston: Houghton Mifflin, 1918; Riverside Edition, 1954.

Haig-Brown, Roderick. *Timber*. New York: William Morrow, 1942.

———. University of British Columbia, The Library, Special Collections Division, "Roderick L. Haig-Brown Collection," box 30, file 5.

———. *Writings and Reflections*. ed. Valerie Haig-Brown. Seattle: University of Washington Press, 1982.

Haig-Brown, Valerie. "Roderick Haig-Brown." *Flyfishing* 13:5 (February 1991), 14-18.

Holbrook, Stewart. *Holy Old Mackinaw*. New York: Macmillan, 1938; Sausalito, California: Comstock Editions, 1980.

———. "Stewart Holbrook Reviews '*Timber*.'" Chicago, Illinois *News*, (25 Mar., 1942). University of British Columbia, The Library, Special Collections Division, "Roderick L. Haig-Brown Collection," box 70, file 3.

Kesey, Ken. *Sometimes A Great Notion*. New York: Viking, 1964; New York: Bantam, 1965.

Robertson, Anthony. *Above Tide: Reflections on Roderick Haig-Brown*. Madeira Park, B. C.: Harbour, 1984.

Books by Roderick Haig-Brown

Silver: The Life Story of an Atlantic Salmon, 1931.
Pool and Rapid, 1932.
Panther, 1934.
The Western Angler, 1939.
Return to the River, 1941.
Timber, 1942.
Starbuck Valley Winter, 1943.
A River Never Sleeps, 1946.
Saltwater Summer, 1948.
On the Highest Hill, 1949.
Measure of the Year, 1950.
Fisherman's Spring, 1951.
Fisherman's Winter, 1954.
Mounted Police Patrol, 1954.
Captain of the Discovery, 1956.
Fisherman's Summer, 1959.
The Farthest Shores, 1960.
The Living Land, 1961.
Fur and Gold, 1962.
The Whale People, 1962.
A Primer of Fly-Fishing, 1964.
Fisherman's Fall, 1964.
The Salmon, 1974.
Bright Waters, Bright Fish, 1980.

Alison's Fishing Birds, 1980.
Woods and River Tales, 1980.
The Master and His Fish, 1981.
Writings and Reflections, 1982.

On the following pages:
The endsheets from the original 1942 edition of Timber.

TIMBER

*A NOVEL OF
PACIFIC COAST LOGGERS
BY
RODERICK L. HAIG-BROWN*

NEW YORK
WILLIAM MORROW & COMPANY
1942

TIMBER

COPYRIGHT - - - 1942
BY RODERICK L. HAIG-BROWN

PRINTED IN THE UNITED STATES OF AMERICA

AUTHOR'S NOTE

In writing a book around a specialized job an author must do one of two things—either paraphrase the technical terms of the job or come right out and use them. I have used them, and my publishers tell me I must make my peace with my readers on this account.

The first paycheck I ever cashed came from a logging company's protectograph. I have been around loggers for most of my life since then, and logging terms come as naturally to my pen as to my tongue; evasion of them would be a painful and artificial process. It might be incumbent upon me to bear the pain and indulge in the artifice were it not for a belief that a man's work, being the greatest part of his life, is also a vastly important factor in his character and behavior. This is more than usually true of loggers and their work. Loggers have all the pride and clannishness of good craftsmen; they talk logging on the job or away from it; most of them assume that anyone who has reached the age of reason will know the difference between, say, a bull block and a cheese block, a tail-hold and tail-track, a screw jack and a loading jack. To have paraphrased such terms in what purported to be the speech or thought of loggers would have been a measure of distortion hard to justify.

Even so, it is still a writer's obvious duty, and it should

be within his technical ability, to clarify most such terms in the normal course of his story. I hope I have made the grade on this. Mr. W. H. Currie's detailed and technically accurate drawing for the endpapers of this book is in itself a whole encyclopedia of Pacific Coast logging; Mr. Currie not only understands all the subtleties of machinery and rigging but expresses the power and vigor of the action as well as the character and type of the loggers themselves in a way that no other artist of my acquaintance has equaled. For the reader who feels that incidental explanation is not enough I have written a verbose but not ponderous glossary of more important logging terms, which will be found at the back of the book. Scholars and students of folklore will forgive my failure to go wholeheartedly into the matter of derivations. This has been done elsewhere. For me these terms are living parts of the American and Canadian language, words which every day pass the lips and affect the lives of modern men.

R. L. H.-B.

Above Tide,
Campbell River,
British Columbia,
December 11, 1941

TIMBER

I

JOHNNY HOLT kept his mind on the sunlight and the blue water, white crested by the westerly breeze, and the green of the timber across the Strait. The smoke of the sawmill village he had left two hours earlier was small against the blue sky above the timber. The little company tug that had brought himself and Ed and Tommy across was tied to the wharf below them, squealing its rubber fenders against the piles as the little swells lifted it. All these were pleasant things, good to see and feel and smell, and he was at pains to use the brightness of them before the time came to go into the gloom of the morgue. When you came out again you would notice them again, just for a moment; then they would be normal and part of the life you lived, not sharp and clear as they were now.

Leaning against the peeling white paint of the little building, he looked at Ed and Tommy. They had their inquest faces on, pale, miserable, smooth with special shaving. Even the clothes they were wearing and his own clothes belonged inside there, in the cold room with the scraping chairs.

"God," Johnny said. "Why don't they come?"

Ed Nelson pulled a watch out of his pocket. "They'll come," he said. "It's ten minutes soon yet."

Tommy said: "Say, Johnny, do we have to go in and look at him, like he was after the turn hit him?"

Johnny nodded. "Afraid so, kid. You don't have to look too close though."

Men began to arrive, walking slowly and reluctantly in the sunshine along the single waterfront street of the town. Jurymen, a provincial policeman, Chris Eldridge, the superintendent of the company, a man from the compensation board. The coroner came and they all filed into the little dim room in the front of the building. The jurymen sorted themselves awkwardly into six chairs in front of the coroner's desk. Johnny sat with Ed and Tommy and Eldridge near the back of the room. The big policeman declared the court open and began to swear in the jurymen.

Johnny watched the jury. He knew some of them. Edwards, the storekeeper at the cannery, the barkeep from the hotel beer-parlor, a guy from the machine shop, Andy Mansell, the hand-logger. Even the two he could not place he had seen before. A quiet enough lot. They wouldn't have many questions. There was nothing difficult about it anyway, nothing to be hidden or explained. Young Charlie had had it coming to him pretty nearly every day of the six months he had worked on the loading crew and it was nobody's fault when it finally did come up with him. Just the same, Charlie was a good kid and you didn't want to make him out too crazy reckless—Ed didn't and Tommy didn't either, so it wouldn't be hard.

The coroner stood up and all the chairs scraped and everyone followed him into the other room, where Charlie was. They had left him on the stretcher and some of the blood on the gray blanket still showed. The coroner was speaking, talking to him, Johnny.

"Can you identify this man?"

Johnny nodded: "It's Charlie Davies."

"Charles Ernest Davies?"

"I guess that was his name."

The coroner became the doctor. He bent down and touched Charlie's smashed head with gentle hands. "I want you to see this," he told the jury. "Death must have been absolutely instantaneous. The skull is very badly fractured in a great many places."

The jurymen watched and understood and everyone filed back into the courtroom. Johnny hung behind and looked again at the big body on the stretcher. You wanted to be able to say something, tell the guy he had been good and it would be a long time before you got another loading crew with four good white men on it. You wanted to tell him it hadn't meant a goddamned thing when you cursed him out for doing something crazy—not a thing except that you didn't want him to get killed. And instead of that the last thing he had heard you say was: "Watch those logs, Charlie, you crazy son of a bitch." He turned again and went back into the courtroom.

They took a long time shuffling and scraping back into the chairs. The big policeman stood up and beckoned to Johnny. "First witness," he said. "Take the stand, please."

Johnny kissed the book and sat down in the chair near the coroner's desk. The coroner was a big man, thirty-five or forty years old, quiet-faced and quiet-speaking. Johnny looked at him and trusted him; most of the boys figured he was a good doctor and they said he tried to get things straight at inquests.

The coroner asked his name again to make sure the stenographer had it right, then said gently and slowly: "Would you please tell us what happened, in your own words, and not too fast so that this lady here can take it down? First of all the time of day."

Johnny felt the words begin to move fast in his head. He knew things he wanted to say, but they were farther on in the story and he might lose them before he came to them. "It was pretty near quitting time," he said. "A little after four-thirty. We were putting the bunk load on the last empty and there was a turn of logs coming in from the woods. Charlie went down with the back tongs and seemed to run right into the turn as the engineer set it down."

"Just a minute." The coroner turned to the jury. "Is that clear? Most of you gentlemen know something about the woods, but I want you to ask questions when anything isn't clear."

Johnny watched the jury. He felt better now because he wouldn't have to say it all at once and there would be time to think and keep things straight. The jurymen were silent, blank-faced except for Edwards, the storekeeper. Edwards moved his feet, then leaned forward in his chair and spoke to the coroner. "I don't get any of that," he said. "I haven't been around the woods and there's a whole lot of words in there don't mean a thing to me."

The coroner put down his pencil and set the tips of his fingers together. "Which are the words?" he asked. "We'll try and explain them for you." He turned to the stenographer. "Read over what you've got there please, Miss Hildred. We can stop and go into anything that isn't clear."

Johnny watched the girl as she read. She was smart and good looking, with thick black hair and dull red lips. Edwards stopped her almost at once. "Bunk load," he said. "What's that? And what's a turn of logs?"

One or two of the jurymen smiled patiently. The coroner said: "A bunk load is the bottom layer of logs put on a car. The five or six logs that rest directly on the bunks of the car." He turned to Johnny. "That's what you meant, isn't it?" Johnny nodded and the coroner went on. "A turn of logs is several logs being hauled out of the woods on a long wire cable by the donkey engine— sometimes just one or two, sometimes half a dozen; depends on how many chokers there are on the cable. Is that clear?"

Edwards smiled apologetically. "I think I get it," he said. "A choker would be some kind of a hook that grabs on to the logs right where they're lying out in the woods, and there's a steam donkey to haul them up to the track. It was these logs coming in that hit the deceased."

The coroner looked at Johnny and Johnny nodded again. "That's right," he said. "There was only two logs in the turn. Mostly we fly just two chokers on a highlead machine unless the timber is awful small. Charlie went down with the back tongs just as the turn came in."

"What's that, the back tongs?" Edwards asked.

Johnny looked at him, then at the coroner. Maybe this guy was going to make some sort of trouble. He didn't seem like it—just kind of dumb and trying to get it all straight, but you couldn't tell. "The witness means loading tongs," the coroner said. "The loading operation—" he turned to Johnny. "Maybe you could explain it better than I can, Mr. Holt. It's your job and I'm not overly experienced in the woods myself."

"Well," Johnny said. It seemed silly not to be able to explain something you were doing every day, but it wasn't so easy when you came right down to it—not when it was some guy asking the questions who didn't seem to know the difference between a skeleton car and a brow log. "Well," he said again. "When a turn comes in the engineer sets the logs down on the rest of the pile on the landing—that's the space alongside the track where we load from—and the chaser goes out to unhook the chokers." He hesitated, trying to get it straight from there. "That's where we start in," he went on. "Me and young Tommy here and Charlie Davies. We've got two pairs of tongs—scissors tongs, like ice tongs only bigger—slung from the guy lines over a car on the track. One loader takes the front tongs and packs them out to the pile and hooks them on to a log. Then the loading leverman—he's up on the donkey—goes ahead so the line tightens on the tongs and lifts the front end of the log up over the car. Then the other loader takes the back tongs down off the car with him and flips them on to the other end of the log. When the leverman tightens again the whole log lifts and straightens round square over the car. He drops it down in place and we go up to shake the tongs." He stopped, still watching the stenographer. She was a swell-looking girl all right, with her mouth kind of smiling like that as though this was all kind of silly;

you wouldn't figure to see a dame like that in a dump like this, but they were always showing up some place where you wouldn't expect them. And it was kind of foolish too when you came to think of it, a guy talking out loud about how to load logs and a whole room of grown people listening.

The coroner said, "Thank you, Mr. Holt. I think that is all very clear." He turned to Edwards: "That gives you the picture, doesn't it?"

"Yes," Edwards said. "I've got it straight now, I think. I'm sorry to act so dumb, but it's no use a man sitting on one of these juries and not knowing what the score is. They should pick loggers."

The coroner shook his head. "I disagree there. The Crown wants the opinion of a group of intelligent citizens, not experts." He turned to the stenographer. "What's the last thing you have on the witness's account of the accident, Miss Hildred?"

The girl read back: "The deceased went down with the back tongs and seemed to run right into the turn as the engineer set it down."

The coroner turned back to Johnny. "You had put on the front tongs?"

"Yes."

"And the front end of the log was lifted up over the car when Davies took the back tongs down?"

"That's right."

Edwards leaned forward in his chair again. "Could witness account for Davies' failure to see the turn of logs coming in? Was it something to do with the lay of the ground, or what?"

Johnny turned his mind sharply to a picture of the landing, searching for the words that would make it clear. The coroner watched him kindly, yet with the question in his eyes. "Take your time, Holt," he said. "Tell it the way you want. I'll check you as we go to make sure the technical points are clear to the jury."

The words came to Johnny and he knew what he had to tell, how it would make things right for everybody, even for Charlie. He felt grateful to Edwards for the chance to get it straight. "It was the way the landing was," he said. "It wasn't a bad landing; there was a good flat place on both sides of the track for the logs to pile on as they came out of the woods. But we were yarding—bringing the logs—up from the downhill side and on the square lead—from straight out at right angles to the track, that is. There's kind of a hump in the ground on that road, not more than a hundred feet from the landing, and a turn of logs can come over it pretty quick if you're not watching, straight down on to the landing."

The coroner said: "You want us to understand that that is what happened to Davies. He went out to put his tongs on the log you were loading and failed to see the turn coming in?"

"That's about right. He didn't know how close it was."

Edwards asked: "Did you know the turn was close when you put the front tongs on?"

"Sure," Johnny said. "I could see by the angle the sky line was pulling on it over the hump. But I could get the tongs on without ever stepping off the brow log, so it didn't make no difference."

One of the jurymen asked: "What's the brow log?"

Hell, Johnny thought, they can go on like this all

afternoon. He saw that the other jurymen were shifting in their chairs and the stenographer was smiling again. "It's a big log we set alongside the track," he said. "Between the empty car and the pile on the landing. Makes sure the logs ride up over the car instead of smacking into it and knocking it off the track. It's handy for the loaders too; makes a sort of step up or down for us."

The coroner looked over the jury. "Is that all clear? Do you want to hear any more from this witness?"

"Yes," Edwards said. He watched Johnny closely as he asked the question. "If the turn was close as that when you put the tongs on, why didn't Davies wait?"

Johnny saw Charlie Davies standing on the half-completed bunk load, his spiked shoes gripping the log, tattered blue jeans stagged short on his strong legs; the smile on his face and the little beads of sweat which meant that all his muscles were loose and right and he was working well within himself. He remembered his own gesture and the words to hold Charlie back, lost in the roar of the big steam donkey bringing in the turn and the slap of the straining rigging. Charlie's smile, shaking off the gesture of warning, his easy movement forward with the tongs held in front of him. "I guess he thought he could make it," Johnny said.

The other questions came after that, as they had to. Couldn't you have warned him? Have stopped him? Was he an experienced man? How long had he been a loader? Was he careless? Hurrying for any reason? They let Johnny go and called Ed Nelson, the loading leverman, then young Tommy, the other second loader, then Dan Evritt, the yarding leverman. Edwards wanted to know just what Dan's job was—the guy was thorough, you had to hand it to him for that. He wasn't mean anyway, either; not looking for trouble, just trying to understand the thing properly.

"When you get the signal from the woods they've hooked on to a log, you just go ahead on the steam and the drum on the donkey winds up the sky line and hauls in the log?"

"That's right," Dan said. A little, tough, jumpy guy, sitting straight up in the chair and twisting his hat in his hands; he'll get sore and make some sort of a smart crack if they keep on at him, Johnny thought. Then there'll be hell to pay.

"Once you get started you don't ever stop?"

"Not unless I get a signal to hold her, or it feels like something ain't right. Why else would I stop?"

"You couldn't have seen in time that Davies was going down in the way of the turn coming in?"

"I could not," Dan said. "And there's nobody else could."

Johnny watched and listened with a sort of numb boredom. That was always how it was at an inquest. The questions went on and on around the same thing, never getting anywhere. But it was easy enough to see they believed Dan. That was one place Dan was sure of himself, about his job; not about anything else in the world, but always about his job. They let him go and called back Ed Nelson, the loading leverman. Ed had the thing on his mind—he was plain miserable with it, had been ever since it happened. He could have held on to the tongs, not let the line run out when Charlie wanted to go with them. That might have checked him. But you don't do things like that with a guy like Charlie. If he's made up his mind

Timber 13

to go he's going, and the chances are he's catty enough to make it. If you try to hold the tongs back on him all you'll do is throw him off balance and likely as not he'll still get it and it'll be your fault. It might be hard for Ed to get that over to a jury, in spite of the way they had all argued it over and over since Charlie got hit. But the jury was letting him go now and they hadn't asked the questions that would lead up to it. The coroner said something and then they were filing out into the sunlight, leaving the jury to make out a verdict.

Johnny stood on the steps looking out over the blue water again. He had forgotten about this break in the middle, this return to clean air and good light with the gray smell and dimness of the courtroom still waiting. It was a good time and you drew close to Ed and Tommy and old Dan, rolled a cigarette, talked a little; the coroner and the big policeman talked together and Chris Eldridge stood apart from everyone, filling his big curved Peterson pipe. Chris was there to watch in case anything came up that looked bad for the company and he was careful to keep it that way—only watching, maybe talking to the man from the compensation board, but nothing more than a "hello, boys" for the witnesses and not even that for the coroner or the cops.

Tommy said: "The poor bastard was sure smashed up," and Johnny saw his hand shaking as he scratched at the big red-headed match with his thumbnail.

Ed said: "A shot of rum would go good right now. Slim Crawford is up at the hotel with a bottle."

Johnny felt the weight of the rest of the day fall away from him. "Slim's back?" he asked. "When did he get in?"

"On the boat last night. I saw him when I went up to get tobacco."

"Soon as we get through here," Johnny said, "we'll go call on Slim."

Slim would be full of his trip to town, full of talk about girls and movies and baseball; he would have bought a new gun or a new fishing rod and the talk would slide away the time on the tug crossing the Strait and the time in the caboose behind the empties on the slow drag up the adverse grade to camp. The door of the courtroom opened and Johnny went in with the others almost gladly. Chairs scraped again, people stood up, hesitated, sat down, stood up again. It was quiet and the coroner read the verdict. "We, a jury empaneled to enquire into the death of Charles Ernest Davies, do find that the deceased was killed accidentally while loading logs at the Bryan and Assalt Timber Company's Camp Number Four on . . ."

The court closed and they filed out into the sun and the brightness of the little quick waves beyond the road. Johnny felt it a part of him again and the acute perception of it all went away from his mind. He thought of Charlie still on the stretcher under the bloodstained blanket, but it was all over for Charlie: the undertakers would come and dress him up, make his body, even his broken head and face, tidy in the gray coffin, then no one would see him again. And it would be in Ed's mind and Tommy's mind and Johnny's own mind, as though Charlie had never laughed on a landing or gone out with the tongs in the proud easy movements that boasted his strength and the sure quickness of his small feet.

2

THEY turned into the hotel and climbed the battered, brass-treaded stairs. Ed walked ahead, peering at the numbers on the doors in the dim light of the passage. He stopped at a door, pushed it open and went in. The others followed.

Slim Crawford threw down a magazine and sat up on the bed. "Come on in, fellows," he said. "It's all over there by the basin—rum and rye and Scotch. I thought we'd have a party in camp tonight, but this is better."

He turned to Johnny and held out his hand. Johnny took it and felt the moment of shyness between them, the knowledge in each that this was something he had looked forward to and the quick fear that it might not be as he had hoped, that a month of different things and places and people might have changed something. But the moment passed and Johnny said: "It's been dead around camp without you, Alec."

"It's no grief to me to be back. For God's sake, have a drink. You all look as if you belonged in that goddamned morgue yourselves."

Johnny went over to the table by the basin and poured himself half a tumbler of rye. Slim lay back on the bed with his own glass. He held it up. "Here's for Charlie," he said. "All the women and all the liquor he didn't have time to use down here."

Johnny laughed and drank. You couldn't wish Charlie anything that would please him better—those two things and a chance to be proud of the way he could handle loading tongs. But Charlie on the stretcher under the gray blanket wasn't handling women or tongs or liquor. Whatever had done that had gone out of him in the moment the turn hit him. Slim Crawford said quietly, "How did it happen?"

Ed Nelson told it, slowly and carefully because he still felt that he could have done something. "I guess I ought to have held back on him," he said at the end, his eyes pleading for Slim's absolution.

Johnny watched Slim's eyes, hard and dark blue under the wide straight forehead, saw the jaw line hard and the mouth tight in the slender face. "Hell," Slim said. "It wasn't your fault, Ed. Charlie would have got it sooner or later anyway, and if you had held back on him you'd have just thrown him off. It's the fault of all the crazy guys that want to show how fast and easy they can do things. Nearly all loaders are that way—look at Tommy here and Johnny, only with Johnny it's so goddamned easy he doesn't know he's doing it."

Johnny said: "Charlie did it easily; he was strong and quick and he liked to make it look good. So we all do, I guess, but Charlie tried to make it too good. Only time he was really happy was when he could get a log to brush his hair or knock the dust off his pants."

"It's just a racket," Slim said. "And you guys fall for it. You keep on falling for it and making money for the companies. If you're hellish good you get by and make wages for yourselves. If you're not you try to keep up and get killed trying or else get fired because you can't make it."

Johnny felt the resistance to the argument growing in him. It was old stuff; Slim had said his side many times and had had his answers, but it had to come up again and be argued again; it would never be decided by talk, only by things happening, but it had to be talked out this time and many other times. "A guy can't just work with half of himself," he said. "He's got to get some kick out of doing a good job or he'd go crazy. Hell, you work fast enough at your own job, Alec."

"That's a whole lot different. I'm working alone a lot of the time, and anyway, a man doesn't get killed or wear his legs out just traveling through the bush."

Ed Nelson said: "Hell, Slim, guys like Johnny have got a good name for getting logs out and that's why they can always get jobs. You can't expect a fellow to work like a cripple all his life just so some guy off a farm can keep up with him."

"Young Charlie was no farmer," Crawford said.

Johnny turned sharply towards him. "Charlie didn't have to get killed either. Charlie was putting on a show to please himself every time he touched the tongs—you know that as well as anybody."

"Yes," Crawford said. "Charlie was just a kid. But can't you see he got his ideas from watching guys like you? You've built up a sort of tradition round the job and naturally every kid wants to fit into it."

Young Tommy, standing near the window that looked out over the Strait, watched the speakers closely. He said: "Johnny isn't careless like Charlie was. It looks good when Johnny's loading and the logs go on, but he isn't taking chances all the time."

"Sure," Crawford said. "You can see that. Charlie wasn't the type to see it, so he's dead."

Johnny hitched his shoulders and turned away to pour another drink. Ed Nelson said: "What the hell can you do about a guy that's naturally reckless? Johnny warned him half a dozen times every day."

"I'm not saying you can do a hell of a lot about one particular case like that. Maybe Charlie would have got it anyway. But a good union would change things. Nobody would have to be scared for his job if he couldn't keep up the pace and everybody would be able to work slower and easier. And a union could get better safety regulations and make sure they were enforced."

"And we'd have a bunch of foreign bastards telling us what to do, same as we did in the strike," Johnny said.

"Maybe that's just what's needed—outsiders to get a little sense into your heads. But once the thing was properly organized you fellows could control it if you would just get in there and do the work."

"We could like hell," Johnny said. "Vancouver would run it. And the East would run Vancouver and some outfit down in the States would have the last word about everything. If we tried to run things our own way they'd put us out of commission in no time at all."

"Johnny's right," Nelson said. "A union is okay when you've got work for it, like the strike. But in good times there's always a bunch of bohunks gets control of it and the ordinary guy who's minding his own business gets nothing but grief. They tell you where you can work and when and how and what for. And if you don't do it you're called a scab and a son of a bitch by a bunch of guys that never saw caulked shoes in their lives."

Crawford sat up and swung his legs over the side of the bed in an angry movement. "You guys make me sick. So goddamned independent you'd drown before you'd catch hold of a chunk of wood to save yourselves." He turned on Johnny again. "Jesus, Johnny, can't you see that if you and Eric and Dick and a few of the others the boys trust would take hold you could run a good union? You did it during the strike and kept those outside organizers right where you wanted them."

Johnny shook his head, then sat down in the room's one big chair. He knew that the others, as well as Slim, were waiting for what he would say, that they wanted him to say what they all felt. But the words weren't there to set against Slim's words. "It's different in ordinary times," he said at last. "The boys can't hang on to a union except when they want something out of it. Soon as they've got what they want they lose interest and the first thing you know the union is bossing them in ways they don't want."

"That's right," Nelson said again. "And anyway, why should a man stick his neck out right now? For the first time in years he can get work at halfway decent wages and if he tries to monkey with union stuff the first thing he knows he's in town and on the blacklist. Unions will come, but not right now."

Johnny nodded silently. That wasn't any way to put it up to Slim, but it was the truth. Unions would come— anybody knew that; they had come every place else and they had to come here—you could feel it in your bones. But you could tell just as easily it wasn't the time right now. That was the sort of thing Slim didn't understand. It belonged with the way people felt, wanting to work and get paid for it, to go on with things as they were for a while anyhow, not be looking for trouble just as soon as trouble seemed to be somewhere out of the way.

Slim said: "Things like unions don't come just by sitting back and waiting for them. Somebody's got to get out and take the grief. And if you let the professional organizers do it you haven't any kick coming when they boss you later on."

Young Tommy straightened himself away from the window. "Hell, that's not right, Slim. You can't make it right for a working guy to get pushed around by some punk that's never even seen the woods. If we've got to have somebody boss us it had better be loggers."

Slim moved impatiently, then got up and went across to the table where the liquor was. "You've got loggers for bosses," he said. "The boss loggers, and most of them never saw the woods either. They sit in Vancouver or Seattle and dope the thing out from swivel chairs. That's the kind of suckers you guys are; you'll take bossing from men that don't give a darn what happens to you. You won't take it from men that haven't got any reason for living except to make things better for you."

"You can always quit an outfit if you don't like it," Tommy said. "You can't quit a union."

Ed Nelson laughed. "You just quit sometime and see how quick you don't get on some place else."

"It's still kind of tough right now," Johnny said. "But

that's due for a change. Most times a good man can get himself a job." He looked at Slim Crawford. "It isn't every boss logger that's a son of a bitch either. Look at Chris—he's square enough. And he's not so different from a lot of the others; if a man minds his own business and does his work he's okay."

"Who said Chris was a boss logger?" Slim asked. "He's just a superintendent, getting paid to do his work same as anybody else and taking orders from the higher-ups. You never even see most of the guys that really own you."

Johnny let himself slump in the chair, feeling the liquor in his blood. It was good to have shaken the inquest so quickly, to be a whole man again and rid of the cold smell of the morgue. But it shouldn't have gone this way, straight into the old argument with Slim, having to defend the way Charlie had died all over again after the inquest had passed off without any trouble—because that was what it had all come up from, the way Charlie had died. And that had been the same as any one of half a dozen other accidents and Slim had admitted it was and then somehow got the thing off on this angle, where everybody but him was at a disadvantage. It didn't help any to talk it that way, to gripe at the bosses and run off a whole line of radical stuff that made a man feel badly about himself for no good reason. He said: "Chris has plenty to say about what goes on at B. and A. What's more, the big bugs in town listen to what he says. I don't see how you get that way, Alec, in your job. You know damn well they're pushing you right on up so you can take over a superintendent's job yourself one day. Hell, you've got a boss's job right now—you're on the payroll as assistant woods superintendent or something like that."

"It doesn't make any difference where I'm going. What matters is that the boys need a union to protect them. And if I'm ever in a boss's job I'll need one to check up on me."

Little Dan Evritt swirled the last of his drink in the bottom of his glass and spoke for the first time. His whispering voice and little creased face were full of his joke. "The boys sure will need protection when you get to be a boss, Slim. You'll have a gallon of rum under every stump and a whore's annex on every bunkhouse."

Alec's face was angry for a moment, then he laughed with the others. "You might have something there, at that, Dan. That's about what it would take for you guys to get interested."

"Didn't notice you ever turn down either of them things," Nelson said. "Only time you get holy is on the union stuff, then you're a regular minister."

Johnny straightened a little in his chair. Slim would get human again now. Sometimes when he got on to unions like that he would argue until you got to feeling real sore at him. He must have been up with the organizers in town and got all primed so that it had to come out at the first chance. "For God's sake let's see that bottle again," he said. "We've been talking like a bunch of soreheaded old women for the last half hour."

"What in hell else is there to do?" Ed Nelson asked. "The tug won't pull out for a couple of hours yet anyway."

"Have a couple more rounds, then let's go look at the town. That's all you bastards are fit for."

3

JOHNNY stood on the wide, squat stern of the tug, watching the evening light on the waves of the dying westerly breeze. The little town straggled its untidy length along the narrow strip of flat land that separated the bay from the slope of the hills. The white of the morgue showed up as though the paint were not peeling and cracked, but the building looked harmless and ordinary at this distance. Young Charlie was still there, tidied up now against the satin lining of the gray coffin. It was bad to leave him alone like that, with the darkening water in the coldness of evening making wider separation. Johnny felt again the tightness of chest and throat that wanted to reach out and back, to say all the words that had not been said and live the years of strong life, of work and drinking and talking and laughing that were shut away for ever now in Charlie's big body. But you could shake that off and be free of it—it would not touch you again after this time, not to hurt anyway; he knew that because he had gone away and left other dead loggers in this and other morgues, and the thing never stayed long—often not even this long, but Charlie had been a good kid. He looked away, along the other buildings of the town, to rid his mind of it. There was the Chinaman's store and the machine shop and the boat-builder's ship, the Shell wharf and the Union wharf and the cannery wharf. Then the Swede's store and the hospital wharf. They looked tiny and far away now, but he had been on or in all of them with Ed Nelson during the dreary afternoon—waiting while Tommy and Slim went up to see the Marion girls in the house on the hill.

Chris Eldridge came silently along the deck and stood beside him—a big man on little feet. He stood without speaking for several minutes. Then he said: "Was that straight dope at the inquest, Johnny?"

"Sure," Johnny said. "There wasn't anything needed keeping back."

"What are you getting up there now?"

"About twenty cars most days. Too many small logs to beat that by much."

"Twenty?" Chris seemed to consider the figure carefully, standing there in the dusk. "Couldn't be pushing the boys any, could it?"

Johnny still watched the distant houses along the shore. He thought, What in hell is this? First the inquest, then Alec, now Chris. You'd think I'd murdered the guy or something. "Hell, Chris," he said. "What's the big idea? If you think there was something phoney about the way Charlie went, why don't you say so?"

Chris shook his head. His voice was slow and calm. "I don't mean it that way, Johnny. Even if I did the thing would come back on me, not you. That's what I'm getting at really. Are we pushing you so you figure you have to push the boys?"

"No," Johnny said. "I'd tell you to go to hell and walk off the job before I'd take that. You ought to know it too." He still felt sore and maybe this was the place to get it out and settled, once and for all. It had been too close to that with Alec up in the hotel room and a man didn't want to have to get sore at his best friend. Chris was a good enough guy, but if he wanted to talk it that way he could take what was coming to him.

"You're still sore," Chris said. "I want to talk it out straight. We've got nothing to gain out of killing a man to get a couple of extra loads. That's not the way this outfit's run. We try to keep a crew together, not drive 'em off all the time. I thought you boys knew that and that was what kept you coming back here."

"Okay." Johnny's voice went on even and hard. "You want it straight. I'm not pushing myself or nobody else. If there's twenty loads coming from a side I'll put on twenty. If they ain't coming I'm not trying to make them come. I don't have to—if you guys don't like my work there's plenty of places that do. And that goes for the guys second-loading for me, too."

"You didn't ever think to can Davies for being careless?"

"Sure I did. But what good would that do? He was better with me in this outfit than down at Hughson's or some other highball camp with nobody to watch him."

Chris nodded. "That's right. Ted told me he was a reckless sort of kid, but good, and I thought maybe you figured to break him into some sense."

"A thing like that doesn't take figuring. It's straight common sense." Johnny felt suddenly that what he had said sounded foolish and somehow small. You couldn't get sore at Chris because the guy never got sore himself—

he just let you talk and listened and made up his own mind from what he heard. "Hell, Chris," he said. "I'm sorry I got sore. But there's been so much talk and figuring going on today a man gets to feeling he's on the spot. It doesn't take talk for a guy to find out if he's right or wrong. He knows inside him what's right and what's wrong and that's the way he acts. Only people seem to think there must be angles to it all the time."

"I know. Nobody likes hanging around all day for an inquest. I should have known better than to tie in to you like that right afterwards. I just wanted to keep track of you and be sure you hadn't changed any. I don't get to see you on the job so often since Slim Crawford took over the job he's doing now—I'm getting to be a regular chair-pounder. But I sure hate to see a kid like Charlie get it and I guess that's what made me want to talk."

"You and me both," Johnny said. "But I haven't got Charlie on my conscience. There never was a guy worked for me yet that I didn't watch out for him all I could."

"Sure," Chris said. "I know it." He turned on silent feet and went away. Johnny stood there, still looking back towards the hills above the little town. He felt tired and sickened by the day, by the touch and pull of so many things that had no part in the ordinary life of working and eating and sleeping, of talk, on the job or in the bunkhouse, of hope and plans and the unplanned things that gave pleasure. The argument with Alec in the hotel room had been the worst thing; he felt battered by it, miserable from it. You had to respect what Alec said. Alec was smart, he had a good education and lots of reading, and when he said a thing there was something back of it. Generally you could see the thing and understand it and know that it was good; but this time it was wrong. You couldn't pin it down and point to what was wrong, but you could feel it—the same way you could feel that what had happened to Charlie was a natural accident, nobody's fault, just something that happened because of the breaks and the way Charlie was.

He felt the tug swinging into the bay, towards the Beach camp, and he turned and walked forward to the bow. The trouble with what Alec said was mostly in the way he said it. Nobody was against unions; they did good work when there was work for them and maybe they had to come as a wholetime proposition some day. But it was the way Alec talked it. He talked like a regular sorehead agitator and always put you in the wrong, as though you were a scab or working for the bosses if you wouldn't go all the way with him; he could even make it seem you were plain yellow sometimes. Later on, like now, you could figure it out and get it straight and know that what he said was just talk. But at the time it made you sore and it felt bad to be sore at Alec; being sore at a man you had no use for was all right, but nobody liked to be sore at a guy as good as Alec was on everything else. Arguing with him didn't do any good because he was such a smart talker, but that didn't make him right. He left things out in his figuring, like the way the boys were feeling and what they really wanted.

As the tug came near the wharf he watched the boommen sorting the logs just dumped from the evening train. The mainline locomotive was switching empty cars, straightening round for the trip back to the woods. In the familiar sound of its steam Johnny felt release from the mood that had held him and from all the doubting misery of the day. The big hoarse-throated locomotive was something real and the men who worked on it, Hank and Dad Hutchins and the others, were men you understood and felt sure of. Sitting in the caboose with the stove going, Hank or the second brakeman talking, maybe taking a swallow of Slim's liquor, would be full return to normal. Slim there and Ed and Tommy and Dan. Talking of logs and loads and maybe of hunting and fishing.

He turned as Slim came up beside him. The tug swung again, straight in towards the wharf.

"Why didn't you come down in the engine room?" Slim said. "The boys put on quite a party down there." He looked suddenly at Johnny and his voice changed. "You weren't sore, were you? I mean about what I said up in the hotel room this afternoon?"

Johnny shook his head. "I wanted to think," he said. "About what you said and the rest of it. A man has to think to himself sometimes. And Chris was up there talking for a while."

"About Charlie?"

"Mostly."

"That guy's certainly a lot different from most of them. Maybe because he was a donkey-puncher half his life and got to know what it feels like. They say he was good too."

"You're damn right he was. Dan Evritt and pretty nearly every other yarding engineer on this claim learned his stuff from Chris. He was the only guy that ever did handle that big skidder they had without breaking rigging all the time."

The tug came alongside the wharf and Johnny stepped out on to the planks with the bow-line in his hands. He made the line fast. "Got your stuff, Alec?"

Slim handed a packsack across the gunwale, then picked up two suitcases and a bundle of fishing rods and stepped on to the wharf with them.

"Hell," Johnny said. "You travel like a goddamned duke."

They walked up to the caboose, climbed aboard and settled themselves near the stove. Hank Parker came in to get his lantern. "Hello, boys," he said, and went out again.

Ed Nelson said: "For God's sake, Slim, did you spend another six months' paychecks on all them fishpoles?"

Slim Crawford laughed. "No. There's only one of them new." He pulled a suitcase towards him, opened it and passed a bottle. Then he found a metal box and handed it to Johnny. "Take a look at them. I got some new feathers from that old guy who was scaling at the lake camp last summer and they made up into swell flies."

The train started as Johnny opened the box and Hank came in again. He looked over Johnny's shoulder at the rows of flies. They were set off against the bright metal of the lining of the box, each hook held in its clip. The first impression was of a deep richness of good colors, silver and red and orange and gold, fine blues, sober grays, clear yellows, soft browns and gleaming blacks. Then the eye focused to detail, catching the subtleties of barred and mottled and spotted feathers and above all the smooth perfection of the workmanship, the flow of hackle and wing back from the head towards the bend of the hook, the blending of colors and marrying of alien strips of feather. Johnny felt a surge of sheer physical pleasure as he saw them, then the old feeling of pride at an achievement of Slim's. Slim had something. This, and the way he knew about books, about the woods, about hunting, about his own job, even about places to go in town. He did things easily, did them right and got a kick out of doing them.

Hank's weathered, ugly face, long-nosed, heavy-lipped, heavy-browed, bent closer to the box. A dark brown dribble of snuff showed at one corner of his mouth, catching the light of the oil lamp. "Boy, those are something. I didn't know you could do that good, Slim."

Ed Nelson asked, "What are you going to catch with them, Slim?"

"Big rainbows," Slim said. "In the river. They were crazy for bright flies last year, so I thought I'd really go to town this year."

Johnny handed the box back. His eyes met Slim's for a moment and they both smiled. Johnny said: "It's like looking at a bunch of chorus girls on the stage."

Slim laughed. "You mean you'd like to go to bed with them?"

"Be kind of sharp company," Hank said. Then: "Say, Slim, how would Arthur Lake be next Sunday? Could a guy get fish there? Me and Joe was thinking of going in."

"It'll be a bit warm this late, but you can always get fish

in the neck between the two parts of the lake. They may be wormy, but you'll get them."

Tommy said: "Can't you guys talk nothing but fishing? Tell Slim about the cougar, Hank."

"It wasn't so much," Hank said. "We was coming down light about a week ago, after dark. Me and Joe was in the cab just this side of the big cut and old Dad hollered to look ahead. We saw him stand there in the middle of the track, looking straight up at the headlight. His damn great tail looked like it was lying across the rail, way out behind him. Then he went off into the brush. Didn't seem a bit scared. Dad stopped the locie soon as he could and me and Joe took the fireman's thirty-thirty and went off to look for him. Didn't see him though. Seemed kind of scary when you got away from the track."

"He likely was sitting behind a stump looking at you," Johnny said.

"That's what Joe and me figured and soon as we figured it we hit back for the locie." Hank turned suddenly to Alec Crawford. "Say, Slim, wasn't Red Henderson a good friend of yours? He's back in camp."

"The hell you say. You seen him, Johnny?"

"Sure," Johnny said. "Just the same as ever."

"How come they let him out? I thought he was in for another year anyway."

"Good behavior. Red says it was a snap in there. Best life he ever hit except there wasn't any way a guy could get rich."

Slim laughed. "Red's ways of getting rich weren't so hot even when he was outside."

Tommy said: "What did they put him away for, Slim?"

"Some guy told him about a warehouse where the cops store all the confiscated dope—opium and cocaine and that stuff. So Red rented a truck and got two or three crazy nuts to go with him and they backed the truck up against the door of the warehouse. They had just broken down the door and started loading the truck when the cops came. Red says he never did get to know if the stuff really was dope—he didn't even think to wonder about that until me and Johnny went to see him in the pen and asked him."

"Hell," Tommy said. "You sure wouldn't think all that to look at him. Just a little slim freckle-faced guy—don't weigh more than a hundred and thirty-five."

The talk went on. More of Red, then hunting and logs, then women, back to hunting and logs again. The caboose clattered its way along behind the straight-connected Baldwin and the string of empties until they came to the switchbacks that led them up the hill away from the beach. Then Hank went out to switch his train through. Ed Nelson had taken out a pack of cards and was playing solitaire while young Tommy watched him. Slim Crawford and Johnny talked together, quietly and intently.

"Listen, Johnny," Slim was saying. "We can go down right after supper on Saturday—ride the Shay when she takes the loads down the lake. We can maybe fish a bit Saturday night, sleep in one of the bridge crews' shelters, then fish all Sunday and flag the speeder when it comes through Sunday night. How'll that be?"

"Sounds good," Johnny said. Something in Slim's serious concern with the plan reminded him of Slim on the bed in the hotel during the afternoon. He seemed to treat this thing as urgently as the other, yet less violently because more surely.

"If the river's anyway right we'll get fish. They were there this time last year and there's been nobody to bother them. They sure are fish, Johnny. When you get a hold of one you'll wish you had your spotting line instead of just a bit of gut leader."

Johnny laughed. "Guess a guy'd need to check the spotting line at that. Tommy tell you what happened a couple of weeks ago? We put five loads of logs and one empty car over the de-rail."

"The hell. How come?"

"It was the shackle really, not the line. You know how we rig them now? An eyesplice at the end looped around the bunk of the first car and back on to the line with a shackle. We had all the brakes loose and Ed was letting them down easy on the line to spot the last car under the tongs when the pin in the shackle broke—no jerk to it or anything; must have been crystallized. Took most of the next day to clean up the mess."

"What did Ted say?"

"He's still sore because he can't figure how a broken shackle is anybody's fault."

"He told Johnny we should have held them on the handbrake," Tommy said. "And there was Johnny riding them right down till the first car was off the track, trying to do just that."

"Ted don't mean anything," Johnny said. "A guy's got to have something to say when there's a pile-up like that."

4

JOHNNY finished eating, piled cup and saucer on to the heavy plate and climbed out from the bench. His mind was free of the previous day's happenings and he felt good. It was a fine day, clear and sunny, but the westerly breeze already stirring up the lake would keep things cool. He had a picture of the landing clearly in his mind: twenty or thirty logs, most of them fair-sized, lying straight out at right angles along the brow log. Nothing piled awkwardly, no boomsticks. The first car a six-log load, after that tens and twelves unless the yarder brought in more big stuff right away. The loading crews would be waiting for logs before the locie came to take out the loads and switch in more empties. They could keep on top of it all day.

The foreman was waiting outside the door of the cookhouse. He was a big man, tall, long-legged and with wide shoulders as square and flat as a board. Johnny stopped beside him. "There's two sets of tongs at the blacksmith's shop," he said. "Okay to have Shorty stop while we pick them up?"

"Sure. Matt's going up to load until the new guy comes. How does she look for today?"

"Good," Johnny said. "Should make twenty-five easy. They'll be changing roads tomorrow."

"Slim Crawford come in with you last night? Chris phoned from the beach that he was coming."

"He went over to the office to look for you." Johnny watched the foreman's stiff-legged awkward walk, shoulders held still and square in movement, long arms loose at his sides. Ted was a good guy and he got the logs out without seeming to get excited about it, like some of them. You could talk to him and say what you wanted to say and get answers the way you wanted to get them. Johnny went over to the bunkhouse, picked up hat and coat and gloves, and went out again to the track. Men were streaming up from the long narrow bunkhouses all over camp. The fallers and buckers came slowly and for the most part singly, some of them carrying sharpened saws or axes, their wrists big from chopping and sawing and wedging, their shoulders bowed by burden of tools. The Italian graders and trackmen came in groups, talking and laughing excitedly. The others—loaders, hooktenders, chokermen, riggers, engineers, even whistlepunks—somehow holding themselves apart, each one aggressively himself, bearing about him a pride in his own quality that showed in some small, effective way. A few swaggered consciously, setting the high heels of their caulked shoes solidly to ground in short, balanced stepping. In others it was a way of carrying a strong body, a flaunting of heavy leather rigging gloves, perhaps a checked shirt or the extravagantly frayed cuffs of raintest pants stagged short of boot tops. Johnny was strongly conscious of them and of the differences that separated group from group and, within the one group, yet more sharply, man from man. He watched Slim Crawford coming up from the office and knew that he again was different. Slim walked with long, easy, reaching strides and a slight spring in his step; he was loose all through, free of the muscle-bound tautness that held most of the men who worked on the machines, as well as the fallers and buckers; and there was a different purpose in the way Slim held his head and looked about him.

The brakeman came down from the locomotive and along the side of the crummy, a converted caboose that took the crews to work. Johnny said: "Stop for those tongs, will you, Shorty?"

"Okay," Shorty said.

Slim came up and stood beside Johnny, rolling a cigarette. Men were talking and laughing inside the crummy and Johnny could hear young Tommy kidding the grade foreman about Mussolini. A few more men straggled up from the bunkhouses and climbed in. Johnny swung himself up on to the rear platform and settled in his usual place, forearms resting on the wheel of the handbrake. Slim Crawford stood beside him, leaning on the iron handrail. Red Henderson came out from the crummy and stood beside Slim. Shorty signaled and the train pulled out.

At the blacksmith's shop Johnny and young Tommy dropped from the train, picked up the tongs, and clattered them on to the platform of the crummy. Shorty signaled and the train jerked into movement again. Johnny stood looking down at the tongs, sliding his caulks along the steel. "Old Ed sure knows his stuff," he said. "Slap those on a log and they stay put until you want them loose." It was good to look at them; the thick, curved, scissor arms, with upturned points sharp and bright, shading back into the blue gray of the arms through the changing colors of tempered metal. Seventy-five pounds of metal to lift five tons of wood and sap.

Slim said: "Remember the tongs down at Mellit Bay?"

Johnny turned round to his handbrake wheel again. "Sure do. That old bastard got his pattern from a broken-down ice man one day when his wife wasn't home."

Slim said: "Are the graders out your way?"

"No," Johnny said. "They're over on Side One."

"How many more settings to the end of the grade?"

"Two—one tree's rigged. We'll be moving next week. Ted send you up to pick out some more?"

Slim nodded. Johnny said: "For God's sake, pick decent landings. There must be flat places somewhere on these goddamned sidehills."

Slim turned to Red Henderson. "How is it, Red? Feel natural to be up a tree again?"

"Kind of tough at first," Red said. "A guy gets soft setting around in that goddamn place three years. But it's sure good to know you've got a few bucks coming at the end of the day. Things is opening up again now. A guy'll soon have a chance to get rich on the stock market."

"You working on Side One?"

"Yes. Raising a tree today. Pity your goddamn survey crew couldn't spot their lines a bit better."

"Wouldn't make any difference," Slim said. "There's nothing over there bigger than piling."

The train slowed and stopped a little way short of the big steam donkey that yarded and loaded the logs on Side Two. The spar tree, bare of limbs and topped a hundred or more feet from the ground, towered its network of heavy steel cables over the donkey, and a burst of white steam shot up from the safety valve against the brown bark of the trunk and among the dark lines. Slim noticed the strong sour-sweet smell of crushed bark and sapwood as he and Johnny walked the edge of the track, passing round the steel bunks of the skeleton cars; you didn't notice that smell unless you had been away from it a while and it reminded you of the things you had left in town—usually of Bess Logan and some girl at her place. It was good in some ways and bad in some ways—not so bad as the slimy smell of the same bark and sapwood at the sawmill, when it had been in the water a while; not so good as the fresh scent of bark and sap and crushed needles that would be a little farther along the track, where the fallers were working.

Johnny stopped at the landing, pulling on his gloves. "Coming down at noon?" he asked.

Slim shook his head. "I've got a lunch. See you at five o'clock."

Slim passed the donkey and the last of the waiting empties and moved over to the center of the track. The steel ran on in wavering uncertain lines, over ties with no ballast between them. He passed another spar tree, rigged with guy lines and blocks, brow logs in place on a steep landing, ready for the machines to move in and start logging. Then the steel ended and he was walking on the bare earth of the grade. There was felled timber all about him, the fresh-cut ends of logs showing redly out of tumbled masses of broken limbs, the bluish underside of the needles making a piled and cushioned background for red-brown bark of fir logs, the gray of hemlock and occasional silver of balsam. Another spar tree, naked of limbs and top but not yet rigged, stood straightly ahead of him; and beyond that, sharply cut as though the woods were a solid, was the edge of the standing timber.

By the spar tree Slim turned from the track and climbed on to a high stump. From there he looked about him, seeing how the little draws and gullies, all the flow of the land on each side of the track, led to the tree; how the fallers had let their trees down along the run of these lines so that the standing tree was a hub with spokes that stretched six or eight hundred feet from it in every direction. Tree 18 on line HW. It had seemed a good one when he and Ted picked it months ago, with the timber standing all about it to hide the lie of the country. It was good to see it now and know that it had worked out so well, that eye and mind and instrument had done a good job of stripping the veiling timber from the contours and finding the right answer. He dropped down from the stump and went on into the standing timber. Behind him he heard the donkey's starting whistle and the clatter of steam as Johnny's tongs lifted the first log of the day.

In the timber it was quiet and cool and the moss and needles underfoot deadened his easy steps. Andy's preliminary line led on from the end of the grade, Art's careful figures in blue chalk on stakes at every hundred feet. "Location's right on it most places," Andy had said. "And I think I kept close enough to the trees we looked at. Can't shift much for trees anyway; there's rock several places and if you want to keep from hauling logs against grade you can't fool around much on those sidehills."

He found the first tree and blazed it with the cross that would protect it from the fallers—he knew that it checked in well with the country and Andy's line was dead right for it. Before noon he had picked and marked six trees, one of them a small hemlock that would be used only to raise a larger tree into position, but the others, good solid firs, well placed to country and track and on ground that would make fair landings. Then he turned up from the line, traveling by compass almost straight against the slope. He felt glad to be free of the line, working again on something not yet set. Chris Eldridge had said there were to be no grades above HW here where the hill became higher and steeper; they would be putting cold-deck donkeys out in the woods to draw logs into piles within reach of the regular yarding donkeys down at the track. Three hundred paces uphill from the surveyed line he took out his compass again and set himself a new course, cutting across the slope and back towards the edge of the timber. He was thinking and watching now on this first time through, marking in his mind the run of the draws, the set of the slopes, flat benches and steep gray bluffs. He checked himself by the cruiser's blueprint, occasionally glancing at compass or aneroid. But this trip there was no need to be exact; tomorrow he would come out and tie in what he found to the line below him and perhaps the day after take Ted through and let him start worrying.

It worked out more easily than he had expected—a series of benches ran along the hill at about the right distance from Andy's line and gave plenty of chances for good cold-deck settings. He came back out to the edge of the timber soon after three o'clock and realized that his lunch was still in the back pocket of his coat. He turned up to the fringe of timber along the crest of the hill above where the fallers had been and followed it along until he was directly above the tree where Johnny was working. Then he settled himself at the base of a big fir and began to eat.

He realized that the concentration of his work had shut other thoughts away from him for several hours. It had been a satisfying concentration and had done good work for him. Chris and Ted had been worried about the Side Two line—worried because they had been caught behind there and knew they must plan the logging in a hurry to keep ahead of the rigging and yarding crews. That was their worry, passed on to him; but there had been a worry of his own. Andy's line had been run without any idea of cold-decking the part of the hill beyond reach from the track, and if it hadn't been for the lucky run of the country there might have been trouble about that. To be rid of those things was a good freedom. There was suddenly time now to remember next Sunday, how the river would be and where the fish would be in it; getting Chong to put up a box of food and borrowing Art's sleeping bag for Johnny. There was time again to look about you and notice things, to feel the strong breeze coming across the logged country from the lake, to see the sunlight on the salal leaves, to hear the yarder straining under a turn of logs and the roar of steam each time Ed Nelson touched his loading levers.

Slim finished his lunch and lay back against the trunk of the tree. He thought back to logging again because it was all there before him, waiting to have a mind on it. It started with himself—no, way back before himself, perhaps with some crazy fool of a timber staker, traveling about the bush with an ax and a sack of oatmeal. Then the timber staker went to town and sold his timber to some big logger from Seattle or Everett or even one straight out from Michigan in those days. And then for years the timber was just standing there, while the big logger sent an occasional cruiser to estimate it and map the country and try to find somewhere nearly as much there as the staker and the first cruisers had said there was. Then the big logger had to decide it was time to start something and survey crews went in to find camp sites and locate railroad. And maybe money had to be raised from somewhere—shareholders and bondholders, trust companies and banks, people who had never seen a skeleton car or a pair of loading tongs or even a log maybe. Then, when the camps were built and the railroads laid and piles driven for the dump and the booming ground down at the beach, the first logs would begin to roll.

I've never been in at the start of an outfit. Must be a sweet mess if it's anything like when we moved Camp Seven to Camp Eight. All that has to happen before I come in—and maybe a whole lot more of backing and filling and speculating and false starts if it's one of those unlucky outfits. After that I come, looking at what they tell me to look at, checking the figures of a cruise or the lie of a hillside or the run of draws and swamps. Then I'm with Andy, telling him where I think his lines will have to go or with Ted up here or Dalberg down at Camp Five trying to tell them where they ought to rig trees and how the country will come to them if they do. Then the graders and bridge crews, following Andy's lines with Art's writing on the stakes. And the steel gang after them.

By that time the fallers and buckers are in and it's beginning to open up and look like this does. Red comes in with the rigging-up crew and they slap guy lines and blocks and loading guys on the tree and run lines out into the woods. All that before a log moves except to drop or roll a few feet when a bucker finishes his cut.

Slim closed his eyes and traced the thing through in his mind. He couldn't remember that he had thought it all the way through before and seen it this way. He saw the logs snaking down the hillside now, following the pull of the mainline to the pile at the landing. Then Johnny on an empty car just spotted under the tongs, his white-gold hair bright in the sun, tan shirt loose outside blue jeans cut short at boot tops. Little feet in spiked boots, dull brown Paris boots with spiked heels set far forward, almost under the instep, to grip on the forward-slanting logs. Johnny looking down at the pile to pick his bunk load, reaching one leather-gloved hand behind him for the tongs that Ed at the levers slid down into it. The infinitesimally brief pose, like a diver's, both hands gripping the tongs, held high and a little in front of him, eyes on the chosen log. Then the few short running steps, the twist of shoulders and body that flipped the tongs on to the log a foot or two from its end and was met by the quick spurt of steam as Ed touched the lever to set the tongs. You couldn't remember the detail of it fast enough, even when you did it yourself. The way Johnny did it seemed to melt all the movements into a single flowing glide. Even the jerk of steam as Ed tightened on the tongs was followed so closely by the longer roar as he lifted that the two seemed one. And Johnny would be not only in the clear but back on the brow log watching the lift of his log as it came up across the car.

Slim pulled his mind back to follow his logs to the sea. If you've never done it, you'd better do it now. Johnny's only a little part, not even as much as you, except that you've worked with him so much and watched him so much that he seems like all logging from start to finish. Johnny's loads go down to the switch behind the Two Spot and hook on to the loads from Side One. Then the Five Spot takes over and runs them down through camp, along the lake ten miles, along the river four miles and over to the Camp Five junction. Hank Parker and Dad Hutchins and the big Baldwin take them there, hook them on to the Camp Five loads and rattle them down to the dump. That's where they hit the chuck, two loads at a time sliding and rolling down the sloping piles into the deep water of the booming grounds. And the boom boys sorting them out, number threes and worse for the mill, the good fir and the cedar for the tugs to take to town.

"Hell," Slim said. "It's quick enough once they start." Half a million feet of logs a day from the two camps. Five or ten acres of good timber in any man's language. He slid forward a little until he was settled squarely on his back at the foot of the tree. The west wind brought the sounds clearly up to him from below, so that he could follow every movement of the work. The sharp rattle of chokers let down on the mainline; slighter sounds of metal on metal as the chokermen pulled them out and set them round the logs. The hooktender's shout and the answering whistle at the donkey. The throaty staccato of the yarder, the slap of guy lines and rattle of blocks on the quivering tree. Logs cracking out of the brush, smashing down saplings, sliding past stumps, thudding on to the landing. Then the easier sound of the haulback at work and the chokers coming out again. And through all the other sounds those sharp bursts of steam and the clink of tongs as the loading crew worked.

Slim sat up and looked at his watch. Hell, he thought. There's all kinds of time to walk over to Side One and see what Red's doing.

5

SLIM lay on his back in the sun outside the bridge crew's shelter. Johnny was putting up a rod and threading line through the rings. Below them, two or three hundred feet through the trees, the wide river sparkled and danced over a rapid. Johnny said: "I wish you had been with me last night, Alec. I was going good, laying it out there like a real fisherman, when that fellow took hold."

Slim looked up at him, squinting his eyes half shut against the sun, his full lips lazy with a twisted smile. "Then you let him break the gut. Great heavy gut pretty near like straw line."

"Hell," Johnny said, "how was I to know the son of a bitch could pull like that? You didn't see it. It looked like the whole bottom of the river coming up when the son of a bitch broke water."

Slim watched the strong white hands bring the line through the top ring of the rod. They were unsteady and clumsy, fumbling to knot the gut to the end of the tapered fly line. He smiled again, gently and happily. It was good to see Johnny fumbling and awkward, clumsy about something for once in his life. "You're scared there's going to be another one take hold of you."

Johnny looked up quickly. "You go to hell. If you

hadn't ever hooked on to anything bigger than a twenty-inch trout in a lake your hand would shake too."

Slim climbed to his feet and picked up his rod. "Guess I'll hike on down to the Triangle Pool. I'll fish below that for a way, but I'll come back and meet you there about noon."

"Okay," Johnny said. "See you then. Don't keep any small ones."

Johnny tied one of Slim's bright flies to his gut and started down through the timber towards the river. He came out to a long smooth pool below the rapid, narrow at the head where the fast water came in, but spreading well towards the lower end. He stood looking down at it in satisfaction. Slim had said it was the best bet in the whole river for a steelhead. It was morning, the start of a day; the new rod that Slim had picked out for him was light in his hand for all its eleven-foot length, and the short hour of fishing the evening before had given him confidence in what he could do with it. He waded in at the head of the pool, feeling the sharp cold of the water as it came in through the broken seams of his old caulked shoes. Slowly he let line out and began to work his fly across the current.

Slim had said that the fish usually lay well towards the tail of the pool, but to try the whole thing through anyway. When Slim said things like that—and they didn't have to be about fishing—you believed him and did what he said. He was a funny guy. Last night and this morning he had been kidding all the time, his red mouth twisted with that smile and his blue eyes looking at you from his smooth, evenly brown face. Slim was like a swell-looking woman sometimes; brown curly hair, always lighter in summer time just above his forehead, where he pushed his hat back; long, round chin, full lips and straight nose. It was good to look at him. But he wasn't ever like any woman you could come near, or any soft woman. Just his face was like the faces on woman statues sometimes are. His hands were big, long-fingered and wide, and there were long hard muscles in his forearms and shoulders, across his back and on his flat belly. It wasn't right to think Slim was like a woman, except for his face sometimes and when he talked sometimes. The way he could talk, telling things and figuring things and explaining things, could make you like him so goddamn much you wanted to die for him or give him anything you had. But he wouldn't always talk that way. Sometimes he'd just keep kidding, saying little sharp things that didn't matter a damn, like last night and this morning. He did that when he was feeling lazy and nothing was bothering him. Right now it was because he had straightened things out for Ted and got things fixed so the fallers could go in beyond Side Two the first of the week. Straightening Ted up would please Chris, and Slim was just like a kid about Chris, no matter what he said about his being a boss logger and just the same as all the rest of them. When Chris said something he had done was good Slim's face would get all red and his voice would be so thick he'd stumble over his words and you could hardly tell what he was saying. That was maybe because Chris had taught him so much of what he knew, but likely it was tied up with the kind of man Chris was—a logger from away back, always friendly and easy with the boys and acting like he was still just running a donkey instead of bossing the whole outfit.

He watched his line as the current drew it and angled the fly across. It straightened below him and he waited, drew a little back into his hand, waited again and lifted. Sixty feet of line came back through the air, straightened behind him, flew forward at the pull of the rod top and curved the fly well out across the current again. Johnny moved two steps downstream as the fly touched, fishing as Slim fished, giving it a chance to get down before the line bellied in the current and began its draw. The line was sinking well, drawing the fly slow and deep. He looked down and saw the flat-topped rock, just breaking water, two steps below him. "When you're right by the flat rock you're in the surest place of the whole pool. Lay it across there as far as you can, straight out. He'll take you on that, about forty-five degrees downstream. And for God's sake don't get to thinking you've got a spar tree and a two-inch mainline." Slim had said that at breakfast. You felt like a kid at school when he told you anything so plainly, maybe like Slim himself had felt when he came up second-loading five years ago, a green university kid putting in a summer vacation. He had grown out of that fast though.

Johnny lifted his line again, made his cast and moved down to the rock. The current drew the line tight and the fly began to work. The pull came suddenly, fiercely, tearing line off the reel. Johnny saw the bright fish in the air, two or three feet clear above the water. His rod was up, bent in a long arc. The reel still ratcheted out and the fish jumped again, twice, well downstream. Then he was suddenly right with it, nursing the reel with his hand, checking the rush, using the rod as it was meant to be used. He wanted the fight over, the fish on the beach, safe. It was jerking unevenly, sulkily, working across the pool, just holding against the current. He coaxed it up, afraid for the gut, for the hook-hold, for every slender thing that linked the two of them together. The fish came on, swimming slowly, then turned sharply and ran again. He brought it up again, level with him, then past him. He put on more strain, guiding it towards shore. It came, resisting, then suddenly jumped in a blinding splash right at the rod-top and went off in a long, tearing run clear to the head of the pool. It came back easily. Johnny led it in on its side, clear up to his feet, bent down, slid two fingers into the gills and carried it ashore. It lay bright on the rocks, a little scarlet blood running down from the gills. Johnny laid the rod down and freed the hook. What happened in the rest of the day did not matter. It had been done properly and without fuss or failure, except in that first frozen moment when nothing was lost. Slim had said a man was a fisherman that could do it and do it right.

Johnny reached in his pocket and got out pouch and papers. He rolled a cigarette, spilling tobacco because his hands still shook. That goddamn Slim. This was the sort of thing he got that other people didn't get because they didn't know enough. Slim knew what kind of rod to buy and how to use it and what fish to look for. And when it was all done the way he said there was a hell of a kick to it. It was the same with other things. Slim had found Bess Logan and the girls. He said it was plain crazy to go pick some whore in a beer parlor that couldn't talk right or act right and then go get drunk with her. Bess Logan's girls weren't like that. You could take them out places, to restaurants and shows and wherever you wanted to go, and have one of them for all the time you were in town. And the way Slim told you to read a book, or explained about how the timber was going and some day there might not be jobs, the way he could figure out a hunt or a fishing trip like this one and show you how to get the most kick out of it—all that showed he had something. Johnny smoked his cigarette and watched the blue of the sky through the green tops of the tall firs. . . .

Slim Crawford walked down to the Triangle Pool, then decided to leave it until later in the day. There were two pools farther down that he could fish through before noon, then Johnny could try the Triangle Pool if he hadn't been able to get a fish up above.

The first of the two pools was on a long curve and he fished it down lazily, sliding the line out in looping roll casts that covered the water from bank to bank. It gave him strong pleasure to do things easily and he was grateful to the light downstream breeze and the perfectly matched balance of line and rod that let him work smoothly and gracefully, without straining or effort. There was a certain rhythm to his fishing, the reaching cast, two steps downstream, the long arc of the searching fly, the careful holding at the end, recovery of line and the new cast. But he broke the rhythm again and again without seeming to destroy it, sometimes shortening line to cover a sunken rock, sometimes reaching farther out, perhaps flopping the forming belly of the line upstream to delay the pull of the current, occasionally stripping line from the reel after the cast was made to let the fly carry down in its line for a few feet more. And when the fish took there was no haste or anxiety in his response. The rod lifted easily into a smooth, springing curve that met and turned the instantaneous first rush; Slim's left hand held the top of the cork grip, his right hand slid down to the reel. He seemed to expect every move, every sharp turn and run and leap, and he controlled each one as it came with light easy movements of hands and body. When he drew the fish in to him it was on its side and perfectly still. He slid his fingers under the gill covers as Johnny had a few minutes earlier, carried it ashore and killed it with a single sharp blow at the base of the skull. Then he too rolled and lit a cigarette.

That rolling of a smoke to honor the death of a good fish was to Slim a rite, consciously performed. Its omission would have reduced the value of all that had gone before almost to the point of nullification. As he smoked he looked down at his fish. It was laid carefully in the thick moss at the foot of a heavy-limbed spruce, on a curve of ground that raised the center of its body slightly above head and tail and subtly emphasized the grace and power of its shape. It was a good place, but long experience in the fulfillment of his rite had led him to it almost without conscious searching. He was glad that he was alone, without need to hold back from his pleasure or maintain any barriers of casualness between himself and the eyes or words of witnesses. It would be all right with Johnny there, but it was better without him. Slim just smoked and looked at the fish. It was a good fish, a little over ten pounds, he judged, smooth-scaled and silver-fresh from the sea. One saw that at a glance. But the delight was in looking more closely, assaying the lovely proportions of the little head, the slender yet rounded body and the wide square tail. This fish had the color too, the faint violet sheen, so delicate as to be imperceptible unless one looked with eyes that really saw, running from tail to gill cover along the side. When you had seen this you had time to look again, at the clean silver whiteness of the belly, at the few little spots—like tiny black crosses when you looked closely at them—along back and shoulders. Slim moved a little, so that the light ran differently along the body of the fish; the change showed him the long lines of muscles, flowing with the body curve and repeating it.

He finished his cigarette and stubbed it out on a stone. Slowly he took out his tobacco and began to roll another cigarette. It would be better to see all that living, in movement under the water. Yet you could never see it closely enough that way. It was good when you saw it, perhaps even better than this, but quite different. In the water the fish blended, as it was meant to, the dark back always uppermost, catching only a fraction of the light; silver belly and glorious sides dimmed to even dullness. The false position of the body, turned to air and unshielded daylight, was necessary before all its beauty could be seen. And then it lasted only a little while, not more than half an hour at full perfection. . . .

Johnny came down to the Triangle Pool just before noon, carrying two fish, and found Slim already there. Slim saw the fish and stood up. "Boy, that's swell," he said. "Hell, Johnny, I'm tickled you got them." He took both fish and laid them on the rocks to look more closely at them. The skin of the first had dried and wrinkled in the sun and wind, but it was still a fine fish. The second was small, not much over four pounds, but beautifully shaped and colored. Slim pointed to it. "You only just got that one."

Johnny nodded. "I came straight down as soon as I had him out of the water." He was out of breath, sweating and very happy. "How did you make out?"

Slim said: "I got a couple. Let's take yours over and put them all together." He was glad now that he had turned the third fish loose; he had done it partly because he did not want to be burdened with an excessive weight of fish, and partly through reluctance to kill. It had worked out well. They laid the four fish together and covered them with moss and leaves. Slim reached into a small packsack and handed Johnny a square packet of sandwiches.

"Sit down and tell about it."

Johnny settled himself in the shade, leaning back on one elbow in the soft moss and looking out at the river. "Well," he said, "I got the big one in the first pool, right where you said to look for him. He scared the liver out of me, but I guess I did it all just about right—nothing broke, anyway. And the other one struck right up at the head of the pool above this one—first cast I made. He acted crazier than the big one—ran and jumped all over the pool and went half way down the rapid before I could get him. So I came right on down."

Slim was watching him closely. "Get a kick out of it?"

Johnny looked up, his face alight with his smile. "Sure did. That beats any fishing I ever saw or thought of."

They were silent for a while, then Johnny said: "Let me look at that box of flies again, Alec."

Slim reached into his pocket, brought out the box and handed it across. "Lose some?"

Johnny opened the box. "No. Broke the hook off one—must have hit a rock behind me. I just wanted to look at them again."

They were bright in the sun, still pretty, but no longer having the luxurious, sensual richness he had felt in the lamplight of the caboose.

"Still like chorus girls?" Slim asked.

Johnny shook his head, looking at the flies. "No. But that's the way they did look, the first time I saw them. Like the way that guy paints girls in *Esquire*—all slick and smooth, and long legs and bright colors."

"Sure. I know. Sounds like you're getting ready for a trip to town."

"That's right," Johnny said. "I should have gone down with you. What did Bess have this time?"

"Just about the same bunch. You didn't ever see Rita, did you? Tall and smooth as they come, with black hair and black eyes. A bitch to bite. Bess let me have her for two weeks straight. We had rooms on Burrard Street and lived as if we were married."

"Jesus," Johnny said. "Must have cost like hell."

"What the hell is there better for a guy to spend money on? I tell you, Johnny, it was slick. I'm crazy about that kid. She's all kinds of good—not just in bed."

"A man could be married all year round just about as cheap."

Slim frowned. "Sure, and bring the girl up to some dump of a camp where there's nothing to do but walk a few hundred feet along the track? And live in some goddamn shack the company calls a house? Or else build one yourself so they can kick you out and take it over whenever they want?"

"Eric makes out all right. They seem happy enough."

"She's a damn good woman and she makes it better than most women could. But she won't be satisfied with it forever, now they've got kids."

"Just the same, a guy's got to get married sometime."

"You're damn right he has." Slim sat up and screwed his lunch paper into a tight ball. "Listen, Johnny. I wasn't kidding with what I said about unions the other day. That's the sort of thing a union could fix up. Right now the companies do everything they can to keep a man from getting married."

"It isn't as bad as it used to be that way, but it's still not so good. They maybe won't stop you getting married, but they sure don't do anything to make it comfortable."

"A good union would fix that."

"Think so? Any union we got would be ninety per cent bohunks and bums. Some with wives back in Europe, some with wives up at a settlement somewhere, most of them without wives and not ever likely to get them. There wouldn't be more than one or two in fifty that would give a damn about bringing wives into camp."

"Lots of those fellows will get married when they're

more used to the country. And anyway, that isn't the only reason for a union."

"I know there's lots of good things about unions," Johnny said. "If the average working guy could keep control of them. But it don't happen that way. You and me and Eric and Ed and the rest of the bunch might start a good union and the next thing you know we'd be out on our fannies. And a lot of foreigners that never saw a pair of caulked shoes except in a Hastings Street store would be running it. And us. Saying where we could work and how we could work and when we had to strike and how much we had to pay the shysters back East. Look how it was in the strike. Remember that long-haired son of a bitch that used to get up every time he thought the boys needed a pep talk? 'Fellow-strikers,' Johnny mimicked the nagging voice. 'Fellow-workers, I mean. . . .' Hell, that bastard never saw work, and if he did he ran to beat hell or went out on strike."

"Well," Slim said, "it's going to come and if good guys would get in at the start and keep busy in the thing they could control it. I don't see why you're so hard against it, Johnny. You're always nuts on safety stuff and getting a decent wage and decent treatment and seeing the other guy does. And any bum who's ever been in a camp with you can touch you for ten bucks in town."

"That's different. It's like the union we had for the strike. There was need of something then. Up till 1930 things were the way they ought to be. A man could get himself a job at a good wage and if he didn't like it he could quit and get another job quick enough. Then she was tough all right. And right on till the start of this year we weren't more than working for board. But as soon as we knew the price of logs was moving up we asked for more wages. And when the companies tried to stall we organized a union, went on strike and got more wages. That's the way I figure it should be."

"Maybe it's not too bad with a good company," Slim said. "A superintendent like Chris is square enough with the boys—just as square as the head office will let him be. But all the outfits aren't like that—look at Hutchins. And you can't ever tell when an outfit's going to change."

"Hutchins was what we struck about. That was the first outfit to start making money and when the boys asked for a raise they turned them down cold. So we struck."

"Sure, but you need protection all the time. And there's other things besides wages that ought to be changed—blacklisting and shut-downs, for instance."

"I can't see it," Johnny said. "Maybe a few wobblies get blacklisted. And there's shut-downs for snow and fire season and bad markets. But a man can get work if he's good on the job, and wages are pretty fair now."

Slim sat forward and reached for his rod. "I know all that," he said. "I can feel the same way about most of it. But you've got to remember that if they can blacklist reds and wobblies they can do the same damn thing to you any time they want."

"I guess there's something in that. I don't know. You can talk it all a whole lot better than I can, Alec, but it still seems to me there would be something phoney about any union we got."

Slim Crawford laughed and Johnny sensed that he had let the serious mood fall away from him. The effort to convince was discarded, tucked away to be brought out again and used at some other time. "The hell with it," Slim said. "I know goddamn well how you feel. Let's go back where we started for a minute. You don't really figure on going to town right away, do you?"

"I guess not," Johnny said. "There's liable to be a shut-down in August if the weather keeps dry. I ought to be able to get by till then."

"Look," Slim said. "Forget about town till Christmas and let's have a real hunt in October sometime. I want to go up Kiltool Sound again and we could have a swell time there. Deer and goats and bear and geese and ducks."

Johnny slapped his strong, thick-fingered hand down on the soft moss. "Boy," he said. "I wouldn't want anything better than that. That's where the bowl in the mountains you told me about is and where your cousin has a farm down on the tide flats?"

"That's right. Put you straight back home on the prairies. You can milk a cow and drive the team and get hayseeds in your hair if you want. And there's cream and fresh eggs and girls—nice girls, that keep their fannies under their skirts all the time." He stood up, threading a new fly line through the top rings of his rod. "We better go fishing again. I left this pool so we could try that new rig I told you about—the floating line with one of those little thin flies in the box there. Just get one fish to take hold that way and you'll wonder why you ever got a kick out of the old way."

6

JOHNNY lay on his bunk after supper, smoking a cigarette and leafing through a magazine. It was September and the evenings were still light. In a little while Slim would be finished making up his notes and would come over, and they would both go down to the lake to see if there were any trout around the float. Then, at dusk, they would come up, have a shower in the bathhouse, talk a little and go to bed.

An old man sat on the next bunk, his elbows on his knees, head down, staring at the floor. There was no one else in that end of the bunkhouse, though the sound of voices came through the open door from the small room where the stove and the drying racks were, and from the other wing of the bunkhouse beyond it. Johnny laid his magazine down and looked at the old man.

"What's the matter, John?" he said at last. "You look as if you had kinked your saw and hit a rock with your ax all at the same time."

Old John looked up from the floor. His face was gentle, heavily lined and long-jawed, with a wide low forehead. His blue eyes smiled a deprecating denial of the gloom his bowed shoulders and drooping head had suggested. "It ain't anything, Johnny," he said. "Just I been an old fool and I guess I trying to figure out why."

"What did you do, John?" Johnny spoke with the unconscious, faintly patronizing gentleness of the young and strong for the old.

"I got me in a poker game."

"Last night? With your paycheck?"

"Ja. With paychecks for five months. I save 'em for grubstake to work on my claims next year. When I was young falla play pretty good poker. Last night no good. He take everyt'ing like I was baby."

"Who did?"

"Big black falla work on rigging-up crew. Black on here." John touched his upper lip. "You seen him."

"Crooked?"

"I t'ank so maybe. Some of the boys say they seen him before. Big Al Farley they call him."

"Anybody else lose much?"

"Sure. They play pretty near every night all week. Not tonight."

"Maybe we can get those paychecks back."

"Bulls you mean?" John asked. "No good. A falla been an old fool like me you better let him. No bulls."

"We'll leave the bulls out of it."

"Don't you go get hurt for me, Johnny. Old John ain't worth it. They's two of them fallas together."

Johnny laughed and got up from his bunk. "That's okay, John. We'll try it once anyhow."

He went out of the bunkhouse and along to where Red Henderson bunked. Red wasn't there but someone said: "I think he went down on the wharf, Johnny." Johnny walked up to the track and turned along it towards the wharf. It was sunset on a still evening and he could see

Red's slight figure against the dull red reflection of the water. Red's voice, frail and light but true and full of easy rhythm, came back to him on the still air. "Molly and me—and baby makes three—in my blue hea-ven." As he sang Red's feet shuffled on the rough planks of the wharf, tracing out little quick dance steps, never completed. Putting him away like that hadn't changed Red a goddamned bit. This evening might have been three years ago, even to the clothes he was wearing—heavy wool underwear, long-sleeved and with no shirt over it, only the wide straps of suspenders holding up raintest pants that stood stiffly out around his legs and failed by twelve inches to reach down to the shiny patent leather dancing shoes.

Johnny walked out along the wharf. Red looked at him and kept on singing. "Do you still dance, Red?"

"Hell, how do you think I got back here with new work clothes? Me and Grace was in a competition and got second. Them judges ain't no good now. Time was they put chalk on the heels of your shoes and when a good couple was waltzing they'd make the guy put a glass of water on his head. Now style don't seem to mean nothing to them."

Johnny said: "You did pretty good to come second."

"Why not? I used to think a man could get rich in that racket. There was a South American woman once, about forty, forty-five and still plenty good looking, but it didn't work out. Guess she figured I wasn't tall enough."

Johnny said: "That guy with the black mustache, Al Farley, is he on your crew?"

"Him? Sure is. Why?"

"He took four or five hundred bucks off the old windfall bucker, playing poker last night."

"The hell you say. I didn't know there was that much dough in camp. Him and that side-kick of his has been cleaning the boys regular all week, but I didn't hear they had hit a jackpot like that."

"Know the guy before he came up here?"

"Big Al? Knew of him. Crooked as a dog's hind-leg. Cold-deck Al some of them call him. Regular card shark."

"Will he stick around or pull out now?"

Red shrugged his shoulders. "That sucker's my big worry right now. That's what I was trying to figure down here. The way he acts on the crew it looks like he wants my job. I've got as far as him or me's going down the road, but I don't see how it's going to be him."

"You can't tangle with him," Johnny said.

"Why not?"

"Hell, he must weigh over two hundred. He'd paste the daylights out of you."

"Might dim a lamp on him while he's doing it."

"You couldn't reach that high on him."

Red shrugged his shoulders again. "If he pulls any of his wisecracks tomorrow he's going to get called."

"Well, don't tangle with him out on the job. Wait till you get back to camp."

"Okay," Red hummed and danced a few little steps on his quick, light feet. "Jesus, Johnny, it's a hell of a note a guy has to make his living this way."

"Don't you like rigging? You used to like it."

"Sure I like it. But it's a hell of a note for a guy that's

got ambition to be shinning up trees like a goddamn monkey all day. You can't get rich that way."

"What would you do if you got rich, Red?"

"Me? God, I don't know. I'd buy me a fancy big car and go and stay in swell hotels. I'd have good clothes, lots of them—nothing flashy, them quiet, custom-made, hundred-and-fifty-dollar rigs like rich guys wear. And I'd have a swell-looking dame with me all the time and good liquor. And I guess I'd get my golf game good again."

Johnny rode with his forearms resting on the brake wheel of the crummy as the train switched in to Side One at the end of the day. He watched the men as they climbed aboard. Al Farley came among the first group and passed inside the crummy. Johnny turned to watch the easy movement of his big body among the benches of men, the broad flat back of his shirt, outlines of shoulder blades and heavy muscles showing in dark patterns of sweat on the faded blue cloth. His legs and feet were good too, sure and light-moving but with heavy calves and heavy thighs above them. Two hundred and ten stripped, Johnny decided, and turned to his brake wheel again. He heard Farley's big voice behind him: "The little sawed-off son of a bitch said he'd see me after supper. Christ, it's one hell of an outfit that'd have that for a rigger."

Red Henderson came up and stood beside him. They watched Slim Crawford coming down the track, striding two ties at a time and smiling as the brakeman kidded him.

"We'll pull out one day and leave you to eat salal leaves for supper," Shorty said.

"Hell, I can walk it quick as this old fog-box can struggle down there," Slim said and swung aboard. Up in the cab the fireman jerked on the bell and the train began to move.

"How did you make out, Red?" Johnny asked.

"Said I'd see him after supper."

"Did you have to do that?"

"Sure did. I canned him about midafternoon and he called me every kind of a son of a bitch he could lay his tongue to. Guess I'll be heading for town tomorrow too."

"Why in hell?" Johnny asked. "That stuff don't go any more. You canned him—let him go even if he does clean up on you. Anyway, Ted wouldn't give him your job."

"He doesn't want to stay," Slim said. "He's got the best part of a thousand bucks in his jeans for ten days' work and he'll be pulling out tomorrow anyway."

Slim waited for Johnny at the door of the cookhouse. "What's the set-up?" he asked.

"Watch the big buy. Soon as he goes out we'll go after him. Know what his side-kick looks like?"

"Sure. Chunky guy with a red and black shirt and a kind of soft-looking face."

"Watch him if anything starts."

They went in and sat down. Slim put food carefully on his plate. Not much. Meat, a little potato, some lettuce. A piece of pie and a cup of coffee after that would be enough. He looked across at Johnny, eating his usual meal quickly. Funny how guys took things differently. Red didn't seem to give a damn either and he was sure of a pasting. A few men were beginning to straggle out of the cookhouse. Red got up, walked to the door, selected a toothpick from the cigarette box nailed to the wall, and went out without looking back. Farley came quickly. Johnny stood up, looked across at Slim and nodded. They went through the door together, in time to see Red turn halfway across the tracks and face Farley's rush. Red's little dancing feet were quick; he side-stepped and put a left in Farley's face. But Farley was good. He moved in and hit Red between the eyes, then on the side of the head. Johnny said: "Let's go, Alec," and a moment later he was holding Red. Red looked back and swore. Johnny said, "Shut up," and swung him back to Shorty and young Tommy. "Take him to the bunkhouse, boys," he said.

It was like watching Johnny load—fast and smooth and easy. Slim saw Farley's partner and watched him. Johnny and Farley stood a few feet apart, watching each other.

"What the hell's the big idea?" Farley asked.

"What do you think?"

"I got no quarrel with you. The little guy called me out. If he didn't want it why did he say so?"

Johnny said: "You got some company checks you'd maybe like to cash for a nickel apiece."

"Looks like it's time somebody taught you to mind your own business," Farley said.

Johnny felt the surge of blood to throat and neck, the sharp readying of muscles all through his body. He led a left into Farley's face and followed with a right. He had worried about Farley. The guy was big and strong and might have been good; professional card sharks often were. But he didn't look good now and he hadn't looked very fancy even against Red. Johnny measured his distance and put another left into the black mustache. Farley rushed and Johnny met it, hard left and hard right at the base of the ribs.

Slim saw Farley's partner moving up. He swung across to face him. "You keep out of this," he said.

"Who says to?"

Slim stood still and said nothing. His heart was pounding; fighting was all right for Johnny—he'd done it for a living once—but most guys didn't like it. This guy didn't like it. His eyes turned away from Slim's and he moved a step back. "Stick around," Slim said. "But don't get funny." He turned back to the fight.

Farley was down on his hands and knees across one rail, blood dripping slowly from his face on to a tie—Slim noticed it was a hewn hemlock tie. Johnny stood over him. "Had enough?" he asked.

Farley nodded, his head still down.

"What about the checks?"

"They belong to me. I won them fair."

Johnny moved his feet. He still had caulked shoes on. "Listen," he said slowly. "You find those checks and hand them over right here and now or I'll kick your teeth down the back of your throat." He thought: I believe maybe I'd do it too, thinking of old John shuffling through the woods bucking windfalls day after day for five months so this bastard can have it easy.

Farley reached a hand back to his hip-pocket and threw

out a wallet. Johnny picked it up and sorted out a dozen of the green company checks. There was a big roll of bills in the wallet. Johnny turned and handed the checks to Bill Harker, the hooktender on Side Two.

"These guys take cash off anyone, Bill, or just checks?"

"Pretty near all checks, I think," Harker said. "Farley had a big wad of bills when he came into camp."

Johnny flipped the wallet back so that it fell on the tie under Farley's face. "Let's go, Alec," he said.

They went up from the track towards Red's bunkhouse. "You did a swell job," Slim said.

"It needed doing. Wonder how Red is."

Red was sitting on his bunk, Shorty and young Tommy standing over him like guards. Shorty said: "Did you finish it that quick, Johnny? Tommy and me was madder than hell at Red here because we figured we might be missing something good."

Johnny said: "Did he hurt you bad, Red?"

"Hell, no. I was just getting started good when you come along."

"Did you really want to fight him that bad?"

Red looked up. One side of his freckled face was red and swollen and he still had the determined, belligerent expression with which he had faced Farley. Then he laughed. "A guy's got to make some sort of bluff, don't he? I don't want the can beaten off me any worse than you do, but it's no use to let everybody see it."

Slim said: "You're a good guy, Red."

"Makes a guy feel kind of small to have Johnny act nursemaid like that."

Young Tommy said. "Forget it, Red. You went after

Timber

the son of a bitch and you didn't back down. If little guys like you could clean up on big guys like that it would be a hell of a life. Little guys is always looking for scraps."

"Some sucker will get Al Farley good one day," Shorty said. "He's pulled too many raw ones."

"You seen him before?" Johnny asked.

"Sure. Al's worked every camp on the coast some time or other and most of the joints in town. Generally he keeps his trap shut better than this time. He's one hell of a good rigger. Comes into camp, does his job, makes a clean-up and gets the hell out."

"Don't the boys ever get wise and run him out of camp?" Tommy asked.

"They don't give a damn mostly. He did get beat up once before, in some haywire camp up in the Islands. But he does it slow and quiet, and he's too big and tough for most guys even if they do get sore at him. If he hadn't figured old John for more of a sucker than he was and then got started riding Red here he'd have gotten by with it this time. There's always some of the boys like a poker game, even when they know they're being taken for a ride."

Slim said: "Going for a shower, Johnny? We missed out last night and Charlie said he'd have a good fire."

They went down towards the wash house, passing groups of men that were talking about the fight. Ted was standing in the doorway of the office. "You ain't forgotten it all, Johnny. That was quick as you took the nigger from Seattle."

Johnny laughed. "I'd take ten of that guy before I'd get in with the nigger again."

Slim said: "What nigger was that?"

"It's old stuff," Johnny said. "Ted used to follow the fights and he saw me fight preliminaries in Vancouver two or three times when I was first out from Alberta. The nigger was good all right. I caught him lucky the first time we fought, but he pasted me all over the ring about a month later. Whitey Jones they called him because he had a strip of white hair about an inch wide running back from his forehead. Whitey might have gone way up if somebody hadn't stuck a knife in him."

They were in the wash house. Slim was already stripped, his brown body lean and angular as he bent forward to look at the fire under the boiler. He straightened up and watched Johnny take off his shirt. Johnny's skin was very white, smooth as a girl's; there was a dull red mark of Farley's fist on his ribs. Slim watched the movement of firm, rounded muscles as Johnny stripped; his body was so smooth that you didn't judge the strength of it at first. Good shoulders, yet not spectacularly wide; chest heavy with muscle, very thick through; big triceps, thick forearms, thick belly leading straight down from ribs to hips; round buttocks, round thighs, thick calves, small, high-arched feet. Then the firelight from the boiler outlined the muscles in shadows and you saw for one sharp moment the marble of the Greek athlete in the corner of Sonby's lecture room at the University.

"You're sure built for fighting," Slim said.

"Short arms," Johnny said, holding them out. "The hell with fighting; I never did like it much. Talk about going up the Sound for that hunt. Did you write your cousin?"

"Should get an answer next mail day. Did you talk to Ted about getting off?"

Johnny turned on the water and stood waiting for it to run hot through the pipes. "It's okay by him—not more than two weeks."

"That's plenty," Slim said. "Hank Parker will let us have his boat."

7

JULIE MORRIS lay on the bunk in the cabin of her brother's boat. The Union boat from Vancouver had turned into the cove at four in the morning. Dal was there with the gas boat and they had started right out on the eight-hour run to Kiltool Sound. She had cooked breakfast for the two of them, then held the wheel through the long run across King's Gulf while Dal stood in the pilot house and told her about the folks and how it was at the farm.

"Enid's big now, Julie, turning into a swell-looking girl. You'd hardly know her from the way she was a year ago when you went down. Dad's just the same as ever, always working like a team of horses and expecting everybody else to do the same. He plowed that forty acres between the two big sloughs this spring and it made a dandy crop—says he'll plow every bit of wild grass under now and seed it to heavy land mixtures. Ma's got a new stove, all white enamel—hell, you know all about that anyway; you picked it out in town and shipped it up. Sorry for swearing, Julie."

Julie had laughed. "That's all right, Dal. Guess I've heard worse than that in the last year."

"Funny thing," Dal said. "Dad doesn't seem so strict about all that as he used to. I guess it's because Enid's

Timber 73

getting old enough for it not to bother. And all us eleven boys about the place mostly getting grown up now too. Danny and Jerry are working down at Hal Johnson's camp—Danny's tending hook and Jerry's slinging rigging for him. Dave's fishing; rigged his boat for trolling and went north in May. Ought to be back any day now. The rest of us are still home, but I guess there'll be more young ones go out in the world next year."

Julie looked at him. "Don't you ever think of going, Dal?"

"Me?" Dal shook his head. "I guess the farm's good enough. It's raised thirteen kids and it's a darn sight better set up than when Dad moved in. A man goes fishing or logging, he just ends up a bum."

"Not thinking of getting married, Dal?"

She saw him blush, dull red along both cheek bones under the brown skin. "Ma write you?"

She shook her head. "You talk like it."

"She's a swell girl. Schoolteacher down at the Cove, Muriel Atkins. Don't tell the kids, will you, Julie? Not yet."

Julie slid her hand over his. "I won't, Dal. And I hope it will work out for you a hundred per cent."

Dal swallowed twice, fumbling for something to say. "Guess I'll go below and get a bit of sleep. You'll be all right for an hour or so, won't you? Till we get near the entrance. Call me if anything's wrong." He went down the steps into the engine room and she heard him moving about with the oil can.

It had been wonderful crossing the Strait alone with the boat, the heavy engine plugging along from sunrise light into full day. There had been wisps of mist at first, straggling over the flat calm water and across the feet of the mountains. Driftwood showed up against the still surface in multiplied distortions of itself. Occasional little rips of tide twisted the boat sharply so that she had to move the wheel to bring it back. Sometimes a salmon jumped from a traveling school and caught the sunlight full silver on his side—cohoes, mostly, she judged, but a few early dogs. Round, gleaming-black heads of seals bobbed up beyond the bow, drew down and came up again astern. Grebes and murrelets dived and scattered showers of bright little forage fish into the air ahead of their swimming. Black and white scoters, heavy-bodied, rose in clumsy water-scattering flight if the boat pointed directly for them, more often dived or simply rode the swell of its passing in stolid easy swimming. Julie wanted to swing the boat to stir each flock to flight, but she knew that by doing so she would bring Dal up to the pilot house. Any faltering or change in the engine's even pound would bring him and she prayed softly that there would be none. The long gash of Kiltool Sound was showing clearly now, running northeastward deeply into the dark green mountains. She was coming home and she would have liked Dal to have slept below while she brought herself all the way, clear through the long hike up from the entrance and into the main slough behind the island at the head, where the little wharf ran out from the farmhouse. But he came up, as she knew he would, when the entrance was just beginning to open to them, still a mile away across the Gulf. She remembered what Danny said:

"Dal can sleep like a dead man and still know where his boat is and everything it's done since he went down."

Dal said: "Sleepy, Julie?"

"No. I'm too excited. Doesn't it look swell, all those mountains. And you've got new snow."

"Yes," he said. "Night before last. It came down about to the five-thousand-foot line. Nothing on the trees yet. You'd better go down and rest, Julie, even if you don't sleep. You'll be played out by suppertime if you don't."

"All right, Dal," she had said. "Just let me stay till we're in the Sound. And call me if you see any goats or anything while we're going up."

So she had come down and now she was lying on the bunk of Dal's boat in her Vancouver clothes. The morning sun poured through the forward-slanting windows, across the bunk, and slapped their shadows almost audibly above the sink on the opposite wall. She wished herself out of city clothes—they seemed wrong on the boat, though Dal kept the cabin awfully neat and clean. You always wore city clothes, all the family did, coming or going from town. It was a kind of uniform that set you apart, made you at once a little less and a little more than ordinary folks until blue jeans or an old house dress let you back again into common life with them. These city clothes weren't much like the ones she had worn to go away. She leaned out of the bunk so that she could look past the engine and see Dal's feet on the pilot-house floor. Then she lay back again and raised her knees until the neat, blue skirt slid away from them and showed her full thighs. She pulled the skirt back about her hips and loved what she saw. The warm color of the satin, then the sheer, tight drawn length of the silk stockings, and the shiny black of patent leather shoes. A year ago I didn't know I could look like that; I didn't know anybody could except maybe in advertisements. I thought it was just girls' faces people meant were pretty. She pulled the skirt forward again, liking the feel of its fine hard weave. She knew how it set on her and knew the freshness that the frothy white blouse and little tailored coat gave to her—nothing could be less like the shapeless black silk dress she had worn to go down a year ago. Ma and Enid had said it looked smart, but she had guessed even then at what it had taken a full year of Dolly's teaching to show her.

She looked at Dal's alarm clock, firmly set in its bracket over the stove. Four hours yet before they could get in. She kicked off her shoes, pulled a blanket over her and settled herself to sleep.

Dickie lay on the end of the wharf, looking down into the clear water of the slough. You couldn't see much down there most of the time—just bullheads and maybe a flounder or two, sometimes a school of shiners a little way out—but now was a good time and you could be pretty sure of seeing salmon. They passed as he watched, half-a-dozen bright dog salmon swimming uncertainly against the lazy flood of the tide; they must have come in on the ebb and now the flood was drawing them against itself back to the main river.

The big yellow collie, lying asleep behind him, flicked its ears. Then it sat up, cocked its head on one side to listen, and barked sharply, twice. Dickie sat up too and listened hard, but he couldn't hear the boat. You never

Timber

could hear it until it was round the point and in the river. But Prince could; Prince knew it was Dal's boat too, because the hairs on his neck were flat and he didn't growl and he was still sitting down. When other boats came he wasn't quiet like that.

Dickie pulled a big knife out of his pocket and began shaving the edge of one of the planks that made the deck of the wharf. Dal was bringing Julie back. Girls. Julie and Enid and Ma would be talking all through supper about things that didn't matter, and Dad would listen and help them, and Dal was getting the same way now. Still, Julie was pretty—prettier than Enid or any other girl—and she was a good sport; boy, she could sure play softball. But he wished it was Danny or Jerry or Davey coming home instead. He could hear the boat now and recognize the steady cho-kuk, cho-kuk of Dal's two big cylinders hitting back from the hill across the Sound. . . .

Julie got up from the bunk, straightened her skirt and put on her shoes. She combed her hair, patted it into place, then reached into her bag again for lipstick—no, she thought, not lipstick. Powder, yes, but they might not like lipstick. She looked at her face in the mirror and wondered what they would think of her. She looked well-cared for, like Dolly and the other girls, as though you had thought about the way your face and body looked and as though it mattered to yourself and other people; and it did matter, a lot. You had to look that way. What will they think of it, though? Will it worry them, or make things different between us? Will they think I'm changed and maybe guess how differently I think and feel now most of the time? I am different, quite different. I've found so many things I didn't know were in me, things they wouldn't like me to feel or know about even to myself. She laughed aloud, a little quick laugh that Dal would not be able to hear above the noise of the engine. I'll bet Mother never kissed Dad the way I kissed Arthur the other night—he would have taken the strap to her if she had.

Julie touched her hair again. It wasn't fair to think of them that way. Dad was strict and Mother always seemed quiet, as though things hadn't been much fun for her, not the vibrant, thrilling fun that kissing Arthur had been. But you didn't know, you couldn't know. That was secret to themselves and they wouldn't talk about it or speak it any more than she, Julie, would show the way she had kissed Arthur. But standing there in the cabin she felt naked, as though Dad could look at her and say: "You've felt things you shouldn't have felt, girl." And the way Dal had looked at her, the amazed shyness, almost awed, and the awkwardness of his welcome to her. But then she was different from a year ago: dressed differently, walking differently, thinking differently, living differently, and not in ways that any could mind. She put her coat on and went up to the pilot house again.

Dal said: "Well, Julie, how does it feel to be coming home?"

"Grand," she said. "Much better than I ever thought. You don't know how a fellow feels about missing things in town."

"That's what you think," Dal said. "I missed everything from Prince to the manure pile that winter I was down. Used to think and think, trying to figure how it all looked—all the little things, like Dad saying they had changed the separator around in the dairy and he was figuring to run a new line of stalls along the north side of the barn. It didn't seem it could all be going on just the same without me there."

"I felt that way too. It was worst of all in berry-picking time. Dolly and I went up the Fraser Valley one Sunday and picked some, but Dolly didn't like it very well and anyway there was nothing to do with them when they were picked."

Dal moved the wheel a little to set the bow for the river as they rounded the point. "They'll hear us now," he said. He waved his hand towards the steep slope of mountain due east of them; Julie saw a raw red square cut out of the green timber and a red gash leading from it a few hundred feet down to the water. "Danny and Jerry and I logged the old Makepeace claim last winter, when Hal Johnson was shut down for snow. Made up five sections of pretty good fir. Danny rigged a swell donkey with that old Chrysler engine I took out of the boat."

Julie watched the valley opening up ahead of her. There were still leaves on the alders that stretched far up the river along the narrow, flat floor between the mountain walls, but they were sparse and dull dark green, without any freshness of spring or fullness of summer. Here and there on the mountainsides was rich color, pale gold of willows, strong red of ground maple against the heavy green of fir and hemlock. Well across the flats at the mouth of the river, close under the sharp climb of the mountains, she saw small red-and-white shapes of feeding cattle.

A little way up the main channel of the river Dal swung over and turned into the slough. "Just enough tide," he said. And then, as they came in sight of the wharf: "They're all down there for you, Julie."

Julie went out on deck, swung herself round the pilot house and ran up to the bow. Just for a moment she thought: They can see me now, what I am wearing, how I look. Then she was waving and laughing. Mother was waving and Enid was waving and Dad had his hand held above his head the way he always did when people were coming or coming back. The boat ran alongside the wharf, Dal's reverse gear grinding; she flipped the bow rope to one of the boys and jumped out on to the planks with her high-heeled shoes sure as though they had known only this. She felt a surge in her for them all, for the place, for the returning to it, for Dal and his boat that had brought her there. It was a time of breathlessness with nothing yet said, nothing asked, the whole of a year waiting to be told. The boys were kidding already, Mother held her very tight and close, not like Mother at all, Dad kissed her hard, first on one cheek, then the other. Enid was shy, holding back, but warm and soft when Julie held her. They were walking up towards the house now. Mother was crying, quite quietly but real tears down on her cheeks. And Julie heard herself talking, about Prince, about the many-colored late bloom of asters along the path, about the new paint on the house.

Dal said: "I'll go milk with the boys, Dad. You'd like

to talk to Julie. Dickie and Freddie can bring her stuff up from the boat."

Enid said: "Supper will be on the table soon as you're through separating."

They went in by the front door that opened into the living room—Julie hadn't gone into the house that way since she could remember. Enid passed straight on through to the kitchen, nervously anxious to show Julie that she could feed the family, though she had been doing it competently for well over a year. She's the one I want to talk to most, Julie thought. I can tell Enid anything and get her to understand and maybe feel what I feel; and when that happens I'll feel as if I belonged with them again. Dad was looking at her, carefully and searchingly from head to foot. She watched his expression, but could not tell from it what he thought—you never could with Dad. He let you know very plainly and very surely when he got good and ready, by what he said or what he did. She felt she wanted to look over to the bookcase, where the strap was. It was seven years since she had last been sent to fetch it, but the seven years seemed suddenly gone and she was again a little scared, a little ashamed, a little angry, very defenseless.

"Julie," he said at last, and even in the one word she knew his tone was frankest admiration. "You've surely come out, girl. You always did promise to be good looking, but minding the way you were running around in working clothes with the boys a year or two back, there wasn't anyone could have thought you'd have learned to make so much of it."

Julie felt all her assurance back. She dipped a little curtsey. "Thank you, sir."

"Sit down and tell Mother and me all about the city till Enid has supper on. Maybe you'd like a glass of sherry wine."

Julie watched her father's great shoulders and thick heavy body as he went to fetch the wine. Mrs. Morris got a tray and three thin-stemmed glasses from the walnut dresser that had survived the trials of Gramma Morris's journey from Kentucky to Saskatchewan and her own later journey to the coast. "Dad thinks a mighty lot of you, Julie," she said. "And I guess he's got reason to. You've made good use of your opportunities and of the brains God gave to you." She set the tray on the lace cloth of the round table in the center of the room and went back to her chair. This, Julie knew, was what Mother had to say—her piece as co-head of the family. Mrs. Morris sighed deeply, so that her frail little body seemed to rustle the print dress. "It makes me real proud just to look at you, Julie," she said. "There's not many that's lucky as I am with my family." She watched her husband come back with the wine bottle held carefully in his hands. "You young folks are all growing up to take care of yourselves and that's something to be thankful for these days."

Filling the glasses, Mr. Morris said: "Your mother likes to think she's getting old, Julie. Ever since Dal took to sparking a girl she's been wondering how it will be to travel around and look at the grandchildren."

At supper they talked freely and naturally and Julie forgot her good clothes, forgot she had ever been away.

The quarrels, arguments and difficulties of a year ago were still quarrels, arguments and difficulties that loomed large and important and filled the minds and drove the tongues of all of them. The dishes in the center of the table were the same and the food heaped upon them was the same—mashed yellow turnips, the high pile of potatoes, squash under its film of melted butter, pickles and relishes beyond count and the great turkey in front of her father. In all the room only the stove was different, gleaming white in its central place, strangely modern yet with a solid dignity fully equal to that of the old stove with its complications of polished scroll work. She heard Dickie's voice, important with news for her.

"Julie, Slim's coming next week."

"Don't call him Slim," Enid said. "That's just a loggers' name."

"What's wrong with loggers' names?" Ray asked her. "When did we get so as we can high-hat loggers with two of them in the family?"

"How long is he going to stay?" Julie asked. "It's always fun when Alec's here."

"He's coming for a hunt," her father said. "And he says he is bringing a friend of his named Holt. Alec must be doing mighty well with the company to get off the way he does pretty near whenever he wants to."

"Who's the other guy?" Ray said. "A logger too?"

"Don't let me hear you say 'guy,'" Mrs. Morris said. "I won't have that word at my table."

"Of course he's a logger," Dickie said. "I've heard Slim talk about him—Danny and Jerry too. They say he's the best darn head loader on the coast."

"It's always loggers," Enid said. "Loaders and riggers and hookers and brakemen and boommen. We haven't had fallers and buckers yet. I suppose that's something to be thankful for."

"That's not a way to judge men," Mr. Morris said. "A man is what he is, not what his work is. That's bad talk, girl, and I didn't think to hear a child of mine use it."

"I didn't mean it that way, Dad," Enid said. "I meant it's always the same when people come here. They talk logs and sections and booms and maybe hunting—nothing else."

"You don't need to worry," Ray said. "They're coming to hunt, not fool with girls. Once Alec gets his face pointed for Gulliver's Draw you won't see much of him."

Julie felt the wrangling conversation draw away from her. Loggers were men, all kinds of men; some were tough and dull so that nothing about them mattered and you kept a distance from them; some, perhaps not many, were like Alec and her own brother Danny—quick, beautiful men that you loved and understood; and some were simple and shy, slow and friendly and sad so that you wanted to touch them gently with your hand, try to show them how good you thought they were and give them some greater love of themselves. Almost all men fitted into those three divisions, even men like Arthur and her father and brothers, and the men Dolly knew in Vancouver. This was what she had learned, the thing that was between her and what they were talking now. But she knew they could not feel it or at least that it was not more

Timber

than they had expected. She saw that Dal was smiling down the table at her.

"Want to milk tomorrow, Julie?"

"Sure do," Julie said. "But not Primrose—Flower and Bess and Daisy if you like; and you or George had better strip them after me."

Remembering the cows and Primrose's bad quarter made her of them again. They took her and held her with them through the evening, through the lighting of lamps and dishwashing, through the children's homework and all her own account of the year in Vancouver. She went up to bed quickly when the time came, breathless with the things she had not told. She and Enid were together in the room they had always had and the light of the oil lamp on shiplap walls and iron bedsteads seemed warm and close, private to them both even though they could hear the movement and talk of the boys in other rooms about the house. Julie sat on her bed and looked about the room. Enid closed the door softly.

"Enid," Julie said. "Let's talk."

"Oh, Julie, yes. Get undressed quickly and we'll leave the light on, like we used to, right up till we want to go to sleep."

They undressed without looking at each other, as they had been taught to from early childhood. Mother said people are not meant to look upon each other's unclothed bodies; remembering the first evening she had roomed with Dolly, Julie felt that Mother maybe wasn't so old-fashioned; Dolly telling her not to be silly, ordering her to turn around, then turn again, saying at last: "You'll do, kid. Once you get wise you can tell from the shape of a girl's body how she will feel. You'll do." Julie blushed now, remembering her own embarrassment which finally broke down into tears, and Dolly's rough, good-natured comforting; you learned quickly that Dolly didn't mean much by things like that; it was just the way she was and the way she looked at life, and it helped to make her be fun to live with.

Julie slipped the nightdress over her head, let her underthings slide away from her beneath it, and jumped quickly into bed. A moment later she heard the creak of springs from Enid's bed and only then did she look up.

"I beat you," she said. "I haven't undressed so quickly in a year."

"You've got a nightdress," Enid said. "I've got pajamas. They take longer." She looked closely at Julie sitting with the blankets drawn up to her waist. "It's a pretty nightdress too."

"Do you really like it?"

"Of course. You've got such lovely things since you've been away, Julie. And you look so different in them. It makes me feel shy of you."

Sitting up in her bed with her arms behind her, supporting her weight, Julie laughed, throwing her head back so that Enid saw the curve of her throat, soft and warm in the lamplight. "Don't be silly, darling. I'm just the same really; just grown up a little. You'll do the same thing—you've done it already, lots."

"Did you put that little necklace on just to go to bed in?" Enid asked.

Julie touched the necklace of tiny pearls around her

neck. "Of course not, silly. It was under my blouse all day. I always wear it."

"They're so pretty they could be real."

"They almost are," Julie said. "They're cultured."

"What does that mean?"

"People do something to make the oysters make them instead of just letting them happen."

"Then they must be expensive." Enid looked across at her sister quickly. "Julie, where did you get them?"

"Arthur gave them to me."

"A man?" Enid's eyes were very wide. "Then you're going to marry him."

Julie shook her head. She hadn't thought that it might come this way and so quickly. "No," she said. "I don't think so. No, I know I'm not."

Enid sat straight up on her bed. Julie felt just as she had felt when her father was looking her over in the living room, like a little girl again, awaiting judgment for some naughtiness. She did not look at Enid. "Julie," Enid said. "What do you mean?"

"Just that Arthur gave them to me. He's nice."

"Then you're going to give them back to him?"

"No. He didn't give them to me because I was going to marry him. Just because he wanted to."

"But that isn't right. Girls can't let men do things like that."

"Yes, they can. Listen, Enid." Julie looked towards her again. "Men all want something they haven't got. They don't know what it is—it's different things with different men. I let Arthur take me out in the evenings and

I let him kiss me sometimes and give me things sometimes. That's all, but it makes him happy."

"Is he old?"

"Not very. Nearly forty. I'd like to do the things they want for other men too—Alec, for instance."

"Julie, you do say awful things."

Julie laughed. The horrified tone had almost gone from Enid's voice and in its place the old admiration for an elder sister's daring had crept back. "Don't worry, darling. I'm not really bad. Sometimes I almost think I'd like to be, but I won't be. I'll get married one day and have lots of babies and be ever so big and domestic. And you'll come and see me and tell me about your babies."

Enid's face was happy again. "You are awful, Julie—talking about babies as though they were practically here when we're both miles and miles from even thinking of being married—at least I am." Then she added defiantly: "But I wouldn't mind if you really were a bad girl. I know you wouldn't be, but I wouldn't mind, honestly I wouldn't, Julie."

Julie swung her legs out of bed, ran quickly across and kissed her. "I know you wouldn't, darling. You're sweet." She turned away and looked quickly behind her. "Wait a minute," she said. She reached back to her own bed, pulled the top blanket away and put it about her shoulders. Then she curled herself at the foot of Enid's bed, arranging the blanket so that it covered her legs and feet. "Now let's really talk. Not about me any more. About you and Dal and Mother and Dad and Dickie and everybody."

"You'll get cold," Enid said.

"No, I won't. I'm warm-blooded." Julie settled herself more comfortably. "What's all this about Dal and some schoolteacher down at the Cove?"

"Muriel Atkins? You must have seen her. She used to be at Lodge Bay when they had a school there."

Julie shook her head. "No. And why doesn't somebody write me about all the interesting things like that?"

"You must have, Julie. At dances and things. She was there two years anyway. I remember her."

"It doesn't matter," Julie said. "Is she nice? Is she in love with Dal? Do you think it's a good thing?"

"Of course. We all think it's good. She's just like us— at least she's always lived on a farm and she can cook and put up fruit and meat and that sort of thing. And she's smart and quick too—just what Dal needs to keep him from settling down into an ordinary old farmer. Dad says she'll run him ragged, but when he's in the right mood he says she'll get more ideas out of Dal's head than he ever knew were there—about how to run the place he means."

"Do you think she'll want to stay on the farm?"

"Dal says she loves farming and always meant to live on a farm when she got married."

"That's what they all say. But do you really think she will?"

Enid nodded. "Yes, I'm sure she will."

"Is she very pretty?"

"Not very. Not all alive pretty like you are. She's got dark hair and a good skin and big eyes, but she's quiet and her face is too big somehow. You can imagine her all settled down with lots of children."

"Will they live here?"

"No. Dal's going to build a house in the clearing over towards the school. It's higher ground there and she's got lots of ideas from magazines. It will be a swell house when they get it all finished—much better than this old barn."

"What about the rest of the family? Any more weddings?"

"Nearly all the boys have got girls except Dickie and maybe Davey. But I don't think any of it's serious yet."

"How about you?"

"Who would there be?" Enid said. "And anyway I'm too young yet."

"Haven't you ever wanted to kiss anyone?"

"Yes."

"Who?"

"Ron Cully."

"He's cute," Julie said. "When did he kiss you?"

"He didn't. I don't think he ever will, he's so serious."

"He's nice looking," Julie said. "He's got curly hair and he laughs a lot and his teeth show all white. I never thought he was so serious."

"He is. He says he's going to make a name for himself as a chemist, then come back and marry me."

"Enid Morris! You let him say that and still not kiss you when you wanted him to? I never heard of such a thing."

"What can I do about it?"

"Tell him straight out to kiss you. And when he does, kiss him back—hard. He'll soon learn."

Enid crept farther down under the blankets. "That's

what I thought," she said. "He's going away again at the end of the month, but I'll see he remembers me when he does. I'll kiss him so hard it will be like biting. That's what I want to do."

Julie looked at Enid's tight-clenched teeth and laughed. "That's my little sister," she said. "Ron's going to be a pretty happy man when he gets through making that name for himself—if not sooner."

8

JULIE pressed her brown hair tight against the flank of the cow and her strong fingers worked smoothly, jetting the heavy streams down into the foam of the bucket in rhythmic alternation. Now, after only a few days, it was easy as it had ever been and she knew that she could milk as fast as Dad, faster than any of the others, without thinking about it or even trying very hard. The smell of the barn was strong about her, in a heavy sweetness that she loved; there was the scent of piled tons of hay, the rich warm smell of the cows and the insistent freshness of the steaming milk. The sound of a slow beast shifting its weight; the sharp rattle of stanchion as a head tossed, the gently scolding voice of one of the boys, the thud of a filled bucket on the plank floor and the clatter of handle falling to rim; steadily over it all the satisfying thunder of milk into her own pail and the even drawing of the other milkers reduced to more credible proportion of sound by their distance from her and the deadening bulk of the standing cattle.

She heard Dal stripping to finish the big Holstein and Ray's footsteps along the barn as he brought his full bucket to the scales. Ray said: "Gee, Dal, that Johnny Holt's a powerful guy."

"He's not so awful big," Dal said.

Timber 93

"No, but did you see how he's built? Thick through like that? I'll bet you can't pull him on the broomstick."

Dal laughed and stood up. "What's that got to do with it?"

Julie's hands worked faster. She heard Ray walking back to his next cow, Dal emptying his full bucket into the big can. She was in a hurry for the evening, to see more of Alec, perhaps have a chance to talk to him quietly. He would have come out to milking, but Dad had kept them both at the house, talking. There would be talk through supper, quick eager talk from everywhere at once, kidding and laughing. And afterwards the boys would be wrestling, pulling each other on the broomstick, twisting wrists, boasting and talking about hunting. But Alec would be lazy, sitting watching it all, kidding them sometimes in his soft voice. And if she went over near him he would talk to her quietly and sensibly. Alec knew more of her than the others did—except perhaps Enid now—from that time in town last summer.

Julie finished milking and stood up with her bucket. Dal said, "That's the works, Julie. I'll milk Rosie if you want to go and help Enid." He laughed, looking at her. "Boy, you sure look different from the way you did when I met you at the Cove the other day."

Julie looked down at the blue jeans and short gum boots she was wearing. "Doesn't feel bad," she said. She knew Dal liked to have her come out to the barn to milk. Dal had said—not so very long ago—that he wouldn't ever marry because there wasn't another girl like Julie. And she had said she would keep house for him and they could run the farm together. She wondered if Dal's schoolteacher would wear blue jeans and come out to the barn with him, then knew that she wouldn't and he wouldn't want her to. Julie laughed.

"What's funny?" Dal asked.

"Nothing," she said and went out of the barn and along the path towards the house. She saw Alec coming towards her with Johnny.

"City stenographer apes country girl," Alec said. "All through milking, Julie? Johnny here is like you, just a farm boy at heart and he wants to see if he can still get milk out of a cow."

Julie looked at Johnny and smiled. "That'll please Dal," she said. "There ought to be something still left for you."

"That's swell," Johnny said. He was watching her as she turned to speak to Alec again. This was the one Alec had said was dynamite—quick and sudden, always bursting with something. "You'll probably like Enid better. She's quieter, deeper maybe, even though she's younger. Julie's open and straight as a man. Can't keep anything she thinks to herself." Johnny felt awkward and heavy standing there while she and Alec talked; briefly, as she smiled at him, some warm thing had flowed from her directly to him. Now he was a stranger to both of them and shut out by the long knowledge each had of the other. They were alike; he had known that in his first sight of her as they brought Hank's boat into the wharf. Now, as they talked together and he could watch her, it was very clear. The girl's face was lighter, softer, yet fuller and more rounded than Alec's, but as her changing expressions lighted it Alec was in each one. Her hair was the same light brown, touched to the same red or gold as the light caught it, and curled back in the same broad waves from the same straight high forehead. Her lips were very soft and full, bright with life under the smooth skin, yet they were shaped as Alec's were. Her nose was straight and slender as Alec's; her chin was rounded and gentle, not like his except in its set. She turned to him again and he saw that her eyes were strongly blue against white and the white was very white and clear against the smooth dark skin.

"You'd better hurry if you want to milk," she said. "And I've got to hurry and help Enid if you want supper."

She went on along the path, very conscious of the tightness of the blue jeans across her hips and on her thighs. She kept her eyes ahead of her; Alec would probably turn and look, damn him, and later he would let her know in some quiet way that he had seen. It doesn't matter with just brothers around but I'm too much woman for these things now. The blond boy wouldn't look; he was shy and quiet, not like Alec at all; one of the ones that you wanted to stroke and gentle and make think better of themselves. But he had something too; you could feel it a little when he looked at you and you knew that he wouldn't be with Alec unless he had. He was beautiful— she liked putting the word to a man; Dolly was always doing it—in some way. His body was so solidly thick above the waist, so light and quick with taut movement below; thinking of him you remembered that rather than his face.

Julie went quickly into the house. Enid was already

working over the stove. "I want to change to a dress," Julie said. "I'll be down in a minute."

"Okay," Enid said. "Hurry." She wanted Julie with her. There wouldn't be much time for talk before the boys began to come in and wash up, but she wanted her there anyway. This new Julie from town made you thirsty for more and more of her; she was the same Julie, full of talk and laughter and quick happiness, but in different, exciting ways. She said things that made you afraid and ashamed, for her and for yourself, but she made you love her more and more and in all she said there was promise of strange, real things only a little way from you. She heard Julie's feet quick on the steep wooden stairs and turned to see her come into the room. She had changed to a short-sleeved dress with big bright-colored flowers printed on a white ground; the dress was firm and smooth on her hips, flaring from these to a skirt that swung and danced about her bare legs; a little collar was turned up on her neck and open in a short V at her throat. Her hair seemed to dance about her head as the skirt danced about her legs and her eyes were bright, her lips parted with excitement.

"Gee, you look pretty," Enid said.

"So do you, darling." Julie lifted her sister's face between her hands and kissed her on the lips. "Now tell me what to do."

"Set the table," Enid said. "I've got everything else under control."

Julie began to clatter out the heavy dishes, counting the places at the long table. Enid said: "Did you see them out at the barn?"

"Met them on the way in," Julie said. "Alec said you told him to say to quit stalling and come and help."

"I did not say any such thing. That Alec can think up more ways to try and make trouble."

"He's fun. What do you think of the other one?"

"I like him. He doesn't say much, but he's nice. Mostly when the boys bring loggers home with them they're so fresh you'd think they own the place. The boys think that's funny. Or else they're so tough they can only speak one-syllable words out of the corners of their mouths— and then all the kids are imitating them about the place for the next six months."

"This one certainly isn't fresh," Julie said. "And I'm not so sure he's dumb either."

Enid went over to the sink and began breaking eggs into a bowl. "Look at the roast when you get through, Julie. It'll need basting. That buck of Dal's is at least a hundred years old."

Dal's voice said from the doorway: "Don't you believe her, Julie. That was a prime beast, fat as if he hadn't moved a hundred feet all summer."

"For a farmer Dal always was a lousy meat hunter," Alec said. "He just looks at horns and never thinks anybody might want to eat what's behind them. If that buck didn't move all summer it was because the rheumatism was getting him so bad."

"Suppose you never put sights on anything bigger than a spike all season," Dal said.

Standing at the stove, Julie listened to the sound of voices growing about her and the tramp of heavy feet across the kitchen floor. Her father had come in and was reading the paper; his spectacles were pushed up on his forehead and she knew he was ready to leave the paper and talk as soon as anyone settled down near enough to him. The boys moved about, washing at the basins along the shelf on the far side of the kitchen, running upstairs to stamp around overhead changing shirts and pants; always kidding, talking, laughing, jostling one another in the excess of energy that flooded in upon the kitchen at this time, no matter how hard the day had been. The activity began to show its effect. Alec and his friend were washed and brushed, sitting on the bench beside the table, talking to her father. She listened carelessly to what they were saying, hearing it through the confusion of other sounds in the room and upstairs.

Mr. Morris asked, "What have they got you doing now, Alec?"

"Most anything," Alec said. "Soon as there's some grief nobody else wants they pass it on to me."

"We heard the other day they had made you assistant superintendent."

"In the woods," Alec said. "Mark Evans, down at the Beach, is the real assistant supe."

"Are you still laying out railroad?"

"No. Andy's doing most of that work now. I pick line ahead for him generally, but he runs it in. Right now I'm checking over that big block of timber around Murray Lake—bringing the old cruise figures to somewhere near right and trying to find a way to bring it out by Camp Four."

"That's only the half of it." Julie heard Johnny's quiet voice and found herself listening more closely. "There isn't a man on the claim knows the country the way Alec does, and he's got them so they're scared to rig a tree or mark a setting without he's checked it over first."

"That's only because Chris is too busy with office work to attend to it," Alec said. "There's got to be somebody tying the whole thing together out on the ground."

He must be doing all right, Julie thought, talking himself down that way and acting sort of embarrassed; it isn't like Alec not to take all the credit for anything he's done. She heard Dal come downstairs and watched him cross the room, a little self-conscious in a new silk shirt and creased pants. Ray came in from the outside room where he and George slept; Julie saw that he had the metal-studded belt and satin shirt at last—the shirt was a full, rich, dark green, gleaming as his muscles moved under it and the light caught it. Her mother came in from the living room, watched Enid for a moment, glanced critically into the oven. "You can put it on the table as soon as they are all down," she told Julie. "Enid should have made more biscuits. We'll be short of bread tomorrow morning."

Julie leaned forward and kissed her. "Go and sit down, Mother. We'll take care of it." She was remembering what her mother had said last night. "You've changed, Julie. You've opened out. I can see you're going to be happy and make others happy and that's how it should be. God always meant young people should be full happy." That wasn't the way Julie had expected it. Dad hadn't said much—probably he hadn't seen or guessed so much as Mother—but she knew he was watching her now, pretending to listen to what Alec was saying, but watching her because he enjoyed the way she carried and moved her body, the way her skirt touched her hips and swung about her bare legs.

They were all in the room now and it was suddenly quiet. Dal said: "When do we eat, Julie?"

"Soon as you all sit down," Enid told him. "You could have had it half an hour ago if you had been ready."

"Enid will make the mother of a fine family," Alec said. "She's got the line already."

"You just leave the girls be, Alec," Mrs. Morris told him. "If you could tend your own business half as well you'd be a better man."

Julie heard them all laughing and heard Alec's gentle: "But Aunt Lil, it's just because we're used to the way you can do it," as she brought the roast over and set it in front of her father. Then she straightened her body and her eyes met Johnny's. She smiled at him again, as she had on the way in from the barn, a full smile that she dimly knew carried much of herself with it. "Don't let them bother you," she said. "They're always like this."

Johnny's quick smile answered her. "I've known Alec too long to pay much attention to him," he said.

Walking back to the stove, Julie asked herself: Why do I do that? He's cute when he smiles, all alight with it and gentle and friendly, but he's only a logger; not even good looking really, with that broken nose and the pale, thick hair brushed straight back from his forehead like that. But he's got something. I haven't heard him say more than a couple of dozen words and I don't know anything about him, except that he's a friend of Alec's, but I can feel something from him; and it isn't just because he's the only man around who isn't a brother or a cousin or a relation of some kind. I'm not that bad.

She came back to the table, set the big dishes of vegetables in the middle of it and sat down at her place. They were talking about hunting now and the trip Alec had planned.

"I want to show Johnny Gulliver's Bowl," Alec was saying. "Whether you find much game there or not it's a swell place to be and a swell place to hunt."

"There's always game there," Mr. Morris said. "Always goats and a few deer. Nobody's ever shot a real big bear in the Bowl or in the Draw either that I know of, but there's bear in there and it's the best chance of a good hide this time of year."

"Johnny wants a goat," Alec said. "He's never had a chance at one yet. I don't suppose we'd turn down a good chance at a bear, but a goat and maybe a real big buck is what we really want."

"You will not turn down any chances at bears, Alec Crawford," Mrs. Morris said. "Do you think we want another whole winter without bear fat? There wasn't a man on this place could get us a bear last fall and that's the first time it's happened in all the years we've been on the ranch."

"But Aunt Lil," Alec said. "We're up here for rest and recreation. We don't want to be packing hundreds of pounds of bear meat down the mountains."

"Be gone with your nonsense," she said. "You'll bring one home and like to do it or there'll be no bed and board here for your fine fads and fancies about what you will hunt and what you will not."

Mr. Morris laughed. "Now, Mother," he said. "Mr. Holt here is not used to the way you treat us boys that do the hunting for you. You'll have him scared to show his face up the Sound again."

Johnny said: "I guess I'm persuaded I'd better make a sure shot of any bear I see."

"It's not for you, Mr. Holt," Mrs. Morris told him. "It's this Alec here with his fancy ideas and making the boys as bad as himself. Why, even Dal here can't go hunt for a bit of meat now without talking about how pretty are the horns on it."

Ray asked: "How long do you figure to be gone, Alec?"

"Four or five days to the Bowl, and we might go up on the Hill for a night or two after we get back."

"Could you make it to be down here for the dance Saturday night?"

"Dance?" said Mr. Morris. "What dance?"

"We thought we could get the Cully girls and some of the folks from down the Sound and maybe a bunch from over at Hill Bay if we got word down there. Like the last time Alec was up, Dad."

Julie looked quickly across at Alec, then down at her plate again. He had not ever remembered it well enough to look at her—or else perhaps too well to let anyone see him look at her. He said: "Sure, Ray, we'll make it. What do you say, Dal?"

"You bet," Dal said. "Even if we don't leave the Bowl till Saturday morning we could get back in time. You bring your dancing shoes, Johnny?"

Johnny smiled. "Guess I've got something will do," he said. "Where do you dance here?"

"In the schoolhouse," Ray said. "It's swell there when we get it all decorated. And you ought to hear us Rhythm Benders go to town."

"You're pretty near two years older than last time," Alec said. "You ought to be a couple of months better anyway."

"They're good," Enid said. "We all went down to a dance at Hal Johnson's last month and kept them going till ten o'clock the next morning."

Johnny looked across at Julie's bare arms against the white table cloth. They were very round and smooth, he saw, a little tanned and with short, soft black hairs curving on them. Seeing the hairs there made her seem suddenly solid and real and very close. He wanted to touch her.

9

FROM the river it had not seemed such a long climb to the head of the Draw. They had left the farm a little before six that morning. Julie had cooked a first breakfast while the others were milking and then had come down to see them load up the big freight canoe and start out. Johnny remembered now the feeling of loneliness that had been in him as they left her there, waving from the gravel bank in the hazy early light and the river mist. Alec had said, "Wish we had Julie with us. Why in hell we think we have to go off and frig around in the mountains instead of staying where it's comfortable, God only knows." From Alec that had seemed funny; Dal had said: "I never heard you talk like that before, Alec. What's the matter? Getting old?" But Johnny knew the feeling echoed what was in himself and you could tell that Dal understood it too.

It fell away from them as the sun rose and they worked the canoe up against the heavy current of the river. Johnny watched Alec's steady movements ahead of him; the plunge of the pole, driven down for grip on the rocky bottom, the brief pause, the heavy thrust. Behind him he knew Dal was following and matching the movements as he himself was. And he knew his own pleasure at each sharp forward surge of the canoe was matched in the others.

Timber

They came to the lake and paddled through its four-mile length in silence, then turned to the poles again for the last two or three miles of river work. It was a different river now, cloudy with glacial silt, and the high mountains seemed to hem it more closely than before. They had had a clear view of the Draw for the last half mile. It was a narrow fold in the dark green of the timber, climbing away above the alders of the river flat for half the height of the mountains, then lost somewhere behind high bluffs. "You're in the canyon as soon as you get round the shoulder of those bluffs," Alec had said. "It's not a bad climb."

They unloaded the canoe at a sand beach below an often-used camp site, where blazed trees faced in towards the blackened circles of old fires. Their packs were light, not more than thirty-five pounds and a rifle apiece, and it was easy and pleasant crossing the flat. They came almost suddenly upon the start of the Draw, where a quick stream leveled out into slow flowing while still within sound of its checked and broken running on the slope of the mountain. It was an easy climb at first, following the ridge on the west side of the Draw among light second growth and salal brush under the tall stand of cedar and fir and hemlock. At the end of half an hour they had stopped to rest and smoke, and again at the second half-hour. But now it was steeper climbing and the gray and yellow of lichen-streaked rock showed more and more frequently in the timber. Johnny watched the other two as they moved steadily ahead of him. Dal was good, heavier and not so easy as Alec, but surefooted and strong, used to the hills. Alec stopped and threw off his pack.

"Time to smoke again," he said.

Dal sat down beside him and looked back down the hill. "We aren't doing badly," he said.

"How far till we come into the Bowl now?" Johnny asked.

"About another hour of this and we'll be in the canyon. It usually takes half an hour through there till you come to where it begins to open up." Dal looked up at the sun. "We should be making camp by soon after three."

"Time to get some meat for supper if we don't see anything we can knock over on the way."

Johnny said: "How low do the goats come?"

"I've never seen them very far down this time of year," Dal said. "Generally well up in the mountains at the head of the Bowl."

"Remember the big billy that fooled us two years ago? I'd like Johnny to get a crack at that baby."

"He might at that. When Dad and I came up after bear last spring we saw a goddamned big old goat right about the same place. He started to fade back towards the rim when we were still a mile away from him."

"What happened the first time?" Johnny asked.

"We never did figure it out," Dal said. "Alec and I circled to get above him—took us nearly all morning to do it—and then made sure we had him. We saw him good before we started to work down on him, feeding out on a flat shoulder of rock as quietly as though he didn't know there was anyone closer to him than the mouth of the river. Next thing I knew Alec said: 'Look!' and there he was, a thousand feet straight up from us, looking back. We chased him right over the rim and had to sleep the night out there, but we never got close enough again to tell which end of him was which."

"The old bastard was smart," Alec said. "It's goddamned seldom they are, too. We better mosey along or we'll be making camp in the dark."

They climbed steadily for another hour, stopping only once or twice to rest and smoke. Johnny saw that the line of the slope was changing slowly and at last they were traveling along it instead of up against it. The timber was sparser and smaller now and they began to cross rockslides, some fresh and bare, some grown up with scrub alder and willow. The walls of the canyon climbed straight above them for two or three thousand feet on either side, gray rock broken by giant fissures and bluffs and rare shelves and shoulders that supported dwarfed, distorted trees. The creek made sound over the rocks of its bed among devil's clubs and salmonberry two or three hundred feet below them. Across it, a steep bank sloped up along rockslides and snowslides, through swales of willow and blueberry, to the foot of the canyon wall. Johnny felt suddenly freer and lighter, as though he had dropped the weight of pack and rifle from him when they left the overhead burden of dark massive timber. It was always that way when you came up past timberline in the mountains. You were suddenly in a strange world that had little relation to the everyday things of sea-level; there was a rawness of change all about, a threat of forces that had little effect elsewhere. Work of frost and thaw, of snow and rain and sudden winds, raging with unmeasured force, was plain all about you, staring from rockslide and snowslide, from the grotesque squatness of little trees, from the very color and shape of the ground you trod, knowing that it would be hidden under snow in a few weeks' time. It was good to feel this, it was what you came into the mountains for; and he was glad when Alec stopped again at the end of a strip of tall willows and Dal said, looking up towards the sudden faint rustle of the upper leaves: "It's going to storm before we get out of here."

"How soon, do you think?" Alec said.

"Maybe tonight, maybe not for a couple of days, but it's always a bad sign, the wind coming up the Draw like that this time of year."

"Hell, I thought it looked set for fine weather when we were coming across the Strait."

"Do you think there'll be snow?" Johnny asked.

"Sure," Dal said. "Up on the mountains and maybe as far down as this. A hell of a wind and a damned cold rain anyway. It can blow like a son of a bitch in the Bowl."

"Oh, well," Alec said. "If we don't like it we can be back at the ranch inside five or six hours."

They passed through a narrow belt of timber and came out suddenly to the Bowl, at the edge of an open slide. The stream twisted and searched its way down from the mountains facing them, across a meadow that was still green and bright with late flowers. A strip of timber ran up the mountainside for five hundred or a thousand feet above the meadow and from there gray rock piled up through three thousand feet to the rim. The rim swept round in a great circle, jagged and broken where the narrow, shallow passes cut through it, but still unnaturally perfect. Beyond the meadows the floor of the Bowl was a tumble of huge rocks, climbing away at the head through innumerable bluffs and benches of rock to the rim again. There was fresh snow at many places along the rim and the snow of other years poured down to the floor of the Bowl in half a dozen broad and massive slides. There was sound of water through the place and the eye searched and found the frail white lines of the creeks that dropped down over the rock to build the stream.

"Boy," Johnny said. "That sure is swell."

Alec nodded. "The slickest goddamned place in the whole of B. C. It'd scare you."

"I didn't think it would be so big," Johnny said. "And so tight closed in. It must be five or six miles from here to the head."

"Nearer twice that," Alec said. "A good ten miles, isn't it, Dal? And if you closed off the canyon here you could have a tight, round lake three thousand feet deep before it started to spill over."

"Why do they call it Gulliver's Bowl?" Johnny said. "Who named the place?"

"Dad," Dal said. "He says it makes you feel so God damned small. That's the only time he ever says goddamn and he says it in two words like that so it means just the way it spells."

They went down and followed the rock-strewn bed of the creek to the meadow and Johnny felt glad of the spongy level surface when they came to it, and of the greenness and richness of the meadow against the hardness of rock all about him. At the edge of the timber Dal said: "This is where we'll make camp. We've got a bunch of trees ringed for firewood and a sort of a shelter."

They threw the packs down, built a fire and boiled coffee. While they were eating Alec said: "You and I can do the bullcooking and get things straightened round for supper, Dal, and Johnny can go look for some meat."

"One of you ought to go," Johnny said. "I don't know anything about the place and you'll maybe go hungry."

"No," Dal said. "It's easy. Just follow up the edge of this timber here and you're sure to see a mowitch somewhere along it. There's a strip of heather a little way up where they go out to feed. And if you don't see deer you'll surely get a grouse. Don't shoot those till you're on the way back, though."

Johnny cut through the timber, angling slowly against the hillside towards the open. He was glad to be alone. Alec had talked so often of the Bowl that you wanted time to look hard at it and try to see it for yourself. At the edge of the timber he stopped and looked slowly over the whole wild place. The sun was almost touching the rim above him, but the sky arched blue above the rim on the other side and only a few wisps of white cloud drifted slowly from south to north. There would be mist over the meadow when they woke up in the morning and it would be a good thing to see a bright sun come over the edge of the rim across from them. A man didn't have time to look at things like that often enough.

He climbed slowly along the edge of the timber, searching ahead of him for the movement of a deer between the trees. He passed a narrow bench of heather, and across it, far up towards the head of the Bowl, he saw white dots which he knew were goats. Before he reached the next bench the sun was well below the rim and the whole hillside was in shadow.

A grouse burst from under his feet and clattered into a tree. A saw it there, craning its neck to look down at him, but went on cautiously towards the bench. The buck was feeding within fifty yards of the edge of the timber. He raised his head as Johnny jerked the lever of the carbine and pumped a shell into the breech. It was easy to see the forked horns and there was a clear shot at the side of the neck in the evening light. Johnny felt the sharp thrill of excitement tense in his forearms and choking dry in his throat. He steadied himself, raised the rifle and fired. The buck dropped.

Running up to him, Johnny felt a shame at the echoes of his shot still carrying against the sides of the Bowl. He saw the bobbing white tails of the other deer that had been feeding near only dimly in the confusion of the moment. But later, as he rolled a cigarette while the buck bled, the peace of the place crept back and he felt for the first time as if he belonged there. The dead buck was the price of his entry, giving him a claim to share what the Bowl held for Dal and Alec. He cleaned the buck, loaded it on to his back and started down the hill. Two more grouse flushed near him and flew into a tree. The shadow of the setting sun had crept up the opposite side of the Bowl clear to the rim, but as he passed under them he could see both birds clearly against the sky. He watched them and kept the deer on his back. It would have been too much to bear a second time the responsibility of fierce sound echoing through all the miles about him.

He saw the light of the fire through the trees below him

and heard Alec's: "Here he is," at the crack of a branch under his foot. In a few moments he was down with them, dropping the buck from his shoulders.

"There's a towel and a chunk of soap down at the creek," Dal said. "We'll have something cooked by the time you get back."

The stars grew out of the night sky above the rim as they ate and Alec said: "I don't think it will rain tomorrow."

Dal looked up. "Maybe not," he said. "But it'll come before we get out of here."

"Where do we hunt tomorrow?" Johnny asked.

"Alec saw a bear track crossing the creek just this side of the Canyon," Dal said. "He thinks we'd better get him and then we'll be free to look for goat. I'm not so sure. It would be safer to get a goat before the weather breaks and try for the bear later."

"No," Alec said. "If we go home and say we passed that baby up we'll never hear the last of it. We'll get him tomorrow, easy, if we all three work at it. Then we can try everything in the book to get Johnny a goat before Saturday."

10

"SHE'S coming today," Dal said. "Surer'n hell."

The sky was a solid gray dome over the Bowl, smooth and even, and against it raced ragged clouds, darker and much lower, but still above the rim.

"It's a bad day to hunt goat," Dal said.

"That's all right," Alec said. "We'll get one anyway. You go get the fat off that bear and then fix up the shelter so it will be good and tight. Johnny and I will hunt the head of the Bowl and if that long-bearded old bastard's where we saw him yesterday we'll get him sure. What say, Johnny?"

"I'd sure like to try it," Johnny said. "Seems a lousy trick to leave Dal here to do all the bullcooking, though."

"Don't let that worry you," Dal said. "When I get things straightened up I can always go out and look around close to camp. I'd like to get a sight of that big buck Alec jumped before we got the bear yesterday." He took his knife out of his pocket and reached into a packsack for the whetstone. "But listen, Alec, don't take chances up there. If it comes on to storm heavy, hit for camp. Just because you like to travel these bluffs in a blizzard it doesn't mean anybody else wants to."

"I'll let Johnny be the doctor," Alec said. "Soon as he says the word we'll hightail for home."

They followed close to the stream bed, keeping below the big snowslides right up to the head of the Bowl, where the steep bluffs began. Long before they saw the big goat Johnny felt himself keyed and ready—it was like the time before a ball game or a fight. They climbed slowly away from the floor of the Bowl, keeping towards the west side. Looking back they had a clear sight between the walls of the Canyon, across the valley and over the mountains beyond it. The sky was darker that way, heavy, solid blue-gray that shaded gradually to the lighter gray overhead, and the wraiths of lower storm clouds grew larger and heavier in their flight from the southeast. Johnny felt the wind about him in shaking gusts and heard it strong amongst the flattened limbs of the few little trees they passed. They had been climbing steadily for nearly an hour, following narrow ledges and draws between the bluffs, when Alec stopped. "There he is," he said.

Johnny followed the pointing arm and saw the tiny white shape of the goat, still above them and fully a mile to the east.

"That's where he was when Dal and I hunted him that time. It's a big wide bench covered with heather and blueberry." Alec turned and looked to the south. "We'll be lucky if we get near him before that stuff closes right in on us. Do you want to try it?"

"You're damn right I do," Johnny said. "Give her all you've got. I'll tag along somehow."

For the next hour Johnny saw little beyond the few square yards of rock immediately in front of him, and always Alec's boots, footing themselves solidly into hold

Timber

after hold, bearing the upward thrust of his weight, moving forward again. Once a few great drops of ice-cold rain splashed down about them and gradully he realized that they were changing direction, by the cut of the wind on his right cheek and then full against eyes and mouth and nose. He kept his mind on the shot, on lining the sights on the wide white neck, on that brief moment when they would be lined there, set and solid, the gold bead nestled down to half its thickness in the wide V of the open backsight. Only when Alec stopped and spoke again did he feel the sweat that soaked his clothes and notice the straining of his lungs and the quivering, melted uncertainty of his hands and arms.

"We can go straight down on him from here," Alec said. "Can't be more than half a mile to where he is and the wind dead in our faces. We've got him cold if we can keep out of sight."

Johnny held out his hands. "God," he said. "Look at that. I've got to get them steady before we're close enough to shoot."

"Lie down flat and relax," Alec said. "Just as if you were on a rubbing table. I'll go take a look over the edge and see where he is."

He crept forward to the start of the bluff and looked over. There was a flat below, then another steep drop and the bench where the goat was feeding. He saw three goats, all of them small, then looked again and saw the big one, well over to the left side of the bench. "Hell," he said. "This isn't where Dal and I came out. Can't be more than five hundred yards." Some guys would try a shot from here. Not with open sights and a thirty-thirty carbine and with his goddamned rear end turned round facing you like that. He whistled softly and signaled to Johnny, then turned back to watch the goat again. Johnny came up and Alec pointed down.

Johnny said, "A guy could pretty near drop him from here."

Alec shook his head. "Wouldn't be better than luck if you hit him right. Look." He pointed again. "You can work down to the next flat round the end of this bluff and you ought to come out within a hundred yards of him. Take lots of time going down and wait till he turns to give you a good shot. I'll go down on the other side in case he works over across the flat."

They separated. Johnny felt the wind cold against him now and his hands were steadier. He went down the narrow draw at the left of the bluff, setting his feet carefully among the loose rocks and testing each foothold to be sure that nothing would slip away from it and clatter down ahead of him. He crossed the flat above where the goats were feeding and came cautiously to the edge, his rifle ready. The sharp rattle of a falling rock above the noise of the wind turned his head sharply to the left, but he could see nothing and looked back to the bench again, searching for the goats. They were not there. The bench looked different from this lower level and he searched it again but still found nothing. He felt bitter disappointment chokingly in his throat. "Goddamn the sons of bitches," he said. "That rock must have been them." He looked over to the right and saw Alec walking towards him.

"Same damn thing as last time," Alec said. "You didn't see him again at all?"

"No," Johnny said. "But I heard him. Over that way somewhere."

"Let's go look."

They walked over and Alec stopped, looking down into the little narrow funnel of rock that cut far away up into the mountainside. "Damn me for a fool anyway," he said. "Not to have figured on that." The goat trail was plain, running along ledges, crossing big boulders, cutting down to the floor of the funnel and back to the ledges again.

The snow came suddenly about them as they stood there, fine and powdery, sharp with the wind driving it. Alec sat down. "Guess that puts the kibosh on it," he said.

Johnny sat down beside him. "God, I hate to let it go like that. Isn't there anything would give us another chance?"

"In this?" Alec pointed across the Bowl towards the Canyon. The first flurry of snow had swept on past them, but the far side of the Bowl was completely hidden from sight and the low heavy clouds poured overhead in surge upon surge of rushing, silent speed. The snow came again, sweeping up the Bowl in a solid wall that was suddenly upon them, enclosing them in its infinite thickness, shutting down vision until they could scarcely see across the narrow funnel in front of them.

Johnny turned his face away from it. "Boy, I sure hate to quit now. You and Dal got another sight of him, didn't you?"

"Let's get the hell out of the wind," Alec said. They

scrambled down into the funnel and set their backs against the north side of a big rock. "Look," Alec said. "We ought to turn around and hit for camp right now. Any guy with ordinary sense would."

"So what?"

"So just that. Let's get the hell on back."

"Hold it a minute," Johnny said. "If you've got some idea about that old billy I'd just as soon know what it is."

"In about two hours we could be back in a comfortable camp. Dal will have a dandy shelter built down there and a big fire going. If he's got as much sense as he looks to have that old goat has picked himself a nice sheltered bed and laid down on it by now."

"That's not it."

"You really want to go on? We won't be able to see fifty feet in front of us first thing we know; these rocks'll be slippery as fir logs with the bark peeling and either or both of us is likely as not to break a leg and freeze to death."

"Okay," Johnny said. "What else do you know?"

Alec laid a hand on Johnny's shoulder. "You've got it bad." Johnny could tell he was pleased; it felt good to have pleased him that way, to have surprised him a little. But it had happened because he wanted to see the goat again, to be holding the sights on him, to set his hands on the short black horns. Alec said: "Here's the way it is. There's a second funnel like this farther up the mountain, above where Dal and I saw him looking back at us that time. If we can find that and if he's crazy fool enough to be still moving in this filth, there's just a chance you might get a shot at him going up the funnel. Whether we get him or not it'll be a goddamn tight thing to get back to camp before dark."

"Okay by me," Johnny said. "Let's get going before we freeze to death."

Alec laughed. "I remember when I used to have a hard time to talk you into going outside the bunkhouse on a wet Sunday."

They followed the funnel at first, finding in it some measure of shelter from the driving snow. It was a small canyon rather than a true funnel, a narrow split in the solid rock that led them steeply up the mountainside. Alec followed the goat trail where he could, but they were forced from it many times and had to struggle over the rock-strewn floor, skirting great boulders that barred the way. Alec took out his compass and checked the bearing of the funnel.

"It's the same line as the one above," he said. "Right to a degree. We ought to get out of it now and make a big offset to the right. Then we can cut back and hit the other somewhere above the flat where that old devil ought to be."

They found a way up the wall of the funnel and into the storm again. Johnny felt a momentary reluctance to set his back so squarely on the camp and Dal's good shelter, but it left him almost at once as he stood at a distance with the rifles and watched Alec hunched over the compass again. The snow was still a fine powder, so hard-driven by the wind that it found no grip on the exposed rock, but it was already piling against ledges and in little crevices.

Alec followed the first leg of the detour carefully,

turning often to the compass. You had to turn to it; a two-hundred-foot sight was a break and even if you managed to follow a good line out and come back on a good line there were plenty of chances the thing wouldn't work out. You might come back right on top of the goat and never see him in this stuff. Or maybe the second funnel was farther up the mountain than you remembered it. But it was too good a hunt to miss.

He stopped and looked at his watch, then brought out the compass again and read the bearing that should take them back to the funnel. This second leg was worse than the first, with the wind full on the left side of your face. The trip back to camp would be a bastard. Johnny was crazy to get that goat; he had been wanting one for two years now and this was the first chance; generally there was nothing to getting a goat, but this one was different—that was why a guy wanted so badly to figure him out.

He stopped again to look at his watch and check the compass. Reaching back for his rifle he saw Johnny's face, red and twisted against the stinging drive of the snow. "How's she coming?" he asked.

"Fine and dandy," Johnny said. "Are we getting there?"

"Should have been there five minutes ago."

They traveled two or three hundred feet and Alec stopped to read the compass again. The hell with the watch, he told himself. Either we hit her or we don't. Then he saw the break in the ground immediately ahead of them. "There she is," he said. It felt good to say that. They went up and looked down into the funnel. There was a thin cover of snow on the floor of it, but in places

Timber

they could see the outline of the worn goat trail and there were no tracks in the snow.

"Looks good," Johnny said.

Alec nodded. "Unless the old bastard went straight up before there was snow there. Look," he said. "We've still got to hurry. You get down tight against the side of that rock, where you'll be out of the wind, and watch the funnel. Keep your hands warm as you can; it'll be a running shot, quick as hell. I'm going to cross farther up and go straight down well over on the other side. Don't move away from here whatever happens. If I don't hear you shoot first I'll be back in about half an hour."

"Suppose you get hurt?"

"I won't. But if I do I'll start shooting. Two shots every five minutes or so. You'll hear them easy on the wind."

Johnny lay behind the rock, rolling a cigarette in fingers that were clumsy with the cold. He lit it, then plunged his hands under his coat, pressing them against the warmth of his body. It was almost warm behind the rock, out of the wind, and he had a clear view of the funnel for at least fifty yards. It wouldn't be an easy shot, if he came. Quick and a bad angle. Just to see him go through there would be enough, on a good day. But with that trip back to camp a guy would want to have something in the packsack to make him feel good. He took the cigarette out of his mouth and buried the stub so that it sizzled and died in a little drift of snow. Then he saw the big goat. It was coming up the funnel at an unhurried trot. Johnny raised the rifle, crossed the sights on the white neck and fired— three times, as fast as he could work the lever. The wind tore the sound of the shots away up the mountain and the goat was down, sprawled in the snow without movement.

Johnny climbed down to him. It had been almost too easy and too quick. He looked at the big body, reached out a hand and touched the long, yellowish, matted hair, then the little black horns, shining and perfect. The head was heavy, wider and more massive than he had expected. To look at the dead goat and touch it gave him a solid, complete satisfaction, quite unlike the thrill of triumph he had known in killing the deer above the camp. Five minutes ago this thing had seemed infinitely far away, attainable only by some remote, improbable stroke of luck. And now, from out of the dim light and harsh sound of the storm, it was here, at his feet.

Alec came down upon him suddenly, when he was still struggling to turn the goat on its back. "Boy," he said. "Is that ever a honey." He spanned the black horns with his fingers. "Not more than a fraction off ten inches, if it is. You did a peach of a job too. Must have dropped him pretty near as quick as you saw him."

"I couldn't do less than knock him over after you had figured it out to put him right on the end of the barrel."

Alec shook his head. "That was one unlucky goddamned animal," he said. "Five hundred feet farther down the hill and we'd have walked right on where he was lying and maybe never seen him. A hundred feet farther than that and we'd be walking yet, still looking for the funnel. I found the start of the funnel down there after I heard you shoot, and his bed was just inside it." Alec pulled out his knife and opened it. "We've got to go to work and get what you want off him, then hit for home. . . ."

Coming out of the funnel on to the bench of rock below it Johnny realized the full weight of the storm for the first time. It forced them to bow their heads and lean forward into it, glancing up only occasionally to look out the ground ahead. The snow closed in about them until it was a solid curtain of driving white less than fifty feet away in every direction; it matted eyebrows and eyelashes and sheeted the front of their clothes, creeping through the closed openings and soaking through to the skin. It balled on the nails of their boots so that they had to stop again and again to kick it away.

They slid down a narrow gully along one side of a high bluff and found a measure of shelter at the bottom. Alec stopped and said: "There's a place over to the right where we could put in the night. There's some wood there and we could get a fire going. I'm pretty sure I could find it."

Johnny shook his head. "Let's make it to camp. We can get to the creek before dark, can't we?"

Alec slipped the pack from his shoulders, looked about him, then walked over and stuffed it into a crevice between the rocks. "We'll come back for that tomorrow," he said. "There's one way we can get out, but we'll have to hump it." He was thinking of the long stretch of steeply sloping rock on the west side of the Bowl. In dry clear weather you could walk that easily and fast, standing up, and come down the rockslide that reached the floor of the Bowl only half a mile from camp. But it was a bad slope and all bare rock; if a guy started to slide he hadn't a prayer of checking himself short of the sheer drop of two or three hundred feet below the shelf. It wasn't bad if you were used to the mountains; maybe it wouldn't be bad if you didn't know about the drop. But it was the only way. The other way, searching round the bluffs, climbing down, finding the gullies and little narrow places that would give a foothold, would keep them long past dark. And there was no way down in the dark on a night like this, when the snow would blanket every trace of lighter darkness even in the sky itself. In rain you could sometimes put your head close to ground and sight against the sky to judge how the ground dropped off in front of you, but not tonight.

They were starting across the ledge now; Alec dropped back alongside Johnny and kept abreast of him but below. Johnny was walking steadily, his head far down into the storm, feet glad of the clear way and the soft grip of the snow. He seemed not to notice the steep angle of the slope. Alec watched him. The slope always does seem less, he thought, if there's two of you walking abreast; changes the perspective or something, I guess. He turned his head for a moment to look forward into the storm and saw the sharp break of the edge of the shelf less than fifteen feet below them. He moved closer to Johnny, edging him up the slope away from it. Johnny felt the change of direction, looked down towards him, saw the break below. He stopped and Alec saw his mouth open to the sharp indraw of breath. "Almighty God," he said. "Where does that go to?"

"We'll be working away from it from now on," Alec said. "Thank God you can't see the way it really looks on a clear day, straight down all the way to the creek bed.

You wouldn't go straight down; you'd bounce and stop somewhere on the next bench, but that's the way it looks from here if you can see it."

Johnny put one foot forward and stopped again. Alec could see the sweat on his forehead, under the brim of his hat. "Jesus, Alec," he said. "I can't move."

"Sure you can," Alec said. He had read the words on Johnny's lips rather than heard them and he shouted his own against the storm. "It's just you're not used to it. You could walk it easy if it was a log."

Johnny spoke again. Alec yelled. "Shout. I can't hear you," and watched the struggle in his face.

Johnny's words came back, strong across the wind. He was breaking out of it. "That looks to go down for ever."

Alec shook his head. "It's nothing. There's another ledge ten or twelve feet down. Just the snow makes it look that way."

Johnny started ahead again, feeling for his footing, stiff-legged, leaning against the slope. "Just walk," Alec shouted to him. "Straight up, as though you were on the level." They began to angle up the slope, away from the drop. In a little while the snow hid it from them again. "We're past it now," Alec said.

Half an hour later they came to the rockslide. Johnny sat down in the lee of a big rock. "Hell," he said. "I'm sorry I was like that."

"Gets me too when I think about it," Alec said.

Johnny looked at him. "How do you keep from thinking about it? You knew that goddamn drop was there all the time. We've only just passed the end of it now. I know that."

"I've been across before," Alec said. "Getting used to it is all that counts. You'd be all right next time."

"Makes a guy feel like there's something wrong with him."

"Bull," Alec said. "You did fine. Lots of guys would be still there frozen tight—literally, by this time too."

They went up and brought the pack down the next day. The storm had blown over in the night and the sun was strong and warm on the floor of the valley though the snow held everywhere on the sloping walls, and high white clouds still raced from the south against the blue sky overhead. Dal wanted the hide of the goat to make a rug he had promised Enid for her room, so they went right up to the second funnel and did not get back to camp until late in the evening. Dal had built a big reflector-shaped shelter the day before, lacing pine and hemlock boughs into a solid weave that the wind could not penetrate, and they lay in it after supper, facing a big fire piled against a rock. Alec dug into his pack and found a full bottle of rum.

"I was saving this for a good night," he said. "That pint of brandy we had last night was just for emergencies."

"You old son of a bitch," Dal said. "You told us you had left the rum on the boat."

"I'm not kicking," Johnny said. "I've had a swell day and I'd just as soon do a little quiet drinking. Last night I wasn't in any shape to appreciate it."

"I always have a good time up this crazy mountain,"

Alec said. "That was a peach of a hunt yesterday, Dal. I wish you had been along."

"I don't," Dal said. "Coming down over those bluffs against a storm like that and getting into camp a full hour after dark, soaked to the arse. I'd have liked to have seen that big old billy though; the way Johnny saw him— along the sights. That's the biggest goat ever came down out of these hills, by a whole lot."

They talked lazily, with the red light of the fire throwing their shadows back against the interlaced branches of the shelter. Johnny felt a good tiredness in his legs and shoulders, a rich pleasure of sensation in the slackening of muscles that had worked his body through four hard days. He hoped Dal and Alec would talk late, until the rum was gone; they could finish it without moving except to put wood on the fire from time to time; and rolling into the blankets would simply mean kicking off a pair of pants and struggling for a moment to get a couple of them out from underneath you.

"Say, Dal," Alec asked. "What sort of an outfit has Hal Johnson got?"

"Like most of the small outfits. Sort of a family affair, friendly as hell. Old Ma Johnson puts up good meals. Danny says the rigging's kind of haywire most of the time, but he and Jerry seem to like it there."

"I thought most of these small outfits were hell to work for."

"They used to be, when the crew packed their own blankets and slept on straw in wooden bunks. I guess some of them are belly robbers and slave drivers even now, but they don't get by with much and most of them have a hell of a time to keep from from going in the hole."

"That's their line anyway," Alec said. "With the wages most of them pay they ought to be getting rich in a hurry."

"There's damn few that do," Dal said. "I never knew one yet."

"Alec figures they ought to have unions," Johnny said.

"Most of the boys don't want them," Dal said. "Just a few soreheads that aren't worth a goddamn on the job anyway."

"That's because they don't know what's good for them. Some of those small outfits pay about four dollars where a big outfit pays six."

"It's a job. And anyway, a guy don't have to work there."

"What does Danny get for tending hook?"

"Six bucks."

"That's better than some, but it's low enough."

"Maybe they could do better with unions," Dal said slowly. "But I don't think this country's right for them. I guess they do a lot of good in factories, for city workers that can't move around much. But this country's too near pioneering. A man likes to think he's his own boss and can work how he wants and where he wants. It isn't so much that way since the depression, but most men that can do a job figure it like that."

"Because they don't know what's good for them. Listen, Dal, wouldn't you be better off if you had a proper market for your stuff and could be sure of a fair price for it?"

"You mean marketing boards and that stuff?" Dal said.

"Hell, no. The way it is now a man can get something once in a while. Start paying a bunch of office guys to tell you what to do and you're sunk right there. I'll tell you something else. You can't argue with snow and wind and tides in country like we farm. And you can't work union hours in seed time or harvest time or if you want to clear land. Count us out of it right there. Dad made her stick and I guess I can."

"What are you going to do with the place, Dal?"

"Me? I'm going to keep feeding and butchering and selling beef. And whenever I get a bit ahead I'm going to buy registered animals till the whole herd's good stuff. I'm going to do more of what Dad did this year—break up the flats and seed 'em down to good crops. And if there's still money to spend we'll put it into the house."

"Don't you want anything more than that?"

"There isn't anything more I can see. Raise a bunch of kids like Mother and Dad did, and do it a whole lot softer. They'll do it softer yet when their turn comes. We'll go to Vancouver once in a while—what the hell for, I don't know. And I'll come up here and hunt. What do you figure a guy ought to want, Alec?"

Alec laughed. "You're all right, Dal. It takes guys like you to make a country. But when she's made it takes unions and marketing boards and a whole lot more to keep her right."

"If they don't graft more off you than they get for you."

"You said it, Dal." Johnny sat up straight on his blankets and reached for the rum bottle. "Alec doesn't believe all he says about unions anyway. He talks it the way he'd like it to be and maybe that's the way it ought to be. But it isn't."

Alec frowned into the fire. "I can't talk it with you, Johnny. I know you too well and you know me too well and it always ends up this way. Trouble with me is I haven't got the stuff to go ahead and put it over—except when I've had a few drinks and then only while they last. But I believe in it—all of it. Just because I can see what makes it difficult doesn't mean I don't believe in it. It's the most goddamned important thing there is for all us fellows—fallers and bullcooks and rigging men and even guys like me—if we'd only get wise to it. I guess I haven't had it hard enough to be able to put it over. And I get a kick out of too many other things like fishing and hunting and tarts in town. Most of the time I'm not a damn bit better than you two."

Dal watched him, his eyes gentle in the firelight. He hadn't seen Alec like this before, not kidding, not sure of himself, planning something or explaining something, but humble, almost bitter in self-depreciation. "If it's needed so badly why is it difficult, Alec?" he asked. "I know the boys are independent, but what else?"

"There's the companies for a start, but that's something every union has to beat. Then there's differences in wages and jobs—a hooker or a rigger getting his seven or eight bucks won't get very het up because a section man only gets forty cents an hour. And the everlasting shifting about—one crew coming, one going and one in the woods; it's hard to build anything solid on that. One month you may have a camp that's sixty per cent fallers and buckers and the next month they'll all be laid off and your camp committee is a different set-up altogether with a whole lot different ideas. Lots of other things like that. They all make it harder, but they can all be worked out. They've goddamn well got to be."

"You think it will come, then?" Dal asked.

"No, I don't think it will come without guys working for it and fighting for it, and there's not much sign of them doing that yet. Take a guy like Al Nickson for instance. Al learned to fight for unions down in Washington, in the bad times right after the war. He was real tough then, but he doesn't seem to give a damn now. He says loggers will never stay with any union if they're getting by."

"That's the real trouble with all of us," Johnny said. "We're getting by, so what the hell." He lay back on the blankets again. "Boy, it's swell up here tonight. I don't know why in hell we don't do this more often."

"Because you're a goddamned wage slave," Alec said. "If you were a boss you'd have a hunting lodge and spend two or three months in it whenever you wanted."

"You would like hell," Dal said. "You'd sit on your fanny in an office all year. Then you'd maybe take two weeks out for a hunt and spend the whole of your time worrying about whether the other guy was beating you out of something while you were out of town. And if you did get out in the woods you'd be so bloody fat and out of shape you couldn't hunt anyway. I know. We've had 'em here."

Alec laughed. "There's something to that," he said. "We had a couple of big boys in camp the other day. Chris and Ted and I were showing them around and Fat ran the speeder over a de-rail and dumped the works of us. He was going slow and it wasn't bad, but one of the big boys broke his arm and the other had a broken ankle and a sprained wrist. Nobody else hurt."

"A man gets old and soft, he can't take a fall," Johnny said. "I'm tired. How about hitting the hay?"

"No," Alec said. "Finish the bottle. We can sleep in tomorrow morning."

"That's right," Dal said. "It's an easy trip out and we don't have to get home till afternoon. No booze at the dance tomorrow night."

"If that schoolteacher's like she was last time I'm going to take her down on the boat," Alec said.

"You better not let Dad hear about it."

Johnny tilted the rum bottle over his cup, then reached for the hot water. It wouldn't do for him to know the way I feel about your sister, he thought. Jesus, I could go for that kid if I just met her out some place—and if she was that kind.

II

JULIE slammed her book shut and stood up. "It's too nice to stay inside," she told Enid. "Let's go out. Let's go up and meet the boys."

Enid stirred on the couch, her eyes still on the open page of her magazine. "I feel lazy," she said. "How do you know they'll be coming?"

"They said they'd be back in lots of time for the dance. That means they'd have to leave the Bowl in the morning and they should be down any time now."

"You'll be too tired to dance if you go running about the woods after decorating the room all morning. Stay home and be lazy."

"No," Julie said. "I want to go out. I'm going up to the Cut and watch them come through the Drop."

Enid looked up at last. "You're not going like you are, in that good skirt?"

Julie looked down at herself. She was wearing a yellow wool sweater, a heavy skirt of brown tweed, yellow wool socks at her ankles and low-heeled brown shoes. "Why not?" she asked. "I'm not wearing pants again unless there's nobody but the family here."

"You'll ruin that skirt. You'll slide down the rocks and tear it or something. And you'll scratch your legs."

Julie laughed, crossed the room and bent down to kiss

Enid's hair. "Darling, you talk as if you were an old grandmother and I was twelve years old."

Enid lifted her face to be kissed again. "Run along, little one, and have fun. Make those good-for-nothings ride you down in the canoe."

Julie went out into the sunlight, along the pathway past the dairy and the barn, then across the big pasture to the entrance of the trail that followed the slough back to the river again. It was shady under the alders, still damp and cool from the storm, and many fresh leaves had fallen on the trail and along the rotting logs on either side of it. Prince had followed her out and she heard him now, off to the right, barking at a treed willow grouse. It was half-hearted barking, not the steady, sharp, repeated summons of his serious hunting, and she knew he would leave the tree and catch up with her farther along the trail. It was strange and good to be going along the old trail in these different clothes and in her new different self. She had passed that way before so many times, wearing blue jeans or an old tattered skirt or an untidy house dress, looking for the cows, carrying the twenty-two for grouse or lard pails for berries, always for some purpose, never just for fun as she was going now. She saw it as a stranger, like somebody up from town, she told herself. Like that pretty girl from the yacht who had walked up to meet the men on their way back from fishing; she had perfume about her and you wondered if she had silk underthings on out there in the woods, vaguely knew that she had and it was her business to be always pretty and silken and perfumed. She and Enid had talked about her, whispering in the dark for a full hour after going to bed that night, remembering her lipstick and powder, the handkerchief at her throat, the extravagant, careful grooming of her hair, guessing at what she might be wearing back on the yacht. Julie remembered sharply that her own thought of the contrast between the imagined silk underthings and the familiarity of the leaves and black earth and rotting wood of the trail had shamed her. And now, she thought, I am walking along the trail and I can feel silk soft and smooth against my skin. It was exciting and she suddenly knew she was young and fresh, full of a rich strength.

She was a stranger as she saw light ahead of her through the trees and came on the water at the head of the slough, and a stranger again when the trail brought her to the bank of the river and showed her the leaping white of the first rapid above tidewater. She stood still and really looked at it, seeing things she had never seen before—the solid green curve of water over a rock, the dancing break as it folded back on itself below, throwing little splashes of spray high in the sunlight; the tremor of bushes on the far bank as the current waves caught their overhanging branches; the rise of the mountains from the straight drive of the rapid where the river curved out of sight at the bend upstream of her. Julie went on, walking a little faster because she remembered suddenly that the canoe might have passed her, out of sight on the river while she was skirting the slough. If that had happened the boys would be back at the farm now and she would be missing them all this time. Not that it would matter; there would be time at the dance this evening, and what she was doing now, by herself, was fun, more fun than it had ever been, more fun than if Enid had come along too. But she still hurried, because the canoe might come along at any time, dancing and twisting down the rapid and she knew she would rather see it at the Drop, where the river gathered itself together into the sudden narrow chute of white water that spent its force gradually in short, tilting waves between the high walls of the Cut. Even walking along the trail she could remember the breathless expectancy and the jolting excitement of the sharp run through the Drop. Dal and Alec could take her up there tomorrow and run down it; Alec would be lazy and say he didn't want to go, but everyone would be arguing and kidding and scolding and in the end he would go.

They might not get down this afternoon. Perhaps they would take an extra day of hunting because of the storm—but Dal wouldn't stand for that because Dad would be mad if they traveled down on a Sunday; you must not hunt on a Sunday and the journey home from a hunt was the same as hunting; that had been argued out in the family long ago. Or one of them might have been hurt in the storm. She remembered when Mr. Temple's party had been late coming down from the mountain and Dal and Dad had gone up to look for them; and later the two canoes coming up to the little wharf in the slough, each with a blanket covering a dead man in the bottom of it, and Dad shouting to Danny to put gas in the boat for the trip to the Cove. But if one of the boys had been hurt in the storm they would have come out with him yesterday, so it wasn't that.

Prince had come back to her and was trotting at her heels as she began to climb the smooth, sloping rock towards the top of the Cut. She came out to the edge of the wall above the water, where she could get the best view of the Drop and see a straight reach of river above the sweeping bend that led into it. The flat place was there as she had remembered it, made private from the land side by a semicircle of low bushes growing in a crevice in the rock. She passed through the bushes and sat down. Enid had been wrong. Her legs weren't scratched; they were brown and smooth and strong, with firm, full calves and round, soft knees. And her skirt wasn't torn either. The girl from the yacht, walking up the trail, hadn't been so much out of place as she had seemed; unless you had work to do, like picking berries or hunting cattle, you didn't need such rough clothes for the woods.

She wondered how long she should wait. It was pretty here, where they had come so many times to swim and picnic. The kids couldn't have used it so much this summer. Generally the bushes had a trampled, bedraggled look by fall; and there should be a blackened lard pail under the log, with some pitchwood near it; and the embers of the last fire in the circle of rocks were very dead, with no flaky white ash still about them, as though they had known a full winter's weather. But she couldn't stay and just look for very long; they might be down at the farm already. And if they came should she shout at them to stop for her at the end of the Cut? Dal and Alec might want to be mean and make her walk and kid her about it all evening; that had happened before. They were different now—Alec had been very different since that time in town—but you couldn't be sure. If they had had good hunting and were feeling pleased with themselves they just would do some smart-aleck trick like laughing and going on down the river—even if they only went a little way, then stopped and waited for her.

She saw the canoe the moment it came into the straight reach above the bend, a dark sliver against the distant white water. She decided instantly that she would not shout. It would be better to hide, watch carefully for something that would prove she had seen them, then do the kidding herself later on—tell them she had been standing straight up on the rock and they had been so blind they hadn't seen her, blind hunters who would have passed up a five-point buck standing looking at them within a mile of home.

She moved over to the bushes and settled herself close against them, lying on her stomach, looking up towards the Drop. She called to Prince and made him lie beside her. "Steady," she told him, giving her voice the same tone as Dal's. "Steady you old devil, right where you are." She watched the canoe; just before it disappeared into the bend above the Drop she could distinguish the men—Dal in the stern, Johnny amidships, Alec in the bow. She spoke to Prince again, setting her hand on his head. "We've got to keep still," she said. "Very still. They've got good eyes—at least Dal and Alec have. I don't know about that other fellow, but likely he has too." She saw the canoe shoot out from the bend, Alec leaning forward to drive his paddle and swing the bow straight for the center of the Drop. You always came fast to the Drop, full speed for steerage way, Dal said, and the speed gave the canoe light, lifting drive through the tumble of the short waves below. It was straight above now, right in the center of the green glass-smooth drive that poured down into broken white. The three paddles were in the water together, driving forward, out, in again, then the canoe was down in the waves, bouncing, throwing spray back over Dal in the stern until he eased it out into the smoother draw of the current where the cut was wider. It was past her, silently and swiftly, the paddles lifting and flashing and thrusting together. They were hurrying, heads down and shoulders heavy against the work, and they had not seen her. Men do things so well, she thought—things like that. They tie themselves right up tight in them and shut everyone else out. They don't fool or talk or giggle, just go right after it and do it, then they are lazy later on, sitting about and talking and laughing and kidding and boasting, trying to make it sound good, but not making it nearly so good as it really is. They were out of sight and she realized that she hadn't anything to say that would prove she had seen them, nothing except the order they were kneeling in the canoe and anyone who knew Dal and Alec could guess that. She hadn't even noticed whether there was a rolled-up goat hide or bear skin among the dunnage, but there might have been one, covered up or in a packsack.

The canoe passed out of sight beyond the Cut and she got up and climbed down from the rock. As soon as she was on the trail she began to hurry, sometimes running over the soft ground. They would be home long before she would, talking and laughing and telling about the hunt. And everything would be hurry and bustle and confusion from now until the supper dishes were cleared and washed and put away.

At the head of the slough Prince left her again, disappearing in a flash of yellow along the trail as though a leash had been suddenly snapped away from his straining; he knew that Dal had passed—Julie had felt his body tense and quivering as the canoe went through the Cut— and he could wait no longer. As she came along the path from the barn she saw that the boys were ahead of her; the whole family was outside the kitchen door, looking down at something on the ground. It had been a good hunt, Julie guessed. Enid was standing in the kitchen doorway, at the top of the steps. "I don't think there's anything so good looking about it," she said and everyone laughed.

"It may not look so handsome right now," her father said. "But it will be something any man could be proud to have when it's mounted." Julie saw him slap Johnny on the back. "I'm glad you showed the boys what their own country can produce. Dal here and Alec like to think there's nobody but them can hunt the Bowl right."

Julie looked down at the big head of the goat, lying on the heavy hide, then raised her eyes to watch Johnny. So the big guy could hunt; that was different from usual; the boys were always bringing in friends to hunt, then cursing afterwards because they couldn't travel or they couldn't shoot or they were scared of the canoe or something. She heard Johnny say: "Alec did everything but tie him up for me." Julie saw he was confused by all the admiration of his trophy and she liked him for it.

"Would you listen to the guy," Alec said. "A running shot at a lousy angle and in a blinding snowstorm after climbing pretty near right out of the Bowl. And he puts three slugs at the base of the neck, fast as you can pump them into the barrel." He turned and saw Julie. "How come we missed you, Julie?" he said. "You must have started down just before we came through."

"No," she said. "I was on the Cut all the time."

"You should have hollered," Dal said. "We'd have given you a ride down."

"I wanted to see how good your eyes were," Julie said. But she knew the joke was flat and she didn't care; they were all there looking at her and she could feel they were disappointed that she had not stopped them. "No," she said. "It wasn't that, really. It was so good seeing the trail and all of it again and I wanted to walk. We can take the canoe up beyond there tomorrow and run back. It'd be fun."

"That's a date," Alec said. "Johnny wants to go through again too."

"Come on in and clean up for supper," Enid said. "There'll be plenty of time to put on good clothes for the dance when you've eaten."

Julie enjoyed the supper. It was always exciting when men came in from the hills with much that was new to talk of. It was fun to be putting good food in front of them and hearing them exclaim at its goodness and compare it with what they had cooked for themselves. And it was fun to listen to the new stories and try to guess which of them would fall into the pattern of family legend, to be told and remembered again and again on lesser days. This hunt of the big goat would be remembered, she knew—Dal might be telling it at that same table in twenty years' time, about the storm and Alec's guess and Johnny's shot, and their journey back to camp against darkness. And they had put Johnny's pack on the steelyards when they came in; two hundred and four pounds he had carried down the mountain.

"You can thank Johnny for your bear fat, Mother," Dal said. "And the venison. Alec and I had our knees shaking with the little hundred and fifty pound jobs we had. If we had been alone we'd surely have had to bring just the head and the two hides and leave the rest."

"You'd have done no such thing," Mrs. Morris said. "If Mr. Holt hadn't been there you would have got no goat. And if you had come down here without bear fat and good meat you would have turned right around to go back and get it."

"Maybe that'll hold us," Alec said. "Just the same, that load of Johnny's was something. It took the two of us to get it on his back and he came down the hill as if he was walking a paved highway."

"I couldn't have made twenty feet with it against the grade," Johnny said. "I guess if you've jumped around enough on logs with a pair of tongs on your neck you get so your legs just don't feel any more. . . ."

It was ten o'clock before everyone was dressed and ready to go up to the schoolhouse. Several of the boys had gone across the river to fetch the Cully girls and Ronald Cully had come over to claim Enid. Julie found herself looking at him closely and critically, trying to see what Enid had told her that first night she was home. He did look serious, she decided, sort of earnest and distant, very carefully polished up in his good clothes. Yet he was also as she had remembered him, a little untidy in spite of the polish, and good looking with his black curly hair and dark brown eyes and the teeth that flashed white when he spoke. When he held Enid's coat for her Julie saw that his face relaxed a little and she remembered him coming out of the schoolhouse after all the others, when they had already started to pick sides for the softball game; the change in his expression was about the same.

Enid said: "If Dal's still not ready we may as well go on ahead of the rest of you."

Holding the door for her, Ron Cully smiled, freely and happily for the first time since he had come into the room. "We'll see you at the dance," he said, and they went out.

Dal came down the stairs and Julie thought: Poor Dal, he's wishing his schoolteacher could have been fetched from the Cove. "Ron Cully surely has grown up," she said. "He's got big too. He always looked so small at school."

"That's one smart guy," Dal said. "He's going places. By the time he gets finished with that college in California he'll be able to pick his own job."

"What will he be?" Julie asked.

"Chemical engineer," Alec said. "Likely he'll get a research job with some big manufacturing outfit—down there if he's lucky. What's he doing up here now, Dal?"

"I don't know. He's leaving the first of next week. Guess he's due to graduate next year."

Alec stood up. "We'd better get moving," he said. "Johnny, you take Julie. Dal and I will come along in a few minutes."

Julie felt a little flutter of excitement and anger in her. So Alec was going after Rose Kenny again; he had made good time with her at the last dance and he thought he could do better this time. He had his nerve, thinking he could arrange things just any way he wanted. "It's time you learned you can't boss everyone, Alec Crawford," Julie said. "Maybe Mr. Holt doesn't want to take me."

Johnny smiled. "May I?" he asked. "Please."

I like you, Julie thought; you're swell when you smile. "You may," she said. "But I think we ought to take time one day to teach Alec better manners."

"Climb down, Julie," Alec said. "No girl ever gets to be a grand lady to her favorite cousin." I might be wrong on that, he thought. Little Julie's growing up all the time and she's got what it takes. Some guy's going to have to watch his step around there soon.

Johnny was holding the door open and Julie went out. It was silly to have been mad at Alec; there was always a lot of arranging about a dance up here, more than there would be for a dance at the Cove or even for one at Hal Johnson's or one of the other small camps—unless it just seemed that way because the family had to do the arranging. It's different in the country than in town though. In town you just go dancing and nobody seems to notice much; in the country everybody notices and if a man takes you to a dance he must ask you for the supper waltz and the home waltz and then take you home after; if there's any slip-up in that people talk, so it means more for a man to take you in the country. And Alec is too bossy anyway.

Johnny said: "I guess you're taking me really. I don't even know the way. Is it far?" He was holding the beam of the flashlight ahead of her, along the worn path across the pasture.

"About half a mile," Julie said. "They built the schoolhouse just off the flat, on the beginning of the hill, so it wouldn't be flooded. Sometimes, in a hot summer, we have water over the floor down at the house. The glacier's bad for that."

"You do? Alec didn't tell me about that; he's told me so much about this place that I feel I've known it for years."

"It doesn't happen so very often and it isn't bad really except for the sand. When the river gets that high the sand doesn't have time to settle in the lakes and it's inches deep on everything when the water goes down again."

Johnny felt closer to her. Alec shouldn't have said it that way down in the kitchen; nothing had been said before about how they were going to the dance and maybe she had wanted to go with someone else—maybe she had wanted Alec to take her. "I'm sorry Alec was like that," he said. "I wanted to ask to take you, but I didn't know how it might be."

Julie smiled in the dark. He wasn't dumb; he could say what he was thinking without being afraid of it anyway. "I just get mad at Alec sometimes," she said. "He always thinks he can arrange everybody's life to suit himself."

"Alec's smart," Johnny said. "I guess he generally knows what's best. He did this time—for me anyway."

Julie dipped a little unseen curtsey. "Thank you, kind sir. I think we'll have fun and put Alec Crawford in his place."

Johnny laughed. "Don't be too hard on him, but don't let him dance with you much tonight. I want to do that."

They could hear the music now and see the lighted windows of the schoolhouse against the heavy darkness of the mountain slope. Julie walked on light feet; it was going to be fun, she told herself. Alec could have his schoolmarm; it wouldn't be any hardship to play the thing along with this Johnny—if he could dance.

"Do you dance a lot, Mr. Holt?" she asked.

"Alec and I always take in any dance there is down at the Beach—there's a lot of families there, working at the sawmill and they put on good dances. And sometimes we go over to the Cove. Otherwise there isn't much chance except in town."

They went into the schoolhouse. The Coleman lamps were bright, hanging from the crossbeams, and the colored paper streamers and heavy green fir and hemlock branches gave the room a rich ceiling. The big silver cardboard bell, souvenir of Mother and Dad's wedding, hung in its usual place of honor over the orchestra. Ray's Rhythm Benders had their uniform of glossy green satin shirts and tight-waisted, bell-bottomed corduroy pants with metal-studded belts. They looked like a real band. She could see that Ray was happy and proud, standing up in front of them with the big white piano-accordion strapped over his shoulder. Dolly would say it was corny, the whole thing, and maybe it was; but it was friendly and familiar and people were going to have a good time. The Cully girls were all there and they crowded over to her excitedly, Jean and Grace and Ruth, Margaret and Ida and Helen, all talking at once. They are all so pretty,

Julie thought; I hadn't remembered that; and they've got pretty dresses—prettier than anything I ever had before Dolly taught me.

Later she was dancing with Johnny. "Everybody's mighty glad to see you," he said. "It's a good thing for me that most of the men in the room are your brothers."

Julie laughed, watching Alec with the schoolteacher. She was a big, strong girl, very sure of herself in the yellow satin dress; handsome in her big-nosed, big-mouthed way, Julie thought, but too dark—black hair, black eyes, olive-brown skin; she looks a little dirty, a little greasy anyway. She's doing things to Alec, pressed up close against him like that with her big breasts and her wide hips. And you can see she hasn't got a girdle on; if Dad or Mr. Cully notices the way she's dancing there'll be a new teacher here before the end of the school year. I wonder if Alec will take her outside, like he did last time. Not till after Dad and Mr. Cully have gone home anyway; she's smart enough for that.

She said: "You've done more dancing than just the way you said. Somebody taught you." She leaned back from him, watching his fumbling for words and the flush that mounted to his square forehead.

"There's a guy called Red Henderson in camp," he said. "A rigger. He's been a professional and sometimes a few of the boys get up a little music in one of the bunkhouses and he shows us things."

"They're good things," Julie said. She could feel his arm high and firm on her back, holding her close against him, and the strong guidance of his whole body through the long smooth steps. He was better than Alec and always before it had seemed there was nothing in the room better than Alec. Dancing with him here seemed more real than dancing with men in town—they always had to be kidding or trying to get by with something. Johnny just held her and danced and the dancing seemed more than dancing.

The music stopped and Ray strutted across to a chair and sat down, to signal that there would be no encore. The pattern of the evening followed that of all northern coast dances in a blending of old and new, of mail-order clothes and working hands and strong, active bodies. There were waltzes and nondescript dances imported from town, occasional polkas learned from near-by Finnish settlements and, more rarely still, the square dances handed down from older generations, danced with the sweating vigor of youth and a freedom of movement perhaps restrained in earlier times. Between encores the couples circled the floor, walking arm in arm; between dances they sat, less stiffly and awkwardly as the evening went on, in chairs around the walls.

After supper Johnny found himself separated from Julie, dancing with a vague succession of Cully girls who held him at a distance and questioned him politely about the trip to the Bowl. Dancing with them, he watched Julie. Many of the older people had left—the Morrises and Cullys had stayed only until supper was over—and Alec had disappeared with his schoolteacher. I would have envied him that most times, Johnny thought, but I don't now. I want something better—that Julie girl; I wanted her that evening on the hill, remembering her arms on the table at suppertime with the little curved black hairs soft against them. I want her here, now; just dancing with her is enough. I shouldn't want her down on the boat the way Alec has the schoolteacher. It's a longer, slower thing than that and more satisfying; just holding her and dancing and hearing her talk is satisfying. She fits with something I like, the way she is, the way she looks and moves and talks. It wouldn't be enough to be with her once and then go away—and it wouldn't happen. She's not that kind.

He saw Julie alone and went across to her and in a little while they were dancing again. It's better late in the evening, Julie thought; your body is looser and warmer all through, wanting more and giving more. She felt Johnny's strength against her and let her body be drawn by it until she could feel her breasts crushed against him and his thighs moving against hers. She knew his face was touching her hair and was glad. She heard the thick difficulty of the words and felt the quickening of his heartbeat when he said: "Alec says you work in town all the time." It made her suddenly free and sure of herself; it would not be all gone in this one evening. She moved her right arm across his chest, pushing her head and shoulders back to look up into his face while their bodies still held close together.

"That's right," she said. "All the time, month after month, except for a holiday once a year like now. Do you get down often?"

"Every six months or so. I'd sure like to see you sometime."

"Why shouldn't you?" she said, and smiled. She let her arm go to his shoulder again, felt him hold her closer than before, and they danced without speaking again until the music stopped.

Going home along the trail they could see the Cully boy's light ahead of them through the trees as he walked with Enid. Only Ray and his band were behind them, packing up the instruments. They walked side by side, a little distance apart on the good footing of the wide trail. I want him, Julie thought, for more than just now. He'll go away and when he goes to town he'll go to some girl like Dolly and I shan't see him. Maybe I shan't mind, maybe I shall only laugh about the way I feel now; but I don't want to laugh and I want to mind. She reached her hand out, felt it touch his big hand and slide into it. He had stopped and she was facing him and the light was out. Then he was holding her tight against him, tight until it hurt and the full length of his body was pressed against the full length of hers. Her head was back and her lips were parted, half afraid, yet wanting everything. She felt his lips against hers, almost gentle at first, then fierce and searching. He drew away suddenly. "Did I frighten you, Julie?"

"No," she said. "Oh, Johnny, kiss me again."

Later they were walking again, side by side but close together, his arm about her. "You won't remember," she said. "There won't be any more of this."

"I will, Julie. I promise I will."

"Will you write to me—not just when you are coming down, all the time?"

"Sure I will, but they won't be awful good letters."

"That doesn't matter. Just write that you love me and you want me. Promise?"

"Promise," he said.

When they could see the lights of the house she stopped again. "Johnny, darling," she said. "Do you want me?"

"Of course I do."

"You can have me you know."

"You mustn't say that, Julie," he said. "Not yet."

12

JOHNNY moved his arms restlessly against the metal of the handbrake wheel, shaking the hard, dead coal sparks away from the sleeve of his coat.

"It's time they gave Eric an oil burner," he said. "Or else make him keep the spark arrester on that damn thing all winter."

"It isn't Eric's fault he hasn't got an oil burner," Alec said. "He'd take Number Five on the mainline any time Dad Hutchins would make up his mind to quit. Chris has pretty nearly promised him the job too."

"Is Dad going to quit? He's been a hogger so long I should think he'd stay that way till he dies."

"He likely will at that. He's been talking about retiring to that house of his in West Vancouver ever since I've been with the outfit and he looks just as solid as ever up in the cab of the Five Spot. But I guess he's closer to meaning it all the time. Anyway, Chris said something to Eric about it the other day when Eric was talking about going down to run locie for Crown Valley Timber—said to hang on till next summer because the mainline job would likely be open."

"That'd be swell for Eric and Marion. It's better for a woman down at the Beach than up in camp. Eric's young yet, but he's one hell of a good engineer and getting better all the time. I like to see a guy like that get a break."

"Did he ask you to go up to his place for supper tonight? Said he was going to."

Johnny nodded. "Yes. It's their anniversary, isn't it?"

It was a late November morning, dark and cold. The locomotive climbed slowly, snorting and struggling to force the long string of empties up against the grade, dragging the creaking crummy with its load of men behind. The light was just breaking over the far hills to the east, showing the heavy, dirty-white clouds in the pause between the rain of the night and the wind and rain of the day.

Johnny said: "Talking about Dad retiring, what's that about Chris?"

"He's bad again," Alec said. "Same thing with his stomach. He said last time the doctor told him he'd have to quit for good if it went bad again. He's got a sister or something down in California and he wants to go down there."

"Is that right he's got cancer?" Shorty asked.

"No," Alec said. "It's ulcers."

"Poor bastard. That's what killed my old man and he suffered bad."

"Who'll they make superintendent with Chris gone?" Johnny said. "Mark Evans?"

"That's what they say down at the Beach," Alec said.

"That long black whore." Shorty spat dark snuff juice back on to the receding track. "He's scared of his job now when he's only assistant supe."

The train began jolting and creaking round the long curve that opened up the full width and length of the valley, away to the mountains at the head of the watershed. Johnny watched the slow sweep of country in front of him, the logged waste of blackened stumps in the foreground, green timber across the stream three hundred feet below the track, mounting away through fold after fold of rounded hills to the steeper slopes of the mountainsides. On the mountains more timber, solid green low down, then white with new snow, then more and more scattered until individual trees stood out, tiny and perfect against the smooth white of snow on clear slopes. The unbroken white of the snow climbed far above the last trees and only became streaked with the black of bare rock on the five raw, jagged peaks of the high mountain at the head of the watershed. The rising sun seemed to have shattered the low clouds, pressed them down into cushions of mist in the hollows or drawn them up, away from the wide valley; but the sun itself did not show and there was no break in the cold gray-white of the high clouds. I go past it every day, Johnny thought, but I don't always see it. Sometimes a guy's talking or he can't see it for the clouds. It's good in summertime—you wish you were out in it then. I've never seen it just the way it is today and it makes you feel good to see it a different way. Somewhere the sun broke through for a moment, not showing itself but touching the eastern clouds and the five peaks of the mountain to pink.

"Boy," Johnny said. "That's swell."

Alec watched the cold colors, leaning on the iron rail. "You're damn right it is," he said slowly at last. "Makes you feel good to look at it. This country ought to grow good people, with things like that for them to look at every day."

"You think that makes a difference, Slim?" Shorty asked.

"Sure as hell ought to," Alec said. "Look at the people in those little European countries, always fighting and raising hell. I figure a lot of it's because they haven't got room enough to look around and see things. Canadians and Americans aren't like that and maybe they're better for being able to see things and get out into a big country. Even in Vancouver you can see mountains."

"Might be something in that," Shorty said. "Like the way a guy doesn't feel so mean when it's good weather instead of raining all the time."

Johnny laughed. "Don't get too mean when you bring the second lot of empties in today, Shorty. She's going to be a dirty one—worse than yesterday."

"Think so?"

Johnny pointed towards the mountain.

"Look there," he said. The pink had gone from clouds and snow, and a heavy gray mass was moving up behind the shoulder of the mountain. As they watched, it poured through the pass, spreading across the face of the mountain, blotting out the peaks, sending squalls of sleet across the timber of the lower slopes. "She's going to be a bitch," Johnny said.

The wind was heavy above them as the locomotive slowed the crummy into Side Two. Johnny dropped down from the step and walked up past the empties to the landing, pulling on his gloves. He climbed on to the sled of the donkey and walked round to the firebox. Dan Evritt and the fireman were already there, standing by the open door of the firebox. "Hullo, Johnny," Dan said. "Want a cup of coffee?"

"Not now," Johnny said. "But it will sure go good later on. God, I hate this time of year."

"What's the matter with it?" Dan asked. His voice was high and wheezy from a throatful of gas at Ypres, and he seemed to keep his little frail body alive only by the constant stimulation of thick black coffee, made in the firebox of the donkey. "What's the matter with it? Not enough swimming and sun-tan?"

"I guess that's it. The weather's worse after the new year but it doesn't seem so bad with spring coming on and no shut-down till fire season. Now, when a guy gets a day like yesterday was and today's going to be he begins to figure why in hell not shut her down right away instead of waiting for Christmas."

"Hell," the fireman said. "You're just getting stakey. That's all is the matter with you."

Dan shook his head. "It isn't that either. There's a woman in it somewhere. I never saw it fail when a guy started writing letters two or three times a week."

Johnny turned sharply towards him, then checked himself. "Hell, Dan, you know better than that."

"Sure," Dan said. "What's her name?"

"Hell," Johnny said. "Aren't you scared of anything?"

"Not of big guys anyway. Takes little guys like me to be real mean. I'd put you off here as quick as thinking—with the steam hose. I've done it to bigger guys."

The fireman said: "Not Johnny you wouldn't put off. Some goddamn big farmer, but not Johnny."

Johnny laughed and put his arm across Dan's shoulders. "Sure he would. He's the meanest little old bastard that's still got a rope waiting for him."

Dan said: "No kidding, Johnny, you thinking of getting hitched?"

"Not so as the other party knows about it," Johnny said. "How in hell's a guy going to ask a decent girl to come and live out in the sticks like this?"

"It ain't that bad," Dan said. "Eric seems to make out all right with that redhead of his."

"Eric's got a chance to get ahead and a hogger can stay on the job till he's halfway in the grave. First thing I know my knees will give out and I'll have to quit loading."

"You'll get ahead just as quick as Eric if you get a woman to keep at you. Young guys like you ought to get married and live in camp. That what's wrong with this whole damned country. Instead of that you make a stake, then go to town and let some goddamn chippy clean it off you before you've even taken up her skirts. Look at young Don; went to town a week ago with six hundred bucks and came in last night clean."

"Did he say how it happened?" Johnny asked.

"Oh, sure. A guy met him coming off the boat and asked him if he wanted to see something good. So Don fell for it and next thing he knew they were kicking him out of the joint because he hadn't got any dough."

"Seems to be getting worse," Johnny said. "There's been half a dozen like that in the last month or two."

Dan reached for the pot and poured himself another cup of coffee. "That right Chris is bad again?" he asked.

"Seems so," Johnny said. "They say he's liable to quit for good and go south somewhere."

"That ain't so good. We'll be a long time before we get another one like Chris." Dan pulled out his watch and looked at it. "Time to yank the old whistle," he said.

Johnny turned away from the warmth of the boiler and went out into the driving rain that had swept up from the southeast. It was a cold rain, streaked at times into colder sleet from low clouds. He pulled off a glove to do up the top button of his raintest coat and ram his hat down. The tongs were hanging over the first of the three empties still to be loaded before Shorty came back from Side One to switch in new cars. Young Tommy and Ron Shelton came down from checking the cheese blocks that held the logs in place on the steel bunks of the skeleton cars. Standing on the first car, Johnny held up his right hand and Ed slid the tongs down to it. The day had started.

It was a lousy show, Johnny told himself, fit for a lousy day. The chokermen were working down in a swamphole, sending in slabbed cedar and kink-butted fir, with a long time between the turns. There was never enough of a pile on the landing to give a guy a chance to pick a good bunk load. He swung down and flipped the tongs on to the one decent-looking log. Ed moved the levers, the log came up and young Tommy went down with the rear tongs. The log swung into the air, jerked up over the car. Ed steadied it and let it down on to the steel bunks, close against the cheese blocks on the upper side of the track. Johnny shook the front tongs free and went down with them to his second log. Ed set it on the car and Johnny went down for the only log in the pile that would balance the first one, a fir butt with a bad kink. He had to roll it three times on the bunk to settle it down in place. Ron Shelton came over to the front tongs and Johnny stepped back and pointed out his next log. The yarder was bringing in a turn; two good logs, he saw. Maybe the boys will be in better stuff from now on.

It wasn't so bad once you got going. You didn't notice the rain and wind and there couldn't be anything much go wrong—just another day, sixteen or eighteen loads out before the quitting whistle blew and the gut-wagon came up to take the crew in for supper. Supper at Eric's would be good; the goose Alec had shot last Sunday and hot rum before and after, all through the evening. You always had a good time at Eric's place; Marion had done a swell job with him. Before he married her Eric was getting to be quite a booze-hound, but she had straightened him right up without seeming to do a thing. Eric could take it or leave it alone now; haven't seen him really plastered since he was first engaged to her, though he'll always take a drink if there's any around. That's part of why he's getting ahead; he always was a good engineer, kept that old Climax running when nobody else could and made it rattle the loads along in good shape. But since Marion has taken hold of him and he's got the Two Spot he's steadier and a whole lot more sure of himself.

Johnny dropped the tongs on the first log of the third bunk load. He unbuttoned his coat all the way down, letting it hang loosely from his shoulders in spite of the driving sleet. A guy didn't notice it once he was warmed up and anyway the coat tied you up when it was all buttoned. Must get a size larger next time—pretty near due for it now. One thing about going out to Eric's, it won't be so easy to get a letter in the mail for Julie. The southbound boat stops at the Beach tomorrow afternoon and if I don't get it into the office tonight that'll be a week gone without one. Wish I could knock off a letter the way Alec can, in about five minutes; then I could make it tomorrow morning and get the timekeeper to put it in the bag. Maybe Julie won't mind, but that isn't the point anyway; it makes me feel good all week if I get a letter away. God, she's a swell kid, and when she writes you can feel the way she looks and the way she talks right out of the letter. It'll be something, to have her to go about with in town. Sure it will, and what about Bess Logan's girls? You going to do without one this time? Just go to the movies with a decent girl and come back to camp after the new year without having had a woman in bed the whole time? You will like hell. It'll work out when you get down there; there'll surely be some way to fix it up.

The loading crew went up and stood by the boiler, letting the wetness steam away from their heavy clothes while the Two Spot switched out the loads and brought in new empties. Johnny bent down, watching under the iron roof of the donkey as a turn came in and the chaser went out to free the chokers. More good logs.

Young Tommy said: "If they keep that up we ought to get twenty-one—nine this morning and twelve this afternoon. Hope the hell they do; I sure hate frigging around on a wet day like we did all yesterday afternoon."

Johnny nodded. "You and me both," he said. "Say, Tommy, you hear anything about Don Henty?"

"Getting rolled you mean? Sure. They cleaned him

good. Says he can't remember a goddamn thing about it except a swell big room with gold mirrors all around the walls and a big glass thing with lights hanging down from the ceiling and a bunch of tarts sitting around. He woke up in some hotel down on Cordova Street. The clerk said a couple of guys brought him in dead to the world and paid for a room for him to sober up in."

"Sounds like the same joint as got a hold of Scotty."

"Sure. And there's two guys in the float bunkhouse say they got taken the same place. Jonesy claims a taxi driver took him there and they showed him a swell time for two days and it didn't set him back more than about fifty bucks—a case of liquor up in the room and two girls around most of the time."

"Does Jonesy know where the joint is?"

"No. He was tight when they took him back to his hotel, but he says they treated him fine."

The empty cars came in and they went out to set up the handbrakes and put on the spotting line. It was cold, out in the wind and sleet again, but the logs came well and Johnny felt the warmth from his body building up inside his clothes, and the loads went on smoothly and easily. Tommy and Ron, and Ed at the levers, made a good crew—better even than with Charlie, because Ron had lots of sense but he was plenty fast too—and the chaser was good, setting the logs down where it was easy to size them up and put the tongs on. A lot of that was old Dan of course; Dan could set a turn down to kill a gnat if he had to, but just the same a good chaser is a help and this little guy Nick is catty; he has the chokers off and himself to hell out in the clear so darn quick you hardly have to figure on him at all. A good crew like that is one hell of a fine thing; it'll break up, one of them will get mad and quit or just quit or get hurt, and there'll be a green man to break in or a foreigner or some guy with lead in his arse, but it's swell while it lasts. It ought to be steadier though, not so many changes. It's good that fellows can move around the way they want, leaving one job and getting another, quitting just to go to town and get their greens or get drunk. But it shouldn't be fixed so they want to do that all the time. Dan's right, more young guys ought to get married and steady down.

Got to get that goddamn big log out of there, Johnny thought; Tommy has to go up over it every time to get in the clear. Make a load by itself with two little sticks to set along against the cheese blocks. He called to Ron to bring the straps and packed the front tongs down to the log himself. The log was too big for the gape of the tongs, but they passed the short strap of steel cable under it and brought the eyesplice at each end up over the point of the tongs. Johnny signaled the leverman to take her up easy and watched the strap bite into the heavy bark. The back end of the log pulled out of the pile and slid forward, and Johnny signaled: "Hold it." He watched Ron and Tommy set the second strap under and bring the splices up to the rear tongs, then jump back into the clear. Ed moved his levers, lifting the big log slowly and smoothly. The spar tree quivered as the end swung round parallel with the track, and the guy lines slapped and strained. Ed steadied the swing and let the log down on to the bunks, slowly and smoothly.

"Nothing to it," Johnny told himself. Some loaders

hate like hell to use a strap; they figure it's wasting time because they aren't jumping around slinging tongs and giving signals. But a man gets the best part of a load in one lift that way and it gives him something different to do once in a while. Big logs are okay so long as there aren't too many of them together, to keep a crew frigging with straps all day and using heavy tongs instead of these seventy-five pound jobs.

Putting on the next bunk load he let his mind back to the crew again. Sure they ought to steady down and make something of themselves, kids like Ron and young Tommy here. They had ambition—talking ambition—but they never made anything of it; at least not many of them. They'll work like hell in camp for six months, then go to town and spend everything they've got in a couple of weeks on booze and chippies. Then they come back and talk about it for six months until it looks good again, then go back and do the same thing over. There's no sense to a guy tearing his guts out for six months so as he can get himself a new outfit of good clothes and set a chippy up in a new fur coat. What got me on to thinking this anyway? Tommy and Ron both figure on coming back after the Christmas shut-down and Dan and Ed will. Nick won't; he wants to buy himself an automobile and get to some camp where there's a road. No, it's that kid Don, and Scotty and those other guys. A month, hell; they don't get a couple of days. That makes you sore; it's goddamn robbery and it isn't even as if the girls get anything out of it—just those pimp bastards that run the joint. Sure, a guy's got to be a crazy son of a bitch to get himself into a place like that. But what the hell else is he going to do?

He goes to town, gets a couple of drinks in him and wants to go places; he'll go with the first slicker that gets talking to him.

Back in the bunkhouse in the evening, changing out of his wet clothes to go to supper, Johnny worried again about Julie's letter. He remembered what she had written last week: "I love getting your letters. You mustn't say they aren't good letters, because they are. They make me remember the dance and the day after when we all went up the river and most of all they make me want to see you again soon, quite soon, in a few weeks now. So you must go on writing them whatever you think about them, because I like getting them." Hell, he thought, it's funny how a guy can get caught up in a thing like that—and get to kind of like it too. There'll be another one from her next mail day and if I don't get one away tomorrow I'll feel bad about it. The hell though, it doesn't mean anything. It would be different if I was thinking of getting married. Julie would be a swell girl to be married to; there's so much of her, all ways, and she's so full of things and she'd keep everything shaped up right for a guy. But what do I want with getting married and what would she want with coming to live in a goddamned uncivilized dump like this, married to a working guy? She's too smart for that. She could have any of those fancy city guys she wanted. Writing letters between her and me is like it was writing notes back and forth with that Phyllis kid in high school. She was a pretty kid and the swellest dresser in school, and that was okay with me. And she wanted me around because I was pitcher on the ball team. But that was all there was to it. This with me and Julie isn't just the same, but it's like it in lots of ways; she's just kidding me along and I can't leave it because I think she's a swell kid. I wouldn't want to leave it. Hell, I'd feel terrible if I thought I wasn't ever going to see her again; but a guy always feels that way and he always gets over it. . . .

Alec Crawford came into the bunkhouse. "All set, Johnny?" he asked.

Johnny reached for his mackinaw and they went out into the heavy rain, along the plank walk between the bunkhouses to the track, then along the track to where the light of Eric's house showed, across from the car shop. The door of the house opened to the sound of their feet on the steps. Marion Denton stood in the lighted doorway.

"Come on in, kids," she said. "You're good to be on time. Eric isn't through cleaning up yet, but he'll be out in a minute."

They took off their mackinaws and hung them on the porch, then went inside. It was a small room, too small for its double function as kitchen and living room, and overcrowded with furniture. But there were bright curtains over the windows and bright cushions on the chairs and it had a good feeling about it of neatness and warm comfort.

"Sit down," she said, "and make yourselves at home. Turn on the radio if you want. I'll mix up something to drink."

Johnny sat down and watched her. It was like that in Eric's house; you just went in and sat down and it was all friendly and comfortable. Some houses you stood around and the women giggled and you didn't know what to do and they didn't know what to do; and it went on like that all evening in a sort of stiff awkward kidding that tried to make out everybody was having a hell of a good time when nobody was. In Eric's house you sat down and Marion mixed a hot rum and Eric came in buttoning his shirt and saying: "Hullo, boys," just as if you were talking to him out on the job.

"Which anniversary is it, Eric?" Alec said. "Fourth?"

"Third," Eric said. "You can keep track of them by the kids."

"You cannot," Marion said. "Little Eric is just two and the baby isn't two months yet."

"What's wrong with that? Add one to little Eric and you've guessed it; that'll be true as long as we live."

"That isn't the way you meant it to sound," she said.

"Don't be mean to him tonight, Marion," Alec said. He was standing by the stove, tall and slim, his blue eyes bright and his face flushed by the rain and wind of the day. He raised his glass high in front of him. "Here's to both of you," he said. "And little Eric and Jean too. And here's hoping Marion will cook the same supper and ask the same people to it forty-seven good years from now."

Johnny stood up and they all drank. "Fill 'em up again," Eric said. "We've got to get the cold out before we sit down."

"No," Marion told him. "Afterwards. The goose will spoil if you sit around any more now." She bent down to open the oven door and brought out the heavy-breasted, dark-brown bird.

The evening passed away from them easily and quickly,

in quiet talking and the comfortable warmth of the pleasant room. Johnny sat deep in a big chair, watching the others as they talked, talking a little and lazily himself, until the dark, glowing brownness of the rum and its rich warm scent became a transparent curtain, soft and warm and rich, through which he saw and heard and felt everything. The same color and richness and warmth was within him, flowing in his mind, lazily strong in his veins, warm in his belly. And I haven't drunk much, he thought, hardly anything at all. I could stand up and let it all fall away from me, go out from here and in a few minutes not know I have had a drink. It isn't just the rum; it's because it has been a tough day, because that was a good meal and I ate too much of it, because I'm not used to a comfortable chair in a warm room like this; and most of all because I like these people and what they are saying and there's nothing else that matters except now, this very minute. This is the way a man ought to live, not that other way with just a bunk and locker behind it and a suitcase under the bunk; and going down to the bathhouse with Alec to talk by the light of the boiler fire, though that can be good too. This ought to be all the time, not just once in months of the other, and a man wouldn't need the rum either—maybe just one, good and hot, when he came in after a wet day, but that's all. That other way is living like a goddamn animal; it isn't human. . . .

Alec was standing up. "We'd better be on our way," he said. "That old Chinaman hammers the bell good and early these dark mornings."

Johnny stood up and all the warmth and color of things

dropped away from him, as he knew it would. "It's been swell with you folks tonight," he said. He looked at Marion. "That was the finest supper I ever had."

Marion smiled at him. "You'll have lots more just as good," she said. Why does she smile like that, Johnny thought. I've seen women do it before, one woman talking to another that's going to have a baby or about a girl that's going to be married; it's sort of soft, kind of with a secret in it that isn't really a secret because everybody knows about it.

They went out into the rain again, the spot of Alec's flashlight shining on the wet rails and ties. The wind was at their backs and Alec said: "It's none of my goddamn business, but did you get a letter away to Julie tonight?"

"No," Johnny said. "I should have done it last night but I didn't know till this morning that we'd be going over to Eric's."

"Do you want to come in the office and write one now? The kid'll be disappointed if she doesn't get one."

"Thanks," Johnny said. "I'll do that." That isn't like Alec, not kidding or anything when he's got the chance; maybe it is though at that; you can't tell what he's liable to do, except that generally he comes out the way you'd like him to—that's what's good about him.

They went into the office. Alec opened the draft on the stove, switched on the gooseneck lamp on the timekeeper's desk and got out pen and paper. "Go to it," he said. "I'll read for a while. Don't feel like going to sleep."

Johnny began to write. It was easier than usual tonight. Going out to Eric's was something to write about, remembering it had been warm and bright there and how Marion had the room fixed and what Alec had said. Julie always said in her letters: "Write me about your job, what you do in the daytime and how the logs were and how many loads you got—I like to hear all that, then I can remember it and imagine it when I'm down at the office." But there was nothing to write about loading, just: "We got twenty-one loads. It was all bum stuff at first but after that it got good and the whole crew was going good." A girl didn't want to hear that stuff, so it was swell to have something like supper at Eric's to write about.

He leaned back in the timekeeper's chair and Alec said: "Finished?"

"Just about," Johnny said and began to address the envelope.

Alec said: "You heard about young Don. What do you think about that? Think it's the same outfit that's been getting all the boys?"

Johnny put the pen down and sealed the envelope. "Sure it's the same outfit. Someone ought to go down and bust those guys wide open."

"That's not so easy," Alec said. "They're smart. And anyway, what good would it do?"

"There's ways to do it; it's been done before and if it's done right it throws a scare into them that keeps 'em quiet for a long time."

"You got something figured out?"

"Sort of," Johnny said. "But I need more dope. You going to town as soon as they shut down?"

"No. I'll have to stay up two or three days to make reports."

"Ted wants us guys to work along the track with the cherry-picker, so we ought to be through about the same time. I figured some of us could get together in town and maybe do something then."

"Sounds good," Alec said. "If you can ever dope out where the joint is."

13

JULIE turned from the brightness of Granville Street into the dim light of the street where she lived. She liked the walk home better than the crowded jerking of the street car that had carried her west every evening before she moved up to room with Dolly, and it was best of all on these evenings when she had stayed late at the office; half a dozen blocks along Granville, past shop windows and cafés and movie theaters at a time when the stir of people coming back uptown was just beginning, walking proudly, her head high, the sound of her heels crisp and sharp against the sidewalk in the quick, short-stepped rhythm of town movement. There was still a little tingle of excitement in turning down to the darker street; sometimes there would be a man there who tried to speak or began to follow her. She had learned to look straight ahead at such times, pulling back her shoulders and quickening her step ever so slightly. You never really saw them and they never bothered you, but it was a little frightening and it made the dark street exciting, even tonight when there was no one there.

She crossed the alleyway in the middle of the block, crossed the next side street and came into her own block. It must be later than she had thought, because there was no light in the cabinet-maker's shop and he was always there until six-thirty. She turned in at the side door next to the shop, ran quickly up the steep flight of dark stairs and put her key into the door of the apartment.

There was a light in the tiny hallway and she saw the letters on the table, with Dolly's note on top of them. "Phil came and fetched me for supper. There's lots to eat in the kitchen. We won't be late and Phil's going right home. Love. Dolly." Julie wrinkled her nose at the note, then smiled and walked into the sitting room. She switched on the light, pulled her hat off and threw it on to a chair; let her coat slip away from her to the floor, then went across and sat down on the couch, her legs curled under her. She thought; it's like Dolly to go out just when I'm late and it's her night to cook supper, but she'll darn well do it tomorrow night. I'm going to read the letters before I do another thing, anyway; that's why I wouldn't have supper with Arthur, because I knew they'd be here.

She held up the two envelopes, one in either hand, and looked closely at them. They were both the same—post-offices envelopes with red three-cent stamps printed on the corners; across one her father's thin, even hand flowed smoothly. On the other Johnny's writing stood out blackly in heavy awkward strokes and small letters. She read quickly through Johnny's letter first, smiling to herself and moving her feet under her on the couch. "He's nice," she said and put the single sheet down beside her. She opened her father's letter and read it, then picked up Johnny's again. I'll bet that redheaded woman can't cook a darn bit better than I can, she thought, and I'll bet that house is a mess—I've seen them, those loggers' houses in camps: a big radio, a breakfast nook set, green and cream, and an open cupboard with some pierced silver wedding presents in it. Poor kid; he just felt good there because he never sees anything but a bunkhouse. I wonder what he'd think of this place?

She looked about her at the room. It was a small room with two big windows looking over the street. Rayon curtains, vertically striped with bold dark red and white, were drawn across the windows now, and the same dull red was all about the room—in the rug, on couch and chairs and the many rayon-covered cushions. A few of the cushions were white, the two little tables were white and the walls were a good shade of pink, soft and warm and not too pale. I thought it was beautiful when I first saw it; it's still nice, a happy room, but a little untidy—I don't mean really untidy, with things strewn about all over the place, but untidy from some of the things I remember about it. She looked across towards the door of the small bedroom next to the kitchen—"my office," Dolly called it; that had seemed exciting too, at first, but it wasn't now—just untidy. On the other side of the room was the door of the real bedroom, where she and Dolly slept. It was a warm room, like this one, but pretty and full of frills—"for us girls," Dolly said. "And nobody else. There'll never be a man inside of it and we can be mysterious and pretty and ever so young and fresh and girlish all to ourselves." Then she had laughed her big, full-throated laugh. "Can you imagine that? Listen to the old warhorse talk, would you? You'll have to make up for me on the young and fresh angle, honey, and I'll show you ways." That was how Dolly was; at one moment proud of her big strong body, her lovely face and gold hair; at the next bitterly contemptuous of herself, saying harsh things that hurt her as she said them, begging for Julie's reassurance, spurning it when it came. She isn't really old, Julie thought; she can't be thirty yet, and she is lovely all the time, whatever she says.

Julie got up from the couch and went into the kitchen. She found everything laid out for her—salad and dessert made, creamed potatoes ready for the oven, even chops in the frying pan. She thought: That's just what Dolly would do when you think she's run out on you; that's why she's such a swell person. She switched the stove on, put the potatoes in the oven and water to boil, then went back to the sitting room and began to straighten it, picking up her hat and coat, sorting the cluttered pile of magazines, patting and straightening the many cushions to a tidy disorder. There's nothing small about Dolly the way there was about all those people at the boarding house. They wanted to quarrel and be mean about every little thing, the bathroom, the seats in the dining room, the food, even the slamming of a door. Dolly took things and gave things freely and naturally; if she gave you something you didn't have to remember about it—she wouldn't; and if you gave her something or did something for her she accepted it happily and neither of you felt that it was an obligation to be matched or paid off sometime in the future.

Julie went back to the kitchen and set the frying pan on the stove. She took the chops out and only dropped them back again when the pan was hot. That sort of thing made Dolly fun to live with too. She had learned everything backwards, for herself, long after she was earning her own living. She could cook grand things and make pretty salads and fancy desserts, but she didn't know simple things like how to cook meat or make bread or cottage cheese or anything like that. I wonder how I would be, cooking for a man and making a home for him and looking after him—by myself, I mean, without Mother there to tell me one sort of thing and Dolly to tell me the other sort. I'm sure I could do it just as well as that Denton woman he thinks is so wonderful. But I'd want it to be nice, like this is, not all dull-colored and messy and poor, and not like it is at home with just useful things everywhere, made out of plain wood, nothing pretty, I'd want to have pretty things, even if it was only a little house; a pretty bedroom and a good comfortable living room with pretty curtains and slip covers on the chairs—that's all a person would want if they had a good little kitchen like this one.

She finished her supper, washed the dishes, then went into the other room and sat down with a magazine. They'll be late, she told herself; Phil will take her to a movie, sure as anything, but I should worry; I like it here and I haven't had it to myself like this for a week.

After only a little while she dropped the magazine from her hand, got up and went over to the couch again. She picked up Johnny's letter and stretched herself full length on the couch. Why shouldn't I think of him, all about him and all about wanting him? I haven't even got a picture of him and it's hard when I try to remember the way he looks. I can only think of touching him at the dance and on the way home, of how solid and strong and big he feels when you touch him, and yet somehow soft—

not gentle; he is gentle, but I don't mean that; it's a sort of firm softness all about him, something you could lie against and rest and be held up and happy. I can think of the way he smiles, too, quietly but with all of his face and his eyes, not just his mouth, and of how it hurts your heart, watching him. But I can't think of the way he looks most of the time and I want to be able to. I'm sure I love him now. Up home you couldn't tell. It was all so quick, seeing him like that and being mad at Alec and going to the dance. But now I think about him and wait for his letters and want him here. I don't want to let Arthur kiss me any more, because it doesn't feel good the way it used to; it feels old and silly and not enough. I want Johnny and I want him to have all of me, for whatever he wants. I want to do things for him and be things for him, things that matter and make me afraid, things that would please him and make him happy.

Julie closed her eyes and let herself down into the warm, close world of her thoughts. It makes your heart beat hard, thinking of him and wanting him so; it makes you thirsty and hot and you can't just lie quite still and think. I wonder if he would love me that way; I know he doesn't now, it was all just a little minute up there at the Sound, but I wonder if he could love me for always and want me for always? And I wonder if I'm beautiful for him? She let her hands slide down her body to her hips, feeling her own firmness and smooth strength under them. Dolly says I'm beautiful. She says any man that gets me will get his money's worth and if they can't see that for themselves they haven't got eyes. But Dolly says things like that; she's so happy and quick and full of life sometimes that they just seem to pour out of her, and you can't be sure they mean anything. Just the same, I do think I'm nice; looking at me in the mirror, I think so; and men look at me on the street and in the office when they come to see Mr. Malley. But you can't tell from that either. Different men like different kinds of girls. He does like me or he wouldn't have held me so hard and kissed me like that, and he wouldn't keep on writing, but that might be just because I'm a girl and not because I'm me.

She heard Dolly's key in the lock, but it was difficult to open her eyes and make her body calm. She sat up, straightening her skirt, feeling discovered and guilty, as Dolly came into the room.

Dolly said: "Hullo, darling. Did you get plenty to eat? I felt like a louse leaving you like that, but Phil wanted me to go." Then she saw Julie's flushed face, her blue eyes bright and distant, lazy with the slow return from her thoughts, and the single sheet of the letter on the couch beside her. "Why, honey," she said. "That man does things to you." She came quickly across the room and dropped to the floor beside the couch.

Julie said: "Did you have a good time? I'm glad you came back early." She felt suddenly very tired, empty of all the warm, strong things that had been in her.

Dolly took off her hat and threw it across to a chair. "So-so," she said. "That man's dull as an old cow. I don't know why I bother with him." She stood up. "I'm tired and my feet hurt. Why don't we get undressed, then have some coffee and talk? I want to talk."

"That would be fun," Julie said. She unbuckled her

shoes and kicked them off, went over to the kitchen in her stockinged feet and put water to boil for the coffee.

From the bedroom Dolly said: "What did they keep you so late for?"

"Correspondence," Julie said. "A whole flock of letters that couldn't wait for tomorrow."

"That naughty old man didn't make passes at you?"

"Who? Mr. Malley?" Julie laughed. "I guess he's past that."

"They're never past it, darling. Too busy sometimes, but never past it. You'll see. One night all of a sudden he'll wake up to what you're made of. Then he'll pat your shoulder or your hair for being a good little girl, all tired out but still working faithfully and loyally for the good of the old store. Next thing after that he'll be crying his eyes out telling how tough it is at home because the old lady don't know what a man wants." Dolly came back into the sitting room, tying the belt of her long satin dressing gown.

"He patted my hair three months ago," Julie said. "And he isn't married. The water will be boiling in a minute. You make the coffee and I'll be right with you."

She went into the bedroom and slipped her clothes quickly away from her. I thought of doing this when I first came in, but I'm glad I didn't now. It's more fun this way, with two of you together and having coffee and just talking. Dolly's going to say something about Johnny; I'm sure she is this time. She has always just teased a little before and pretended it didn't amount to anything, but she saw me when she came in and now she really will say something. I'm glad, but I'm scared too.

Julie felt grateful for the cool smoothness of the nightdress against her and she stood in front of the long mirror while she fastened the snaps of her high-necked dressing gown. It makes you feel cool and fresh all over again and when you are tired it's nice to go on talking and yet be all ready to jump into bed whenever you want. We'll talk for a little while, then I shall write quickly to Johnny, just with one light on the little table in the sitting room, and that will be the very end of the day, with nothing more to be done.

She went back into the sitting room and Dolly came in from the kitchen. "Lie on the couch, darling," Dolly said. "And I'll wait on you hand and foot to make up for leaving you all alone." She brought the coffee and poured it out, then threw some cushions to the floor beside the couch and sat down on them. Julie watched her: She's such a big girl, yet she's so graceful. I'm big too, big and strong and smarter than she is in lots of ways, but I feel little and young when I'm with her. She's so sure of herself all the time, she holds her head so high and talks so straight out at you. That's how she looks behind the counter in the store, straight and big and cool and lovely, ever so efficient and quick; and yet you know all the time she's big to hold you and love you. It's no wonder men fall for her and let her boss them; she's half a mother all the time, even when she takes them into the little bedroom.

Dolly said: "So you've fallen for him all the way, this big he-man of the tall timber. He must be some guy to put it over like that in one little letter."

"I don't know what you mean," Julie said. "He didn't say anything."

"Of course not, not even the littlest thing, to make a girl go all soft and starry-eyed and brimming over with love. He just wrote about the weather, I suppose: 'Not so good as this time last year, but we mustn't complain, really it's very seasonable.'"

Julie suddenly felt she wanted to cry. "He didn't say anything," she said. "Really he didn't. Just what he's been doing."

Dolly reached up and touched her. "So that's all it takes. Come on, Julie. Break down and tell a pal. I won't be mean any more."

Julie handed her the letter and Dolly read it. I want her to know, Julie thought, I want her to know every little thing about it, for times like now; but not for times when she's got men around. And I'm afraid she's going to say I'm crazy. I know she will and that's why I'm crying—that and because I'm happy with loving him and miserable because it's all so far away.

Dolly finished the letter and nodded her pale head. "It's bad all right. You got to thinking about how much better you could do for him than that redhead. And then you got to thinking how it would be, married to him and all, in a little house of your own. Right?"

She looked up and Julie nodded, smiling with the tears still standing in her eyes. "But you're not going to do it," Dolly said. "Not going to marry a logger and live in a shack when you can have pretty nearly any man you want just for looking sideways at him."

"He didn't ask me," Julie said. "He didn't even say he loved me even."

"Of course not. He's not wise to it himself yet—not on top. Only way down inside him."

Julie sat up. "Do you think so?"

"I know it," Dolly said. "When he wrote that letter he was thinking just the way it made you feel. He knew damn well that about the redhead would start you off."

"He did not," Julie said. "He's not like that."

"I don't mean he figured it all out. Men aren't smart enough for that. But he knew it without thinking, inside him."

"Then you really do think he loves me?"

"He's crazy about you. So are half the men that ever saw you. All you've got to do is pick the one you want, give him a little push and he'll fall right in your lap. Arthur, for instance."

"Oh, him," Julie said.

"What's wrong with him? He's got a fine job and a big car, he's careful and steady and sensible and he's going to get a whole lot richer before he's through. On top of that, he's kind and thoughtful. He'd make a darn good, solid husband for any girl."

"You can have him," Julie said.

"I would if I thought I had a dog's chance with you around." Dolly looked up at Julie again. "Maybe you really are crazy about this Johnny guy. Johnny indeed. I'll bet that isn't even his real given name and I'll bet you don't know what his real name is."

"I do too; and it is Johnny. John Gordon Holt, but everybody calls him Johnny and I like that. It seems sort of natural."

Dolly shook her head slowly. "What a reward for a

woman who thought she was making something out of you. A goddamned logger."

"They're just as good as anybody else."

"Well, they've got a good half of what a girl wants. Big, strong, healthy brutes. But they sure as hell miss out on the rest of it."

"You're awful," Julie said. "He's not a bit like that. He's gentle and nice."

Dolly knelt up beside the couch. "I know he is, darling. I just wanted to see how you love him. If that's the way it is you shall have him. We'll see to that."

"How?" Julie asked. "He doesn't want to get married or anything. He likes the way he lives and getting girls just when he comes to town. They all do."

"Oh, no, they don't. There isn't one of the poor devils wouldn't like to get himself a good wife and settle down to raise babies. You've just got to handle them right. You could take that guy up the aisle as easy as taking him to a drink or I miss my guess."

"I wouldn't care," Julie said. "He could have me just the way I am, tonight if he wanted. Except that I want to be with him always, not just for a little while. And I want to love him lots of ways, not just that way."

Dolly held up a finger. "You're a naughty child to talk like that, and don't let me hear you do it again. If you want a man, you make him wait and get you the proper way. I've told you that before. Don't give them anything just because they want it."

"You do."

"That's different, and anyway I don't. You give yourself away to this guy and you'll lose him sure. You just stand way off and put him through the hoops."

"I don't want to fool him into anything. I want it all open and natural."

"They don't. They like to be strung along a bit."

"He's different."

"No, he's not. He may be good, but he's not different. Listen, darling, when you go up that aisle you're going to be a nice, fresh, sweet little virgin, just the way you are now. And don't you dare get any other ideas."

"You make me feel such a baby."

"That's all right," Dolly said. "So you are. I'm going to bed now. When is he coming down?"

"He hasn't said properly. Just before Christmas, I think."

"Well, go ahead and write your letter. And tell him to call here as soon as he gets in—give him the number. Don't be long coming to bed."

Julie got pen and paper and pulled the little table close to her. "Johnny darling," she wrote. "Dolly has just gone to bed and I'm all alone in our sitting room. It's nice here, with only one light on and most of the room dark. I loved your letter about the Dentons and that good supper you had. No, it doesn't 'all sound rather rough' to me. I like things nice, but it doesn't have to be a palace. You saw how we were up home.

"We worked late in the office today. All the orders for Christmas make a lot of extra work. Dolly says the floor of the store is so crowded all day long you can hardly breathe (she works at the perfume counter on the main floor, you know, and naturally all the people going to the top floors have to go past there). I think it's swell though, because it's nearly Christmas and you will soon be coming down. I wish you were here now and I could hold you like I did that day up the river. I want to hold you, darling, ever so tight and hard, for ever so long. Come soon.

"Your,
"Julie."

14

JOHNNY lay on one of the beds in the hotel room, his shirt open and his tie pulled loose at his neck. He knew that Alec was moving about the room, taking things out of the suitcases, but he kept his eyes closed. They had eaten breakfast on the boat and come straight up to the hotel, as they always did, to make some place their own before they went out into the city. The first day is always flat, Johnny thought, before you get things lined up. But it's a whole lot worse than usual today. Julie's not three blocks away, at that place where she works, but I can't see her before tomorrow anyway—maybe not then if things don't break right for us tonight. And Alec won't want to go up to Bess's place and get fixed up till tomorrow either. It's something that we've got to see Red Henderson and young Tommy anyway.

He opened his eyes and looked at the polished toes of his black shoes, then over to where Alec was still sorting ties and shirts and socks into drawers. "How bad did that guy say Red was?" he asked.

"He didn't say how bad he was. Just said he was sick in a room at the Stratheden Hotel."

"That dump on East Hastings? It's a hell of a place for a man to be sick. What time will we go see him?"

"Any time, I guess," Alec said. "What time are we supposed to meet Tommy?"

"Three o'clock at the Montenegro. He's going to see his cousin down at the Albatross this morning."

"Why don't we go down there and see him ourselves?"

"That'd queer things sure," Johnny said. "Any guys that work a place steady, the way they say these sons of bitches work the Albatross, are sure to have a waiter or a clerk or somebody in with them."

"I guess that's right too," Alec said. "It would be a hell of a note if they were laying for us."

Johnny sat up and swung his legs off the bed. "If they're laying for us our own mothers won't be able to identify us when the cops pick us up tomorrow morning." He looked around the room. "Hell," he said. "You're the damnedest guy to make yourself at home. Give you half an hour and you'd make a cell look like you'd lived there all your life. Books and pictures all over the room and papers all over the desk. It's no wonder you need an extra box car to carry all the gear you travel with."

"Like it?" Alec asked.

"Sure I do. It feels good. What say we go and see Red right now, then get a bite to eat and meet Tommy?"

Coming out of the hotel, they went up two blocks, then turned along Granville. Alec said: "Better swing over one more. That Dolly woman that lives with Julie works on the main floor of the department store and it wouldn't do for her to see us go by."

"Would she recognize you?"

"I guess so. She was up at the place when I went to see Julie last summer. No sense to taking chances anyway. What they don't know don't hurt them and there'd be one hell of a holler if Julie knew you were in town and didn't call her up tonight."

It feels good to have him figure that way, Johnny thought. I wonder if she really would give a damn; it maybe won't be the way a guy figures at all; she might be high-hat when she's in town and there must be other guys around—white-collar guys with cars and good clothes, that know how to act. You can't ever tell how a thing will be ahead of time.

They turned along Hastings Street, threading a way among the Christmas crowds that shuffled about the doors and windows of the big department stores. Johnny said: "Hold on a minute," and stopped to look at the window of Paris's bootstore. "I've got to get me a new pair of caulked shoes," he said.

"Me too," Alec said. "We can stop on the way back. Red's place is only a little way along here." He pointed along the street to where a red and yellow sign, almost lost among a hundred others like it, spelled out "Stratheden Rooms."

"Jesus," Johnny said. "The poor guy must be broke as well as sick. He generally stays at some halfway decent place like the Northern when he's in town."

"He had a pretty fair stake when he left camp," Alec said. "But he wasn't feeling so good even then. Remember how he kept coughing?"

They turned in at the open doorway under the sign and climbed a short flight of stairs to a dark hallway with a little office boarded off from it. No one was in the office, but there was a bell beside the window and Alec pressed on it. Some time later a door slammed and a gray-haired, gray-faced woman came shuffling along a passageway. Her hair was in ragged, uncombed wisps about her head and she had on carpet slippers and a drab dress she had been sleeping in. "Looking for somebody?" she asked.

"Does a man named Henderson stay here?" Alec asked her.

"No," she said. "No one of that name here." She looked at them with narrow eyes. "What does he look like?"

"Little guy with red hair and freckles," Johnny said. "Red Henderson they call him."

"Are you his friends?"

Alec moved impatiently and Johnny touched his arm quickly. "Sure," he said. "We heard he was sick."

The gray face in front of him lost some of its grim defensiveness, and the lines in it relaxed to weariness again. "Along at the end there," she said. "Number five. He's bad. There's death in his face. You better do something for him."

They went along and stopped in front of a glass-paneled door with the illegible black lettering of the name of some business firm still on it. Alec knocked and opened the door. Johnny looked back along the passage as he went in and saw that the woman was still watching them.

Red was lying on his back in the bed, his eyes tight closed, his breathing short and heavy. His face was white and thin so that the freckles stood out very sharp on it and the red hair seemed redder than ever before. The pillow and bed linen were dull and dirty, gray near the fierce, stretched whiteness of Red's face.

Johnny said: "Red, it's us. Johnny Holt and Slim Crawford. How're you feeling?"

Red's eyes opened slowly. "Christ, I thought it was the old lady. Sure is good to see you fellows."

"How do you feel, Red?" Johnny asked again. "Couldn't you let a guy know you were sick?"

Red shook his head. "I'm okay." His voice was a straining whisper. "They been good to me here. Made too much trouble for you guys already."

"Listen, Red," Alec said. "We'll get hold of a doctor. And if he says to we'll move you up to the hospital right away."

Red shook his head again. "No money," he said. "Broke to the wide." His face lighted and he tried to get up from the pillow. Johnny held him back. "Listen, boys," Red said. "This is good. I had her made this time. On the market—new gold mine on the West Coast. She was going good up in camp there, so I quit and came down. Had her figured right all the way too. Then I got sick and the big guys must have run her down right while I didn't know a damn thing about it." His face was white and still again and his eyes closed. "Guess I'll have to look out the caulked shoes again soon as the camps open up."

Alec said quietly, "I'll go for the doctor, Johnny. You stay with him."

Johnny looked at Red as the door closed, then turned away and walked over to the big window that looked out on the noisy, sign-crowded street. It was cold in the room, so cold that he did not open the window, though the air was dead and foul. He heard Red's voice from the bed and turned round.

"Did he go?"

"Yes," Johnny said.

"That's one swell guy," Red said. "He's deep too, and smart; he's had schooling. You're a good guy too, Johnny. They don't come any better."

"Can it, Red," Johnny said.

"No, listen. I'm not just talking to hear myself. Slim's a smart guy and he'll get rich some way; he don't need help. But you're dumb like me, see, and you've helped me out a whole lot of times. Now I want to help you. You listening, Johnny?"

Johnny came close to the bed. "Sure, Red," he said gently. "Sure I'm listening."

"That gold mine, see? The Double Tree Mine it is. The big guys have run her down now and they'll pick her up again. You get on to it now, when she's down, and go up with her. She's good and you can ride with her, 'way up. Look at Cully Egan and Al Davis and C. O. Hally. They was bums like you and me till they picked the right one and now look at 'em. Race horses and yachts and department stores and jobs in the Senate. They own this burg and they was just bums."

"Thanks, Red," Johnny said. "I'll watch her. You'll have time to get back in there too; all kinds of time. But you need rest now, and plenty of it."

"That's right too, I guess." Red's eyes closed again and his harsh breathing was loud in the room with no voices against it.

Johnny heard the footsteps along the passage, then Alec was back with the doctor. The doctor was quick and confident, strangely clean and powerful in the square, dirty room. He bent over Red with his stethescope. In a little while he looked up.

"How long has he been like this?"

Alec looked at Johnny. "He tell you?"

"No," Johnny said. "But he had that cough before he left camp; hell of a cough it was. That must be two or three weeks ago."

"You boys know if he's got any family?"

"None that I ever heard him talk about," Johnny said. "But you don't have to worry about that. Slim here and me will take care of it. You just get him to the hospital and fix him up."

The doctor shook his head impatiently. "I don't mean that. If he's got any family they'd better get here quick if they want to see him. . . ."

In the hospital it was calm and warm and clean, and their footsteps echoed in the wide passageways.

"Jesus," Johnny said. "It feels better to get him into a place like this."

The doctor came out of the room. "He's as comfortable as he can he," he said. "You're sure he's got no family?"

Johnny said: "If it's going to kill him we'll try and find out. That right?"

"Yes."

"The cops will know," Johnny said. "He was in the pen inside a year ago. But look, Doc, you can make them keep quiet on that if he goes, can't you?"

"How do you mean?"

"Not get it in the papers all about him being in the pen. He's a good little guy. That's not the way he is."

The doctor nodded. "Sure," he said. "We can fix that. When will you fellows be coming back?"

"This afternoon," Johnny said. "You don't think he'll go that quick if he's going?"

The doctor shook his head. "No. He's strong. If he gets through tomorrow he might make it. But you don't want to count on that."

Tommy had said: "Chuck says to get down early. They come in any time between nine o'clock and closing time." At the hospital the nurse had said: "He's resting quietly. You can't see him, but you can come up just before you go to bed and someone will tell you how he is."

Sitting with Alec at the round, mustard-yellow table, Johnny looked about him at the Albatross beer parlor. He was slouched in his chair and he made his movements slow and awkward; even through the stale-beer smell of the place he could smell the whisky they had purposely spilled down Alec's coat and shirt. Wish they'd come, he thought. I feel good now, good and sore; I'd like to sock somebody and tear something apart, but another hour of this and all I'll want is to go to sleep. Thinking of Red keeps you sore though; the poor little bastard dying up in that room and nobody calling a doctor or giving a damn. They throw a guy like that into the pen and wear him down till he's not strong any more, then kick him out to go back to the job. And when he gets sick because he isn't strong enough, nobody gives a damn.

Alec straightened himself in his chair and reached clumsily for his beer glass. "They won't come," he said.

"We've been here an hour now and there isn't a goddamned reason in the world why they should come."

"Sure they'll come," Johnny said. "That barkeep says they come in just about every night and take a look around."

"One thing, if they do come we haven't got much competition. Looks like we're the only two drunks in the place."

"Can't miss," Johnny said. "One of these goddamned waiters will tell them anyway. They've been watching us ever since we came."

Alec put his glass down. Johnny slouched farther down in his chair while the waiter brought fresh glasses and took away the empty ones. "There's three of them," he said. "But Tommy says only two come most nights. A big fat guy with a red face and a flat nose and ears all over his head. And a dark guy, fancy dresser with a little mustache and lard on his hair. That sounds like the same two that picked up young Don."

"And we'll go up and see how Red is after we've broken up the joint?"

"That's right," Johnny said. "And don't forget it's going to be dark in there when we get started. Feel for a place to hit with your left hand, then smack it hard with your right. And if the chippies get rough, don't be scared to smack them down too. And break anything you get your hands on."

"It ought to be good with all those mirrors. Don said they were right around the whole room."

"May be hard to tear them loose." Johnny watched the

door of the beer parlor. "Looks like that might be our party now."

The two men stood for a moment in the doorway, then walked across and sat down at a table. A waiter brought them beer. The fat guy looks pretty nearly respectable, Alec thought; if someone hadn't pushed his nose cock-eyed and thickened those ears you'd think he was a salesman or a publicity man or something like that; looks kind of friendly too. You'd pick the dark guy for a slicker though; he's good looking and powerful, but he's got a kind of mean look to him. I sure hope this works out right; Johnny's goddamned sure of himself, but one of us is likely as not to end up with a knife in his ribs. I don't know why we do it, except it will be exciting while it lasts and a peach of a story afterwards. If I were alone or with somebody else I'd skip the whole business, but I can't back out on Johnny and he's too cold-blooded mad to change his mind. He can stay cold mad the longest of anybody I ever saw and it's always about the same sort of thing—some little guy getting gypped or hurt some way. That's why he'd be such a damn fine union man, except that he's always got to know the guy's who's been hurt.

He saw the men get up and start across toward them. His heart was pounding and he thought: Why don't we clean up on them right here, instead of sticking our necks out into their own damned claim? Johnny wants to wreck the joint, but we could have it over in ten minutes if we started right here.

The dark man said, "How's chances to sit with you guys?"

Johnny looked up at him with drunken suspicion. "What for?" he asked.

"Just for company. We'd like to buy you a drink, wouldn't we, Norm?" He turned to the fat man, who nodded and beckoned to a waiter. They both sat down and the dark man said: "You boys are loggers, aren't you?"

"Any business of yours?" Johnny asked.

Alec said. "They're okay, Johnny. Why shouldn't they buy a drink?" He turned to the dark man. "Sure we're loggers. My name's Slim Crawford and this is my pal Johnny Holt."

The dark man held out his hand. "My name's George Riggs and this is Norm Green. Meet Mr. Crawford and Mr. Holt, Norm."

Johnny straightened a little in his chair and reached for a glass of beer. "Here's looking at you," he said. "If you sons of bitches want to sit with us I guess there's nothing I can do about it."

The fat man said: "Don't be that way, Mr. Holt." His voice was high and squeaky. "You boys are out for a good time, aren't you? Maybe we can help some."

"We only got in this morning," Alec said. "And didn't figure any place to go yet. The old town seems kind of dead."

Riggs leaned forward. "Norm here and I know the way around. Maybe we could all go some place together."

"Girls?" Johnny asked. "Must have girls."

Riggs glanced over his shoulder, then turned back. "Not so loud," he said. "Sure, we know where there's girls."

The fat man laughed and slapped his palms down on his short thighs. "Do we know or do we know," he said. "Just name what you want, short or tall, fat or thin, black or white or yellow. Name your choice, me and George knows 'em all."

Johnny looked across at Alec. "We going with these guys?"

"Sounds good to me," Alec said.

Riggs was suddenly less friendly. His eyes were hard and narrow. "Got any money?" he asked.

Johnny straightened himself angrily and reached into his hip pocket. "God Almighty," he said. "What do you think we are, pikers? Take a look at that." He held out a roll of bills.

"All right, all right," Riggs said. "No offense. It's just that some guys think they can buy themselves a good time for a couple of bucks."

"How about another round before we go?" the fat man said. "You boys been celebrating a little?"

"We had a few drinks up in the room," Alec said. "But we're okay. We won't make trouble any place."

"Sure, sure," Green said. "Just enough to get feeling good, not enough to get mean. A man needs a drink after he's been out in the sticks four or five months."

They drank the beer and Alec stood up, stumbled and knocked his chair over. Riggs was at his side instantly, helping to pick it up. "Your pal walk all right?" he asked.

Alec laughed. "Sure," he said. "He's not bad. That's just the way he likes to talk." He saw Riggs nod to the fat man.

"I'll go call a taxi," Green said.

Timber

In the taxi Johnny slumped back on the seat. They were going west from the Albatross. That's all right too, he thought. Means that once we get out of the dump we'll be pretty safe. If it was some joint in the east end of town you might have to go like hell for a dozen blocks before you could feel safe. Got to watch that fat guy, get him good the first time; they look soft, bastards like that, but they aren't. Why in hell do we have to do this, go and break up a chippy joint and waste a whole evening? I could have seen Julie by now and maybe gone places with her. I want her more than this. Jesus, though, I hate these goddamn suckers; it would feel good to kill one of them, sitting in town getting fat off guys that have been out working in rain and filth for six months.

The taxi turned into an alley and stopped. Can't be but three or four blocks from Granville, Johnny thought. They climbed a long flight of stairs, Riggs in front, the fat man behind, and stopped on a small landing. Riggs looked round and winked. "It's a swell place, boys," he said. "You're going to like it. Everything fixed up real fancy."

He put a key in the only door on the landing and pushed it open. Johnny went in, stopped just inside the door and leaned drunkenly against the wall. He could feel the blood hot in the palms of his hands and the pulse of it fast on his neck; the muscles of his shoulders and back felt solid and good against the wall behind him, tight and ready to go. This is it, he thought. Gilt mirrors all along the far wall, leaning out a little—they'll come off easy. Little gilt chairs with red seats about the room; they'll break up. Flimsy little tables. The big glass chandelier over a heavier, polished table in the middle of the room. One other light, over between the two windows. The chippies right here and ready to go, four of them—no, five—and a soft-looking drunk with them; and another guy, not drunk. He'll be the third pimp.

Riggs was walking across the room towards the women. Alec was keeping a little behind and to his left. He'll be jumpy, Johnny thought, and that guy's heavier than he is. The fat man was talking.

"Come on, boy, get a hold of yourself and meet the girls. That's what you came here for and we want to show you a good time."

Johnny jerked himself up from the wall and began to follow the fat man. Right by the table he planted a left behind the fat man's ear, hard and solid. "Let's go, Alec," he shouted. The fat man's face was turned towards him, open-mouthed, very red, not scared at all. Johnny put his right on the side of the hanging jaw and felt the jawbone crack sideways. The fat man went down, flat on his back, and Johnny jumped both heels square on his face. One of the women was screaming. Two others were trying to pull Alec away from Riggs. Johnny saw the third pimp in front of him, hit him twice, stepped over and swung his forearm around Riggs' neck, under the chin. "Hit him," he told Alec. "Right on the button. All you've got." He felt the shock of the blow and felt Riggs' body go slack against him. He heard running steps somewhere in the back of the apartment. "Jump on him," he said. "I'll get the big light. You get the other." He dropped Riggs, jumped on the fat man's face again and from there to the table. The big chandelier was in easy reach and he tore it down so that it crashed on the polished surface of the table. He saw the door open as Alec got the other light, and he went down to it as though he were going off the brow log. That's just how it feels, he thought. Something heavy hit him on the left shoulder, but he stuck his left hand out, felt a man's face and brought his right over. Then he closed, jerked his knee up and hit again. The man groaned and went down.

Johnny stood quite still for a moment, balanced on the balls of his feet, listening. The women were quiet. Alec was fighting on the floor over by the windows, where he had broken the lamp. Alec said: "Go ahead and break it up. I can handle this bastard." Johnny started for the mirrors, stumbled against a chair, picked it up and broke it against the floor. He found the first mirror, tore it down and stamped it to pieces. He heard the crash of another mirror on the far side of the room, then gave himself over to breaking anything he could reach. One of the women began to scream again and he went over and slapped her with his open hand until she stopped. He tripped over the crawling figure of a man, got up, came down on its back with both knees, slung it over with a half-nelson and beat a dozen blows into the upturned face. That wasn't the fat guy, he told himself. He got up again and felt his way over towards the door. Another mirror crashed somewhere in the room and the women started screaming again. "That's good enough, Alec," he said. "Let's get the hell out."

He heard Alec coming across the room and opened the door to let light in from the hallway. Alec had one hand up to the side of his face and Johnny saw the blood coming through his fingers. "Keep going," he said. "Down the stairs."

He looked back into the wrecked room. "Shut up, you crazy bitches," he said. "And tell your boy friends it was loggers did that. And tell them to lay off loggers or they'll get the same again. We got the number of this joint now."

Out in the alley Johnny stopped and looked back. "Only light in the place," he said. "That's a break. You hurt bad, Alec?"

Alec shook his head. "No," he said and vomited. He walked two or three steps, then put a hand against the wall to steady himself and vomited again.

"Jesus," Johnny said. "What did they do, kick you in the guts? Jesus, I'm sorry, Alec."

Alec straightened himself. "I'm okay," he said and began to run, still holding the side of his face.

They ran through several alleys, slowing to a walk at the cross streets, then Alec turned and went along two or three blocks. "I know most of the drivers with this taxi outfit on the corner," he said.

He went up to the first of the line of parked cabs and looked into it. "Hello, Mike," he said. "How's chances for a ride?"

The driver peered at him. "Hello, Slim. What the hell hit you?"

Alec said: "Drive us around a bit, Mike. We got to recuperate."

In the cab Johnny said: "Let's look at your head. What happened?"

"I don't know," Alec said. "He hit me with something. There's a lump there like a haul-back block and it's bleeding some. Doesn't feel too bad."

"What made you vomit like that?"

"That Riggs guy. I jumped on him the way you said, first on the ribs and then in the face. I didn't like it. Felt kind of squashy, as though things broke."

Johnny's face was set and angry. "I wouldn't lose any food over that," he said. "I wish we'd had time to do a real job on those suckers." He looked down at a long cut in the palm of his hand. "We better get cleaned up and go see Red. We'll have a drink too."

Alec said: "I could use one. Jesus, Johnny, you're a tough guy."

Johnny laughed. "I'll forget it in a minute," he said. "A dump like that makes me so sore I'm not natural. . . ."

It was very quiet in the wide passage at the hospital. The nurse said: "I'm afraid he's a sick boy. We've done everything we can for him, but you had better come back first thing in the morning."

"No good to see him?" Alec asked.

"No," she said. She looked at the bandage on his head. "You look like you've been in trouble yourself. Who put that on you?"

"I did," Johnny said. "How's chances to get a better one?"

"Fine," she said. "Come along to the office."

15

JOHNNY stood on the busy corner where the street from his hotel crossed Granville Street. I may as well look at it good, he thought, while I'm here. Back in camp it's going to seem a long way off. It was a mild night and still early. The lights of the drug store on the opposite corner were very bright and the big street cars rattled and banged across the intersection, around the steep curves; they take them slow, but they make it, he thought; you sure wouldn't get a load of boomsticks round a curve like that. Ted's still hollering about that ninety-degree curve on the spur above camp and that must be six or eight hundred feet long. It's kind of good, feeling the people all bunched against you; then, when the light goes green, brushing past you and you standing there still against them; makes you feel heavy and solid like a rock in a river. They sure hurry and they're sure close, touching you like that; even good-looking girls standing touching you one minute and gone the next without knowing it. Yet if there were just two of you alone in a room touching that way, or even alone in the street, things would happen out of it.

He crossed Granville, bought a paper and turned to watch the intersection again. Another ten or fifteen minutes would give Alec lots of time to get away with that

Dolly girl. I don't want to see them there tonight, just Julie; seems kind of silly, but Julie shouldn't be with that other girl anyway; it isn't right. Dolly's a good kid, big and happy and good looking like that, but she's too tough for a girl like Julie and when she's around it seems kind of different. It's like the way I don't want to go to Bess Logan's this time. Seems crazy to come to town and not have a girl for more than just to go to the movies; it isn't really right either; a man needs more than that. But it wouldn't fit with seeing Julie, and wanting that makes you feel you don't want the other. Crazy is right, he told himself. What are you going to do, marry the girl or something?

You couldn't marry her; and suppose you could, what in hell would you want with it? Tied down to working steady in the same camp all the time, saving money, not drinking, fixing things around the house evenings. And kids maybe. It wouldn't work out, not with a live girl like Julie, stuck away in a dump like that with nothing to see and no place to go. But why not, at that? Getting married seems like a hell of a big thing when you just say it and don't stop to figure what it really means. But guys do get married and the wives live in camp and get a kick out of it—or stand for it anyway; Eric and Marion seem to think it's okay. Of course, to make it stick a guy ought to be ambitious, always looking ahead to something; but with Julie that would be easy; everything would be easy with Julie and it would be swell to be with her always like that, warm and alone together in the evenings, talking about things with her instead of trying to write down little bits of them. And having her like that, in your own house, all to yourself, all of her you want, watching her walk round the table with her apron on or sitting down in a chair or undressing to go to bed. And nobody else but the two of you.

I feel like I'm halfway plastered, he thought, all hot and ready to go and away from everything round about; and I haven't had a drink since last night. Why don't you think about it properly? There's nothing coming out of it, nothing like that anyway. She's a swell girl and it's fun being with her and talking to her, it's going to be fun tonight. But it doesn't mean anything. Girls like that don't marry loggers and go to live in shacks back in the woods. And when they do, it doesn't work out; look at that swell kid Carl brought back to camp and how she ran off with that college boy. That isn't true about Julie! if she started on it she'd stay with it right through. But why in hell should she start with a goddamned logger; if I'd stayed with playing ball or even with fighting it would be different—except that I'd never have been better than a bum at either one. A guy ought to be in some white-collar job where he can live like a human being and maybe have some chance to get ahead.

He took out his watch and looked at it, then turned and started along Granville Street towards the apartment. When he turned off Granville he kept to the left side of the street so that he could see the light behind the red and white curtains of the apartment. It was a warm light and exciting. He wondered if Alec and Dolly would certainly be gone, and what Julie would want to do with the evening. They could eat somewhere and go to a movie or to the hockey game; but there might be something

Timber

else that she was thinking of; that was one of the good things about Julie; she was like Alec, you couldn't tell about her because she thought differently from other people and knew about different things.

He crossed the street and went up the dark stairs to the door of the apartment. Julie opened it. "Hello, darling," she said. "They've gone."

She was standing close against him, almost as tall as he was, and he put his arms around her and held her and kissed her. She met his kiss warmly and gladly, with her mouth and her whole body, then pushed him away. "You're trembling," she said. "Is that because you love me?"

"Because I've been thinking about you all the way here. Sure I love you."

"Silly," she said. "Shut the door and come on in."

In the light of the room he saw that she was still wearing the skirt and blouse she must have worn at the office. "I didn't give you time to get straightened up," he said. "I'm sorry. I didn't want to be late because I thought you'd want to go some place and eat."

"We're not going any place," she said. "We're going to eat right here. And I'm going to wear just what I've got on. Afterwards, if you're very good, maybe I'll put on something nice for you. How does that sound?"

"Sounds swell to me, if that's what you want."

"Sit yourself down and I'll have supper ready in a few minutes. Make a drink if you want. Alec left lots of everything here."

He followed her out to the kitchen. "I never want a drink when I'm with you."

Julie laughed and he caught her and kissed her again as she threw her head back to speak. "Make one anyway," she said. "And go away and leave me alone."

"Can't I help?"

"No."

"Can't I stay here?"

"No," she said. "Go in the other room and sit down. And put some water and ice in that. You can't drink straight whisky here. Dolly won't have it. She says it burns the inside of your stomach."

Johnny settled himself in one of the big chairs in the sitting room. There was a small table in the middle of the room with a white cloth on it and glasses and silver for two people. It was warm in the room and he liked the quiet light and the dull red of the curtains and cushions. God, he thought, this is elegant; who in hell wants to go and get in a booth in some café when they can eat here? It's a hell of a note in a way, though. What would those old people up at Kiltool Sound think if they knew about it? Old man Morris would take down the shotgun and go right after any guy he caught doing what I'm doing. And yet it's perfectly okay. That's the queer part of it. I'd no more do anything wrong with Julie than stand under a log when I figured the tongs weren't holding right. Yet I'd go all out to get lots of girls I haven't wanted half so bad. Julie would be better than anything has ever been, so much better that there's no measuring it. She's so warm and strong and real, and she's so darned beautiful, like a queen. She'd mean anything she did, hard and all the way and I've never had any girl you could figure that about. It's always been just play, but

Timber

Julie's deep and there would be all of her in it, deep, deep down and through so that you couldn't find it all in just once or in a hundred times.

He got up from the chair and went over and stood in the doorway of the kitchen.

"What do you want?" she said. "Go away."

"Can't I watch?"

"No. Go away and relax. I'll have it out there in a minute."

"I want another drink."

"You can't have one. Not till afterwards. I don't want a drunken logger on my hands all evening."

"Okay then," Johnny said. "I'll just watch."

"No, really, darling, I want you to go away. You can kiss me once—then go away and wait. I won't be long."

Back in the sitting room again Johnny fumbled for tobacco pouch and cigarette papers, then remembered the pack of tailor-mades in his pocket, took it out and lit one. Julie came in and he watched her setting things out on the table. In a little while she said: "There it is. Come and get it."

She watched him sit down, a little awkwardly in the light chair, and was happy. Everything was triumphantly the way she had wanted it to be. The thick steak was perfect, evenly brown and swollen with red juice, the Brussels sprouts and broccoli were drained and dry, richly dark green against the white dish. The potatoes were a concession to what men liked, golden brown and crisp, fried in deep fat. They should have been creamed or mashed, Julie thought, maybe even baked with lots of butter; but this is the way you would have to do them for Dal if you wanted to make it a party.

Johnny said: "Boy, that's a swell-looking meal. You sure can cook, Julie."

"I'd be awful dumb if I couldn't," she said. "After years of putting on meals for that houseful of men at home."

"You didn't learn to set a table like that up there, and make it all look so good."

She wanted to say: "Dolly showed me how to do that," but she knew somehow that would spoil it for him and she said: "Sometimes we used to do it carefully up there; Christmas time and weddings and maybe when there was a new preacher came up on the *Columbia*."

"You wouldn't have me mixed up with any of your old preachers?"

"No, I would not. And they weren't all so old at that." She thought: Something big is going to come out of tonight. This isn't all it is, just sitting here and eating and talking a little. I don't know what it's going to be, but it's going to make everything different; it's got to.

After supper she let him help her with the dishes and cleaning up the kitchen, then they went back into the sitting room. Julie went to the little radio and twisted the dial until she found good dance music.

"Do you want me to change into a dress?" she asked.

"No. I like the way you are. Do you want to go out some place?"

Julie shook her head. She felt suddenly that she wanted to cry because she was afraid for it, for the whole evening she had planned and whatever unnamed thing she had thought would come out of it. Then the feeling passed and she knew it was going to be all right. I'm not trying to fool him or do anything bad. I don't know what I'm going to do or what is going to happen. I just know that I want to be alone with him now, for this evening and in this place.

"Do you still feel so bad about Red?" she asked.

"No," Johnny said. "I felt bad the day we buried him—sure, he was a good friend of mine. But not now. It's no use to keep mourning about a guy that's dead."

"What was he like?"

"He was a little guy, kind of simple, and funny in lots of ways. But he was good-hearted as anybody can be, and he was good on the job, and he was square."

"Alec said he was in jail."

"That's right. But not because he wasn't square, just because he didn't figure right. Red had a hard deal all the way through and he didn't have much chance to learn what the score was in big things. But that didn't make him any worse guy to know or be around with."

Julie sat down on the couch and swung her feet up. "You're nice about him," she said. "I like it when you talk like that."

They talked on quietly. There was only one light burning in the room and the radio played faintly behind the dim glow of its dial, so that neither of them was conscious of it. Johnny thought: I want her, but I'm afraid to go over there and touch her and hold her. I wouldn't want anything to happen; it wouldn't happen, but she might be afraid of it and that would spoil everything. But she isn't afraid; she made us stay in here and wanted it, and she isn't the scared kind anyway. He went over and sat on the arm of the couch above her head. Julie reached up her hand and he took it in his.

"Kiss me," she said. "I've waited so long for you to do that. You aren't afraid of me, are you?"

Johnny laughed softly and felt the laugh the way it sounded, deep inside him. "No. Afraid of me."

Julie sat up straight. "You mustn't be. You wouldn't be like that with other girls. You haven't been afraid of anything other nights."

"This is different. We shouldn't really be here like this."

"Poor darling," she said gently. "You want a girl, don't you?" He looked down at her quickly. "Of course you do. I know about men; why shouldn't you want one?" Suddenly her voice was fierce and strained and she was breathing quickly. "But you haven't had one, have you? Not this time."

Johnny knelt quickly beside the couch. He felt the blood in his face and in his throat and strong all through his body so that his forearms quivered and tightened. "Julie, you mustn't talk like that. It's not like you."

She smiled at him, calmly and confidently now so that he felt like a child, under her, waiting to be told, to be shown. "Yes, it's like me," she said. "It is me. You can have me, darling. You know you can."

Johnny felt her shoulders warm through his coat against his left arm and he lifted them and kissed her. Her body strained up to him and his right hand went to her waist and all the while he was kissing her, searching for the very soul of her and all her being. There hasn't ever been anything else like this, nothing ever, anywhere; you don't feel any part of her quiet and still, it's all alive and used and driven by something inside her. And you don't feel it just with your body, but all flooding in your brain and beyond you. He let her back to the couch, very gently, still kneeling. "God, Julie, I love you. For what you said then. But I don't want it to be that way."

Julie looked up at him, smiling a little, her eyes lazy, and now he felt strong over her, sure of himself and what he wanted. "Why not?" she said. "What other way is there?"

"I want it to be different with us," he said. "Not like other times—not going away quickly. I want us to get married and be together always."

"I want that too. But why not now anyway?"

"Because it's not like you. It's not the way you are. But I love you because you want it."

"When can we get married?"

"I don't know. Maybe I ought to get to be something different first, more than just a logger."

Her eyes opened wide. "You mean work in town or something like that?" She shook her head slowly. "No. I wouldn't want that. Why would I?"

"You don't want to marry a common logger and live in a shack in camp when you've been used to all this and knowing white-collar guys."

Julie laughed and he felt her laugh warm in him and beautiful so that he wanted to see it and touch it. "Darling," she said. "Darling heart, being a logger is part of why I love you. I'm not afraid of your shacks or your woods. I just want you."

Johnny said: "We could maybe get ahead. I can always hold down a job, any place, and we could maybe save and get something of our own."

"Of course we will. But I want it always logging. A little haywire camp somewhere in the islands."

"It wouldn't be haywire."

"I just meant haywire for little, not for really haywire. We'd make it highball and get rich and get a bigger one."

"If we didn't go broke and have to go back to day wages."

"I'm not scared. Let's do it soon, really soon."

"What about your folks?"

"Dad thinks you're swell," Julie said. "They'll be surprised and Mother will worry if she can't get down, but it will be all right in the end."

"You mean as soon as that? Before camp opens up?"

Julie nodded. "Why not? What good is waiting?"

"I don't know," Johnny said. "Seems as though people always do."

Julie reached up and pulled his head down to her. "You're so darling." She clenched her strong teeth and locked his head tight against her. "You're a beast," she said. "You turned me down and I ought to hate you. Instead of that I love you harder than before."

16

ALEC CRAWFORD came down the hill fast, over and through the tangle of felled timber. He kept his eyes just ahead of his feet, glancing up only occasionally to check his direction towards the track. When a fallen tree lay near the line he was following he ran quickly along it, picked out another, jumped to it, used that and reached for yet another. Occasionally the good footing of the logs ran out into a tangle of broken, twisted limbs and he had to force his way slowly for several yards through a breast-high clutter of green needles and gnarled gray branches. Once he came upon a dozen trees evenly spaced at right angles to his line and jumped from one to another of them with the easy striding of a hurdler, carried on into each new leap by the unchecked momentum of the one before it. The smooth, swift motion and the sharp bite of his caulks into each successive log pleased him so that he glanced back over his shoulder as he stood on the last of them, to judge the space he had covered. He came on the track in a shallow cut and dropped down at once to the unballasted ties.

Walking the ties he still hurried, settling into a quick-footed walk, many times checked and broken, that kept his caulks rasping into the unevenly spaced, hewn hemlock faces. Damn Andy, anyway, he thought; running his line into a jackpot like that and leaving me to straighten it out. And now Ted's rattled about Side One and if I don't catch the locie back to camp this trip we won't get that straightened out till God knows when; and he won't be fit to talk to till we do. Should make it though, if that was them hooking on to Johnny's loads when I started down the hill. If they were leaving empties I guess I'm out of luck.

He rounded a curve that brought him in sight of the spar tree, and heard the locomotive struggling against the grade with the empties. He slackened his speed a little and took the ties more easily. There was ballast between them now and he could look up ahead towards the spark-arrester of the donkey engine, showing squat and black beside the red-brown spar tree. Two sharp spurts of steam showed white above the donkey and the shrillness of the whistle reached him a moment before the first clatter of power as Dan Evritt pulled down the throttle. Alec watched the lift of the heavy sky line, jerking to pull the logs free of the brush, drawing smoothly, jerking again as they hit a stump and slid round it, straining heavily as Dan's hand summoned full-throated power to bring them up the sharp slope below the landing. It's like playing a fish, Alec thought, except that it's always coming in, no running out; but you can break just the way you can in a fish, if you try and horse them in too hard; things happen when you break in one of those things, with three or four hundred feet of steel mainline to whip in and coil up on the landing; if a man gets a piece of that wrapped around his neck he can quit worrying. Talking about safety in a logging camp is nothing but a goddamned joke. There's Johnny, three or four months married to Julie and standing under that every day. If it did come he'd probably be the hell out of the way, under a car or something—he's done that before now and he can do it again. But that's only one thing of a hundred things that could happen any hour of any day of the week, and just one of them would be enough to make Julie a widow with a forty-dollar-a-month pension.

Yet a person doesn't worry about Johnny. He's one of the few guys that really seems figured out for that job—goes into it naturally and handles it easily. Most of them are sweating at it, driving themselves, shaving it thin all the time, but Johnny's on top of it. It isn't just that he's big and powerful; Gil Harrison is a honey of a leader and he's only a little bit of a guy; nor that he's catty, quick and sure on his feet—lots of them are that. It's more in the way he takes it, so sure of himself all the time, always one jump ahead of whatever is happening. The ordinary man isn't built to work like that; he can do it, sure, watching himself and sweating, and get by for a time if he's lucky. But you don't feel that about Johnny; he's been at it ten years now with nothing worse than that time he slipped and bruised his knee, and he's good for ten more, twenty more if you like; there isn't a log in the pile he can't think ahead of.

It's kind of queer how you get to think so much of a man like that. I feel something the same way about Chris —maybe it's because they can both do things. I can figure things out better than either of them—away better than Johnny can and better than Chris most of the time: get Chris in standing timber and he doesn't know where in heck he is. But they're right on the job when it comes to doing something or moving something; they think of blocks and wire rope and donkey engine sizes and tailholds instead of just in figures, and the first thing you know the thing is done. I can do it—I get better at it all the time—but with them it's just as natural as eating; they say they figure things out, but they don't figure a darn thing; they just know it in the back of their heads, what two-inch cable will stand, how much a ten-by-fourteen donkey will pull, how to hang a block so it will give them the purchase they want. It's good to run into that kind of thing and now that Chris has gone there isn't enough of it around this dump.

As he came up to the machine he realized he was thinking of Dolly. He tried to trace the thought's connection with what he had been thinking of Chris and Johnny and found it at once; she's the same way they are—she doesn't have to figure things, she just plain knows them. She knew that night how it would go with Johnny and Julie and knew it wasn't any time for us to go back there. And she knew where we could go to have a good time ourselves without butting in on them too soon. I like that woman. You can rest with her and be quiet when you're feeling in the mood and yet when you want more than that she's got everything. That's why I never went back for Rita this time; Rita's never satisfied with anything else than all you've got, from the day you hit town till you go out again. She's a crazy woman for it and I guess I'm getting too old for that kind.

He stood on the brow log, watching while Dan set the turn down and the chaser freed the chokers. It scares you, he thought, even when you're used to it, all that weight dropping and lifting and sliding and rolling as though it were nothing at all, particularly now when the bark is all loose with the sap running and they can slip out from under each other or tear loose from the tongs any time. But you get a kick out of it because it is big, and being a touch scared makes it exciting. Second loading for Johnny that time down at Mellit Bay I was scared, yet I didn't think of being scared most of the time after the first few days; it was just there, somewhere in back of you, and that made it all the better to be doing the job—made it mean something when you went down with the tongs and flipped them and saw them catch.

Johnny jumped from the track to the brow log and stood beside Alec. "What fetched you out so early?" he asked.

"Told Ted I'd be in camp to go out on Side One with him," Alec said.

"Trouble?"

"Some. They were late getting the deck on that trestle and the rigging crew can't get ahead. Ted's kind of sore about it. I think Mark Evans is riding him plenty these days."

Johnny pulled out his tobacco pouch and turned to watch the empties coming slowly up past the brow log. "You brain guys sure got a dirty deal when they switched that prick over on you in place of Chris."

"Didn't we all?" Alec said.

"He don't bother a working plug like me. No one's seen him on this side since he got to be superintendent."

Alec laughed. "You'll break a couple of cars or dump

a load one day and he'll be down your neck wanting to know for why. You can't break a choker hook around this dump any more without he wants to know about it." He started along the brow log towards the locomotive. Johnny said: "Coming up for supper tonight?"

"You bet. Haven't set eyes on Julie for pretty near a week."

He jumped down from the log, went along the track to the locomotive and climbed into the cab. "How's chances for a ride?" he asked Eric.

"Sure, help yourself. Going right through to camp?"

"Told Ted I'd be down this trip."

Eric leaned out of the cab and stared back along the line of empties to where Shorty and Johnny were talking, then turned back into the cab again. "Been up to Johnny's place lately?" he asked.

"Going tonight," Alec said.

"It's darn good to have a new married outfit in camp. Marion gets a great kick out of that cousin of yours. They're in and out of each other's houses all day long."

Standing with his caulks grating and insecure on the steel plates of the cab, Alec leaned back and watched Eric and Stevie, the fireman. Locomotive crews were so damned sure of themselves in the cabs of their locomotives; all loggers are that way out on the job, with familiar things about them, things they know they can use and control properly—I guess all men are that way, he thought—but locomotive crews especially. Perched up on that damned leather cushion, with all the worn, shiny brass and steel handles in front of him, Eric's like a king or a lord or something; you can't get near him. Out of

Timber

the cab he's just an ordinary man. Even young Stevie's got something up here, leaning out of the cab for the brakeman's signal, reaching up for a casual pull on the bell rope and nodding across to Eric. And Eric, pushing the johnson bar forward, easing off the brakes, touching the throttle to set seventy tons of locomotive rolling out on the grade. . . . They don't come better than Eric, now he's settled down a bit—steady and wise and confident, yet young enough still to make them roll.

They stopped at the Y, where the Side One spur came in, and coupled on to the loads from both sides. Shorty went along the train, looking over the couplings and airbrake hoses, then came back to the cab and climbed in. Eric's hand went up to the bar and the train moved out on to the level stretch below the switch.

Alec stood holding on to the steel ladder that climbed up to the tender, looking out from the cab across the deep valley below the track. He watched the floor of the valley, searching eagerly for quick glimpses of the tumbled water of the stream that flowed along it, trying to judge from them how the fishing would be over the week end. Under this, he noticed Eric's handling of the heavy train, matching it against the conception he had formed, when the line was still no more than a row of stakes through the standing timber, of how the run would be. Plenty of throttle on the level below the Y, getting the loads rolling; easing off, feeling brakes, just before the first stretch of downgrade; through that smoothly to the next few hundred feet of level track, then the downgrade dropping steadily through curves, along the sidehill, steep below and sharp cut on the upper side of the track, down to lake level at camp. Sounds and movement about him fitted comfortably into the forms his mind had set for them, sway of cab, clatter of wheels over the rail joints, hiss of brake air, the throb of steam, released and checked, released and checked. Stevie reached a lazy shovel back for coal, and that too was planned or at least foreseen—easy firing all the way down to camp and a full head of steam for the long pull along the lake shore.

He felt the biting grind of wheel flanges on the start of the big curve. Then the sharp jolt of brakes, urgently applied, almost tore his grip from the steel of the ladder. He saw Eric's tense back and his quick hands fighting the momentum of two hundred wheeling tons, then, past Stevie, he saw the speeder coming up and the man on it, alone, reaching to throttle and brake and gears. The man jumped clear a moment before the speeder stopped, and went out of sight over the steep downward drop on the lower side of the track. The train slid on, every wheel locked, caught the speeder, threw it back and away from the track. Eric stopped his loads, jolting and jarring on flattened wheels, a hundred feet beyond. Alec dropped to the track, ran back and went down the steep slope. Ted was lying awkwardly on a pile of split rock and the wrecked speeder was on his legs. Shorty came down with the second brakeman.

"Think we can move that off him?" Shorty asked.

"We can try," Alec said. "On this end and she'll maybe slide over some." He got a good grip, both hands on a piece of iron under the step. They lifted together and it came up; Alec slid his knees under, found a new grip and the others changed and lifted again and it rocked and rolled over a little, out of the way.

"Go up and get the stretcher," Alec told the second brakeman. "Tell Eric to come down and let Stevie stay with the locie. It'll take four of us to get him up to the track."

He turned back to Ted and saw his eyes were open. "How do you feel?" he said, and knelt beside him.

The gray eyes were hurt in the pale face, but Ted's voice was easy and calm. "Don't seem to pain much," he said. "But I can't seem to move."

Alec dropped a hand quickly to his shoulder. "Don't try," he said. "Take it easy. The boys are getting a stretcher and we'll get you down to camp in no time." Jesus, he thought, you can't tell what's the matter with the poor bastard. Likely his back's broken. There's no blood any place except that cut on his head and that doesn't amount to anything. Guess that's what put him out. But he's hurt pretty bad, you can tell that just looking at him. His face is all old and tight and gray, not like Ted a damn bit unless he was starved or something. Sure makes a fellow feel helpless when you want to do something for a guy and he needs it the worst kind of way and you don't know what in hell to do. Got to figure it's his back and move him carefully, keep him still and level on the stretcher.

He took off his coat, folded it flat and slipped it under the foreman's head. "Don't try to move any part of you," he said. "We'll fix you up when we get you on the stretcher."

"Jesus, that was a fool thing to do. I figured I could be up at the Y before Shorty started down with the loads."

They came down with the stretcher and lifted him on to it, supporting his long, square-shouldered body as firmly as they could. Alec straightened himself and looked up towards the track. "Better go up on a long angle," he said. "And slow. Then come back along the track."

It was an awkward, straining job, walking the uneven, rocky ground and trying to keep the stretcher level and solid between them. Coming along the track, past the loads, there was only room for two men and Alec went ahead with Eric. At the cab he said: "Better blow seven."

Eric said: "That's three for the locie and three for the push. The locie's right here and it's a cinch the push can't get away on us."

"Sure," Alec said. "But it'll let them know in camp somebody's hurt."

"I guess that's right," Eric said and climbed into the cab. Alec stood looking back along the track as the seven long whistles rolled out, mournfully down and across the valley. There's always that stillness before them, he thought, and the slow counting wait to see what it's going to be. Shorty and the second brakeman came up and Stevie came down from the cab. They lifted the stretcher on to the plates, keeping it level, and Alec asked: "How was the ride, Ted?"

"Okay, but she's hurting some now."

Shorty said: "We better uncouple the loads and run down light."

Timber

Ted's voice was quick from the stretcher: "You will like hell. There's enough time lost now. Take 'em into camp."

The door opened as Alec started up the steps and Julie was standing there. God, she's a swell-looking kid since she married Johnny. She just seems ten times as good as before, sort of overflowing with herself and full of life; she always was full of life, but now it hits you like one of those big breakers down in California and surges right over you, fresh and strong and full of colors. That's an awful lot for a man to own all to himself, but you've got to hand it to Johnny; he made it, most of it, made it or woke it up, and he can take care of it.

Julie had said: "Hello, stranger, where have you been for a week?" And he had said: "Working, sweet cousin, working. Slave to the green eye-shade and the yellow-cedar draughting table, night after night."

Inside the house, Johnny said: "Sit down, Alec. Julie says we can eat in ten minutes. Did you hear how Ted is?"

"No. They got him across to the hospital and he seemed pretty good, but they hadn't taken the X-ray when Nolly Davis called."

"Who is Davis?"

"Don't you know Nolly? First-aid man down at the Beach and a swell guy. He said he'd stay over there till the doctor made up his mind and then call through again from the Beach."

"How did he seem when you picked him up? Do you think he'll pull through?"

"Hell," Alec said. "I don't know. I think his back is

broken, but they say a guy can live through that. If other guys can do it, a tough Swede like Ted can."

Julie said: "Do you like him, Alec?"

"Sure I do. You couldn't ask for a better guy to work with than Ted. Good-natured and easy-going, and one hell of a smart logger."

"How did it happen he was out on the speeder?"

"It's kind of hard to figure that out," Alec said. "When we picked him up he said it was his fault, he reckoned he could beat the train up to the Y and save time. It's kind of like Ted, at that; he gets impatient sometimes—not with other people, with himself—and then he's got to jump on his horse and go."

"That's right," Johnny said. "Remember that time we loaded a spar tree for Side One and had trouble getting it round the big curve? I thought he was going to jump in there and pack one end around himself."

"What did he do?" Julie asked.

"Well, we had her loaded on two skeleton cars—one end on each car, about eighty feet apart. Going round the curve she jumped the rear car off the track. We put it back on and it jumped again. Ted came up there when the locie blew for him, walked all round the layout figuring so hard you could pretty near hear him, then said: 'Hell, leave her the way she looks, let the top ride along the ties.' Old Tom Davidson said: 'Yeah, and tear out half a mile of track.' But it didn't bother a damn thing."

Julie said: "That doesn't sound so much."

"I'd like to know who they'll send up to take his place," Alec said. He was thinking: No, it doesn't sound much, to anyone but a logger. Just moving a tree a hundred and twenty feet long and four feet on the butt. That's what a logger is, moving things quick and easy, things so big and heavy and awkward they aren't meant to be moved at all.

"They'll fetch some guy in from outside," Johnny said. "Plenty of good men in town these days."

"Not good camp foremen. I'd like to see some guy who's got guts enough to stand up to Mark Evans and tell him where he gets off at."

"Do you expect Evans to pick one out like that?"

"He won't be picking anybody out. Dachman and them at the head office will do it in town."

"I wish you two would talk something else besides logging," Julie said.

"Why not?" Alec said. "You look like a million dollars, Julie, and so does your house."

"Like it? It isn't finished yet."

"Sure do. It's streamlined. I never saw a house like it in a camp." It is good too, Alec thought, no fooling. Nice bright curtains and things painted white, clean looking and simple; those covers on the chairs are good too.

"Johnny made the tables and shelves," Julie said. "And he's making fly screens for the summer now. I'll bet you didn't know he was a carpenter like that."

"He was raised on a farm. Ought to be some use around the place."

"Julie drew pictures of the way she wanted things made," Johnny said. "I couldn't have figured it out that good myself."

"It's slick anyway. Next thing you know you'll have it all cluttered up with brats."

Alec saw them glance quickly at one another. Julie looked down as quickly. Hell, he thought, they've made it already.

"Shall we tell him?" Julie asked. "He knows anyway."

"Sure. He's got a right to know if anybody has."

"I think it's October," she said. "Isn't that terrible?"

"I think it's swell," Alec said. "Go get the bottle, Johnny. You're a goddamned piker not to have had it ready before."

"Alec," Julie said. "You wouldn't dare swear like that in Mother's house and you're not to do it in mine."

"I'm not scared of you like I am of Aunt Lil."

"Leave him alone, Julie," Johnny said. "He's only a tough logger anyway. He doesn't know any better."

"I don't care," Alec said. "So long as she doesn't try telling us we wouldn't dare pull out a rum bottle in the bosom of the Morris family." He thought: That's part of why she looks so swell tonight; they say it does that to a woman. I don't believe it though; it's what goes before that counts. That's just what Julie needed, a guy like Johnny, and it's working out a hundred per cent. He makes a full woman out of her instead of just a green kid, and she'll make something out of him too at the same time, if I know Julie. He won't be loading all his life. Seeing them like that, so close together all the time, makes a man feel sort of lonely. I guess it's knowing them both so well and then knowing they know each other better.

"When are you two going fishing together?" Julie asked.

"Do you still let him loose for that?" That's mean, Alec thought; it wasn't just kidding, even if I made it sound that way, but it came so close on what I was thinking. He said: "I was sizing up the creek coming down on the locie this afternoon. It looks good for next Sunday. How about it, Johnny? Want to try it?"

"Sounds good," Johnny said. "Julie says she can cook fish like nobody's business, so we can come back here and eat what we catch afterwards. That's something was missing before."

Alec lifted his glass. "Here's to the son and heir," he said. "And here's yourself, Julie." That sounds natural and decent, he thought, and it isn't a damn bit. I stuck it on there because I'm crazy about her the way she is now and I want her and want her to know it. She got it that way too. It doesn't mean anything—pleases her and pleases me, except when I stop and think I'm such a heel about women I even want my best friend's wife.

Julie said: "Did you hear them say anything about the shut-down yet, Alec?"

"Have a heart," Johnny said. "We've only been working three months and it's a wet spring so far, knock wood."

"Log market's kind of good," Alec said. "They won't hurry any unless it gets really dry—end of June, maybe. Why?"

"I thought maybe we could all three go on a camping trip somewhere. Around here or up at home."

"That's a swell idea," Alec said. "But you wouldn't want me around."

"Sure we would."

"We could take two tents."

"And I could figure out when to make myself scarce."

"Don't be mean," Julie said. "That's settled, then. I haven't been camping for a coon's age."

"Do you really think they'll run till the end of June?" Johnny asked. "It would be the first year they have since the depression."

"I figure they'll want to, if they aren't scared."

"How scared?"

"Scared of the union."

Johnny put his glass down and slid his chair back from the table. "Is that going to come up again? Just when a guy's got a chance to get a bit ahead?"

"I don't know," Alec said. "I don't figure it's the right time, but there's something moving. They say Dalby fired two guys down at Camp Five because he figured they were union men."

"He didn't say he fired them for that?"

"No, he's not that crazy. But the boys figure that's the way it was. The guys he fired were good enough on the job, but they were both talking union in the bunkhouse at nights."

"You can't tell about a thing like that," Johnny said. "It's mostly just talk."

"You know Tim Vendra?" Alec said.

"Second brakie at Camp Five? Sure."

"Well, he used to get the union paper. Evans called him into the office one night—Dalby was there. Evans had Tim's copy of the paper in his hand—took it right out of the mail—and he said: 'See here, Tim, I won't have this red radical stuff on the claim.' Then he threw the paper in the stove."

"The hell he did," Johnny said. "That's kind of raw."

Timber

"I didn't think they could do that kind of thing," Julie said. "Dad sure doesn't like unions, but he'd be hopping mad if he heard about that."

"They can do anything they damn please, if they're giving you a job."

"But not that. Not taking people's mail and burning it up."

"Who's going to stop them?"

"I would," Julie said. "If they did it to me."

"Tim Vendra's got a wife and two kids. Tim wouldn't want to be blacklisted, sitting on his fanny in town for a couple of years."

"Do you think it will make trouble?" Johnny asked.

"Not this time. The boys aren't stakey enough. But a couple more little things like that and the companies will be looking for a chance to shut down to keep them from getting stakey."

"Even if the market's good?"

"Even if the market's good," Alec said. "If she's good in June and everybody shuts down she'll be just that much better after fire season."

"Suppose they didn't all shut down?" Julie asked.

"They would. Near enough to all of them. That's the sort of thing they get together on."

"Never mind," Julie said. "If they shut down early we'll just go camping that much longer and save money."

"You want to watch it," Alec said. "Or that kid will turn out a worse timber beast than his dad."

17

THE fire had started nearly a week before, within two or three hundred feet of where the cold-deck machine was working on the lower side of the track. It had seemed completely unimportant at first, just the worry of a small crew of men who would have to keep it under control until it died from their attention or a change in the weather. The weather had held obstinately fine and the fire had smoldered as obstinately within its few hundred square foot range until yesterday afternoon; then a heavy west wind, pouring through the open length of the lake and on into the hills, had torn it away from the watching men and set it free for as long as daylight lasted. Now it was dull and subdued again after the cool stillness of the night, but it was no longer unimportant.

Working at the landing to get the yarder loaded and away from the fire, Johnny said: "Slide it under there, Tommy, and you'll get a good lift on her." He dropped the heavy jack and straightened up to watch the locomotive coming light along the track. The smoke was thick already, smarting in his eyes, smelling of pitch and cedar. He turned to look at it, rolling up thick and dirty from the deep draw on the lower side of the track; he could hear the snap and crackle of burning wood and feel the heavy heat of it from six or eight hundred feet away. Not a goddamn chance to hold it when the wind comes up, he thought, and if she gets away it means a week of fire-fighting, then a shut-down while they fix the trestles and the track—likely a shut-down till fall, the way things look right now.

He went down from where they were loading the yarder and stood beside the track. The locomotive came up to him and slowed to a stop. Eric leaned out of the cab. "How does she look?" he asked.

"Not so good," Johnny said. "She's hotter than hell down in the draw. All set to get away on us soon as the wind starts up. We aren't loaded here yet. You'd better go on up and get the rigging goat."

Shorty had come round from the step and was standing beside Johnny. "Evans said to forget about the goat and get the unit out," he said. "He came through from the Beach just before we pulled out of camp."

"Good God," Johnny said. "Go get the goat. She's all loaded, lines taken up, everything. Run the son of a bitch down to the Y and we'll be ready for you here by the time you get back. Those trestles are safe till this afternoon anyway."

"Who's going to take responsibility for that?" Shorty said. "You?"

"Where's Slim? He's supposed to be running things on this side."

"He rode up with us to the second trestle and went down from there to the fire."

"Sure I'll take responsibility."

Eric laughed, looking down from the cab. "Attaboy, Johnny. You tell 'em. It's time somebody around this joint said something that made sense, and stuck with it. The supe is rattled all to hell and Halversen's not much better. Wish we had old Ted back on the job."

The locomotive moved off. Johnny looked again at the smoke below the track. I could be crazy, he thought, but I'll be a son of a bitch if I am. There isn't a way in the world that fire can work up to the track before noon, and if we hold it down longer than that we ought to have the whole works out, even the cold-deck machine. That's where Alec will be, stepping on their tails to make them get the lines in and start the machine up the hill. Soon as we get loaded here I can take the bunch down and give him a hand, unless he wants us to start cleaning out under those trestles. Should get that done first thing after the machines are out.

He turned back to his crew. The smoke was heavy about them, choking dry and hot in the nostrils, griming faces and laying fine gray flakes of ash on shirts and hats. Could use a whole damn crew of loaders, Johnny thought; those chokermen of Tom Davidson's are laying down on the job already. Chuck and Mel are okay, but those other two—the big guy and that guy with the fancy shirt—don't seem to give a damn. He went over to the big man and stood watching him; he was moving a jack clumsily and awkwardly, setting it at an angle against a low part of the donkey sled.

"She don't look like she'll bite good there," Johnny said. "Try her a bit farther along."

The big man looked up at him. "What in hell's the difference?"

Timber 233

"I'd just as soon get this machine moved out of here when the locie gets back," Johnny said. "That's what."

"It's no skin off my arse if she rots right where she is."

Johnny took a step towards him. "Listen, Mac, move that jack along where I said to, and do it in a hurry."

The chokerman moved the jack. "Okay," he said. "Okay."

Johnny walked round to the other side of the machine and found Tom Davidson, the hooktender. "Looks like you can have her loaded easy enough by the time Shorty gets back," he said. "Slim Crawford is down with the cold-decker. I figured to walk down there and see what's on his mind."

"Go ahead," Tom said. "It's time we knew what the score is."

Johnny started down the hill. The smoke was still thick and lazy, but he saw that it was rising from the heat of the fire in a solid, heavy column that slanted forward. He judged that high up, hidden by the diffused smoke about him, the column would be breaking into a billowing white plume along the line of its slant. There's wind of some sort moving it already, he thought, maybe not much more than its own wind, but the lake wind will come soon now. There isn't a god's chance they'll have it under control by night and that means we'll be working straight through. They could get a relief crew in from Camp Five, but they never do that until the last moment. That makes me sore now; I'd have griped about it any time, just for the sake of griping, but getting in a whole lot of extra time would have seemed okay and it's kind of nice out on a fire trail at night sometimes. But now it makes me sore because I want to get back to my own house and be with Julie soon as work is over every day; it would be all right if there was nothing they could do about it, but when you know damn well they could get a bunch up from Camp Five it makes you sore.

He heard the cold-deck machine grunting and straining to pull itself up against the steep slope, and swung to one side to avoid the taut lines that he knew would be somewhere ahead of it. He saw it suddenly, the massive runners of its sled tilted far up over a break in the slope, boiler and spark-arrester leaning back like a man straining against a heavy pull, all of it huge and dim through the smoke. The steam coughed out slowly and painfully, with a halting power too flexible to die, then the runners slammed sharply down and the steam found new life in itself and the whole machine began to move almost smoothly across the flat bench towards the next slope. Johnny found Alec near the machine, his face streaked with the black dust of the fire.

"How's she coming?" he asked.

"Lousy," Alec said. "We broke a line back there and the donkey started to slip back down the hill. Don jumped and broke his ankle. The damned thing only slipped about ten feet, then stopped."

"Where's Don now?"

"We took him up to the Y. The speeder will be up behind Shorty next trip."

Johnny could see the red of flames below them now in the smoke, and make out the forms of men moving on the cleared trail around the fire. "How will she be to hold when the wind comes up?"

"We can't hold her there," Alec said. "That's just for now, while we get the cold-decker out. I've got them started on a good fire trail twelve hundred feet farther over and as soon as the machinery is out of the way we can backfire from there. That'll pinch it right tight into the draw and make sure of saving the trestles on this line. Wish to hell Jake would hurry that bull-dozer through."

"You mean you haven't got it yet? I thought it came up last trip."

"No. They're stalling for some damn reason—Mark and Jake. If they don't get it up here soon we'll have a hell of a job to get that trail cleaned out in time."

"You got enough men to load the cold-decker?"

"Sure. Where's the locie now?"

"Ought to be coming up to fetch the yarder out."

"Then he can get this one next time. I could use a good man down on the pumps at the creek though. Send Ed."

"Okay," Johnny said. "How's to help out on your main fire trail with the rest, or shall I take them up to clean out under the trestles?"

"Take them to the trestles. They're sure to have the bull-dozer on this trip and once that gets here the trail will be clear in no time at all. If a spark got into that pile of brush under the first trestle it would go off like powder."

Johnny started back up the hill towards his crew. Alec shouted after him: "Come on down as soon as you're through. Once we get the backfire started we're going to need all the men we can get to chase spot fires."

As he climbed the hill Johnny heard the locomotive through the smoke. Down near the Y, he thought;

they'll be up there pretty near as soon as I am; hope to hell Tom's got that machine loaded. There's something haywire there in that crew; loggers aren't like that on a fire—they'll gripe plenty, sure, but they don't lay down on the job like that big guy was doing and the other bastard in the pansy shirt. Tom Davidson met him near the track, within sight of the loaded machine. "She's all set," he said. "And I can hear Shorty coming up now."

"Good stuff," Johnny said. "Slim says to go up and clean out under the trestles, then get down on the main fire trail soon as he starts the backfire." He looked straight at the old hooktender. "What's the matter with that crew of yours, Tom?"

"Them two sorehead bastards, you mean? They only came up from town last week and they'd be going out on the next boat if it wasn't for the fire. Maybe they'll go anyway, but I stepped on their tails plenty while you were down the hill and I'll keep right after them."

"It'll take all of that," Johnny said.

Alec came up the hill when they had been at the trestle only a little while. Johnny saw that he was sweating and angry; he thought: You don't often see Alec sweat; what in hell's gone wrong now? Alec said: "Did Jake come through yet?"

"Haven't seen him," Johnny said. "Why?"

"That goddamned train's been up and gone back and I still haven't got the bull-dozer."

"Maybe we'd better move down and help with that fire trail."

Tom Davidson said: "Here's Jake now."

Johnny watched the foreman coming down the steep

slope at the side of the trestle. He doesn't look like he's worrying, Johnny thought; maybe Alec's rattled too soon. I never have figured Jake was so dumb; he's not the man Ted is, but he knows his stuff and he seems to take things quietly—most of the time you hardly know he's around.

Alec said: "How about the bull-dozer, Jake? That wind's coming soon and if I don't get my backfire started from a good trail we'll never in God's world save these trestles."

"Bull-dozer's down at the Y," Halverson said. "Mark wanted to run a good trail right down the sidehill there and make sure of bottling everything up in this corner."

"Suffering God," Alec said. "What does he want to do, let the trestles go? I've got a peach of a set-up to pinch the fire right down into the creek if you'll just let me have that cat for half an hour, like I told you."

Watching Halverson, Johnny saw his quick moment of hesitation. The guy doesn't know his own mind after all; he's just got a way of looking like he did. "I'll go see Mark," Halverson said. "That sounds like a good bet."

"Well, for God's sake, hurry," Alec told him. "That's what you said when I told you what I was figuring two hours ago. I'll take Johnny's and Tom's lot down to the trail right now."

The foreman started up the slope again towards the track. Alec turned to Johnny. "Goddamned everlasting buck-passing," he said. "Let's go. If we don't get a backfire started it won't help a damn bit to have the trestles cleaned out."

Down on the fire trail Johnny found himself listening for the clatter of the bull-dozer's tracks and the muttering power of its diesel. Alec's got the right idea, he thought; if we don't pinch it off and save those trestles it will mean a shut-down right away, likely for the whole summer. They could have sent the cat right up here and still have had all kinds of time to make a second trail down at the Y. It's hard to figure what in hell the idea is. If we have to go back that far to fight it, the Side One trestles will be out too.

He saw the foreman and superintendent coming along the trail. Alec had seen them already and walked up to meet them. The three men came together and stopped. Evans was looking critically along the fire trail. Alec said: "What do you think of her, Mark?"

"Looks pretty good to me. If you get a good backfire started from here you ought to be able to hold her. And if anything goes wrong with that you can fall back to the main fire line near the Y."

"I'll need that bull-dozer in a hurry. The wind is starting up already."

Evans did not look at him. "I'll be keeping Reg down on the main trail," he said. "Got to have a real job there."

"You mean you won't send him up at all?"

"You've got a good line here. Go ahead and start your backfire. That wind won't wait for you all day."

"Start it from this?" Alec pointed down at the narrow strip of bare earth they were standing on. "Hell, we can't depend on holding a campfire with this against that wind. It doesn't even run clear down to the creek yet."

"Got to take a chance somewhere," Evans said.

"That's not taking any chance. That's burning out those trestles for sure, and a whole lot of jobs with them."

"That's better than letting it run right down the valley and burn out the camp and all the equipment. You go ahead and fight fire. I'll do the worrying."

Alec turned to Johnny. "Take your bunch down to the creek," he said. "And finish out the trail. Send Tom up with his outfit to help the other boys back with the pumps. I'm going up to round up the rest of them and we'll start backfiring as soon as everybody's in the clear."

Without looking at Evans and Halverson again he started off into the smoke. He could feel the hot wind stirring against his face, searching for strength and with the promise of strength already in it. I'd sure as hell like to know what's in that bastard's mind, he thought. Seems like he wants to burn out those trestles. That could be it too, with Jake stalling me like that earlier on; Jake knows we've got a good show to hold it here, but he didn't say a word when Evans was talking. I'll bet that's just what it is; burn out the trestles, shut-down to fix them, keep shut down all summer for fire hazard and have the boys come back to camp good and broke in the fall. Now go ahead and try to prove it, he thought; that's just a crazy bit of guessing, the sort of thing the agitators use and nobody more than half believes. But I'll bet you could find it written down somewhere; that came from the head office; Mark never thought it up for himself.

He rounded up the men from the makeshift firebreak that circled the heart of the fire and started them back for the new line. They were mostly graders and section men, slow-moving and talkative, and he asked the Italian foreman about the cold-deck machine.

"The rigger, he came back down little time ago," Tony

said. "He say if you come up to tell you cold-decker ready to go out. They walk down along da track and find you."

"Where's Charlie?" Alec asked.

"Who?"

"Charlie, the bull-bucker. The guy who looks after the fallers."

"Oh, him. He just go down deesa way, minute or two ago."

Alec started in the direction of Tony's pointing finger. He caught up with Charlie a little way along the trail. Charlie was a big, heavy-footed man who gave out his words slowly and reluctantly through the massive droop of a white mustache. It would be a comfortable thing to talk to Charlie, even for a moment.

"Can you get your fallers out in a hurry?" Alec said.

"Sure, I guess so." Charlie spat snuff juice. "Where to?"

"Behind the next fire line. We want to start backfiring."

"Hell's damn," Charlie said. "They won't have all them snags down."

"Doesn't matter. Evans and the push said to go ahead with it anyway."

"Hell's damn, one of them snags'll throw sparks a quarter mile if she gets to burning good."

"Can't be helped. Evans will be sending for you to come back to the Y anytime now."

"Okay," Charlie said. "What in hell's damn do they want to do? Burn out the whole claim?"

He disappeared into the smoke and Alec went on down the fire line to make sure that the men and the pumps were all moved out. The smoke was heavy and depressing about him and the noise of burning brush was loud in the thick silence. Occasionally a gust of wind swirled from somewhere in the fire and brought live sparks with it; he noticed that there were already several little holes burned in his shirt. God, he thought, it's a fool business. Here we've been riding the dog a whole morning and talking our fool heads off about a little bit of a fire that we should have had corralled by now. I haven't got the guts—I didn't think quick enough anyway—to tell that black whore he was just fixing a shut-down and to go peddle his stuff some place else. And it wouldn't have done a damn bit of good if I had. I'd just have got myself cornered and they'd have run the thing their own way anyhow. Why in hell did Chris have to get sick? You knew where you were with that guy; anything he said or did made sense and you didn't have the feeling there was something back of it you couldn't get hold of. You could take chances then, too, so long as you used your head a bit and didn't do anything plain crazy, because you knew darn well he'd back you up. Now it seems like you've got to watch every move you make for fear some son of a bitch will be blaming his bull-headed boners on what you've done. Damn Chris and his stomach anyway; if he had taken the trouble to put water in his liquor once in a while it might never have happened. Alec laughed to himself. That's a fool thing to think—Chris doesn't drink any harder than the next guy, poor bastard. It's queer how you can get sore at a guy and start cursing him out just because he's so good you need him.

He turned from the trail and climbed a log that slanted high over a stump. For a moment he stood at the end of it, staring into the smoke, trying to see something of the fire. Then he turned and came back to the trail again. You'd think they'd have sent one of the forestry guys up by now—no, you wouldn't either; there'll be one up tomorrow and he'll just look wise and talk big and make most of the boys sore. There's not one of them in a dozen knows anything about fighting fire anyway. None of us knows much more; we just try out the old stuff, firebreaks and backfiring, and sometimes it works out and sometimes it doesn't. But this time it was a set-up, easy as picking ripe apples. And they have to go and ball it up, burn out three or four miles of track and as many trestles and several square miles of country all because they're scared of a strike if the boys get stakey—or else because the superintendent's scared of his job. They'd tell you a company ought to be able to burn its own trestles and its own property if it wants, but that's just crazy. They're burning other people's property too—men's jobs. There isn't a damn thing they can do, not even employ a scared superintendent and a weak camp push, without affecting men's jobs. But that's what these guys like Johnny and Dal and the rest of them can't see.

He came to the creek and turned along it, following the wide path the crews had made to carry the pumps out. He found the pumps set up at the start of the new trail, their intake hoses in a deep pool of good water. He went up the freshly cleared trail a little way and found Johnny. The wind was coming steadily out of the fire now and growing stronger. "Soon as I make sure Charlie's got his fallers out we'll start to backfire," Alec said.

"I saw him. They're all clear—on their way back to the Evans line," Johnny said.

"That what you call it now?"

Johnny laughed. "Sure, Evans line, Crawford line, liable to be a Halverson line any minute now."

"Well," Alec said. "If everybody's out we may as well start to backfire. You'll have Tom's crew and your own and Tony's to look out for—and the pumps. If she breaks through anywhere take them out down the creek to Evans' line. I'll get the rest of them out by the track."

He started up the hill, traveling fast. The wind was strong on the left side of his face and already it was carrying larger pieces of ash with it. The fire would be building its own updraft now, and the flames would be quicker and liver. In a little while the spot fires would start up behind the cleared trail, and the boys would have to keep humping to hold them down. It feels better now that there's something to do, he thought, better all the time. Maybe we can hold her here after all; no reason against having a damn good try anyway. Maybe Mark is just plain dumb, not mean at all, and they won't shut-down if the trestles don't go out. He spoke to the straw bosses of the various crews as he climbed along the trail, telling them when to start their backfires and how to get out if the fire got behind them. Half way up the hill he saw a big fir snag through the smoke, the bark hanging loosely from it. The smoke closed round it again and hid it from sight. Hell, he thought, not two hundred feet from the trail and no time to set fallers on it. Charlie sure as hell passed that one up—twice, at that; you wouldn't know there was a law in these goddamned woods that logging companies are supposed to fell all snags as they log.

He came through to the track and found the rigger with the cold-deck crew and his own crew. "Any sign of the locie yet, Curly?" he asked.

"No," Curly said. "We been ready for her pretty nearly an hour now."

"She'll come," Alec said. "How's to put your crew along the track and douse spot fires on the uphill side? We've started the backfires along this trail."

"That's jake with me," Curly said. "Figure you can hold her?"

"We got some show. Could've made her sure if they'd sent the bull-dozer."

"Heard they held that out on you. What's the idea?"

"I'm a son of a bitch if I know," Alec said. "You'd better ask the superintendent that one."

He turned and started down the hill again. Holy God, he thought, now they've got me doing it, passing the buck like all the rest of them. There's too many bosses around this joint and everybody knows it; talking like that just makes it all the worse. What in hell do I want anyway, to avoid blame for not saving those trestles or to save them? Or do I care if I save them? Maybe I only want to get credit for saving them. A guy's got a hell of a time to tell why he does anything when you come right down to it. I'd like to save them, first to show up that goddamned Mark Evans and then because I'd like the boys to have a decent run of steady work. And letting everybody see something's haywire is no way to save them. There's always plenty of guys ready to lay down on the job fighting fire and if you give them the least excuse they sure as hell will lay down. Some of them can see that saving company property is saving their own jobs, but a lot of them figure it's just saving company property and what the hell do they care anyway.

He saw that the backfires were cutting back into the wind well enough; there was already a good swathe of smoldering blackness all along the windward side of the trail. He passed from straw boss to straw boss, kidding the crews, talking easily as though it were all smoothly planned and running right. But the wind was steadily stronger and he could see the spot fires from the main blaze jumping up here and there in the path of his backfires. And behind him a man was already shoveling dirt on to a spot fire on the wrong side of the fire trail. He looked for the big snag but could not see it in the smoke. Johnny met him well up from the creek. "Ed says the big pump has blown a cylinder head," Johnny told him. "The others are pumping fine."

"Dump it in the creek if you have to pull out," Alec said. "How's the backfiring?"

"Swell. Seems to cut right back into the wind in fine shape. We've had a few spot fires but nothing to amount to anything."

"There's snags still standing. You want to watch her when the wind gets real heavy. Give yourself lots of time to get out; she could cut you off in there."

"What about eating?" Johnny said. "Some of the boys are getting hungry."

"If things look good when I get back up to the track

I'll see what we can get. Otherwise you'll just have to eat with Mark."

"Could be hungry enough to do that in another hour or two," Johnny said. "I'll be seeing you."

Alec watched him start back down the trail. It feels lonely when he's gone, he thought; he could handle this a whole lot better than me except for not knowing the run of the country so well. That man's solid as a rock in everything he does, so damn confident and on top of it all. It's a crazy thing he's still loading. If Chris had been here he'd have put him up in Ted's place instead of Jake Halverson, but Mark could never see a thing like that. You haven't got to do more than talk to him to feel good, when he's out on the job. He'd never have let Charlie get away and leave those snags right on top of this line; and he'd have got that bull-dozer some way.

Climbing the trail again towards the track he knew that they couldn't hold the fire. He could see the big snag now, burning dull red through the smoke. The heavy wind was bending the saplings far over and as he watched, it carried a shower of flaming bark far out over his head. He turned and went back, telling the straw bosses to start moving the men out to the track. Tony had already started down towards the creek with his men.

There was fire on both sides of him as he climbed the hill—hot and heavy with smoke and sparks upwind, beyond the smoldering of his backfires, spotted here and there on the downwind side and spreading fast. He caught up with the last group of men on the trail and one of them said cheerfully: "Where's the next stop from here, chief?"

"Somewhere down near the Y," Alec told him. "We can walk the track."

"It's hotter than a son of a bitch," the man said. "I guess them trestles will go."

"They've got pumps there," Alec said.

Curly met him at the track. "She's getting hot," he said. "I've got the boys on the trestles. The locie's gone up for the cold-deck machine."

"Are the pumps okay?" Alec asked him.

"Fine so far."

They started along the track towards the trestles. Alec heard the locomotive behind them. "They'll make it in plenty of time, anyway."

"There's one hot spot up there, but they'll make that okay," Curly said.

They reached the first trestle and turned to look back. The locomotive was in sight almost at once, wheeling and rocking with the towering bulk of the donkey engine swaying crazily behind it. Shorty waved from the front step, his teeth white in a blackened face and Eric waved from the cab. The load rattled over the gleaming wet deck of the trestle and passed out of sight around the curve beyond.

"Guess that's the last train will go over there," Alec said.

Curly nodded. "Smoke's too bad to stay there much longer. What in hell's the idea of letting it cross the track like that?"

Alec looked gloomily at the jet of water from the hoze nozzle, breaking to spray against the ties. "Don't ask me," he said. "They haven't used the track any place to speak of. They've put every goddamned thing back on this one line down by the Y." He felt suddenly tired and depressed. He said fiercely: "I hope to hell there'll be one of them stay on the job this time, to run his own crazy scheme."

Julie stood in the open doorway of the house as Johnny came up the steps. He looked terrible, she thought, just like all the others with that black on him and the sweat caked on his shirt and his eyes bloodshot. But when he reached the top of the steps he put his arm about her shoulders and looked down at her, smiling. "I won't kiss you, honey," he said. "You look so cool and clean and I'm dirtier than a mudhole."

"Are you very tired?" she asked.

"No, we got some sleep out there last night. Just let me get cleaned up and give me something to eat and I'll be in fine shape. I haven't seen you for so long that I want to talk. We can go to bed later."

"Kiss me once for now anyway," she said. "And I'll fill the bathtub."

She uncovered the tin bathtub and began to fill it from the reservoir of hot water at the side of the stove. Johnny peeled off his shirt and began to walk about the room, looking at things on the tables and shelves. He opened the bedroom door and looked in there, then walked to the back door, opened it and looked out into the woodshed. Julie watched him. He likes this place, she thought, he's been missing it; gosh, but I love him for that. I love him and want him so hard all the time it's just crazy, but I want to keep on doing it and I'm going to. There isn't anything else that's important anyway, and if there were I wouldn't want it.

"Gosh, darling," she said. "I've missed you."

He looked at her quickly and smiled. "You've got nothing on me," he said. "Heck, you've even had company." He touched her waist.

"Oh, him. He's not the same. He never will be."

"When you really get him you won't give a damn if I come home or not."

"I will too. Can I stay while you have your bath?"

"Sure, why not?" He began to take his clothes off. "Better lock the doors. If somebody came in your face would be plenty red."

"I shouldn't mind as much as you would," she said, but she locked the doors. She watched his wide back and the easy movement of muscles under the white skin. "What happened?" she asked.

"At the fire you mean? It's safe enough now, but we burned out every trestle we could burn out and let it loose over half the countryside. Alec had it bottled up once if they had just given him the bull-dozer soon enough."

"Was it dangerous? I was scared."

Johnny looked up and laughed. "Dangerous? I'll say not. They never are; just darned tedious."

"Your hair's singed and your clothes are full of holes."

"Little bits of sparks," he said. He held up his arm and showed her the red welt of a superficial burn. "That's the worst I've had out of any fire and that was carelessness. I leaned it on a hot limb."

"They took Shorty down to the hospital."

"Shorty's too much of a hero. He didn't need to ride

the front step that last trip down. He isn't very bad either."

"No, that's what they said. But it sounds dangerous just the same."

"That train crew did a peach of a job," Johnny said. "A bum crew would have let two of those donkeys burn —maybe more." He climbed out of the tub and began to dry himself. Julie watched him. I'm happy, she thought, more happy than anyone has ever been. This all feels so natural and right, having him come back and talk to me in his own way, quietly, about the things I want to hear. Other men would be tired and grouchy. And I love seeing him like this, with nothing between us except the good strong thing that you can feel—that he can feel too in the same way. He'll be too tired for that, he must be after all that time, nearly seventy hours, out there; but he will love me anyway, gently and with his strength held inside him; he'll hold me and talk and touch me, or if he's tired enough he will let me hold him.

"There was a letter from Mother last mail," she said.

"How are they up there?" Johnny asked. "Anything new?"

"Enid's going to marry Ron Cully right after New Year. He's got a good job down there as soon as he graduates.'

"That'll be a big day at the Sound. You'll have to go up there for it."

"It won't be there at all. Ron can't get away from California so Ma and Enid are going down. The Cullys have relations there, but Ma doesn't seem to like the idea much."

"Shouldn't think she would. That means both of you will have got married away from home."

"I know," Julie said. "Maybe that's why Mother wants me to go up home to have the baby."

Johnny looked up from drying his legs. "You're not going," he said. "It doesn't make any sense to go when there's a perfectly good hospital over at the Cove."

"I thought maybe I ought to go."

"Forget it. You can go to Vancouver if you want, but you're not going up there. Tell the old lady she can come down and be with you right through."

"Who'll look after the family if she does that?"

"Hell, let them get their own meals. I'll pay for a housekeeper if that's all it takes. But you're not going to have that baby any place but in a hospital. It isn't civilized."

Julie laughed. "Darling," she said. "I never knew you had such modern ideas."

"That isn't modern. It's just civilized and decent. Nobody has babies born in a common ordinary house any more."

While Johnny got into his clean clothes, Julie set the table and put supper on. When they were eating, she asked, "Will there be a shut-down right away?"

"In a few days. There may be some cleaning up to do, but that's all."

"For long?"

"All summer, so they say."

"We'll have a good summer then," Julie said. "We can make that camping trip, and go up home for a while and do everything we want to do."

"We'll have to go easy on the money."

"Who cares?" she said. "We shan't need much. And I'll have you all to myself, all day and every day and you won't ever be too tired."

Johnny laughed. "It sounds good when you say it like that. Just the same, we could have used another six or eight weeks' work."

"When will they open up again? Before or after?"

"Before that anyway," he said. "Early September or late August if it rains."

"That's all that matters, isn't it? So long as we're working then we can keep up with the doctor's bills and all those things."

"Sure. It just would have been easier the other way."

"Why will it be so long?"

"Alec figures they want it that way, to keep everybody broke so there won't be a chance to strike. He thinks they wouldn't let him have the bull-dozer because they wanted those trestles burned out."

"That's the sort of thing he gets so awful mad about, isn't it? Do you think he's right?"

"Shouldn't be surprised, the way it happened."

Julie was silent for a moment. She reached for his cup and poured coffee into it. "Johnny," she said at last. "If it is that way—I mean if they really do that sort of thing—doesn't that make Alec right about the rest of it? Don't the men need an organization to protect them?"

"It kind of looks that way."

"Would you help with it?"

"Why, sure, I guess so. If it got started right."

"Wouldn't you help with starting it?"

Timber

"That's not my kind of rig. I'm too dumb to do anything except tag along."

Julie stood up and began to clear away the dishes. "I think you could do it better than anybody."

"No. I can't get up and talk or figure things out ahead like they do. It takes one of those sorehead guys to do that."

"But you always say the boys haven't got any use for that kind. You haven't got use for them yourself."

"That's right," Johnny said. "But let's skip it for now. Alec will be on it all summer." He watched her as she moved about the kitchen; she was already heavy with the child, but straight-backed and proud, her strong legs and thighs carrying it easily. He thought: I surely picked me a good one. She's worth ten of me, any time, and yet I'm what she wants and we fit. They talk about married folks always quarreling and scrapping, but that doesn't happen with Julie; there's nothing about her a man could quarrel with. You always feel safe with her and sure about her because she's got sense and she wants the same things you do. If you say anything you know she'll understand it and if she says anything it's plain and straight and means what it says. "Honey," he said. "You sure are good to look at."

She turned round to him, smiling. "Like this?" She pressed her hands on her belly. "I'm huge and horrible. But I'll be slim for you again soon, darling, and you must want me hard."

"I want you hard all the time," he said. "It makes me proud just looking at you like that."

18

MARION DENTON slipped out of bed in the darkness. She could hear the hum of the locomotive's generator and knew that Stevie was firing up. Eric could sleep another fifteen or twenty minutes and it was better to let him. I'd like to wake him up and hold him and talk quietly for a little while, she thought, but he ought to sleep all he can. He'll be even more tired than usual tonight if he's got to get used to a new head brakeman.

She pulled the belt of her dressing gown tightly about her and went quietly into the kitchen. The locomotive headlight shone through the window on a slant against one wall and the hum of the generator was louder. I like the mornings, even the cold dark ones like this, and to be moving about and doing things while people are still asleep. I used to like it before I was married, going up to the school and getting things straight for the day with no one around; it's exciting for some reason and gives you a good feeling that you are getting a head start efficiently and quickly because there are no interruptions.

She lit paper and kindling in the woodstove and slipped several sticks of fir wood on to the red flame. Then she went across and opened the door to the children's room. They were still asleep, and that was good too; it always turned out a smoother day when Eric got away before

Timber

the children were up; and it only happened now, on the darkest mornings of the midwinter months.

She went back to the stove and stood by it for a minute or two, enjoying the sharp crackle of the cedar kindling. The kettle was full and she lifted a lid and set it over the naked flame. The humming whine of the locomotive's generator went on, as strong in the room as the sharp white beam of the headlight. When you switched the houselights on, the headlight was shut out and the sound of the genator seemed to fade with it unless you listened carefully. That was all right, but just now it seemed a good sound, the summons to a new day, a common, ordinary, good day. Sometimes—when Eric had to go out on a bad night for instance—both light and sound were different, sharper and with a pitch of breathless urgency that could be terrifying.

But it isn't quite an ordinary day. I've got to talk with Julie Holt this morning, try and find out what the boys are planning to do and how much she's had to do with it. It isn't like Johnny to be paying attention to strike talk at a time like this when we've only been working three months, but Eric says he is, and what Johnny does Eric will do. It must be Julie and that precious cousin of hers, and somehow I've got to talk sense into her. It won't be so easy either. She's nobody's fool, is Julie Holt, and she can be good and obstinate. But with that new baby she ought to see some sense. Part of the trouble is with me too; I always could handle boys more easily than girls and Julie's a lot like one of those big girls in school that you couldn't quite tell what to do with—too big to punish and too sure of themselves to listen to reason. And

I'm not going to quarrel with her; it wouldn't do any good and she's what makes this camp a place worth living in, after years of no one else but old Mrs. Tom Davidson and those squealing Italian women.

There was a good heat from the stove now, so she closed the draft, went back into the bedroom and lit a lamp. Eric was awake. "What time is it?" he asked.

"It's early still. You needn't hurry to get up."

"Come back for a minute."

She shook her head and smiled at him.

"Just for a minute."

"No," she said. "We'd stay too long and then you'd be hurrying off without a proper breakfast. Tonight, maybe."

"That's a long time away."

She began to get dressed. He said: "I forgot to tell you last night. Old Dad's talking again about quitting the mainline run."

"That seems to be as far as he ever gets with it."

"No, he says he really means it this time. He told Mark Evans a couple of weeks ago and he says he told them in the head office too."

"Do you think Evans will give you the job?"

"Dad told him and Dachman that that was what Chris was figuring on. He says there's no one else in line for it."

"That's a good reason for being careful, isn't it? About this strike business I mean."

"Oh, that. I wouldn't be any more than stringing along with the crowd anyway."

"That's not true, Eric. You know you've got a lot of influence."

"Well, I shan't be saying anything—just listening and voting in a secret ballot. I'm not even sure it will come to a vote; most of the boys seem pretty luke-warm about it so far."

"It's men like you and Johnny and Alec will make the difference."

"No," he said. "The bohunks don't pay any attention to us. They just do what the agitators tell them to. The rigging men and train crews might pay some attention to what Johnny and Alec say, but in a camp like this with a big crew of fallers and buckers that don't mean much."

"I still think you ought to be careful."

"Sure I'll be careful," he said. "I don't want to see a strike right now—for that matter I don't believe Johnny does either."

"I hope that's the way it comes out," she said. She finished fastening her dress. "Breakfast on the table in a few minutes."

Marion went back into the kitchen. It isn't good enough, she thought; he's too easy-going and if they work on him properly they can talk him into anything. What Alec Crawford said about the high-paid men not caring is worrying him now, but it isn't right he should worry; we've had our hard times, looking for jobs, waiting in town, going into debt, and now we've got the children to think of as well as ourselves. There was all that time before we were married when Eric wouldn't steady down and it looked as though no company would ever trust him to keep away from drinking. And then he got steady and they saw how good he was, until now he's almost sure of the mainline run. I ought to hate myself for thinking like this; generally I'm the one that is preaching to him about being unselfish and doing things for other people, but I'm not going back to all that misery of waiting and being nobody; it's all so good now and we can hold it together and begin to see ahead a little. You've go to look out for your own sometime and I'm the one that has to do the looking out for this family.

Eric came in and she put his breakfast in front of him and poured a cup of coffee for herself. "Do you know the new head brakeman?" she asked.

Eric nodded. "Kid named Stoney. Last I heard he was second-braking at Camp Five. Must have been to town and got his papers since then."

"It's a pity Shorty had to quit."

"Shorty needed a change. He's a good brakeman, but he's been sore at this outfit ever since the fire and he was getting so he didn't give a darn. A lot of the good guys have been getting the same way since Chris left."

He finished breakfast quickly, picked up his gauntlets and the faded blue coat and came back to kiss her. "Don't forget," she told him. "Let the others do the talking. You listen and do what you have to do, but no more."

"Don't worry," he said. "I'll watch my big mouth."

"I know you will. You're a swell person, Eric, and I've no right to tell you what to do. It's just that I'm worried for the children and all of us. Things are going so well now."

Walking the few steps from his house to the locomotive Eric made himself think of what she had said. He

Timber

glanced at the lighted window of Johnny's house; if Johnny goes for it, he thought, there's something to it; that's one square guy and if you let yourself go the way he goes you won't be far wrong. Just the same, what Marion says makes sense too; there's no call to stick your neck out—not when you've got a wife and family to think of.

He swung up into the cab of the locomotive and answered Stevie's good morning. The steel of the plates felt good under his thin-soled shoes and he thought: a guy worries too much about things outside the job. He gets to feel like somebody's pet dog instead of like a man. He looked about him at the cab, seeing the green leather cushion and the dollar watch that had been with him in other locomotives. The worn brass and steel handles, the hot smell of iron and steam, the warmth from the closed firebox, these things seemed to enclose and welcome him, to shut away all those other things that confused him and reduced him. He glanced at the steam gauge, then looked across the cab at Stevie. "What's that two-gun guy shooting up now?" he asked.

Stevie closed the pulp magazine and put it under his seat. He smiled apologetically. "I don't get the same kick out of it I used," he said. "Seems like they're all the same."

"I get more of a boot out of the detective ones. Them Westerns is kind of old-fashioned."

"I'm getting to feel that way myself," the boy said. "Say, Eric, you know anything about the new guy?"

"He's okay. Seems like it's his first time out head-braking. We could do to watch him close for a day or two."

Stevie nodded. "That's what I heard," he said. He turned in his seat and looked back from the cab. "He's there now. Switch is open. Want to go?"

Eric looked up at the dollar watch. "Sure."

Stevie reached up for the bell. Eric pulled the johnson bar towards him, released his brakes and touched the throttle. The train backed slowly into camp and pulled up. Stoney climbed up into the cab.

"How's she going, Eric?"

Eric pulled off a glove and shook his hand. "Fine," he said. "Meet Stevie Peters. Stevie's been firing for me over a year now." He looked down from the cab and saw Jake Halverson standing at the edge of the track.

"How are you fixed up there?" Halverson asked.

"Side One got empties at quitting time. I guess Side Two will be looking for them first thing."

"That's right. Johnny says he's loaded now. You can take the first train through to the foot of the lake, but you'll have to wait in camp for clearance. There's two speeders coming through from the Beach. Mr. Dachman ought to get in before you come down, but there's a load of surveyors going out on the lake spur."

"Okay." Eric turned back into the cab and glanced again at the dollar watch. "About time to pull out," he told Stoney.

Pushing the big Shay up against the grade, Eric felt fine. Getting a straight run down along the lake was a break—a couple of hours away from bullcooking, the everlasting switching and juggling of loads and empties that filled so much of every day. That's one thing that makes the mainline run worth a whole lot—that and having a hundred-and-twenty-ton straight-connected job instead of this geared-down outfit; not that the old Shay is a bad locomotive, he told himself, but she's built for this stuff, grades and bullcooking, a short haul and plenty slow.

As they switched the empties to Side Two Johnny came along to the cab. He said: "The organizers are coming in today." He was rolling a cigarette, looking at his hands.

"Hell," Eric said. "Dachman's coming in too. What's it going to be?"

"Not much, this close to a shut-down. I guess they'll hold a meeting tonight. Maybe start a strike fund." He was looking up now, smiling easily, as though Eric should find more in the words than he had spoken.

"You going?"

"Alec's set on it."

Eric saw Stoney's signal and reached forward to ease off the brakes. "I'll be seeing you," he said.

At the Y they coupled seven loads from Side Two to eight more from Side One. Eric got the brakeman's signal before he expected it. "The boy's fast," he told Stevie. Stevie nodded and gave a careless pull at the bell. Eric used the throttle and the train began to pick up speed on the level below the Y. Feeling the rolling weight behind him he thought again of what he had said to Stevie; hadn't remembered Stoney as any hell for fast—Jimmy Hart was always beefing about his being slow down at Camp Five. Suddenly he reached forward, shut off the throttle and began to ease on the brakes. He saw Stevie look across the cab in surprise. The train slowed a little, but not enough; then they were on down-grade. She began to pick up speed again, right away, with steam shut off. Eric tried the air again and the engine brakes. He thought quickly ahead along the line; half a mile of down-grade, a short level stretch, then the big curve where we met Ted that time; and after that, grade breaking down again all the way into camp. He grinned across the cab at Stevie. The boy's face was white and his eyes seemed very big and dark. Eric saw him jerk his head towards the window of the cab and knew he was asking whether to jump. He shook his head and shouted across to him above the clatter of wheels and gears and the sounds of steam.

"No. We can hold her when we hit the level. Lots of sand and I'll use the bar."

Stevie nodded. They came to the level. Eric released the flaming engine brakes, pulled the johnson bar back all the way and eased the steam to her. He gave her more. Plenty of sand. He could feel her holding up a little. But if she once gets over the hump, past the level and on to the down-grade, there'll be no arguing with her. She might make the big curve, but if she does she'll have too much speed for the one above camp. A guy could jump here and maybe get by with it. The wheels were gripping, sliding, gripping, then sliding again. He stared ahead, not wanting to look at Stevie, trying to judge his speed against the distance to the end of the level. She's slowing all the time. It's not so good to think of riding her till she jumps; but leave her now and she might make the curves and find open switches all the way down to the lake; that would look like hell. And if she got

Timber

beyond camp there are those speeders somewhere on the loose and it could be she'd even ride down far enough to find Dad Hutchins coming up. She's down as slow as she'll likely come now. If there's anything left of the engine brakes they ought to hold her. He shut off steam, centered the bar and tried the brakes. Couplings clattered behind him and he felt the bucking weight of the fifteen loads of logs. The locked wheels slid a little farther, then held the train back to a jarring stop. Eric sat, staring straight ahead, his hand still on the brake handle. Stevie stood up and seemed to shake himself.

"The son of a bitch," he said. "No wonder that coupling was fast."

"That's right," Eric said. "He never put the air through." He got up and let himself down from the cab. Stoney was standing at the side of the track, waiting for him.

"You goddamned son of a bitch," Eric said. "What do you want to do? Kill us all?"

Stoney said: "Go on, say it. You've a right to."

"I ought to knock your goddamned block off and then turn you in." Getting it said doesn't feel as good as it ought. What's the matter with me? Am I mad at this guy or just mad out of being scared? "Holy Jesus, man, there's lives on this train besides yours. And more of 'em down on the mainline. Getting out logs don't mean a thing alongside that. It's a damn cinch somebody's got to see you don't hire out with brakeman's papers again."

The second brakeman said: "Lay off the guy, Eric. He won't do it again."

"I shoulda learned something," Stoney said.

"I'd turn you in if I didn't know they'd blacklist you," Eric said. "Put the goddamn air through and let's get the hell out of here before somebody sees us."

He turned to Stevie and the second brakeman as Stoney went back along the train. "You guys keep shut about this. If they'd blacklist him for risking lives I wouldn't give a damn. They wouldn't; they'd do it for risking company property."

From the cab he looked back along the train and saw Stoney's signal. He set the bar forward and the train rolled again. Son of a bitch, he thought, he can ride the back end of her. Forget it, he told himself, you can't stay sore; you know the guy isn't going to do it again and there was nobody got hurt, was there? He leaned out of the window of the cab. Not even a flat wheel by the sound of it, hell knows why. Just forget the whole damn thing; you've got a break for once, a nice easy ride along the lake and nothing to worry about. You may as well enjoy it.

In camp he stopped the train between the office and the woodyard. "Show Stoney the track phone," he told the second brakeman. "We've got to get clearance from the Beach. There's a speeder out somewhere." He leaned back in his seat, put an elbow on the sill and settled himself to wait. Then he saw the little group of men in the woodyard. Stevie came across the cab and stood beside him. "What in hell's the performance?" he asked.

"Organizers," Eric said. "The guy doing the talking is McKenzie."

"A good guy?"

"No. A goddamn ranter. Glieverson's the only good one of the works. I guess he didn't get up here yet."

Stevie went back to his seat. "I don't go much on that stuff."

Eric looked over the group of men listening to McKenzie. The bullcook was there, and the night watchman; two or three wood-buckers, and a few men from the cookhouse. He turned back into the cab. "That McKenzie would shoot off his mouth to a couple of school girls if they'd stop to listen," he told Stevie. "We're liable to wait here ten or fifteen minutes. Let's see one of them Western books."

Inside the office Frederick Dachman stood with his back to the timekeeper, looking out the window. He turned from the window and asked abruptly: "What's that train stopped there for?"

The timekeeper said: "Clearance, I expect, Mr. Dachman."

Dachman turned back to the window. He was a large man, pale-faced and with pale hands. He wore a loose fawn topcoat and a broad-brimmed, dark green felt hat that looked new. His shoes were a pale tan color, square-toed—one noticed the clothes before the man or his face. He had blue eyes, a good nose, a soft, nervous mouth. His chin was closely shaved and the skin of his whole face suggested barber shops, hot towels, care and attention. Standing there at the window, he kept shifting his big weight impatiently and nervously on his feet. He did not like having to come up to the woods camps. In the Beach camp and at the sawmill he felt as comfortable and sure of himself as in his Vancouver office, but in the woods camps he felt always confused and at a loss. When Chris Eldridge was superintendent it had seldom been necessary to come up, and when it was necessary, Chris was always there as a support. Mark had been busy this morning and anyway Mark didn't give you the same feeling of confidence. Chris would have known what to do about these agitators. It seemed agreed that some concession had to be made at the moment if they were to avoid trouble after Christmas. Letting the organizers come up to camp had seemed a good gesture; but now, seeing them here, the whole thing seemed different. There was McKenzie talking in the woodyard to men who should have been working; and now the train, stopped alongside them, waiting for clearance, the timekeeper said.

He admitted to himself he was worried. It was one of those times that might call for some positive action and when such action might make the whole difference in the way things would go. Chris would have known what to do and when to do it. Chris would go out there and tell the train to move and the other men to get back to work—or he might, for some perfectly good reason that he would explain to you, decide to let things straighten themselves out.

Dachman turned away from the window, paced the length of the office and came back. He was tortured by some half-forgotten sensation and his mind struggled to place it. Somewhere, years earlier, he had felt it intensely —as strongly as now. It had touched him since then, but never strongly enough to demand recognition. He traced it back now through those half-felt moments. They were moments, he found, when he had been faced with some strong disagreement that tended, however remotely, towards physical violence—discharging a man, meeting a drunk, watching a street fight. Body contact. That was a phrase they used about games like football. Memory grew back into his mind, then flooded it so suddenly that his mouth was dry and he swallowed; the palms of his hands were sweating. That first year at college. "You're a big man; why don't you turn out for the football squad?" Kidding him about it. Being friendly about it, coaxing him, flattering him. Sometimes less friendly, even threatening. His own loathing of the close sight and sound of body crashing against body, of being held and hurt in front of people who would laugh and sneer at his frightened incompetence. The hate of it with him for weeks after they had all forgotten and left him alone.

He tore himself away from the memory and turned to the timekeeper again. "If they're waiting for clearance why in hell doesn't the brakeman come over and phone for it?"

"They use the track phones now, Mr. Dachman—it's a line straight through to the despatcher's office."

"Yes, yes, I remember," Dachman said. He turned to the window again. It was clear enough anyhow. They were stopped just to listen to the damned agitators. Denton had been active in the last strike—he had their names clear in his mind even now: Denton, Holt, Crawford, Davidson, Nelson, Nechak and a whole raft of others; too many to fire and Chris had said they were good men, but it was all on the files and it would be important to see how they behaved this time. He glanced along the string of loads; practically hundred-per-cent fir, and good logs too. Every stick of fir saleable now and for the next few months with the new C. and E. contract. At least they didn't know about that. And they said the trouble wasn't too strong—wages chiefly; that could be settled. And they would ask for union recognition and abolition of the blacklist—they always did. Queer how they hate the blacklist. It doesn't affect more than a very few of them and you would think they'd see that men with big investments have to protect themselves.

He looked at his watch. They've been down there at least fifteen minutes; that's time enough. If they can stop a train of logs in the middle of camp to listen to agitators they might as well be on strike now. He thought of going out, walking across, round the front of the locomotive, down to where Denton would be sitting in the cab—if he was in the cab and not down in the woodyard. Denton would be very sure of himself up there in the cab, in his big gloves and greasy overalls—they always were, those men, sitting in their locomotives, handling levers of donkey engines, standing easily on sloping logs; they were never hesitant or afraid. There could be some reason for the locomotive to stop there—so many things happened around a logging camp. Rigging breaking, trouble with the track or a trestle, with switching or a load off the track. Things you couldn't guess at or quite understand, and daren't open your mouth about for fear of showing you didn't understand.

But it wasn't anything like that now. It was simply a breakdown of discipline. Because the company had let the organizers come into camp they thought they had the upper hand and could do anything they liked, in or out of company time. Anything might grow out of an attitude like that. It was essential to keep things moving normally, prevent the organizers from gaining too much confidence. The right move now might make the whole difference to the eventual outcome of the thing. He straightened his shoulders and tightened the belt of his loose coat. "I'm going to see what's holding them up," he told the timekeeper.

Eric closed the magazine and tossed it across to Stevie. "Sure is a line of bull," he said. "Don't see how I ever used to get such a kick out of the stuff."

"Comes of marrying a schoolmarm," Stevie said. "She must have got you educated."

Eric laughed and looked out of the cab again. Stoney and the second brakeman had been listening to McKenzie and now they had turned away, laughing together at something. Stoney started along the track towards the phone box. Eric glanced at his watch; liable to be too soon yet; the despatcher had said twenty minutes. He looked out of the cab again and saw Dachman coming round the front of the locomotive. He thought: What in hell does he want? Going to try and run McKenzie off? Or maybe just wants to keep track of what he's telling the boys.

Dachman came down until he was standing under the window of the cab. "What in hell's the idea of stopping here?" he asked. "Holding everything up."

Eric felt a sharp surge of anger. "Orders," he said carelessly. Who in hell did the son of a bitch think he was, talking to a guy like that?

"Where's the fireman?" Dachman spoke sharply. Take the fellow off balance. Get him moving again before he knew what was happening.

Eric waved his left hand lazily towards Stevie. "In the cab, like he always is."

"Tell him to pull the bell and get to hell out of here. You can't keep a locomotive idle half the morning."

"Go tell him yourself." Eric spoke the words slowly and carefully, very sure of his ground. The guy was talking out of turn, telling a man to pull out without clearance, without even a brakeman on the train. What was the matter with him anyway? Trying to show his authority or scared we'll hear what McKenzie is saying or what?

Dachman had turned sharply and gone away. Stevie watched him go up the steps and into the office. He turned to Eric as the door slammed. "God, Eric, what did you have to do that for?"

"When a guy's that ignorant somebody's got to tell him."

"You sure enough told him. I guess he figures he's got some say if he's general manager and owns a slice of the company."

"If he's God Almighty he's still got no call to give orders he don't know nothing about." Eric thought: I could have let him down easier, I guess. I thought I was over getting sore like that, but it seems like everybody wants to wreck this train today. Anyway, he took it, didn't he? Must have known he was in the wrong.

Stoney came back along the track. "She's clear right through now," he said. "He says the Five Spot should be at the junction with the empties about the same time we get there."

"Okay," Eric said. "For God's sake, let's get moving." If the Five Spot's down there I'll get to say hello to Dad Hutchins. A couple of cracks from that old bastard is just what a guy needs to keep him from going bugs on a day like this. Him sitting there like a big fat frog in the cab of the Five Spot and talking slow and not giving a damn.

19

ALEC pushed up one of the gooseneck lamps, threw down his pencil and brushed the crumblings of eraser away from his map. He set his brown, long-muscled forearms on the edge of the drafting board, looked contentedly down at them for a moment, then moved his head to study the network of fine lines and neat figures on the wide sheet in front of him. It was a strong relief to be working on something new after the endless series of annual reports he had struggled over in the last weeks —plans of railroad construction, of logged acreage, spar tree by spar tree, figures on construction costs, details of the new trestles, comparison of cruise figures with water scale. Art handled the worst of the detail, thank God, but there were still plenty of loose ends to be pulled together once he was through, and somebody had to think up something pretty for the big boys, some new way of saying or showing the same old thing—Art hadn't much imagination for that stuff. All it adds up to is toys for the rich guys, so they can sit at a mahogany table and smoke cigars and talk awful wise about efficiency and cutting costs. Boy, how they can talk too; you'd think every one of them had put in at least ten years fighting hangups on a sidehill if you didn't listen too closely. At that, they do come through with a bright idea once in a while, so maybe it's worth it. And I guess they're entitled to know what in hell we've been doing with their good money.

It's the new stuff a guy gets a kick out of, though, like this map of the Snake Creek timber. They'll buy on that and it's a good job—cruise figures checking on the old 1914 cruise, broken down forty acres by forty acres into fir and balsam and cedar and spruce and hemlock. Contour lines checked too, and close enough to accurate. The main spur sketched in, switching off the Side One line around station 290—line 4KS it will be on the plans from now on. He leaned forward and worked quickly for a few moments, then sat back to look at a cross that marked the first spar tree on the spur and a lightly shaded area of timber that would come to it. I know that one, a big fir standing between two cedars; and the next one after that can be the spruce just beyond Mosquito Creek. Ted would have liked that line; there's big trees handy to it all the way along. And Chris would have liked the whole darn set-up as far as that goes—he always did like it. Every so often, when things weren't going so well, he'd say: "Wait till we get in that Snake Creek country; we'll sure make 'em roll then—we'll be running two shifts on the mainline locomotive if the market's anyway decent." And now here it was, all down on paper, better even than it had looked and the market fair enough and improving almost steadily; and no Chris to see it. I sure miss that guy. He's the only one of them that would understand what we've got here and jump right in and go to town on it. Evans will hum and haw about it, crab at having to bring in a skidder for the sidehill stuff, moan about not having enough cars to handle three sides and generally stall around till the cream of it is wasted. Chris says he feels a whole lot better down south, but I wish to hell he'd get to feeling good enough to come on back. It would be swell to go over all this with him and hear him spot the good points and figure how he could get the best out of it all.

I should worry about Chris though; I'll be damn lucky if I get to work on this proposition myself. Right now I wouldn't like to bet I'll ever see a stick of timber move out of there—not me or Johnny or Ed or anybody else who was at that meeting the other night, except maybe Charlie and old Tom Davidson. Not that it wasn't a good meeting—it went fine and Glieverson handled them just right, not too radical and yet not soft. But there weren't enough there; not more than twenty at the outside, and that leaves the works for us who were there right on the spot. And it isn't as if Dachman didn't warn me plenty right before, the prissy-mouthed bastard.

He thought of walking into the office and Dachman sitting by the stove, calling him over. "Got a minute to spare, Crawford?"

"Sure," walking round the counter and across the room.

"Sit down. That was a splendid job you did, getting us up into that good timber behind Camp Five. We thought we were going to have to switch-back twice to get in there, before you found that low pass behind the shoulder."

"Somebody had to stumble on it sooner or later."

"No, I don't think so. You stumble on those things too often for it to be just luck. That's what I wanted to talk to you about. You know, Crawford, you have what practically amounts to an executive position here. The company appreciates your value, but some of us feel you could be a little more co-operative in some ways."

"I try to figure it out the best way I can."

"I'm sure of that; we all realize you are thorough and conscientious. But we don't feel we have quite the close contact with you we should have. Of course, we see your reports and can judge what you are doing from them. But Mark Evans complains that he sees very little of you."

"Most of my work depends on co-operation with the camp foreman and the engineers. They see Mark whenever he's around."

"That's quite true. But it might be as well for you to go down to the Beach of your own accord once in a while. And I'm quite sure that if you found it necessary to come to town occasionally to talk things over with us at the head office, it would be very well received by all the company officers."

Boy, did that one ever have you fooled. A trip to town at the company's expense every so often and lots of time between boats to see Dolly or maybe Rita if Dolly wasn't in the mood. Trying to keep from grinning like a satisfied monkey when you said: "I ought to be able to work that out easily enough."

And then, and only then, the real point of the whole darned interview. "There is one more thing," Dachman's voice so soft and smooth you didn't realize what he was saying at first. "We haven't always felt that you have quite the right attitude in labor matters. I need hardly tell you that your future is very much bound up in this."

Why couldn't you tell him to go to hell right then? Tell him Morecombe's offered you better wages during the shut-down last summer? And Bill Chambers had said there was a job for you with his outfit any time you felt like a change? Because that's cheap stuff to talk, and after all the guy hadn't said anything bad by his reckoning. If you had a responsible job with the company you had one, that's all, and they had a right to tell you what they expected you to do. Just the same, it was a plain enough warning even if it wasn't straight talk. It left a guy so that he couldn't back down out of going to the meeting and couldn't even keep his mouth shut while he was there without feeling lower than a snake. If it had been a big meeting with the whole camp there, that might have been all right; but a little meeting made every guy there seem like a radical sorehead son of a bitch. And there was no protection for anybody.

Alec looked at his watch. Johnny and Julie wouldn't be in bed yet and it would be good to talk with them for a while; there hadn't been much chance since the meeting. He took the green eyeshade off and threw it down on the table, then reached for his mackinaw and went out. It was a cold night and the stars were bright all over a clear sky; a break in the weather, he thought, and thank God for it. I can make a long trip up Snake Creek tomorrow and blaze that line ahead some more; the creek will be plenty high after the rain and a guy ought to be able to get some idea of what those bridges will have to stand. I sure hope I get to see that line go in; it's a honey of a show up that valley and if they'll let us have the skidder from Camp Five we ought to be able to make it look like something. The other business is liable to blow over anyway. It's more than a week since the meeting and nobody's been fired yet.

He knocked on the door and Julie opened it. "It's Alec," she said and he saw that she was laughing and happy.

Johnny stood up and moved his chair. "Come on in. Once you get started on that office work we never seem to see you."

"How's young Alec?"

"He's asleep," Julie said. "You can see him at ten o'clock if you promise not to wake him up too much."

She moved a chair and Alec sat down. "Have you heard from up Kiltool lately?" he asked.

"Last mail day," Julie said. "They're all fine. Dad got a big silver-tip somewhere past the fork above the second lake and Dal shot two wolves on the way down. Mother says she's coming up to camp to see the baby soon as she's back from California. She's been planning ways to get to see him again ever since we came down that time after I got out of the hospital."

"When is the wedding due to come off?"

"Which one? Dal or Enid? Dal's pretty near finished building now and they think they'll get married the middle of next summer. Enid has set the day and everything —February eighth."

"Ought to be quite a show," Johnny said. "They do things right in California."

Alec laughed. "All of California isn't Hollywood. If there's part of the Cully family running it they'll keep the super-colossal angle down to size."

"They're rich," Julie said. "They own oil. That's how

Ron got his start so soon after getting through college."

"I know, but they're still U. E. Loyalists from New England, and that's steady stock."

"Enid's going to be happy with that man," Julie said. "She's always been crazy about doctors and chemists and scientists. And ever since she went down to high school in Vancouver that time she's wanted to get out and see places."

Alec nodded. "How do you feel?" he asked. "Not about Enid. I mean after the baby and all that."

"Fine. They take good care of you in the hospital and another good thing is the way they tell you how to look after the baby. He's no trouble at all when you do it right. It was swell having Mother there all the time too, and being up at the Sound after."

"That went the way it should," Johnny said. "It's certainly a whole lot better for women than it used to be." He moved his chair, reaching for the tobacco can on the table. "What did you really think of that meeting, Alec?"

"It was all right as far as it went. There was more sense talked in an hour and more business done than in any other half dozen I've been at. But there weren't enough guys there to make a good committee, let alone a union."

"You've got to start somewhere," Julie said.

"A start like that is as good as a finish," Alec told her.

"How do you mean?"

Alec lit a cigarette. "Just that. There's no reason on God's earth why the company can't fire every man that was there inside a month or two."

"That's the way I figured it," Johnny said. "We were

just plain sticking our necks out. But why didn't more come?"

"Different reasons, I guess. Mostly they thought it was the start of a company union or else a rigging men's union. Something a bit phoney some way. And I guess a lot of them were just plain scared."

"Big Mike was there. He packs a lot of weight with the fallers and buckers."

"I'm not so sure about that. They know Mike'd go any place with a smell of trouble about it. No, I kind of think we were the wrong guys to be running it."

"I don't," Julie said. "I think you were too easy about the whole thing. You didn't go after it hard enough and make enough of it. You were as scared as the rest of them, so you tried to treat it as if it was just something ordinary."

"You think we're out on a limb now?" Johnny asked.

"I know damn well I am," Alec said. "Dachman good as told me that before the meeting. I don't know about the rest of you."

"They aren't going to fire good workers just for going to a union meeting," Julie said. "They aren't allowed to anyway, by law."

Alec laughed. "No? There's plenty more good workers in town, guys that have been hungry for long enough to be sure and toe the line."

"Not men like you and Johnny, there aren't."

"Honey child," Alec said, "the way they're scared of unions they'd put an old-age pensioner to load Johnny's logs sooner than a good union man."

Someone knocked at the door and Julie went over and

opened it. Tom Davidson was standing there, awkward in his dark blue fisherman's sweater, his hat gripped in both hands in front of him. "I seen you folks hadn't gone to bed yet," he said. "I thought I'd come in to pass the time of day."

"It's good to see you, Tom," Johnny said. "You don't come over often. Where's the missus?"

"She's to home. Said she was kind of tired. She don't get around like she used since the rheumatism got bad."

He sorted himself out gradually, working slowly across the room as he talked until he found a chair and sat down. He was a short dark man, with calm eyes and a big mouth over chin and cheeks that seemed black with shaven beard. You could give that guy your heart, Alec thought, and he'd hold it gently and hand it back to you in better shape. But there's something on his mind now; he didn't come over here to be sociable. He's a real old-timer and he'll never get over being scared of having cute tricks like Julie and Marion around camp; he still doesn't know how he came to get hitched himself, let alone bring the old lady up to camp with him. Right now there's something special he wants to talk about.

Tom looked at Julie. "The missus said to be sure and ask how the baby is. I guess she thinks an old roughneck like me will forget about them things."

Julie said: "He's fine, Mr. Davidson. Mrs. Davidson has been awful good about helping out with him and he seems to have taken a real fancy to her."

"What's on your mind, Tom?" Johnny asked. "You look like somebody had taken your last dollar."

"I thought maybe you hadn't heard they let Eric out."

Timber

Alec sat forward sharply. "Eric?" he asked. "When?"

"Tonight, when he went up to the office for his paycheck."

Alec laughed, a short, hard laugh. "There she is, my children. The first head to roll into the basket."

"But he wasn't even at the meeting," Johnny said. "Marion talked to Julie about it and we told him to lay off till we had things under control. Who fired him, Tom? Jake?"

"No. It come from down below. Jake had a letter to say about how there was another engineer coming up and the Two Spot hadn't been run satisfactory—not responsible or something."

"That doesn't make sense. Eric's the best engineer on the claim, bar old Dad. Hell, he's better than the old man. I heard Chris say he was."

"They say he talked back to Dachman when he was up here," Tom said. "And there was a runaway up there below the Y and he didn't ever report it."

"You figure that's what it was?"

"Could have had something to do with it, more'n likely," Tom said. "Eric was on the strike committee a couple of years back and the company don't forget them things."

"He's only got to go to town to get another job," Johnny said. "Eric can hire out with most any outfit on the coast."

"He maybe can and maybe can't. It ain't always so easy to hire out again when one of the big outfits ties a can on you."

"God, I sure feel bad about that. Seems like there ought to be something a guy could do."

"Yes," Alec said. "Such as what?"

"If it was Ted or Chris we could go and talk with them."

"If it was Ted or Chris, Eric would be still on the job. Chris would have told Dachman to go chase himself sooner than fire Eric. Go talk to Mark Evans and see how far it gets you."

Listening to them, Julie felt for the first time that the union and all the talk about it was something real, something strong and dangerous, no longer an exciting plaything that might one day help to straighten out things that seemed distantly irritating and unfair. She was standing behind them and her hands went down to smooth her dress over her hips; she felt the firmness of her flesh and touched her belly, newly hard and flat, seeking the pleasure in its restoration that had grown in her daily since the child was born. The pleasure was no longer important, but she looked down at herself and thought: This is me, Julie; I'm a nice person and people like me, but this is happening to me; I'm a part of what they're talking about and it's real and it scares me. It's like having a baby in lots of ways. At first you think: That's such a big thing, for grown-up people, not for me. And then you start to do it and it doesn't seem so much after all, just exciting and fun, but not real. And then you begin to feel bad when you get up in the mornings; and after a while that passes but the baby is heavy in you and it gets in your way and makes things difficult, but you fit it into your life and it begins to be big and real. And you get scared, but you've got to go on, there's nothing else you can do about it. That's how this will happen—I know that now, tonight. In a little while I shall forget it and not know it, but it will be there and real, waiting to come back hard to me at the right time.

She said: "I thought when things happened like Eric getting fired, then the rest of the men went on strike. I thought that was how it's meant to work."

They had turned round and were looking at her and she felt she had said something silly and simple. Johnny said gently: "Yes, that's the way it's meant to work. But you aren't going to make them pay much attention to a dozen men striking out of two hundred and fifty."

"Couldn't you get more members?"

"Not quickly. If they give us till spring we'll have them. We could be ready for most anything by March or April."

"What was the trouble with the boys the other night, Tom?" Alec asked. "Why do you figure they didn't turn out?"

Tom Davidson looked down at his hands, clasping and unclasping the thick, awkward fingers. "They're queer animals, loggers," he said. "Right now they're like a bug between two fingernails. They don't know which scares them the most, the bosses or the organizers."

"They trust Glieverson."

"Sure, Glieve's all right. But they're remembering those other long-tongued shysters. It will be a long time before they forget the ride they took from those guys in the last strike."

"You don't think they figured it was a company union or just something for rigging men?"

"Some of them maybe. But mostly they're just scared. Jobs has been scarce a long time now and most of them are just beginning to get a little ahead."

"Then you think it isn't a good enough time to get a union started?"

"After the New Year it might be all right, like Johnny says. But mostly you can only get loggers to pull together when things is so bad they got to or so good they get feeling like they're Hughie himself and all his angels. Right now it's neither one thing nor the other."

"Did Eric say anything about when he'd be pulling out?"

"Soon as they get packed up, he said. He's good and sore because Dachman wasn't man enough to tell him to his face he was fired."

"Have you seen Mrs. Denton?" Julie asked.

Tom nodded. "She was in talking to the missus when he come back from the office. Seemed like she was going to take it pretty bad at first, then she got a hold of herself. But you could tell she was awful mad—not just sore like him, but deep down angry and no let-up. You could see it in her mouth and the way her eyes was; it scares a guy to see a woman mad like that."

The old hooktender stood up. "I'd best be moving," he said. "I just thought I'd let you folks know."

Julie saw him out of the door, mechanically easing him over the difficulties of his good-by. Poor Marion, she thought, you're going to hate me so you can't speak to me; but we didn't do it, any of us. The boys told him

Timber 285

to stay away from the meeting, almost forced him to. I did everything I told you I'd do that morning you came here. I understood what you meant and how it would be for him to lose that mainline job and why the children make it all so different. She turned to Johnny.

"Isn't there anything we can do?" she asked.

Johnny looked across at Alec. "I still think it ought to do some good to talk to Jake."

"All you'll get out of it is your walking papers," Alec said. "Don't ever think they aren't gunning for you just as hard as for anybody else. And who in hell do you think Jake Halverson is anyway? The guy hasn't got enough sand to tell his grandmother where she gets off at."

"I'd as soon go talk to him anyway. What do you think, Julie?"

"I don't think it will do any good, but I think you ought to try."

"Don't be a fool," Alec said. "You'll just be laying your neck on the block is all. Stick around and keep your mouth shut till the spring and maybe you'll have a chance to do some good. They know you can load logs like nobody's business and they don't figure you for a wild-eyed radical like they do me."

"You haven't got any feeling," Julie said. "All you think of is getting that union ahead and you don't care how many people it wrecks."

"I'm thinking of you," he said. "And little Alec. And I'm thinking of me and Eric and old Tom and Johnny and every other slave that drags logs out of the bush till he's too old or too crippled or they make up their minds to blacklist him. It's a racket you can't beat by any quiet talk with the damn push."

Johnny was putting on his coat. "I'll go up there anyway," he said. "I can't get any worse than fired. And if this is getting to be an outfit where a guy can't say what he thinks I don't know as I want to stick around it."

He went out of the door and started along the track towards the office. He could see there was a light still burning there. Jake isn't such a bad sort of guy, he thought; always seems reasonable enough and ready to meet anybody halfway. He is kind of soft with the big bugs—gives in to them easy and never seems to have any say of his own when they're around. Ted wasn't like that; I've seen Ted and Chris go at it hot and heavy for quite a while before they made up their minds who was going to have it his way. And when you talked to Ted you had a kind of feeling you got inside him; talking to Jake's different—he'll be agreeable and say "yes" and "sure" and "that's okay," but you feel it's all on the outside of him; he means it maybe, and he'll do it, but he hasn't got to know what you mean the way Ted would and he doesn't care much.

He pushed open the office door and went in. Jake Halverson put down the paper he was reading and said: "The door should have been locked. Timekeeper's gone to bed." Then he took his spectacles off. "Oh, it's you, Johnny. Want something?"

"Sure," Johnny said. "Got time to talk a few minutes?"

"What's on your mind?"

"About Eric Denton. Is that right he's let out?"

The foreman got up and walked over to the counter.

"I don't see how come it's any business of yours," he said. "But that's right. Denton didn't handle his job the way he should and he's going down the line."

Johnny took his elbows off the counter and stood up straight. "That's not the way you figured it."

"Maybe it is and maybe it isn't."

"Look, Jake," Johnny said. "They don't come much better engineers than Eric. Everybody around here knows that and firing him is just going to make bad feeling." He thought: Jesus, this is soft kind of talk. Seven or eight years ago a guy getting fired didn't mean a thing; he was ready to quit any time and a foreman had to be pretty damn quick to beat him to it. And when he was through with an outfit he just went to town and hired out somewhere else. But now it's not that way at all with most of them; seems like everybody's scared.

"It's no use talking to me," Halverson said. "I didn't fire the guy. That came right through from the head office."

"What did he do wrong?"

"Lay off it, Johnny. You don't have to know that and you're just making trouble for yourself."

"Yeah? What kind of trouble?"

"There's no need to get tough. I'm just trying to help you out."

"When I need help I'll holler for it. What kind of trouble, I asked you."

Halverson shrugged his shoulders and walked over to a filing cabinet. He searched through a sheaf of papers in one of the drawers, found a letter and threw it down on the counter. "I shouldn't show that to you," he said.

Johnny looked down at the single sheet of paper. "Attention Mr. Jake Halverson, Foreman, Camp Five," it read. "Complaints have been received that a high proportion of loads from Side Two at your camp have been bunk-bound, resulting in some cases in cars going off the track. You are urged to take immediate steps to remedy this and if the trouble persists you will replace the head-loader concerned." Johnny looked up from the letter in slow surprise. "Lovely God," he said. "Would you just tell me how many Side Two loads have jumped since you been running this camp? Go on—you tell me."

Halverson was looking down. "I don't know," he said. "I shouldn't have showed you that."

"I'll tell you. One load, back in October, down by the junction. A broken spring did that."

"Somebody must have kicked."

"You heard any kicks?"

"No, but there must have been some."

Halverson looked up quickly and looked away again as he met Johnny's hard eyes. Soft, Johnny thought, God Almighty, soft is right. The poor goddamned old son of a bitch hasn't even got guts enough to back it up. "What in hell ever made them think you could run a camp?" he asked. "You have the timekeeper make her out tomorrow morning, see? There's lots of outfits can use a good head-loader."

Halverson looked up again. He looked suddenly old and gentle and hurt, like an abused storekeeper. "Don't quit now, Johnny. You don't have to. I'm telling you for your own good. Just forget it and go back to work tomorrow."

"You aren't such a bad guy, Jake," Johnny said. "You mean well, but you're just an old woman, you let everybody climb all over you. Well, I don't. You see he has her made out tomorrow morning or I'll bust this goddamn office in little pieces. You're trying to tell me I'll get blacklisted. Okay, I'm calling that bluff too. I'm going to find out for myself, once and for all. And when I find out I won't forget."

He turned and went out of the office. Walking along the track towards the light where Julie and Alec were waiting he thought: You didn't have to tear it like that, you crazy bastard. Can't you ever get sore without breaking something in pieces; can't you learn to think, like Julie says, farther than just the way you feel when you're mad? That poor old sucker tried to give you a break, didn't he? Then he shook his head, answering the unspoken questions. No, a guy can't change when he's old as I am, not that much anyway. Bunk-bound loads. Hell, a man would have had to smile good and plenty when he said that two or three years ago if he didn't want to choke on his teeth. When an outfit gets to figuring that way about a guy it's time to pull out. You're only beating them to it anyway. If that poor old bastard didn't get up guts enough to fire you they'd do it over his head before long. I maybe shouldn't have done it, for Julie and the youngster. But I can tell Julie and she'll know how it was. Lots of women wouldn't, but Julie will. He smiled to himself in the darkness. She'll be just as goddamned mad as I am and when she calms down she'll tell me I shouldn't get mad.

20

ALEC came out of the main doorway of the big office building and stood for a moment in the pale January sunlight. There was no special place he had to go, nothing he had to do, but he didn't want to stay there; Chalmers might come out for some reason and see him, or there might be someone else he knew passing in or out. He turned along the street, walking towards Victory Square. When he came there he knew that that too was the wrong place. He thought: it's where all the bums end up when they get tired looking for a job—good and handy to the *Province* and *Sun* offices, the Employment Office, and all the big logging company offices. But not a bad place, at that, with the tiny space of green behind the white War Memorial and the pigeons always there and paths running diagonally across. He sat down on one of the benches.

The hell with Bill Chalmers. That was easy to say, but getting turned down by him was bad—"Nothing much around, let you know if anything turns up"; the usual put-off. And he always seemed like a pretty human sort of guy. Of course, he might be genuine and there are plenty of other chances without him; but it doesn't look so good, makes you think a bit. This hanging around town is bad anyway—no place to go, nothing to do all day long and having to watch the money end too. Two or three weeks is just right, everything's new and you don't see how you're going to get around to doing the things you want to do; but after that a man begins to feel kind of useless. There's Dolly, that's one good thing, but I'm not too sure I like the way it is there. And there's Johnny and Julie, but they don't want me hanging round their place all the time. Something I haven't done yet is go and look up Eric and Marion. Maybe I'd be smart not to—if Marion's still mad it would be kind of miserable and it would be liable to break things between us for good and all. But not going to see them is just as bad; that's the easiest way there is of breaking things up, standing off and figuring the other guy may be mad at you and letting that pile up between you until you never could climb over it to get back.

He reached into the pocket of his coat and pulled out a crumpled envelope with an address penciled on the back. Three blocks, straight up from here. Johnny says it's a lousy rooming house, worse than the one they're in. You'd think in a city this size they'd keep those things out a ways, hide them somewhere instead of parking them right in the center of town, next to all the big office buildings and the good stores.

He got up from the bench, walked the length of one of the diagonal paths and started up the street named on the envelope. It was a street of ownerless poverty—not the aggressive, squawling, child-ridden poverty of the slums, not the genteel poverty of a gradually deteriorating residential district, but the poverty of frame houses that had outlived their lives and been left to go on living. The paint had cracked or peeled or washed away from most of them, exposing the aging grayness of weathered lumber; they tottered on crumbled foundations, rotten steps sagged from porches without a full complement of boards, the lines of siding and shingles and gutters shambled out of level in a tired monotony of confusion. Some guy owns them, Alec thought, or some bank or real estate company waiting for a rise in property values. They rent them to poor people for more than poor people can afford to pay, so you get these everlasting signs up—"Room for Rent," "Housekeeping Rooms," and so on. And that sticks because it's a quiet street and close enough downtown for people to want them.

He found the house number, climbed the shaky steps and knocked at the curtained pane of glass in the door. Someone moved inside almost at once and the door opened sharply to a foot-wide crack. A woman's face, still young but hard-set and suspicious, asked briefly: "Well?"

"Mr. and Mrs. Denton home?"

The face disappeared but the door held rigidly at its narrow opening. Alec heard her shout back into the house: "Mis' Denton. There's a caller for you." He heard an answer and the door opened wider. "You're to go right up. First door straight in front of you at the top of the stairs."

Walking up, Alec thought: She's pretty near as bad as the old lady that was minding Red. She was used to having plain-clothes cops inquiring around, but you wouldn't figure that was true here. Maybe it's salesmen or just naturally protecting the house from scandal. If you don't know your boarders too well I guess you have to be suspicious of their callers. Sure is a hell of a way of making a person feel welcome though.

He knocked at the door and Marion opened it. "Why, Alec Crawford," she said. "Come on in, stranger."

Alec smiled. "I was wondering whether I hadn't better throw my hat in ahead of me."

"Hardly. We were talking about you only this morning and wondering when you'd show up."

Eric crossed the room behind her, his hand held out. "Sure is good to see you, Slim. I was beginning to think you never would come out of hiding."

Marion closed the door and they sat down in the small room. Alec said: "Where are the children?"

"Up at Mother's place," Marion said. "It's better for them there and we're better here while Eric's looking for a job."

"Nothing turned up yet?" Alec asked.

Eric shook his head. "No. And they're most of them operating again now. It's hard to get on."

"Shouldn't be. I've never yet seen the time there was too many good locomotive engineers."

"There's plenty of good men," Eric said. "But we ought to be able to get on some place sooner or later."

Marion uttered a little sharp sound of disgust. "Plenty of good men indeed. It took two good men to fill your place at Camp Four."

"That right?" Alec asked. "Have they put another locie on up there?"

Eric nodded. "They brought in the Climax from Camp Five and rented another Shay from some place to take over her work. They put old Pearcy to running the Two

Spot and he always was kind of slow, but he's a good man just the same."

Marion had begun to put out dishes for a meal and Alec said: "I didn't come to eat off you. I've got to move on right away."

"Nonsense," Marion said. "You can give us a couple of hours anyway. You're not that busy."

"I wouldn't want to claim to be busy," Alec said. "But I could have picked a better time to happen around."

"What did you do up there?" Eric asked. "We heard you quit."

"Just beat 'em to it, that's all. If I hadn't quit they'd have told me not to bother coming back after the Christmas shut-down."

"Over the strike meeting? Marion and I have been figuring you must be sore at us for running out on you, and that was why you hadn't shown up."

"Me sore at you? That's kind of good. I've been scared green to show myself because I thought Marion would still be sore at me. Johnny and Julie said she wasn't, but I figured they didn't know."

Marion shook her head slowly. "You were right all the time," she said. "I've learned my lesson now. I'll never hold back on a union again."

"Why so?"

"Didn't we get thrown out on our ear for no good reason at all after nearly seven years with one outfit? And aren't we blacklisted now so we can't get on there or any place else for the Lord knows how long?" Eric moved in his chair and she turned towards him. "Don't bother saying it. We don't know we're blacklisted. Of course, we don't. What difference does that make, except to make it worse and keep us hanging on here and expecting and hoping maybe we aren't when we really do know we are all the time? No, that maybe wasn't any time for a meeting, but it was a mistake in the right direction. The real mistake was not hanging on to what we had after the last strike. And I'm one that's not falling again for any soft line about holding on to the job and watching out for the kids. That's slavery, if it stops you doing what you know is right."

"I always knew you were the most solid of the bunch of us when it came right down to it," Alec said. "But I thought you were right holding Eric back when you did. I still think so, for that matter, because you had a good thing up there and there wasn't any sense in taking a chance."

"And look where not taking chances got us. At least you and Johnny managed to quit. We got fired."

Alec and Eric laughed at her. "Nothing like that to gripe a logger," Eric said. "Having some guy fire him before he can get around to quitting."

"For women," Alec said, "Marion and Julie are the darnedest old-fashioned loggers I ever saw."

"If you live long enough around the tame apes, you're bound to pick up some of their habits," Marion told him. "Did Johnny find anything yet? It's more than a week since we've seen them."

"Not so far as I know. We aren't any of us what you could call in demand."

"Hell," Eric said. "You can always get work. You don't have to hire out the way we do."

"You might be right, but there's nobody falling over themselves to hire me right now. If I don't get something in the next two or three weeks I'm going to head north and take a look around. I wanted to go up Kiltool before the duck season was out, but Johnny and Julie wouldn't go."

"That's where they ought to go," Marion said. "Julie and the baby anyway. Maybe Johnny would want to stay on in town to keep in touch with things."

"Julie won't go without Johnny and he says he won't go up and live off her folks when he's got no job. If he knew for sure there was something coming up it would be okay, he says, but not the way it is now."

"He's as bad as Eric. Eric figures he has to pay the folks for the children's board because we haven't got work, and they've stayed up there a dozen other times and there's been no talk of board."

"That's different," Eric said. "They were just visiting then. Now there's a need for them to be there. . . ."

It was dark when Alec left the Dentons. He felt better for having been with them. It was good to know Marion wasn't sore and at least Eric wasn't rattled about the way things were; worried maybe, but still kind of sure of himself and expecting something to break. They're likely all right for money, after those years of eleven-hour days— that three-hours' overtime for the train crew, hauling men to and from work, mounts up to quite a bit over a period.

He felt too good to go back to his own room and let it all drain away in an evening alone. The only thing was to make a night of it, go and see Dolly and talk her into going some place to dinner and then a movie; she'd be home by this time. He started up the street, walking fast, then turned off and went down several blocks to Granville. If you've got to be in town you may as well get the most out of it—see the lights and the people and the store windows; that's always good and warm and friendly and it sets you up somehow, like a couple of quick drinks.

He could see the light along the edges of Dolly's curtains when he came to the house—you used to be able to see it through the old ones, but these new ones were thick and heavy—and he went straight up. He heard her coming across to the door—the solid, proud set of her heels on the floor and the rustle of the long house coat he knew she would be wearing; just that made the blood hot in his face and excitement strong in his body. Then she opened the door and he saw her quick frown.

"Alec," she said. "What are you doing here?"

"I just came up. I thought you might like to go places."

"I told you always to phone first!" Her voice and eyes were angry. "That doesn't seem much to ask." She moved her head as though to shake the groomed hair back about her shoulders. "Well, now you're here I suppose you may as well come in."

She turned and led the way into the living room. Alec shut the door and followed her. So that's the way it is, he thought, she's afraid I might stop in some time when Arthur Dealy's here. If she wants to get sore about that I can get sore too, good and sore.

Dolly turned and faced him. "You just haven't got any consideration at all, Alec. I ask you a simple thing like that, just to phone before you come up, and you can't do it. I don't know why I didn't slam the door in your face."

"What's so bad in not phoning? I was up this way so I thought I'd stop in. Do I have to get a permit or something?"

"You know perfectly well why I asked you to do that. The trouble with you is you think you can do anything you damn please just because a girl has once said she can stand the sight of you. It's not that way around here."

"That goddamned Arthur," Alec said. "How many guys do you think you can keep on strings at one time?"

"If you don't like it you know what you can do about it. Nobody's asking you to stick around."

"I don't see what difference phoning would make. Suppose he answered the phone?"

"He wouldn't," Dolly said. "He's too much of a gentleman for that. Anyway, I don't want to argue about it. That's how I want it and if you don't want to play that way you can keep out altogether."

"What's the guy got that I haven't got? Why don't you make him phone to make sure I'm not here?"

"He does, only he doesn't know about you."

"So that makes a dandy set-up for you to two-time both of us."

"I'm not two-timing anybody. I'm going to marry him. Don't you understand?—marry him. That's different."

"I see. And until then you just hold hands and he gives you expensive presents and God knows what all else."

Dolly sat down on the couch and began to cry. "Damn

you, Alec. Why do you have to be so mean? You do things your way, why can't I do things my way without getting called names? I give you what you want, don't I?" She looked up at him and for a moment she was proud and angry again. "More of it than you can ever use. And I give Arthur what he wants. What's wrong with that?"

She was crying again. Looking down at her crumpled magnificence, Alec was suddenly sorry. Damn me for a fool, he thought, why do I have to do things like that? I've never wanted her this way, all beaten down like that —that's not the way she is, not what she's for. And what the hell claim have I got on her? I've never said I'd marry her or even bought her a present that amounted to anything. He knelt beside her and put his arm around her. "I'm sorry, Dolly," he said.

"Oh, it's all right. Nothing like that really matters. It hurts, but it doesn't matter."

"Are you really going to marry this guy?"

She nodded without looking up. "Sure I am. What else is there to do? Go on working in the store till my feet drop off or I get fired or something?"

"Do you like him?"

"Sure. He's swell in his way—he doesn't want much and he's kind and gencrous and easy-going. He's the sort that takes care of you no matter what happens, and he'll always be in a position to take care of you."

"Would you marry me if I got a good job and promised to look after you?"

Dolly looked up. Alec saw she was laughing now. "I should say I would not. You don't know how to look after a girl. You will one day, maybe, but right now you don't. You're the sort that has to be looked after."

"Hell, I'm not that helpless."

"Yes, you are. Most men are, the interesting ones. They sometimes learn as they grow older, but you don't find them running round loose then."

"How soon are you going to marry him?"

"Pretty soon now. Sometime in the summer. He's building a house for us."

"How do you know he's not kidding you along?"

"I know," Dolly said. She got up and went into the bedroom. A moment later she came back and threw a little box across to the couch. "Take a look," she said. "I'm going to straighten my face."

Alec picked up the box and opened it. The center of the ring was a fine sapphire and on either side of it two large diamonds were nested in clusters of small diamonds. Damn the guy anyway, he thought, how does he get so he can give women that kind of thing? I don't even begin to know what it's worth—could just as well be five thousand as five hundred for all I know. Looking at the bright thing he was suddenly conscious of the heavy, exciting scent that Dolly used, all about him in the room. It sort of chokes you with wanting her. If I smelt that anywhere in the world, any time, I'd start wanting Dolly. That's the kind of a woman she is—almost any man is bound to want her. I wonder if Dealy knows that and what he figures to do about it. And what is she going to do about it, because it isn't just men wanting her. Hell, she's doped it out some way. She's too smart not to have.

Dolly came back into the room and he saw she had

fresh lipstick and powder on. "What do you think of it?" she asked.

"They don't grow on trees."

She sat on the couch again, then reached over and took the ring out of the box and put it on. "It's beautiful. You can see a man's pretty nice when he gives you a thing like that because he's going to marry you, can't you? Especially when you know he's not so rich he doesn't feel it."

"Makes me feel like a heel," Alec said. "Maybe I ought to go."

Dolly looked at him quickly, her eyes wide and almost frightened. "Don't be like that, Alec. I need you. He's not the same as you are—you know that."

Alec looked down at her face. He let himself see her wide eyes, the full smooth lines of her cheeks and neck, the straight nose and waiting mouth; and all of it against that pale perfect hair, knowing the crown it made was the crown of a body fitted to bear it. He reached down and brought her up to him. "What difference does any of it make?" he said. "We're ours for now and nobody can change that." After a little while she leaned back from him and he asked her: "Do you want to go some place?"

She shook her head, smiling. "Not now. Later, maybe. You'll be hungry then, darling. We both will."

21

THE April sun was bright across the room through the open window, lighting a wide square of the ugly smoke-subdued wallpaper with a brilliance that cleansed it and gave it life. The baby was lying wide-eyed and silent in his crib, watching the gleam and movement of dust specks in the light. Julie stood at the little ovenless gas range, stirring something in a pot and stopping occasionally to taste it. She turned towards the crib and saw the baby's open eyes. "Why didn't you say you were awake?" she asked. "You're too good, honey. If you don't learn to holler you'll never get anything in this world."

At the sound of her voice the baby made a little gurgling sound and raised his arms above his head in a quick, jerky movement. Julie came quickly across the room and picked him up. Then she sat down on the bed, opened her dress and began to feed him. He fed eagerly, pushing his fists against her breast and sucking hard at the nipple. She held him away for a moment, then let him come back. "That's for being too rough," she said. "This has got to stop soon anyway; you're getting too big. For six months before you were born you made your mother look like an old squaw and now you've been using her this way for another six months—no, more than that now. There's other people besides you in this family have got a stake in the way Julie looks."

He looked up at her as she talked, his round blue eyes wondering and content. Julie forgot him and looked about the room. It isn't bad, she thought, with some of our own things out and the sunlight in it today. That smell of everybody else's cooking is bad, but you get so used to it you don't notice it most of the time. I suppose I ought to be miserable—people are supposed to be when they are like us, out of a job for months and months—but I'm not, even a little bit. I'm just plain all-the-time happy. Of course, we don't have to be very scared about money yet. There's the doctor's bills and the hospital bills, but we had those worked down before we ever left camp. And we've been careful, so there's still enough for room rent and food—for a while anyhow. I wish Johnny could get work where he wants, but he doesn't mind so much as I thought he would. He used to get mad at first, when he thought maybe they didn't want him because he wasn't good; but there's Eric and Alec and him and some of the others too, all trying to get work and not getting it, and he knows they're good. That makes him mad too, but a different kind of mad that doesn't hurt him the same way as the other. The only think I'm afraid is that he'll give up trying and get himself work in town somewhere. I don't want that. He wouldn't be happy that way, and it wouldn't be right. He's too good a logger not to stay being a logger.

She felt the baby's gums hard on her nipple and looked down at him, smiling. "That's naughty," she said and moved him a little. It is naughty, too, she thought; it's like—well, it's like something else and I like it. I wouldn't think that if I was a nice person. Yes, I would though;

people can't help what they think, they just think it before they know and there it is; a nice person would pretend she hadn't thought it, but that's just silly. It's kind of fun anyway and it doesn't seem so very bad. He came out of people loving that way and one day he's going to love a girl that way himself. I hope she's beautiful and does things for him, does them hard, hard, like I do for Johnny. That's what people are for; it's just a waste being beautiful and young and not loving hard. That's why I'm happy and why Johnny's happy and why it doesn't matter not getting work for a little while.

She heard Johnny's steps on the stairs and moved the baby again as he opened the door and came in.

"Hello, darling," she said. "There's something good for dinner. I'll give it to you in a minute."

He came over and stood watching the baby draw the milk from her. "Boy," he said. "He's strong. Look at those fists."

"Why wouldn't he be?" Julie asked. "You should have seen him when he started in. He's almost asleep now." She stood up. "Here, you can have him while I put dinner on the table. He's not hungry any more."

Johnny put the child back in the crib and began to play with him. "I went down to the Employment Office this morning," he said.

"No good?"

"Nothing with the big outfits still. There's some contractor with a gyppo outfit on the mainland wants a head loader and a second. It wasn't on the board—the guy at the desk told me."

"Did you take it?"

"No. He said it would be okay to think it over till tomorrow."

"What else?" Julie asked.

"How do you know there's anything else?"

"I just do."

"A guy told me a way to get a union card and get on longshoring."

Julie was reaching across the table to set down a plate. She stopped, still holding it. "You're not going to?"

"I thought it might be better than a haywire outfit. Staying in town that way a person could go on looking for a real job."

Julie shook her head. "No," she said. "It would be wrong. You mustn't change like that. People aren't meant to—not when they're good."

"Seems I'm not good enough to get on with a decent outfit."

"You know it isn't that."

"I'm not sure. Eric isn't either. Alec is, but then Alec would be."

"Did you see him this morning?"

Johnny nodded and came across to the table. "He's talking about joining the Mac-Paps."

"What's that?"

"Some outfit that goes over to Spain to fight in the civil war. Alec says there's quite a few loggers gone with them. Seems Glieverson's mixed up in it some way; he's not going himself but he helps with getting them organized to go."

"That's the craziest thing I ever heard of," Julie said.

"That's what I told him. I said there isn't any sense

to going over to Europe to get killed in a quarrel that isn't any of your business anyway, and he said it's everybody's business what's happening there. I said maybe that was right with both sides murdering all the ordinary, common people and then calling in other countries to help with the murdering. And that made him kind of mad."

"Do you think he'll go?"

"No. It's just an idea. He's feeling low right now because he heard Morecombe's were looking for a check cruiser and when he went up to the office yesterday they told him they hadn't got anything. That's the outfit offered Alec higher wages to go work for them only last summer."

Julie got up from the table. "More?" she asked.

"Sure. It's good. What is it?"

"Stew."

"I know that, but what's it got in it?"

"Pot-herbs," Julie said. "Thyme and marjoram and something else. Mrs. McCormick grows them in the backyard and they're just coming on now."

"Makes it darned good," Johnny said. "Another thing Alec said. There's a brother of yours in town." He watched her, smiling a little. She pushed her chair back and looked across the table at him.

"John Gordon Holt," she said. "Do you have to take a whole meal to tell me that? Which one is it?"

"Which one do you think?"

"Dal?"

"No."

"Don't be mean, darling. I'm not going to go through the whole nine of them trying to guess. Tell me."

"It's Davey. He brought his boat down to do some work on it before the trolling season. I'm going to meet him and Alec at the Montenegro later this afternoon and we'll all come back here for supper."

"Can we have a party, Johnny, a real one?"

"You bet your sweet life we will. I'll pick up a couple of bottles on the way home. You go out and buy grub this afternoon and get Mrs. McCormick to help you."

"What about money?"

"We can loosen up a little. Inside a week now we'll be loading logs or loading ships, one or the other."

"Loading logs," she said.

He walked round the table, lifted her out of her chair and held her hard to him. "You want that? At five and a quarter a day?"

"I'd take it at three," she said.

"It won't be like Camp Four. It'll be a lot worse dump than that. Still want it?"

"Yes."

"I'll see how it is then."

Johnny went early to the beer parlor and sat alone with his beer, waiting for the others. It was good to have a reason for being there, to know that there was going to be something happy and new for Julie in the hours ahead. Julie likes good times, he thought, nothing crazy-wild, but just good times and she's sure been swell all this time, living in that lousy little room there with nothing to do and nothing to think about. A guy can do a lot of figuring and not get to know why she's the way she is, so much with a person all the time that she's a part of him. She's never seen a log put on a car so far as I know, yet she'll listen about the job and talk about it better than most loaders; and she knows how a man feels about the woods and wanting to keep working there because that's what he knows. There isn't any goddamned reason I can see why she wouldn't be far better off if I was to get work here in town, but she doesn't want that—or she says she doesn't. No, it's right she doesn't, you can tell that; but it's hard to see a reason for it, except that she's part of you some way you can't tell about.

He pushed his glass away and leaned back to look across the room. There were few people at the tables but as he looked a man got up and came across to him. He was an elderly man, with untidy gray hair, stooped and thin. Johnny looked at the long face, loose-jawed and with sharp downward-drooping nose; I know the guy, but who in hell is he? The old man dragged up a chair and sat down. "Mind if I set here?" he asked.

"Help yourself," Johnny said. He's one of the guys at the Employment Office, clerk or something.

"Name's Dennison," the man said. "Hilary Dennison, God knows why. I know yours from the Office."

"That's right," Johnny said. "I've seen you there." He held up two fingers and a waiter came over with more beer.

Dennison lifted his glass and took a long thirsty swallow. Johnny watched the thin neck gulping; you like the stuff, he thought—more than's good for you. Dennison put the glass down and looked at Johnny with his tired, bloodshot eyes. "So you didn't get out yet, eh, son?"

"No. Seems like your outfit's quit hiring loggers these days."

The old man laughed. "You might have something there, boy, that's a fact you might." He stopped laughing. "But you ain't," he shook his head slowly. "They're still hiring out loggers."

"Sometimes you wouldn't know it," Johnny said.

The old man leaned forward, then glanced back over his shoulder and beckoned to the waiter. "Two more," he said. "I'll buy this one." He leaned forward again. "Listen, son, I been watching you. Somebody ain't wised you up yet. You better take what you can get down at the Office. You ain't going to get out with one of the big outfits."

Johnny leaned back in his chair and when he spoke his voice was slow and edged. "Who says so?" This is it, he thought, and when it comes I'm going to want to paste someone, good and hard.

"I'm saying so. You don't have to take it if you don't want, but it's straight stuff." Dennison reached forward for the fresh glass and drank it down. "I've watched you a long time, longer than you know about. I seen the time you fought the nigger from Seattle and I sure hate to see a good guy get the brush-off the way you're getting it."

"What's the matter? Some son of a bitch figure I can't load logs any more?"

"Could be." The old man spoke cautiously, stopping to glance over his shoulder. Then he laughed his weak, rattling laugh again. "But it ain't. The big outfits got something on you. You know what, or maybe you don't, but this is straight dope I'm giving you, straight as you'll get."

"I've a mind to choke the rest of it out of you."

Dennison shook his head. "You wouldn't do that, bud. You know when a guy's trying to help out. You hire out with the first thing that comes up, like that gyppo at Yellow River this morning."

"Your brother got a stake in that outfit or something?"

"That's okay," Dennison said. "Joke all you want. But you take her the way she looks, even if it ain't so good. It won't be for long if you keep a tight mouth on you. Not more than two or three years. I've watched it lots of times."

Johnny signaled for beer. Dennison shook his head and got up. "I've had enough," he said. "Maybe too much. It's time I got out of here."

Johnny held out his hand. "Thanks," he said.

Dennison took the hand and looked down at it. "God Almighty," he said. "That's the one put the nigger down, ain't it?" He dropped the hand and turned away. "God Almighty," he said again.

Johnny watched him shuffling his way among the tables towards the door, head down and shoulders bowed. I guess that's as close as a guy'll ever come to the straight stuff, he thought. I might have known that was the way it would come. They've sure got the thing sewed up tight the way they want it—you can get sore as you want and there isn't a damn thing to pin it on. You can't do anything about it, just take it, that's all. I guess I'm lucky. They say some guys can't get on anywhere ever again and so they just lay in town and rot. Not good guys though;

Timber

it couldn't be with good guys because there aren't enough of them. That talk about guys that haven't worked for years, Alec and McKenzie and the rest of them, but they aren't guys you've ever heard of. But that's the way it is; you don't know whether they are good or not; you can't ever be sure. That's the way they want it. Alec says it doesn't matter whether a guy is good or not; if he's a logger he ought to be able to get out in the woods and get paid for it. But I've seen Alec fire guys—he fired that compass man for being slow and he fired half a rigging crew when he was side-push for Ted that time. If he doesn't want them, who else does he think is going to want them? Hell, I can't figure it out the way he does at all.

He saw Alec come in through the swinging door and hesitate a moment, looking about the room. A young, slim, brown-faced man was with him. They came over to the table and Alec said: "This is Davey, Johnny."

"Glad to know you," Davey said. "They talk enough about you up home."

"Julie talks plenty about you," Johnny said. "So does that kid brother of yours at the Sound."

They laughed and Johnny watched his brother-in-law as they sat down. Davey's face was gentle, almost delicate, yet the even features were very strong. He leaned back now, looking about the room and paying no attention to what Johnny and Alec were saying. He's like Julie and Alec, Johnny thought, but it's all smaller and lighter, less real somehow. He watched the sharp, straight nose and the soft mouth, shaped as Julie's was but not full-lipped like hers; the brown skin over the face was thin and fine, very smooth and tightly stretched. The eyes, turning back to him suddenly, were dark and straight, so that you looked into them and saw nothing else. "Alec says things are kind of tough in town right now," Davey said.

Johnny watched the dark eyes cautiously. He felt suddenly a need to defend the way he lived. If he was a good man a logger could always get out somewhere; and if things were kind of haywire for the time being and not the way they used to be a guy didn't have to go shouting it all over hell. "She's been kind of slow," he said. "But I've seen it worse."

Alec laughed. "Worse is good," he said. "We've only been hunting jobs since December."

"I figure to get out around the end of the week," Johnny said.

Alec straightened in his chair. "The hell you say. Doing what?"

"Head-loading. Up at Yellow River. They pay five and a quarter and there's a call for a head and second down at the Employment Office."

"That's a jerkwater outfit if there ever was one," Alec said. "Run like a second-rate comfort station. You'll be lucky if you work four days a week with that bunch of haywire they've got for machinery."

"May as well give her a try. Julie wants it and I'm sure enough sick of hanging round that Office."

"It's a job," Davey said. "That's something when a guy's been around town a while."

"It shouldn't be," Alec said. "Not when a man is one of the best in his line."

"That don't seem to count for much now," Davey said

quietly. "They want guys they can depend on to knuckle under."

Johnny looked across at him. The quiet words were hard and bitter; Alec might have said the same thing or McKenzie or Glieverson, and it would have been mechanical and easy, not the way Davey said it at all. "Is fishing the same way?" he asked.

"They find ways to make it tough for a guy with too many ideas."

"You've got a union," Alec said.

Davey laughed. "Half a dozen of 'em. And there's half a dozen different kinds of gear fishing. The boys never know whether they're sorest at the cannery owners or the guys using different gear from themselves. That's the real trouble. Too many people trying to catch too few fish."

"You get your share."

"I make out. I've got a good boat and I've been at it awhile. Just the same I'd like to see some sort of control on salmon—like there is on halibut for instance."

"That's something different. That's conservation."

"Gets back to organization again. It'll have to come from the guys down below—the owners will never do it. Same with you loggers—there's too many of you making a living off too few trees. One day it will catch up with you and then nobody will be making a decent wage."

Johnny signaled for more beer and he and Davey went on with the argument. Alec thought: What in hell's got into Johnny that he's figuring on going up to Yellow River? He's never worked any place except big outfits before and he hates haywire worse than anyone I know.

There's something got into him to change his mind since this morning.

He reached for his beer and stared gloomily at the full glass. Staying in town with Johnny and Julie gone will be plain hell and it sure doesn't look like I'll get out in any hurry after what old Jack Morecombe said yesterday. How was it he said that at the end? "You may find it difficult to get a position right now, Crawford. There's not much opening up, and the companies are mighty particular about finding steady, dependable men." And I was slow enough to let that go without calling him. That's the sort of blacklist I'm on—some guy like Dachman just has to say a couple of words at a lunch club or a meeting somewhere and they all know they don't want Alec Crawford until he learns some sense.

Johnny said: "What's the matter, Alec? You look like somebody was dying on you."

"Can't a guy think?" Alec said. "Let's get going, for God's sake. We've got to stop at the liquor store and we don't want to be late for Julie's meal."

Sitting in the room after supper, Alec said: "Where do you want to go, Julie? A movie? Or we could get two more girls and go dancing?"

"Let's stay right here," Julie said, "and talk the way we used to up at camp. It's so long since I've seen Davey he's like a whole new person I've never talked to before."

Johnny sat down on the bed. "It may be your last chance to go places for quite a while, Julie."

Julie felt her heart suddenly quick and light in her. "Do you mean we'll go up to that job?"

"Likely. If it's still open tomorrow."

"That's the best thing I've heard since we left camp."

"What'll you do?" Davey asked. "Pull out right away?"

"Guess I'll have to look around up there before Julie comes," Johnny said.

Pouring hot water on to the sugar and rum in the glasses, Alec thought: Then they really will be going. That'll be bad, so goddamned bad I'm going to have to do something about it, get the hell out of this lousy burg on the first hitch that offers. That's crazy too. There's Dolly—I can't just walk out on her when it's better than it's ever been. And yet why not? It's got to break up sooner or later; I can't stay in town forever unless I'm going to starve, and even if I could she's set on marrying that guy in a couple of months and I'm not going to stick around after that. There's plenty of people to see in town besides Dolly—Eric and Marion for two and the bunch from the blueprint office. But it's been years since I didn't count on seeing Johnny the next hour or the next day or the next week, some time soon enough so it didn't matter anyway. And I guess it's been more than ever that way since there's been Julie as well.

He turned round suddenly, the kettle still in his hand, and looked across the room at Johnny. "Did you say they could use a second-loader up there too?"

"That's right. Why?"

"How's chances to come along?"

"Sure. Four bucks a day in a haywire outfit. Don't be a fool, Alec. You were through slinging tongs years ago."

"Why can't he come?" Julie said. "That way we could

stay together and when something breaks it will break for all of us."

"There's some sense to that," Alec said. "Good for you, Julie."

Johnny shook his head slowly. "You're crazy. You've only got to stick around town a bit longer and you'll get what you're looking for."

"Let him come, Johnny," Julie said. "He can quit as soon as something turns up."

"Hell, I can't stop him. I want him to come. It just doesn't seem right, that's all. There's plenty of weak heads and strong backs to sling tongs."

Davey watched them, smiling his quiet smile. He felt something between them, close and strong, that left him out. They're loggers, he thought, all three of them, Julie just as much as Alec and Johnny; that ties them together the way trollers tie together in a bunch of other fishermen—or in a logging camp for that matter; get two or three trollers working out a winter in a camp and they'll always hang together. And then there always has been something between Julie and Alec. They used to scrap all the time when they were kids up at the Sound, but they always used to go off together up the river or in the woods and if one of them got in a fight with the other kids the other would always come in to help and they'd be together again then. I used to think they'd get married one day, especially when Julie went away to town and had a chance to change and grow up where Alec couldn't see her. But they're still just about the same as they used to be and Julie thinks the whole world of this big blond guy—he's a swell guy too and away different from both of them; perhaps that's been the trouble; they're too much alike, more brother and sister than anything else.

Julie said to him: "You're keeping awful quiet over there, Davey. What do you think?"

"I think you all worry too much about a little while. If Alec wants to go up, why shouldn't he? I'm darn sure of one thnig—he's too ambitious to stay there any longer than is good for him."

"How long do you figure to stay, Johnny?" Alec asked.

"I don't know. I guess I wouldn't be in any hurry to quit if they treated a guy right."

"By Davey's figuring that makes you out kind of unambitious."

"No," Davey said. "It's different for Johnny. He's got ambition but it doesn't work out the same way yours does."

Alec nodded. "That's right too. Every once in a while you see a guy like Johnny and you think he's just coasting along, rigging or loading or tending hook, getting no place in particular. Next thing you know he's a camp foreman. And likely he's a superintendent a few years later."

Johnny laughed. "Maybe that's the way it looks to you," he said.

"You know you would have had Ted's job if Chris had still been around," Julie told him.

Johnny shrugged his shoulders. "I figure a man will get some place in the end, if he's good enough."

"You've got to advertise," Alec said. "Talk yourself up every chance you get."

"Most everybody says that." Davey got up and walked across the room to fill his glass. "But you don't even go by it yourself, Alec—look what you said just now about quiet guys getting ahead just when you think they're in some little job for life. And one thing everybody says about you is you don't play up to the big boys enough."

"Sure, and look where it got me." Alec pulled out a pack of cigarettes and passed it to Julie. "Old Stevens, the first engineer I ever worked for, used to say: 'Son, if you want to get ahead you got to remember to give the big boys lots of chance to know what the score is and look wise.' He wasn't so far out."

Davey said: "I still think a guy can get ahead just being good. It builds up for him without him knowing it. The other kind get ahead too, but they don't always last."

"Just being ambitious isn't much good," Alec said. "It doesn't get any special job done."

"That's more like the way you used to talk. You used to say a couple of hundred a month and an interesting job is all any man needs."

"I still think that's about right."

"You used to say it was worthwhile working hard to be famous," Julie said. "Like great painters and musicians and statesmen. But not just to make money."

"Sure, that's worthwhile," Johnny said. "If you are a genius like that it helps people long after you are dead and they remember you."

"What about religion?" Davey asked. "And getting a reward in the next world and all that?"

"It's all right if you believe in it," Alec said.

"It helps a lot of people. It makes a big difference to Mother and even to Dad, but especially to Mother. You see that often; almost any woman up the coast is religious when you really get to know her."

"Do you believe in it, Julie?"

"Sure I do. I'm going to be a Catholic, like Johnny is."

Alec set his glass down hard on the table. "Well, for the love of Pete, would you listen to that. 'Like Johnny is.' And here's me known the guy for ten years and never found it out."

Johnny looked across at Julie and smiled. "They say you can't ever change. If you start out that way you finish up that way. I guess that's right."

Alec shook his head slowly. "What about you, Davey? You holding something out on us too?"

"Nothing you wouldn't expect," Davey said. "I guess I'm still a Christian. I keep a Bible on the boat and I read it a whole lot; I like reading it. But I haven't been to a church service in a coon's age."

"Do you believe in the soul and life after death and all that?"

"I guess so. I don't think about it so much, but I kind of feel it often. A guy isn't put here just so he can go to nothing; he sees too much and gets to know too much to have it all go to waste."

"When do you mostly feel it?" Alec asked. Julie saw he wasn't kidding any more; he was talking the way he did when he was trying to work out how to log a piece of timber or planning a hunt or a fishing trip, leaning forward in his chair, watching Davey, speaking almost sharply. "Feeling like that is important. There's got to be something back of it."

Davey thought carefully before answering. "It's mostly when I'm alone on the boat," he said slowly. "It wouldn't be so much in the middle of the day. In the early morning or towards sunset. You know how it gets up there on the trolling grounds sometimes, very calm except for the big swells, and voices coming clear across the water from 'way off, so far that you can't even see the boats when it's nearly dark. And the sky all light on one side of you, mauve and violet and all kinds of colors, and dark the other way. That's one time."

"Yes," Alec said. "When else?"

"At daybreak sometimes, but not when I'm fishing. Just when I'm going some place alone in the boat. I think it's mostly when I'm out of sight of land, but it happened last time I went up the Sound, right in between the mountains there. And it comes when it's blowing hard and I'm kind of scared. You know how you can get to thinking in a little boat when she's real dirty in some place like Hecate Strait. You're inside there and you can see the spray blow off the white caps and they come following after you and left up the whole boat and then go on past so you can see the backs of them all streaked with foam. All of a sudden you think: This is only a crazy little wooden tub and just one of those over the engine would douse it for good and all. Or I could forget for a minute and let her get broadside on instead of quartering. I could even do it on purpose, just move my hand a little on the wheel, not more than enough to pass a plate to somebody, it's that easy." Davey looked up and Alec saw that his hands were shaking and there was sweat on his forehead. "You feel it then," he said. "Because you could do that so darn easy and you don't do it."

They were all watching him. Alec said at last: "That

Timber

was swell, Davey. Go get another drink; you've sure earned it."

Davey got up slowly and walked across the room. "Heck," he said. "I didn't mean to say all that. You've no right to get a man started that way, Alec."

"It was swell," Alec said. "I haven't ever heard any body say it better."

Davey came back to his seat on the bed. "You make everybody talk and don't say anything yourself. What do you believe in?"

"How do you mean?"

"Well, do you believe in people having souls and being immortal and all the rest of it?"

"Sure I believe everybody's immortal, right here in this world."

"How do you mean?" Julie asked. "Spirits and ghosts and things?"

"No," Alec said. "It's much simpler than that, Johnny said something just now about painters and musicians—geniuses or whatever you call them, how what they do goes on helping after they are dead. It's the same with everything anybody does. Everything you do is immortal or so near it as makes no difference. It goes on and on and on and never stops. But everybody's so used to it they don't notice it."

"I can't see that," Johnny said. "You make a thing and somebody uses it and that's the end of it."

"No," Alec said. "That's not right. Take simple things. You load a log. Because you've put it up there it has to be hauled away and dumped off and towed to a sawmill and cut into boards. And that's just the beginning. One board, say it's a piece of shiplap with a knot in it, goes back to the prairie and gets built into a farmhouse somewhere. A kid sleeps in the room and looks at the knot every night. That maybe makes a difference to that kid some way and he can pass it on to this person or that person so that it would still be around long after you were dead. That's one way. Another way you can say because you loaded the log somebody else didn't have to do it. And that person did something else and that made a difference to somebody else and so on pretty nearly right around the world. Or you could say that because you loaded a whole lot of logs a whole lot of farmhouses were built on the prairies. And all the children that were raised in those houses would pass something of it on to their kids and they would pass it on to theirs long after the houses had rotted away."

"There might be something in that," Johnny said. "But if I hadn't loaded the logs somebody else would have."

"That doesn't matter. The point is you did load them. And if you hadn't been loading logs you would have been doing something else that acted just the same way. And that's only a simple thing. Take when Davey catches a big spring salmon some place; that's a simple thing, too, but there's no end to it. That fish was going to spawn somewhere. Because Davey caught her she doesn't. Maybe another fish will spawn right where she would have—but there's a difference right there; it's another fish. It's going to mean that different fish will be in different places and maybe doing slightly different things for years. And that's going to make a difference to other kinds of fish and small stuff in the water and to fishermen as well. By itself it isn't much, nobody notices it maybe, but it's there."

"It still doesn't seem very important."

"Who said it was? It doesn't need to be. But then you take your whole life, or Davey's whole life, all the things you've ever done, all making their little differences, some of them maybe not so little, and I think you've got something—likely just as much as the man who paints a fine picture that's looked at and remembered for hundreds of years. Take what Davey said here tonight. You heard it; Julie heard it; I heard it. It's made a difference to each of us. I know it has to Julie because I was watching her. Some way or other part of it will get to little Alec and it will make a difference maybe to hundreds of things he does in his life. And those things will make their differences."

Davey said: "It's a hell of a big idea, Alec, but it's not immortality. Even if the differences we made went on clear to the end of the world, that still wouldn't be immortality; because that would be the end of them right there."

"You might be right," Alec said. "But it's as close as I can come. And it's close enough."

Nobody said anything for a little while. Then Johnny said: "When did you first think of that, Alec?"

"After young Charlie was killed. When I first heard of that I thought: There's the end of that guy. But I saw the log that hit him, sitting on a car at the Y two or three days after. They must have missed loading it before somehow. There was blood on the end of it and I thought of how the blood would go on through the grain and they'd cut the log into lumber and Charlie's blood would get to be part of somebody's house. And if that didn't mean anything, maybe a guy in a sawmill somewhere or a carpenter or a plumber would see it and it would make him mad. And if that didn't make any difference either then there was everything else Charlie had ever said or done going on and on and something of it would stick somewhere."

22

IT was a hot day, late in June. Standing on the load, Johnny watched Alec go down with the back tongs. He passed over the log, sliding the tongs away from him so that they dropped neatly and accurately into place. The leverman loosed his quick jolt of steam to tighten on them, but they tore loose and flew up, swinging wildly on the end of the clattering cable. Alec turned back, swearing. "For God's sake, take her easy, Bob," he said to the leverman. "You know those goddamned icehooks won't bite into a powder puff."

The leverman shrugged his shoulders and let the tongs back down to him. Alec set them on the log again and held them until the line was tight. He moved back a little and signaled to go ahead. The leverman lifted and the log came up a few inches, then the tongs tore out again, flying up to hook over one of the guy lines. The leverman shook them loose, steadied them, let them down again. Johnny watched Alec's face, red with the heat of the day and his own fury. "Don't mind it, Alec," he said. "It's not your fault. Just take your own time."

Alec took the tongs and set them on again, catching one point in a crevice of bark and bringing the other well round the curve of the log to give it full chance to bite through the bark and into the sapwood. The leverman lifted gently at first, then swung the log up over the load and dropped it into place on the peak. Alec climbed up, kicked the tongs loose, then pulled his heavy gloves off and threw them down into the shade of one of the runners of the old loading donkey. "Well," he said. "I guess that's her, and a lousy bitch she's been."

"We haven't done so badly," Johnny said. "Four loads average about twelve logs apiece, and it's a long way from noon yet."

"Could have doubled it with halfway decent rigging, and not worked so hard. What do we do now? Holler for more cars?"

"I guess so. We won't get them, but it'll use up some of Mac's steam and make him good and mad." He jumped down from the load to the brow log and went over to the yarder. Alec followed slowly, pulling tobacco and cigarette papers from his hip pocket, and ducked into the shade near where he had thrown his gloves. The leverman was already there. "I'm sorry I yelled like that, Bob," Alec said. "But those tongs are enough to drive a man crazy."

"That's okay. I know how it feels out there."

Johnny came back and sat down with them. "What's the matter?" Alec asked. "Won't he blow for them?"

Johnny laughed. "No. He says, 'ye can use up yere own damned steam. Ye havena any be'er use for it.'"

"The old bastard knows damn well our whistle's busted," Bob said.

"Sure he does. He'll blow when he gets good and ready."

Alec said: "Everything around this goddamned outfit

Timber

is busted or on the ragged edge of busted. Every time you go to splice a piece of cable the end drops off into jaggers; the mainline breaks every second day, every car has got a couple of flat wheels and the locie's held together with old tobacco cans. But I wouldn't give a damn if we had a set of good tongs. Putting them on half a dozen times for every log you load gets me down."

"That last log was a bad one for size," Bob said. "Even good tongs might have come loose once anyway."

Johnny shook his head. "It isn't good enough, trying to work with gear like that. That's the way a man gets hurt, sooner or later, trying to make up time around a joint like this where you put in more hours patching rigging than you do moving logs. I kind of figured to go into the blacksmith's shop some time and make us good tongs. How's to strike for me, Alec?"

"Any time you say."

"Hell," Bob said. "Is there anything around a camp you can't do? First week you come here you rigged that cold-deck spar and last month they put you tending hook up there when old Rain-in-the-face walked off the job. Slim here says you got papers to run donkey too."

"I wouldn't want anybody should stack me up alongside a real blacksmith," Johnny said. "But I know how tongs ought to look and that's more than this guy seems to."

"If Vern Sparkhill ever gets wise to himself he's liable to set you to running this outfit."

"Johnny's the guy could do it," Alec said.

Johnny took the cigarette out of his mouth and spat. "I know better ways to walk into the crazy house than that. Nobody could run this bunch of junk out of the red."

Alec looked at him quickly. "You aren't figuring to quit, are you? At least it's a railroad outfit and they've got steam donkeys."

"One tired locie and a few miles of track. That's right though, it could be worse—remember, we figured it would be trucks and gas donkeys when we came up here. Just the same, I'm going to pull out before winter—before Christmas anyway. It isn't right to ask a woman to live in a tent through the wet weather, not when she's got a small kid."

"Why don't you put up a shack?" Bob said. "You quit here and I'll never get another head loader that knows the difference between a shackle and an eyesplice, leave alone one that knows his own mind about how he wants a load built."

Johnny shook his head. "I've laid out all the money I want in shiplap walls and a floor for that tent. A guy's got to be nuts to build with an outfit that's going flat on its arse inside a year."

"You might be right at that." Bob got up slowly. "Guess I'd better go blarney old Mac into blowing them whistles."

Johnny watched him go. "You hear anything from that guy in the mail last night?" he asked Alec.

"Yes. They can use me to cruise spruce in the Queen Charlottes about September. He says all their summer crews are out already but he'll let me know if anything comes up."

"What'll you do? Stick it out here till September?"

Timber

"I guess so. Maybe longer than that. The Queen Charlotte job won't amount to much—six or eight weeks at the outside, but if I do a good job there they might give me something else; if it wasn't for that I'd as soon not take it at all."

"You've got to take it," Johnny said. "Unless something else comes up before then. You've no right sticking around a job like this, not with your education. You know damn well you could have got something else in town if you'd kept trying."

"Not the way I wanted it. Not around a decent logging operation, where you can see something come out of what you are doing. That's the trouble with all that cruising and survey work—it's too damn far from producing."

"Just the same, that's more what you ought to be doing. You'll go crazy loading in a haywire show like this all summer."

"I know it," Alec said. He thought: If it weren't for having to be away from you and Julie I'd have quit the first week—hell, I'd never have come up here at all. We'll never get another set-up like we had at Camp Four. "I kind of like working around the machines though," he said. "I always did. Remember when we were loading at Mellit Bay? That was a swell lay-out."

"You were only a kid then and you could figure it was experience. You don't need experience now."

"I was thinking last night, one thing I hate about this job is never getting out in the woods any more. I never thought I'd get to feeling that way, but I sure do."

"Why don't you go, then? We've got a three- or four-day layoff coming soon as we're through with this tree—

they're going to check over the machines before moving. Sparkhill would let you go if you asked him; they aren't short-handed any more now."

Alec buried a cigarette-end in the dirt. "Boy!" he said. "That's a swell idea. Old Pete Marsh has got a cabin somewhere up the valley and I haven't seen him for years. How about you and Julie coming?"

"I'd sure like to, but there's no one Julie would leave young Alec with and I ought to do some more fixing up around the place. It's not fit to live in the way it is now."

The leverman came back and sat down with them. "Did he blow?" Johnny asked.

"Hell's fire, didn't you hear him? Three good long ones, more steam than Mac's given anybody in all the rest of his life put together. What good is it for a guy to be foxy enough to talk that Scotchman out of something if he's not going to get any credit for it?"

"That wasn't you," Alec said. "He only did it because he's sore at his fireman today."

"You had time enough to talk him out of a couple of good nickels," Johnny said. "What's he got on his mind this morning?"

"He's thinking about quitting. Says he heard from a guy he knows that works over on the Island that things is getting good again."

"Whereabouts on the Island does this guy work?"

"Alberni way somewhere—I forget the name of the outfit. He says wages are as good as in twenty-nine and she's not so darn highball as then either. He lives in Alberni and drives to work in an automobile every day."

"What does he do?"

"He's a leverman. Says they run two loading crews—two head loaders, two seconds, shift half an hour off and half an hour on right through the day."

"Must be yarding from a cold-deck pile," Johnny said. He rolled another cigarette and lit it. "Does Mac think he can get back on with a big outfit?"

"He's a good engineer when he's sober. Trouble is you can't ever tell when he's going to start on a drunk."

"Except it won't be more than a month or so away," Johnny said. "Every company on the coast must have a line on Mac by now."

"He figures they're going to need men real bad before long. Says there's a big war coming up over in Europe and they'll be buying lumber for God's sake."

"He might be right." Johnny got up. "When in hell are we going to get cars? I guess nobody around here heard about that war yet."

Alec picked up his gloves and got up with him. He felt good. Two or three days in the woods, and a few more months of this will look easy. It isn't a bad outfit in some ways; a man could stand the haywire if they didn't do such fool things, cheapskate things like leaving cars with flat wheels and not paying enough to get a blacksmith who can make tongs—and running in their lines the way they do, Sparkhill going out in the woods with a Jacob-staff compass and marking off a dozen stations at a time. In a month or six weeks I could put good lines through all the timber he owns and save him thousands of dollars getting it out, but he's too darned tight to pay a little extra for that. Same with rigging, as far as that goes; if he'd scrap some of the worst of it and get new stuff he would save the price in labor in a few months. Likely, though, he dragged his credit out as far as it would go the first year he was up here and has been running on a shoestring ever since.

They heard the rattle of wheels on the track below them and Bob said: "That'll be the boss coming back up. Must have gone into camp over the trail."

"Did he go up this morning?" Alec asked. "I never saw him."

"Must have been you weren't watching then. You can't miss that guy. Sure, he went up with the rigger."

The speeder stopped and Sparkhill came towards them along the loads. "They'll be up with cars right away," he told Johnny. "That farmer on the boom donkey knocked two off the track when they were dumping. How come you took so long to get loaded? We figured you'd be sounding off for cars pretty near an hour before you did."

"We weren't more than plain lucky to be loaded then," Johnny said. He pointed to where the tongs were hanging above the last load. "Any time you get to ten and twelve log loads with those goddamned meat hooks you'd better be some sort of a fancy lawyer to talk 'em into grabbing hold."

Sparkhill cocked his head on one side and squinted up at the tongs against the sun. He was a heavy man, bigjawed and with a thick neck that swarmed up from the throat of his shirt to reduce the thrust of the jaw to little more than a double chin. He wore a small battered hat set somehow on a round head and over an untidy mass of graying hair. Still looking at the tongs, he reached up to his hat, lifted it and set it down again so that it covered a different area of hair. "What's the matter with them?" he said at last.

"Nothing," Johnny said. "Except they won't grab on to a log."

Alec laughed and kicked a piece of loose bark. Sparkhill's big neck seemed to swell and his jaw came forward. "How much longer will you guys be at this tree?" he asked.

"Couple of days, I guess," Johnny said. He watched the yarder engineer set down a turn and the chaser go out to free the chokers. "Hey, Mac," he shouted. "How much longer at this one?"

The little leather-faced Scotsman leaned down from the machine, cocking a deaf ear forward with his left hand while he held the other hand still on the throttle. "What's that?"

"How much more we got at this tree? Two, three days?"

Mac turned and looked along the skid road towards where the chokermen were waiting, nodded acceptance of the chaser's signal that the chokers were free, then looked back towards Johnny again, holding up three fingers.

"Hell," Sparkhill said. "I guess that's out, then. I figured I might have you go up and rig the next tree, Holt, but we've got to put logs in the water all we can this week."

"What's the matter with the rigger?" Johnny asked.

"Son of a bitch walked out on me this morning."

"You lost a good rigger then. That guy knew his stuff."

Watching Sparkhill, Alec knew that what Johnny had

said had annoyed him—not the way you'd expect either, he thought; it's not just that he's sore at losing a good man; what Johnny said gave him a kind of a jolt, as though he had something the same idea in the back of his own mind and there was some reason why it didn't sit so good. Maybe his backers have been riding him about losing too many men, but how in the hell do they expect him to hang on to them at the wages he's paying and on a show like this? I'll bet there isn't a man on the claim wouldn't quit if he thought he could get on anywhere else. Sparkhill said: "The train's down at the run-around now. I've got to get the speeder off the track."

He started down and Johnny turned back towards the loading donkey. "I didn't think that rigger would stick it long," he said. "He was too good for a lousy outfit like this."

"There aren't half a dozen riggers anywhere that knows logging the way Farne does," Bob said. "But he's kind of sour. Never stays long any place."

"Did you know him before?"

"Sure. Knew him when he was a punk—he was a hell of a live kid one time, too. But he dropped a tree he was raising and killed two guys and that kind of soured him. Notice the way he don't want to talk to anybody more than he has to? He's been like that ever since."

"He seemed civil enough," Johnny said. "Just kind of gloomy."

"Sure. He wouldn't bother anybody—liked to keep to himself, that's all. Just the same it isn't like him to walk off a job. He'll move on out of any place in pretty short order, but generally he waits for the end of a month or the end of a week or some time like that. Him and Sparkhill must have had some kind of a run-in."

They were loaded again by midafternoon, working in smaller logs where the faulty design of the tongs did not matter so much. Alec wiped the dust of powdered bark from his sweating face. "Boy," he said. "That felt almost like logging. We were going real good there for a while."

"Looks like we got through in good time to help the yarding crew change roads," Johnny said. They went out a little way along the old road and found the hooktender. "You guys sure know how to time it," he said. "We're all set to start logging again."

"Go to it," Johnny told him. "If they get around to bringing more cars before dark we're liable to break some kind of a record today."

The hooker spat black snuff juice at a stump. "That's one for the book, records around this joint. Just the same, we'll have you guys humping next week, when we get moved to the next tree. You been up there?"

"No."

"There's some real stuff there. Big logs. Most of it number one fir. If Vern don't make money out of that, he never will make any."

Alec was looking down the slope towards the river. They had logged right up to the near bank and he could see it, clear and fresh and tumbled, below the standing timber on the far side. Hell, he thought, I've been getting house-bound or job-bound or something, not to go out long before this. I haven't been fishing more than three or four times since we've been up here and never more than a mile from camp. There's no God's reason why I couldn't have gone up the valley long ago—any other time I came to a new place I would have done it. A man's bound to get feeling low, just going out from a bunkhouse to the job every day, then back to the bunkhouse again at night. Julie told me last week I haven't got any ambition any more and I guess I know now what she meant. I wonder if it was her that put Johnny on to telling me to go out over the layoff?

The idea pleased him so that he smiled and the hooker said: "Well, for God's sake, if Slim here don't look happy. That's the first time since I been here I seen you smile as if you meant it."

"It must have been I was thinking of how we got through too late to help you guys," Alec said. They went back to the machine and found the leverman sitting in the shade. "I could of told you they was all through," he said comfortably. "Locie's down at the run-around with more cars. You better sit down and get a smoke while you've still got the chance."

"What did you find out about Farne?" Alec asked him.

"Hell, I don't know. They say him and Sparkhill was chewing the fat for a while first thing this morning. Then Farne put on his spurs and went up the tree, but he come right back down again. And then they chewed the fat some more and Farne walked off. Sparkhill must have said something to make him sore. The way he is I guess that might not be hard to do."

"Did he quit camp already?" Johnny asked.

"Packed his stuff and hiked right on down to the wharf.

Some guy he knew had a gas-boat tied up there and they pulled right out."

"Maybe that was it," Alec said. "He knew he could get a free ride, so he figured it was a good time to quit."

The leverman shook his head. "Be a son of a bitch if I know. I guess it just ain't no use to figure you got a guy doped out. I never seen that guy get sore, not even so he'd talk loud. And I must have seen him pull out of half a dozen different camps, but I never noticed him in any tearing hurry to get to town."

"I didn't know the guy," Johnny said. "So it's no use me figuring." He stood up as he heard the locomotive slowing to couple to the loads. "Looks like you ought to get away Friday morning, Alec. That'll give you three days and you can still be on the job Monday morning."

"That's what I'm planning on. I ought to be able to make it clear up to the divide and back again by that time."

The leverman climbed slowly on to the donkey, still talking. "Only way I can figure it," he was saying, "Sparkhill must have canned him. But he said the guy walked off." He shook his head slowly and went to look at the steam-gauge.

23

ALEC swung the pack on to his shoulders, picked up his light pole ax and started down for the crossing log that spanned the river just below camp. It was still early, but the Chinese cook had made him breakfast and started him on his way with a hundred little attentions that sought to return Alec's own past services—a letter written, Alec remembered, a good word spoken for Chiang Kai-shek and, once, a gift of fish. That's one thing about a Chinaman, if he once makes up his mind you're okay he can't do enough for you. I like Chinks anyway, always have since I got to know Charlie Kung up at B. and A.

Across the river he was at once in standing timber, and within a few minutes the trail had curved out of sight of the camp. His feet reached forward over the soft, dry ground and he felt his shoulders thrusting into the broad pack-straps as he climbed a quick slope of the trail; quite consciously he shed from his mind all thought, for the time being all memory, of the small details of camp life and work. For three days, he told himself, it's nothing at all to do with me, it can't touch me or bother me any way at all. From this moment there isn't a soul alive who knows exactly where I am or where I'm going. I don't have to stay on this trail, I don't have to stop in to see

Pete if I don't want, I don't even have to get back to camp Sunday night. I don't have to keep walking—I can stop any place I want and make a camp—and I don't have to think about a darn thing except what's right in front of my eyes.

He watched the toes of his boots against the worn surface of the trail, step after step reaching out in a freedom of movement that had seemed lost. It's a good trail, he thought, but it was wider and better one time. I'm lucky not to be walking the track; most times a logging road will follow pretty close to an old trail, close enough to wipe out all sign of it anyway. That's what should have happened this time—the country comes naturally to a mainline on this side of the river, not over where Sparkhill put his. But I guess he couldn't get hold of this timber; looks like a good show, too; some dandy cedar here on the flat and a heavy stand of fir for a good way up the sidehill—you can see that from where we're working.

He began to notice plants of red clover and the small white flowers of Dutch clover along the sides of the trail. Packhorses, he told himself; must have been quite a bit of traffic along here one time. I wish Johnny were here; I'd tell him that and he'd ask, "How in hell do you know?" And I'd show him the clover and he'd say: "Maybe there was one horse up here once, or a cow," and I'd say: "Not with a plant every few feet along the trail and all kinds of timothy as well as the clover." I'm glad he's not here though; it would be swell to have him along, but that would make it a different sort of trip altogether. I want to be by myself for some reason. Seeing Pete will be more than enough company for three days.

The trail had climbed away from the river and he could see the railroad across on the far side, passing on from among the burnt stumps of the previous years' logging into the baked and bleaching slash of the new season. The stripped spar trees stood at regular intervals, tall and graceful even without their tops, the lines of the skid roads leading in to them from every side. He saw the two donkeys, Mac's yarder and Bob's loading unit, black and distant under the rigging of the tree they had finished up yesterday. It wasn't a bad one, he thought; those two long gullies came down to it nicely and the landing was okay—better than I could ever find up at B. and A., but that was a whole lot different country from this. This is a set-up, here in the flat, while she lasts; if he only had some gear and a few guys who knew their stuff, there isn't a goddamned reason why that Sparkhill shouldn't make money. He saw the new tree, already topped and partly rigged, the little gas donkey they used for rigging up nestling close at the base of it. The new rigger got away to a good start, he thought; he must have done most of that yesterday. Wonder if Bob's still worrying about whether Farne quit or got canned? Seems like he'll never get tired trying to make up his mind about that.

He paused out of sight of the last signs of logging and there was heavy timber close all about him. The trail dropped back near the river again, following it closely so that he could see the pools and the broken runs of fast water between them, and the timber thinned out a little into cedar and alder and spruce, but he could still see the good fir climbing away above him on the slope. He wondered about the river. Probably it would be a bad time now, this far up anyway, but there were good cutthroat trout down at the mouth and they would run up at certain seasons—probably a man could find a few big fish even now, left behind in the best pools. They would come up again in a few months' time, following the salmon. No sockeyes in this stream—there isn't a lake on it anywhere except away up at the head, on the North Fork. But the humpbacks will run and cohoes and dog salmon; probably they can't get up past the Canyon, but even so that would make good trout fishing in this part, especially in the spring when the young fish are coming up out of the gravel.

He came to a place where a small stream came down off the sidehill, dropping over a dwarf fall of limestone rock thirty or forty feet from where it joined the river. He dropped his pack and stood looking at the little fall; it was cool and fresh in the sunlight that came in between the tall white trunks of the alders and the sound of it pleased him. It's going to be a hot day, he thought; no sense to killing myself when I'm going to get rid of half this pack up at Pete's. After that I'd like to get going, really hike until I feel as if I can't move one leg ahead of the other. That ought not to be so hard right now either. Four or five months of lying around town, then loading, using different muscles in all that short stepping and jumping; I ought to feel a bit of real traveling pretty quick.

He sat down with his back against a big alder, but stood up again almost at once and went down to the river. He squatted by the edge of the water and began turning over the rocks, searching for caddis grubs and mayfly nymphs and the other small insects of a troutstream. It surprised him to find stonefly crawlers still there and he began to search with a new interest, turning over rock after rock until he had found a dozen or more. He put one hand down in the water and held it there until the cold became uncomfortable. That'll be it, I guess, he told himself; cold enough to make them late. Yet this stream doesn't come off a glacier; it's clear as glass. That's something Pete will know, why they call it Yellow River. Can't be so awful far up to where Pete is from here. Bob said he reckoned he wasn't more than about ten or twelve miles up right from the salt chuck and I must have come close to six miles, judging by the way the railroad runs. I wonder how far up this trail holds out? Pete was always a hell of a guy for not giving a damn about trails; that trapline he had in the Wolverine valley just wandered along from set to set through the bush, with hardly even a blaze on a tree to tell them by.

He walked slowly up to his pack again, picked it up and slung it on to his shoulders. He wanted to stop and look at the little fall in the creek, but found the habit of conserving strength was too well rooted in him. It was wrong to stand still with a pack on your shoulders, letting its weight tire you while you advanced it not a step; but to set it down and hoist it up again would use at least as much energy as standing still for a few minutes under its weight. He laughed softly, recognizing the absurdity of a habit that denied him what he wanted, but he went on, happy in the powerful lift and thrust of thighs and legs that carried his own weight and that of the pack against the short, steep grade that climbed away from the creek.

Timber

After following the same bank for another two or three miles the trail cut down to the stream again and crossed on a log jam. Alec looked at the place, judging its possibilities as a site for a trestle, but the sun was hot out on the peeled and whitened logs of the jam and he went on to the far bank. It was flat and low, only a few feet above the river, and the bed of the trail was on fine gray gravel. On either side there was good timber, big firs and cedars and spruces, too well spaced for clean height, but smooth and impressive through the first forty or fifty feet of their trunks. Under the trees there was a thick growth of light-green moss on top of the gravel, making the whole place like a park rather than part of a coast forest. Deep-orange tiger lilies drooped far out over the trail and occasionally there was the strong scarlet of late-blooming columbine. It'd be a swell place to put a cabin and bring a girl to, Alec thought. Hell for flies in the evenings though, big mosquitoes coming up out of all that moss, and it floods in winter. There'll be another channel somewhere over by the sidehill and likely a big log jam farther upstream that backs up the water in freshet time.

The trail climbed a few feet above the level of the flat and he came suddenly upon the cabin. A little white dog began to bark at him, dancing angrily and nervously near the cabin, ready to run but determined to give warning. Pete came to the door and stood looking down the trail. Alec raised one hand and Pete answered him, then scolded the little dog into silence. The old devil hasn't recognized me, Alec thought. He said from a distance: "Hello, Pete."

Pete peered forward as Alec came up to him, then said

at last: "Well, for God's sake, if it ain't Slim Crawford. I thought sure it was one of them bulls."

Alec slipped off the pack and held out his hand. "What's on your conscience now?"

"Nothing much that wouldn't stand looking at. Bulls is okay, but I'm sure glad it's you and not them. Where did you come from today?"

"The Beach."

"Did you eat yet?"

"The Chinaman gave me breakfast at Sparkhill's camp." Alec pointed to the pack. "I brought in some of your stuff that was down there."

Pete lifted the pack. "You shouldn't have done that; it made a pretty big load. But I'm sure glad you did. I've been figuring for a couple of weeks I'd ought to make a trip out for that stuff." He turned into the cabin. "I'll make something to eat. How about a batch of hotcakes?"

"No," Alec said. "I'm okay till along about noon. Then I'll eat with you."

"There's a pot of coffee on the stove."

"That would go good."

Pete brought out the coffee and two cups and they sat down in the sunlight outside the cabin.

"What are you doing in these parts?" Pete asked. "Looking at timber?"

"No, working for Sparkhill."

"The hell. You own a slice of that outfit?"

"No, just work there."

"Doing what?"

"Second-loading."

"Come again," Pete said. "I don't kid that easy."

"No, that's right," Alec said. Answering Pete's questioning, he told the outline of the story.

"You and Johnny and Eric," Pete said at last. "They sure cleaned the old place out. I might have known them ideas of yours would get you in trouble some day."

"Why?" Alec asked. "What's the matter with them?"

"Nothing, except you're kind of mean with them—mean and tough. That don't go with a guy in your position. You've got to be diplomatic. That way you can do some good. Kind of helping from outside."

"Stringing along with the company, you mean?"

Pete nodded. "That's right. That's what makes the wheels go round for the boys, takes the hard feelings out of it."

"You've got to have hard feelings to make a start against the kind of opposition we run into. They don't listen to any soft stuff and the boys don't go for company unions."

"It's somewheres in between both them things. That's the way it has to be to start without a whole lot of grief."

"You could be right," Alec said. "The way we tried it didn't help any." He was silent a moment, thinking back over the way it had happened. "Some of the boys figured part of the trouble was the set-up we had looked too much like a company union. It's hard to say about that, but it wouldn't have happened the way it did if we'd had a better turnout that first meeting."

"You acted kind of simple, calling a meeting cold that way. You should have built up to it gradual with meetings on the quiet. Another thing, trying to mix up rigging men and train crews and fallers and bullcooks and flunkeys all at one time ain't so hot either. That's something else has got to come gradual."

"How do you figure that?"

"Hell, you know as well as I do there's two different sets of guys around any camp, one kind like Johnny and Eric and all the rest that work on the trains or around the rigging, and the other kind, pick-and-shovel guys, fallers and buckers, all the bohunks and foreigners. You can't mix sand and water, not and make it last, so you've got to get one bunch together first and then maybe bring the others in later. You could start with a rigging men's union and build up on that."

"AFL stuff," Alec said. "That don't go so good these days."

"You got to start somewhere and I figure that's right where it is. I always have figured that. But what in hell's it got to do with you, Slim? It ain't your line at all and never will be."

"I'm not so sure about that." Alec watched the break of the river over the rocks, and the heavy, close green of the timber on the opposite bank. "It's time somebody helped the boys get things started. This country's twenty years behind every place else that way—loggers are, anyhow—and if a guy's got some sort of brains he ought to use them to help."

Pete shook his head. "You ain't got the right kind for it," he said. "Or maybe you got too much of other kinds. You just don't think right for it, and you got too many other things to think about. You can help, sure, and you oughter help—the way I said, from the outside."

Alec felt a surge of resentment in him; he's trying to

say I belong with the bosses, not with working guys at all, and that working guys won't trust me. But Pete went on: "You can do what most other guys can't even make a pass at doing. You can size up a piece of country and dope out the way it ought to log just as easy as dumping a canoe. You can figure out where railroads ought to go in and shape up the whole organization of an outfit just about perfect right from the start. That means making work for other guys and the right kind of work, that gets results. You haven't got no right to quit that. Maybe some other guy has got just what it takes to dope out a good union; then you'd say he ain't got no right not to work at it. It's the same for one as it is for the other."

"Everybody's got a responsibility for getting unions working right."

"And everybody's got a responsibility to help out with producing stuff the best way he can."

Alec laughed. "Hell, Pete," he said. "I never knew you thought so hard about things."

"When a guy's by himself eleven months out of the year he gets plenty of time for thinking. You know something else? You oughter get married sometime soon. A man's only half a man without a woman."

"What about yourself?"

"Look at me," Pete said, spreading his hands wide apart. "Pretty near sixty now and just an old woods bum. I was a darn good hooker one time—you know that. If there had been a woman around to keep me minding my business I could of been running camp long ago instead of up here keeping company with the bears and cougars. I tell you, up till he's around thirty a man's got ambition to coast on. After that he needs a woman to keep him at it—and kids too, don't ever forget that."

"You're happy enough," Alec said. "You like the bush and you're your own boss up here the way darn few men ever are. If you had a woman you'd just be driving day after day, getting no place in particular."

"It's different with me from how it is with you. I never did have no brains nor education. Just the same I don't figure to go on being a bum all my life, not even at my age." He looked sharply at Alec. "I got something up this valley, something pretty damned good I reckon. And when she comes in I'm going to advertise and get me a widow-woman for a housekeeper—you seen them advertisements in the paper, the ones that always ends up 'object matrimony'?"

"So that's who it is writes them." Alec put his head back against the logs of the cabin and laughed contentedly. "It could be a swell racket. Soon as you get tired of the first one, another advertisement, another good-looking widow, a little more housekeeping, then change over again. I'll bet that's as close as you'd ever let yourself come to matrimony."

"No," Pete said seriously. "I mean it. Soon as I get her made that's what I'm going to do. And I won't be so godawful hard to please. A good straight woman with a little sense in her head is all I'll ask for."

"What is it you've got up here?"

"I'd want to show it to you," Pete said. "If you like the look of it you're welcome to take on some yourself."

"Copper?"

Pete shook his head. "The hell with that stuff. Silver

and lead. You know that trail you come in on? Some guys had a mine up here, about two thousand feet up on the hill from this cabin and four or five miles up the river. It never amounted to nothing beyond a good showing here and there. They tunneled in a dozen or more places, but never could find any body of the stuff."

"You found something out of that?"

Pete nodded. "I hit the lead again higher up. In plain sight it was and I've followed it out for a thousand feet or more, right on the surface."

"Anybody seen it?"

"One guy from C. M. S. was up this spring, but there was too much snow around for him to see it right. I look for him to come back next month sometime."

"Well," Alec said. "I sure hope she comes out good for you."

"How's to come up there with me tomorrow and look her over?"

Alec shook his head. "Not this time. But I'd sure like to later on—likely there'll be a shut-down in a few weeks, soon as she begins to get real dry."

"What's on your mind this trip?"

"Nothing much," Alec said. "I just wanted to see what sort of country there was in back of me. How far does this trail go on?"

"She begins to angle up from the river not more'n half a mile from here and just runs in to the old mine. I've got a trap trail clear up to the lake at the head of the North Fork and another one pretty near to the divide on the South Fork. They ain't any hell though."

"You never were much of a trail blazer. Could a man

make it up to the lake, cut across to the South Fork and get out down to the Beach by Sunday night?"

"When's that?"

"Night after tomorrow."

"You might. I don't know as any ordinary sane guy would want to try it."

"Where does the South Fork come back in?"

"Not more'n a few hundred feet above where you crossed that log jam. It's just out of sight from there and you don't notice it from this side the river."

"Why do they call it Yellow River?" Alec asked.

"I don't know," Pete said. "She sure looks clear enough, don't she? I guess there must have been a slide come down somewhere to make her muddy when the first guy seen it."

After eating at noon Alec went on. Pete had been surprised, almost hurt that he would not stay longer, but Alec had found a determination in himself beyond anything he ordinarily knew. Most times I'd have stayed with the old devil, he thought, just for being asked twice. I like Pete and there's plenty to talk with him. There's no reason I should keep on going just to make the trip through the valley and along the divide, but if I didn't do it I'd sure feel lousy when I got back to camp. I don't know why that is either, except that I owe it to myself somehow to do what I figured on doing. And I want to really travel, keep going till I'm played right out, then knock off and sleep the night and start right out again next morning. I want to see that country too, for some reason, get it all clear in my mind like I used to have most of the country at B. and A.

He walked fast under the lightened pack and felt the mild sweat break out on him, a different sweating from that of the quick uneven movement on the landing. His hands were hot, but he could set them inside his shirt and feel his chest cool and on the soft undersides of his forearms and feel those cool too. His body was loose and free, moving well, and Pete's trail was easy to follow, with little brush and few windfalls to impede or break his stride. He let his mind think as it would, easily and lazily of the things immediately about him. He felt a sense of speed and power from the light breeze of his passage against his face and the flow of the ground under his feet. There was satisfaction in this and he drove himself faster, searching stronger satisfaction.

It was nearly dark when he stopped, by the side of the little stream that flowed in at the upper end of the lake. He opened his pack and set to making camp without a moment's pause to look about him. His movements were simple, efficient, automatic from long use. He was very hungry and cooked himself a great mess of beans and bacon and a full pot of coffee, then ate and drank until he was completely satisfied. He cleaned up a little, made more coffee and brought a pint flask of rum from the packsack. As he smoked after the meal he drank two more cups of coffee, well laced with the rum, then rolled into his single blanket and slept.

He woke soon after sunrise the next morning and made breakfast quickly. The mood of the night before was still on him and as he ate he studied the country, searching out the way that would lead him across to the South Fork. Above the lake the valley had narrowed sharply and the timber was sparse and stunted on steep rocky hillsides. Even with the sun gradually flooding one side of it, it was a gaunt place, hard with the erosions of extreme weather. From his camp Alec could see nothing beyond the steep northward-facing slope and he knew that he would be able to judge little of the day ahead until he had climbed it. He felt an eagerness to know that made him hurry in cleaning up his camp and starting out again.

Less than a mile farther along the stream he found a deep-cut gully that seemed to run clear to the rim of the valley, and turned up into it without hesitation. He had to pick his way over broken rock against a steep slope, but he drove into the work with the same hard energy that had maintained his steady, swift striding through the whole of the previous afternoon and evening. He reached the head of the gully without resting or looking back and found himself at the foot of a twenty-five-foot bluff. He stood still, searching along it carefully until he found a break that promised some chance of ascent, then sat down and rolled a cigarette.

He had expected to be high enough to see out over some grand sweep of country, perhaps across ridges of mountains towards the north, perhaps clear down to the Gulf of Georgia and across to Vancouver Island in the west. But the turns of the gully and the narrow valley below still hemmed him in and the steepness and closeness of the opposite face revealed only a single snow peak above it. It's better that way, he told himself; I didn't come up here to see far away any more than I came up along the river to fish. It isn't that kind of a trip, somehow. I shall see out, later on today, but there won't be time to really look and it's not important. I didn't look properly at the lake where I camped last night, yet it's clear and sharp in my mind, the little swamp at the head and beyond that the still smooth water with the queer light on it, all through the straight slim trunks of the little trees. I could have looked hard at it for an hour and not seen it better or remembered it more clearly.

He crushed his cigarette out against a rock and stood up. The break in the face of the bluff looked less promising, but it was the only one and he went up to it and started to climb. Ten minutes later he was at the top, looking down over a long easy slope towards the base of the peaks that headed the valley. Beyond them he could see clearly a distant gap that must be the line of the South Fork. He started towards it without resting, traveling fast over the bare rock slope.

Once he was away from that first slope the going was constantly bad—across slides, under the faces of towering bluffs, across uneven, rockstrewn, sloping ground that reflected back the heat of a white and brilliant sun. But the Gulf of Georgia was blue far over on his right, Vancouver Island hazy beyond it, and to the left of him the close peaks were hard and massive, mounting blackly into patched snow. He sweated and worked with the single purpose of getting across the country, and while his hands gripped and his legs strained his mind was vigorously active, shutting him closely in upon himself with a ceaseless pattern of probing thought.

There came back to him, again and again during the day, a clear picture of Julie—Julie cool and fresh and desirable, Julie in a print dress moving about the tent where she and Johnny lived, Julie holding her son, Julie laughing, Julie talking; but always a Julie that a man's arms would reach out for and in whose body and mind was promise of everything a man could need. I'm just crazy in love with her, he told himself, that's all. You do that, when you're hot and straining and thirsty like I am now, think of some girl and of being with her where it's cool and easy and comfortable. Yet there's something different about this; I'm not thinking of her the way I've thought of other women at times like this. I think of her with Johnny and Johnny with her, both together as though they were the same thing; and I feel jealous of both of them, not each one separately, but both together.

He worked slowly along a narrow ledge of rock, facing in towards the bluff above him, watching his hands as they groped for holds. I've got something there, he thought; I haven't figured anything out that clear in six months. I'm not in love with Julie. I'm crazy fond of her and I'm crazy fond of Johnny and I'm crazy fond of the two of them together. I want to be with them and watch them all the time, I'm jealous of them, not of either one of them separately but of what they've got together. That's why I had to come up and work for this goddamned Sparkhill outfit, that's why I was half praying all the time in town that I wouldn't get a job some place where they couldn't be. When you see it like that it's plain foolishness, but it jibes with what Pete was saying about a guy getting married. That's what I'm looking at— two people married the way people ought to be married and that's what I want for myself. Not Julie, but to be properly married the way they are so that it isn't just a word people use but something as solid as this goddamned rock in front of me.

He came to the end of the ledge and dropped down on to the start of a broad rockslide that poured from a thousand feet or more above him. The trouble is you don't hit Julies every day of the goddamned week. There's no reason you should find another one like that in a lifetime of looking. And what the hell chance have I got? All the women I know are numbers like Rita and Dolly—they're good kids all right, but they haven't got a damned thing you'd want outside of a few fancy ways in bed. Just the same, Pete's right, a man's got to get married to amount to anything; and it's got to be to some woman who's solid and real or he's worse off than single.

Thinking that way straightens up the other stuff. Hanging on to Johnny and Julie is no good to them or me; I've been doing it because I'm too damned yellow to stand on my own two feet and make for myself what they've got. And I don't have to hang on to anybody—I'm good in my way as Johnny is in his. The thing that scares me is having to go back and crawl around those Vancouver offices, getting put off by guys like Bill Chambers and Roy Peasley; but why in hell not take it and go some place else when they freeze up like that. It's a cinch it can't be a tight thing with every outfit on the coast sewed up from now till kingdom come. Sooner or later one of them's going to have a piece of country to figure out and nobody to figure it out right.

And when you do get back in there you can go after the thing from a different angle. There's no need to string along with the bosses. A union is a legal thing; what's illegal is a company trying to put it down. So a guy ought to be able to go at it quietly and give the boys a hand the way they need it most. What Pete said is right there again; different guys are fit for different things. Take Glieverson for instance; that guy really knows the score on unions in ways I never will. He doesn't give a damn for anything except the union—that's his job, what he's trained for and what he gets paid for. He's set to take grief and he's got backing when grief comes.

He looked up at the sun. It was afternoon already, but he was walking a series of gently sloping benches that topped a line of high bluffs, and the deep cut of the valley was plain and sharp, not more than three or four miles ahead of him now. He could feel the strain of the day through his body, but it was not a tiredness that would slow him down or affect him in any way for several hours yet. He had not stopped to eat in the middle of the day, but he gladly let his hunger build up in him. The sensation of it fitted his mood closely and seemed to free his mind to more and more vivid thought.

The picture of Julie was clear again, very clear and suddenly safe to him, without shame. It was of a disembodied Julie, a Julie that was not Julie, only a woman having the shape and stamp, the whole quality of Julie. And though the picture was always clear and vivid so that he felt he had seen the woman beyond ever forgetting her, he could find nothing in it for his mind to grasp upon— no detail of face or figure or color that he could name to himself or recall at will. Only when he checked all effort from his thought was the picture there.

The country grew more and more savagely broken

across the line of his journey. He crossed a succession of deep gullies and came into bluffs again, broken ragged bluffs that would sort themselves into no reasonable pattern of benches and walls. He held to the line of his chosen point on the wall of the South Fork valley and fought the rock with hands and feet and every last muscle of his body. The ceaseless, draining effort released his mind to the recurring pictures of his desire and he felt nothing of his body's struggle until he stood at last at his chosen point on the wall of a deep canyon and looked down at a white thread below him that he knew was the South Fork. The whole of the canyon was already in shadow, and looking away from it he saw the sun, huge and red, far down towards the Gulf. He felt softness under foot and found that he was standing on a heavy blue-green mat of juniper; he stepped back from it, ashamed to have crushed it under his caulks, and looked down at his bleeding hands. He tried to wipe them clean on his sweat-soaked shirt, and stared again as the fresh blood started up on them. His body was still hot and loose and he started at once down into the valley, working now with mind and body solidly set to the task of getting down to the stream and making his camp before dark. God, he thought, I must have been crazy to come across country like that; I'm scared half to death of going down this place now and it's like somebody's backyard compared to what I've traveled over in the last couple of hours. There wasn't any real sense in doing it either. I could have angled the slope all the way, following down the ridges and picking easy places to cross the draws, and hit the fork three or four miles farther down. That's kid stuff, doing a thing like that, except it makes you think things straight. Or does it? Hell, I don't know. Doing a thing like that last bit is a whole lot like being with a woman—you do it with the whole of yourself so that there's nothing else anywhere except that one thing you're doing. And you think things that look swell to you at the time and likely enough don't seem so hot next day.

He had reached the stream and followed it down to a good place to camp. He made camp quickly, boiled coffee and cooked his meal. As he ate it and drank the rum and coffee after it he found himself thinking calmly and easily of Julie and Johnny. It was still as clear to him as it had been that morning, clear and logical and completely satisfying. He knew now that he would go away from them, if only for a short while, but that he could go or stay as he chose, without fear.

He had broken camp and started out long before the sun broke over the wall of the Canyon next day. Before noon he reached the crossing on the log jam below Pete Marsh's cabin, but he kept on down the main trail, walking smoothly and fast, feeling the full reawakening of exultant pride in the strength of his own movement that had lain unused within him through the last months.

I am myself, he thought, Alec Crawford, and I know my own job the way damned few men know it. I can get any son of a bitch of a thing I want to go after and from now on I'm going after things. One more week with this cheapskate outfit so I won't be walking out on them, then I'll hit for town. God, he thought, I feel good. It's like coming out from six months of being dead. He looked at the cuts on his hands, touching them gently as he walked.

They belonged with some pleasure he had had, some intensity of thought he had felt was good. He began to search his mind for whatever it had been, struggling to bring it back, to pin it down and make it real for himself.

24

JULIE stood in the doorway of the tent, shading her eyes against the sun to watch for Johnny as the train slowed down in the center of camp. He rode outside, as he always had up at Camp Four, and usually he was the first off as the train stopped. She saw him now, coming up the narrow trail from the track and knew from his walk that the day had been a good one. When it's been a bad one he walks kind of slow and dragging, with his head down; but he's coming quickly now, the way he does when he wants to get supper over and have a long evening.

"Did you get finished moving?" she asked him.

"You bet," he said. "All set to start in tomorrow morning." He kissed her, then held her off from him. "You look swell, honey, right out of a fashion magazine. I don't know how you do it in a dump like this."

She slid her forearms to his shoulders and held his head hard between her hands. "You'd better notice it," she said and he saw her white teeth clenched tight together and felt the shiver through her body as she pulled his head down and kissed him again. "And keep on noticing, or I'll break you buying clothes to make you notice."

He slid his hands along her body to her hips and held them there. "You know easier ways. You haven't got a thing on under that dress."

"I have too," she said. "Go and wash up." She turned back to the stove and added: "The mail came in. There's a letter from Enid—from Yellowstone Park. Ron got a summer vacation after all and they're using it for the honeymoon they didn't have before."

"We never had a honeymoon." Johnny spoke between his hands, leaning over the wash basin and soaping his face. "Want to go to Yellowstone?"

"Sometime maybe. There's a letter from Mother too. She says if we're going to stay on here she's coming down to see the baby as soon as Dal and Muriel are settled in."

"You know the answer to that one better than I do," Johnny said. "Are we going to stay on?"

"Till fall anyway, I guess, if there's no shut-down. Supper's almost ready. Did Alec say he would come up?"

"Sure," Johnny reached for a towel, then walked over to the crib and stood looking down at little Alec. "How do you get him sleeping so much? Before we had him I thought kids were always yelling their heads off from morning to night."

"They sleep if you feed them right," she said. "He's tired now anyway; he spent all afternoon turning this place inside out. Why wouldn't Alec come last night? He must have known we wanted to hear about his trip."

"He said he had to write letters." Johnny walked back across the room and hung the towel on its rack. "That trip did him a whole lot of good. He's quitting the end of this week."

"He is?" Julie stood still in the middle of setting the table. After a little she said: "I'm glad for him. But it's going to seem funny without him."

"He's too good a man to be wasting his time loading logs. I hate to see him go, but I never did think he ought to have come up here in the first place."

"Maybe we'll all get together again in some other camp one day. I often think how swell it would be if Alec got married—except then I suppose she and I would quarrel or something and break it all up."

"You wouldn't."

"I'm not so sure," Julie said. "You see, I wouldn't figure just any girl was good enough for Alec. And if I didn't think he had the right one I might want to scratch her eyes out."

"I'd beat you if you did. Hard."

Julie laughed happily. "I wouldn't care," she said. "Here's Alec now." She went to the door and stood waiting for him as he came up the trail. "How's the woodsman?"

"Swell. I ought to have made you folks come along. That was a peach of a trip."

He came in and they sat down at the table. "Where did you go?" Julie asked.

"Up the river clear to the head of the North Fork, then across to the South Fork and straight down the valley back here."

"Wasn't it a hard trip, going across like that?"

"Yes, but it felt good because I didn't have to do it."

"You can't have stayed long at Pete's place," Johnny said.

"Two or three hours," Alec said. "He's still the same old Pete and I'd have liked to have stayed a week. But I wanted to make that trip right around the head of the valley and I knew I had to keep going or I wouldn't be back here Sunday night."

"What sort of a place has he got up there?"

"Good enough. A dandy cabin just above the fork of the river and what looks like a pretty fair line, for Pete. He's actually cut out a little along his trails."

"Bob says he thinks he's got a mine."

Alec nodded. "He might have something, from what he told me. It's good enough to have a C. M. S. man coming back to take another look."

"I'd sure like to see the old fellow strike something worthwhile," Johnny said. "You never saw him, did you, Julie?"

"Yes, I did. He went up our valley one summer when I was just a kid." She thought: This is really Alec tonight, the way he used to be. He's sort of right with things again and happy, not all muddled and gloomy the way he's been ever since we came up here. In a way that makes it not so bad he's going; if he was still like he was even a week ago I'd have been worried about him, afraid for him being lonely and lost away from Johnny; but when he's like he is now it seems silly ever to have thought that way at all.

Alec said: "I didn't get a good look at those tongs this afternoon. Did you make new ones already?"

"No. I just went down to the shop and worked over the old ones with Matt. The old guy's all right when you get to know him and he's a pretty good blacksmith too. Trouble was nobody ever showed him about tongs before."

"If you'd do that sort of thing more often," Julie said,

"instead of swearing and being unreasonable, you'd be a whole lot farther ahead."

"Johnny's not unreasonable. You ought to hear most guys when they have to buck bum rigging."

"There's something to what Julie says. We all get mad too soon—it's kind of a habit. I didn't think I was so bad as I used to be, but I guess I still get sore pretty easy."

"If you do your part of the job right it seems as though you ought to be able to expect the other guy to do the same."

"It works that way most times," Johnny said. "But it kind of opened my eyes to see what Matt can do when he's shown. And here we've been calling the poor guy everything that's no good for two or three months now."

"You made him come through at the right time anyway. If we had to start on that new tree with bad tongs we'd have a pile on the landing that we wouldn't see the bottom of in weeks. With good tongs we'll be okay as long as they keep the empties coming through."

"Sparkhill says he'll see we get cars. He wants to put everything he can in the water before the fire hazard is too bad."

Julie said: "Johnny says you're going down the end of this week."

"I kind of think I will. It looks like things ought to be opening up from now on, and if a man's down around there in the next month or so he ought to be able to pick up something good for when they start up again in the fall."

"Sure you will," Johnny said. "I still think you could have got something in the spring if you'd kept trying."

"It wasn't good enough," Alec said. "Hanging round those damned offices and being handed the same old line day after day." He thought: I'd like to tell them about meaning to look around for the right kind of woman somewhere, but you can't tell people things like that; it would just sound plain silly. Sitting here now I feel as if I could tell it and make it sound right, but I know it would sound like hell once I started. You couldn't tell them all that about thinking of them together up on the mountain and that's really the thing that makes it hang together. It even sounds crazy to try to tell them that you've changed pretty nearly everything you think just from having talked to an old fellow like Pete; it is crazy too when you come right down to it, because I've been set for some sort of change for quite a while; Pete just gave her a roll at the right time, got me thinking along that way when I had time to think.

He said: "If I do get on with a half decent outfit we'll have to get together again."

"What makes you think they'd let us?" Johnny asked. "If we've been blacklisted they'll still be keeping track of us and they'll make damn good and sure we don't get a chance to gang up again."

"There might be something in that, but if things open up the way it looks now they won't have to be too high-hat about taking on good men when they get the chance."

"Alec," Julie said, "what's going to happen about that blacklisting? I mean if things get bad again or if they don't open up the way you think? Is it just going to go on and on with people being let out of their jobs and not able to get anything else?"

"No," Alec said. "There'll be a union. It's bound to come in the end, and once you get a strong union they can't make blacklisting stick."

"I still kind of like the old way." Johnny pushed his chair back and began to roll a cigarette. "When a man quit or got fired and all he had to do was go to town and hire out somewhere else."

"There never was any old way like that, except in times when they were so short of labor they'd grab at anything. You could have been blacklisted years ago if they'd had any reason for wanting to do it. And you're lucky at that. If it hadn't been they know down at the Employment Office you're a good loader you wouldn't even have been able to get on with a gyppo outfit like this."

"I guess you're right. It's kind of hard to take though, that idea a guy's got to have something protecting him all the time." Julie began to pick up the dishes and he stood up, moving his chair out of the way. "What have we got to do then? Keep on sticking our necks out and hope one day there'll be a union come out of it?"

"No," Julie said. "I should say not. You never will get anything that way."

"Somebody's got to take a chance somewhere if we're ever going to get things started."

"Once is enough of that kind of chance. I'd like to see some sort of result from it before we went into all that grief again. And what use are you anyway, if you can't even get out to work in a camp?"

"Julie's right," Alec said. "You don't have to figure that any of what's done is wasted—it all counts up in the end. But it's about time we began to be a little smart. Pete was saying just about the same thing. What he figured was that maybe a few guys working quietly among themselves could get a start on a union for rigging men and train crews. Then things could spread from that."

"That sounds okay, if the rest of the bunch would ever come in on that kind of union."

"They would if it was handled right. And Pete says guys like you and me aren't the ones to handle it. He figures real organizers, professionals that know the job and get paid for it, ought to do most of the work."

"I don't go much on those guys," Johnny said. "Except Glieverson maybe. Half the time they're just playing the boys for suckers. They don't ever want to settle anything—they just want trouble all the time."

"That's the way we've always figured it, and there's a whole lot to it. But that's why guys like you have got to stay in the woods. We've always kept saying unions ought to be run by loggers, not from outside, and if all the good loggers get themselves fired and blacklisted there won't be anything but bohunks left to run the damn thing."

"What you mean then," Julie said, "is men like you and Johnny should keep on doing your jobs and just help out with a union when you get the chance?"

Alec nodded. "And as soon as the union looks like being something we ought to be in there and running it. I don't mean me and Johnny necessarily, but good guys, that aren't either scabs or soreheads. Another thing Pete said makes sense: if a guy's a square-shooter and he's up in some boss job he can maybe do more to help the boys by minding his own business and keeping in right with the company than he can by going off the deep end."

Julie clattered dishes angrily in the dishpan. "Sometimes you make me sick, Alec Crawford," she said. "Do you have to go way off in the woods and see some ignorant old trapper just to find that out?" She turned to Johnny. "You're just as bad. Look at the two of you. You're supposed to be kind of smart, better than the average dumb logger anyway, and you sit there, solemn and slow as a couple of owls, figuring out things any ordinary person would have seen months ago."

The two men looked at each other and Alec said: "It isn't so darn simple, Julie. Once the boys get to figuring a man's stringing along with the company what he says don't go down with them any more. You've got to watch that. Look at that last strike; the boys wouldn't have anything to do even with good guys like Ted. Just because Ted was a camp-push they'd try to make out he was the same as a boss logger. A camp-push is just a working plug, getting paid a wage same as anybody else, but they can't seem to see that."

"If it happens that way you've got to learn to take it," Julie said. "What they think about you doesn't matter so long as you know you're doing the best you can for them. I know I didn't have the sense to see it all that way when we were up at Camp Four. Marion Denton did though, and I can see now how right she was. Do you know what she said about you, Alec?"

"No, what was it?"

"She said you were a starry-eyed crusader and they ought not to let you in around married men at all."

Alec laughed. "I guess you weren't talking much to Marion about it when we were all in town," he said. "She's kind of changed her mind again since things broke up there at Camp Four. You want to remember she was a going concern in the 1934 strike, and she was talking like 1934 again last time I heard her."

"Just the same, I know what she meant. She said you're not practical—you don't use the things you've got the way they'll do you most good, and that's pretty nearly what you've just been saying yourself."

"Well, I'm learning then." Alec had gone over and was drying the dishes. "That's something, isn't it?"

"It's awful slow learning," she said. "For a man that's supposed to be so smart."

"Lay off him, Julie, and let's talk about something else," Johnny said. "Every time we start talking about unions one of us gets mad. It used to be Alec all the time and now it's you."

"I'm not mad, am I, Alec? That's just good sense, isn't it?"

"Most of it. We had to get a start somewhere and do our learning sometime. I'm quite ready to try a different angle from now on, something slow and steady and a bit more foxy maybe. And I think I'm going to hold it down so it doesn't interfere with the job." He walked across to the crib and stood looking down at young Alec. "How's chances to wake up young Baldy here?" he asked.

"He's got hair all over his head now," Julie said. "It's just fair, so you can't see it. No, he's going to sleep until it's time for his bottle. You can play with him then if you want to stay that late."

Standing beside Alec near the crib, Johnny said: "Tomorrow's going to be a tough one, with all those good logs lying there right at the start of a new setting. Maybe we ought to hit the hay kind of early tonight."

"I don't care," Julie said. "You still can't wake him."

Alec looked at Johnny and smiled. He bent down over the crib, lifted the sleeping baby and passed him into Johnny's arms. Then he turned quickly and barred Julie's way as she came across the tent towards them.

Johnny dropped down from the train and started along the track towards the new spar tree. As he came near the tree he looked up at the tongs hanging in readiness above the first car, their newly drawn points bright in the sunlight. He thought: It just naturally makes a man feel good, getting out on a halfway decent show for a change and having some rigging that looks like it might do a job for you. We've had it kind of soft here in some ways, waiting on cars, patching up haywire rigging, riding the dog one way or another a couple of hours out of every eight. But a guy gets sick of that awful quick; I like to get a start when the whistle blows and quit when she blows again, and keep going in between. Most guys do when you come right down to it; Alec likes to sit and smoke and talk—so do I as far as that goes—but even he gets fed up on it pretty darn quick. That's why he's quitting, I think, more than anything else. And that's why I'll be goddamned glad to get back on with a real outfit again.

Alec caught up with him as he stopped opposite the brow log. "That's a hell of a looking tree," he said. "It's a pity he couldn't take time to raise one when he comes to a lousy son of a bitch like that."

Johnny looked up at the tree against the bright light of the sky. "She doesn't look so hot. But I guess she'll stand anything the rigging will stand; that's still the same goddamned mainline we were breaking all the time at the other tree."

Alec laughed. "I guess there's something in that; it's no use crabbing at the smoke when the barn's burning down. Just the same, I'd have liked to have seen Ted's face if I had ever marked a tree like that for him up at Camp Five."

"Conky?" Johnny asked.

"I'd take a long bet on it," Alec said.

The whistle blew and they began to load at once. The first load went on smoothly and easily, six logs all of about the same size. The second load was exactly like it and they kept pace with the yarding crew until the bunk load was on the third car, slipping the tongs on to the logs almost as the chaser signaled and Mac pulled the chokers free. Alec was laughing and happy, riding out confidently with the tongs, flipping them over and down on to the logs in the easy certainty that they would bite and hold.

Johnny shook the front tongs from the peak log and saw that Alec was already on the load again, freeing the back tongs. They went down and freed the hand-brakes, then stood together at the side of the track as Bob spotted another car under the tongs.

"If they'll only keep cars coming," Alec said, "that rigging crew will never get the jump on us. We'll be able to keep the landing clear till they get back a bit."

Johnny smiled and shook his head, pointing back to a big log on the landing. "A few more babies like that one'll slow us up some. We're liable to have to put straps on it."

"Think so? I've got a notion these tongs'll take her."

"Maybe," Johnny said. "But if they do there'll still be something bigger a bit later on. We're doing swell, though."

They were loading again. Johnny picked his bunk load, four logs, a little smaller than the run had been so far. He thought: I'll put two on those and we ought to be able to make the big one for a peak log; it'll be okay if we can get the son of a bitch out of the way that easy. He watched Alec go out and down with the back tongs. It's swell to have things going right for once and see him getting a kick out of it. Not that it will last; something's bound to go haywire sooner or later and they'll start to catch up on us and we'll have a son of a bitch of a pile on the landing. If we're lucky it might be the rigging crew will get trouble first, but the chances are it will be us.

He went down with the front tongs, set them on the big log and signaled Bob to take it up easy. The tongs held and the front end of the log came up. Johnny was up on the last load to watch the big log into place as Alec went down with the back tongs. He heard the harsh rattle of the yarder as Mac opened the throttle to bring in another turn and looked up at the tree. He shouted at once, his voice quick and sharp: "Watch her." He was up on the balls of his feet, ready to move and he shouted again: "Go under the cars."

Out of the corner of his eye he had seen Mac and Bob and the firemen go down, but he still watched the tree.

Two great chunks broken off by the whip-back were sharp and clear, broken ends jagged against the sky for a moment, well out from the track, then falling. He tried to see Alec, could not and shouted to him: "Keep running, Alec, for God's sake." Then he saw the break below the buckle guys, so slow that tree and rigging seemed as though they would hang there for ever. He dropped to the brow log and threw himself down under a load. He heard the rattle of the falling guy lines and rigging, then felt the heavy jar as the big chunk hit the ground. Almost as it hit he was out again, standing on the brow log.

At first he could not see Alec, only the hooktender and chokermen coming in, running along the skid road, jumping from log to log. Then he saw him, fifty or sixty feet beyond where the big log hung slanting in the tongs. In a moment he was beside him, feeling over his body for life or injury. He could tell nothing, only see that he was unconscious and that one of the smaller chunks from the top of the tree was across his thighs, pinning him down. He tried to roll it off and could not, then he was running back towards the machine. He felt his heart fast and sick inside him and his eyes were blurred with furious tears so that everything about him seemed indistinct. "Bob," he shouted. "Where are you? Get back up there, for Christ's sake, and slack away on those tongs."

He knew that the last break in the tree had been above the loading guys and as he ran back he saw that the loading jacks were still up and clear in the tangle of rigging. The big log started down as he reached it, but he was on it in one jump, riding it down, kicking at the tongs to release them the moment the log touched ground and the line slacked. They came free easily and he held them. "Give me line," he told the leverman. "Plenty of it and fast." Then he went out in what seemed a single long glide, carrying the tongs high and all the sagging weight of line behind them. He reached Alec and set the tongs on the chunk, then signaled to Bob. The leverman lifted, gently, in one slow, even pull and the chunk swung away, it's free end levering against the ground. Johnny pushed a chokerman out of the way and went to Alec. The hooktender was kneeling beside him and looked up. "He's dead," he said.

Johnny looked at him with bitter, hostile eyes. "What in hell do you know about it?" he said and bent over Alec. He felt the limp body again, putting his hand under the shirt, feeling the heat of the body and the wetness of sweat, but no heartbeat. He felt for the pulse at wrist and temple and touched the still moist lips. Christ, he told himself, what's the use? You know it's true. But you can't see where he's hurt, where anything hit him. He looks so goddamned natural there, except his face is pale and his eyes are shut. His mouth is so red now with the blood gone from his face; it shouldn't be red like that if he's dead. And he looks so goddamned much like Julie, more than he ever did. Oh, Christ, forget it. He's dead, just as dead as though you could see his brains all smashed out over the ground and he was bleeding a hundred places. But he said: "He don't look to be hurt bad."

The hooker said gently: "He didn't feel nothing anyway."

"No," Johnny said bitterly. "Maybe that's something." Oh, Mary, Mother of God, he thought, if you could have left just a piece of life in him, just a small piece of all he had, it wouldn't have mattered how he suffered.

The hooker said again: "If a guy's got to go I guess that's the best way it could happen."

"For Christ's sake, shut up."

Then Mac started on the whistles, seven of them, long, slow and mournful in the sunlit air, sounding across the valley and down along the hills.

25

JOHNNY went up the path from the track to the tent, trying to walk easily, without betraying the heavy, dead sickness he felt through his whole body. Julie stood in the doorway of the tent, her face pale, and he saw Alec's dead face again.

"Who was it?" she said. "Not Alec?"

He nodded, glad that he need not say it, and went past her into the tent. "How bad?" she asked.

Nothing bad, just dead. He didn't know what hit him, it's a good way to go. How in hell do you say it? Just dead, dead for ever and ever. "We killed him," Johnny said.

Julie put out a hand to touch him, drew it back, and he saw that she was crying. She went over and sat down on the bed and in a little while she said: "Tell me about it."

He told her, slowly and carefully, in short sentences, and she listened, her eyes dry now, staring up at him. At the end he said: "He knew it was a bad tree. He said so first thing when we got out there this morning."

"Why did you work on it, then?"

"I don't know. Once a tree's rigged and ready to go you don't think about it much. And we aren't in much shape to do any hollering."

He sat down and began to roll a cigarette, watching the

movements of his hands. Across the room young Alec tried to pull himself up on the bars of the crib, failed and sat back hard on the mattress. Johnny put the cigarette in his mouth, went across the room and picked him up.

"It seems all the worse," Julie said. "Because he had things straightened out for himself and he wouldn't have been here in two or three more days. I know that's silly, but it does make it feel worse."

"I know that. That's all I've thought of since it happened."

"It wasn't your fault. You didn't want him to come up here in the first place."

"That wasn't because I thought he would get killed."

Julie got up. "Let's not talk about it any more now. I'll make something to eat."

It was hot in the tent during the afternoon and Johnny lay on the bed. He thought: It's kind of queer none of the boys comes up to talk about it. Maybe they don't like to because they figure Alec and me were kind of closer than most guys are; likely they think I'll get tough with them the way I did with that hooker this morning. The guy meant well and I guess I ought to have been easier with him; Jesus though, to hear him talk you'd have thought it might have been just anybody at all lying there, not Alec. With Alec dying there's so much dead, all at once, as dead as if it had never been alive at all; everything you knew about him, all the different things you've done with him and seen him do, everything he knew and the way he could tell you about it and make it all add up to something. Then there's the way people felt about him, people like me and Julie and Davey and

Mr. Morris, like the boys up at Camp Four, Ed and Stevie and Eric and the rest of them, like almost anybody who ever knew him better than just to say hello to. That dies slowly, in people's minds; but they won't be feeling good any more for something he's just said or the way his laugh sounds or the way he looks and moves. That's what makes it different, more than anything else; I guess it depends on how live a man is how much it means when he dies, and Alec was about the livest person anywhere around.

He felt his mind groping for something, something he had thought in the moments before he knew Alec was dead, and had lost immediately in the violent, confused pain of the next hours. I was sore then, sore enough to kill somebody even when I was going back to fetch the tongs and lift that chunk off him; and after I knew he was dead that all seemed plain silly and small, because being mad couldn't help Alec any. But that isn't the end of it; that goddamned tree never ought to have been rigged and that's a thing somebody should do something about.

From where she was sitting on the other side of the tent, Julie said: "Johnny, we aren't going to go on working here, are we?"

"No," he said. "I've been thinking that."

"How soon can we get away?"

"You can take the boat right out of here tomorrow morning. Get some place in town and I'll come on down as soon as we get finished here." He didn't want to say the word inquest; it didn't belong with Alec, all the slow, awkward misery of it and the dead smell and the group of people who would listen and not know that this was a different time from all the other times they had done the same thing.

"Where will it be?" Julie asked.

"Down at the settlement, I guess. There's a policeman there and some kind of magistrate."

"How long do you suppose we'll be in town?"

"Not long. I ought to be able to get something right away."

She looked at him. "Do you really think that?"

"No," he said. "It's just a chance; you can't tell. But I wouldn't work another day with this outfit." He swung his legs off the bed and stood up. "There was something phoney about that tree. More than just it was conky, I mean. I can't get it straight why I think so yet, but I do think it."

"Is that the first tree you've known to break?"

"No. We had a piece come off the top of one at Mellit Bay. Every once in a while you hear about one breaking somewhere. It isn't just the tree breaking so much as feeling they're trying to cover up something."

"You mean somebody knew ahead of time the tree wasn't right?"

"Maybe. I can't pin it right down. Sparkhill acted kind of funny when he came out there this morning."

"That isn't much to go by," Julie said. "And nothing is going to help Alec now. I'd like to see us go right away from here now and hire out somewhere else as soon as we get to town."

They heard the leverman's voice from the doorway of the tent: "Anybody home?"

Julie stood up quickly and Johnny said: "Sure. Come right on in and sit down, Bob."

Bob Filling was a thin, dark, stoop-shouldered man of about forty. Crossing the floor of the tent he held his large hands awkwardly in front of him, but his little dark eyes looked sharply about him with the quick, humorous cunning of a child from the back streets of a big city. Julie watched him as he sat down, and wondered why he had come. "I'll make a cup of tea," she said and turned away to fetch the pot.

Johnny pushed a tobacco can and cigarette papers across to him. "You've kind of fixed the place up since I was here last," Bob said.

"Some. Just in time to pull out and leave it."

"You going down? I thought maybe you would. Mac quit this morning too, soon as he got in."

"Anybody else?"

"Not that I heard of. Most of them's like me—got no place else to go if they did quit." Bob laughed.

Putting cups on the table, Julie asked: "Are you blacklisted too, Mr. Filling?"

Bob laughed again. "I'd be glad to know that for sure myself, Mrs. Holt, same as the rest of the boys. I was secretary to the union up at Gimlet in thirty-four and this is the first place I've worked since I got let out up there."

Johnny said: "I wouldn't stay on here even if I knew I couldn't get a job any place else."

They talked and Julie listened, cutting and buttering slices of bread. He came here for some special reason, she thought, something that's worrying him and he doesn't know how to say it. It must be something about Alec and

Timber

whatever it is it's going to make trouble. Johnny's so miserable he's savage. He's just looking for something or someone to get really mad at—that's all he was doing just now, wondering about Sparkhill. And if he ever finds what he's looking for anything is likely to happen. She heard Johnny say: "Has there been much talk in the bunkhouse?"

Bob Filling's bright little eyes seemed smaller and sharper than ever. "About what?" he asked.

"About that tree breaking."

"The boys have talked about it some. They always will when anything like that happens. I know Slim was a pretty close sidekick of yours and I seen you felt real bad about it this morning. That's why I come up."

Julie saw Johnny's strong hands clenched hard, very white against the brown of his forearms because his heavy rigging gloves kept them always shielded from the sun. "Okay," Johnny said quietly. "Go on. What do you know?"

Filling's eyes shifted awkwardly about the room. "I don't know nothing more than I told you already. Farne didn't quit. He got fired."

"You mean Sparkhill fired him because he wouldn't rig that tree?"

"Figure it out for yourself. I don't know a darn thing more than you do, and I ain't sticking my neck out any, not for no man. But I kind of liked young Slim and seeing he was your pal I figured you'd want to get wise to anything there might be in it."

"You know where Farne is now?"

"No. One guy on the rigging crew heard him say he

might go back East to see his folks sometime. Before he got fired, that was."

"How about the guy on the gas-boat that took him out of here?"

"He took him straight to town. Said he didn't speak more'n two words the whole way down there. That's like Farne all right."

"Know anything more?" Johnny was standing up, looking down at Filling.

Filling's eyes met Johnny's and held, calm and still for a moment. "Not another darn thing. That's the truth."

Julie saw the tightened skin of Johnny's hands slacken a little and heard his voice, suddenly easy and good-natured again. "Thanks, Bob. You're a good guy. I just had it figured for a minute you might be holding something out on me."

"I'd like to see you get it all straight," Bob said. "You won't, but it'd be fine with me if you could. I done my part quite a piece ago now and didn't get nowhere with it; but that don't mean I don't want to see it come through in the end."

Watching Filling as he went down the path towards the bunkhouses, Julie said: "What are you going to do, Johnny?"

"I don't know. If I could find that guy Farne I'd sure know what to do; but without him there isn't a darn thing to pin it on."

"Suppose you did find him. What good could you do?"

"We could make it look pretty bad for them at the inquest."

"How would that help? It couldn't bring Alec back

and it would make trouble for us so we never would get on anywhere else."

"It might save some other guy's life later on."

Julie shook her head. "I don't think that's how things happen. If they really did know the tree was a bad one this time, they rigged it because they were up against it some way and thought they had a good chance to get by. There will always be times when people figure like that."

Johnny looked at her. "That could be Alec talking," he said. "Saying what you don't expect him to and making it sound almost right. But it isn't right. It isn't right anyone should be able to kill a man just because of trying to save a few bucks."

Please God, Julie thought, please God, help me. He isn't angry; it's almost all right, if I can only say just a little more and say it the right way. He wants to be angry and it won't come and he's going to try and make it come. And if he does there won't be anything left for us—for him most of all. "I know," she said. "I know it isn't. Perhaps you have to find Farne and make it all come out in the open—if there is anything. But I want you to see it this way, honey, the way Alec tried to tell us the other night. You can help most by being a good logger; if you stop being a logger you've helped just once, for a little bit, and then you've stopped helping."

"I don't see you're helping any if you won't stand out for what you believe in."

"If you've got something. If you find Farne and know everything that happened. But otherwise—well, if you had been running camp here this wouldn't have happened. You can stop it from happening some place else, and maybe lots of other things like it. That's easy to see, isn't it?"

Johnny walked over to the door. "I'm going down to the office," he said. "If you're going to be ready for the boat tomorrow maybe you'd better start packing."

Julie stood still, her hands at her sides, the tears starting hot in her eyes. "Please, Johnny," she said. "Please."

He turned back. "Please what?" Then he looked at her. "What is it, honey? You don't have to cry." He came back to her, put his arm about her and held her close. "What is it?" he said again.

"I don't know," she said. "I'm so afraid for us. If another thing happens now it's going to be so hard for us to go on. We won't be us any more, not loggers, not anything."

"Nothing is going to happen, nothing we can't make stick anyway."

"Do you mean that? You're not going down there now to fight? You won't do anything without finding out properly first?"

"No," he said. "I'm getting different all the time. One day I'll even be smart maybe. Right now I wouldn't want to hurt anybody because I don't think I could stop short of killing them."

She looked up at him, frightened again, and saw he was smiling—not the grim, purposeful smile she had expected, but a smile turned in upon himself in some way, making him seem suddenly big and sure and solid beyond all the power she had learned to know and love in him before. "Darling," she said.

He bent down and kissed her. "I won't be gone long."

Walking down to the office he could feel the anger hot and strong in him again, readying his body and tensing his muscles. The sons of bitches, he thought, the dirty, penny-pinching, ignorant sons of bitches. And you can't pin it on them. You never can. If it was me that had got killed and Alec was here, he would know what to do. He'd work it all out and have it all plain and straight in no time at all. I can't do that; I'm just a damned bull and if I get sore I know I have to go in there and hit, and if I don't get sore I know I don't have to. But it's different this time. I'm sore, sure I am, sorer than I've ever been, but I don't know who I'm sore at. One minute I'd like to paste Sparkhill's goddamned face in till his head comes loose from his neck, and the next minute I know that won't help any; I'm not even sore at the guy that way, when you come right down to it I haven't got anything on him. Same with the new rigger. He says he didn't see anything wrong with the tree when he rigged it and you kind of believe the poor bastard, the way he says it. The only guy could really tell you would be Farne and that's what a man ought to do, get ahold of him and make him come through. That makes sense. What Julie says makes sense too. Knocking the daylights out of Sparkhill till he'll come through with what he knows makes sense too—if he knows anything. That's the way it is; too many things make sense. Always before it's been kind of easy, a man knows what to do and he goes straight and does it. But this time there's too many angles.

He walked up the office steps and pushed the door open. Sparkhill and the timekeeper were standing behind the counter, talking. "You can have her made out for tomorrow morning," Johnny said.

The timekeeper nodded and Sparkhill came over. "That was too bad, what happened this morning," he said. "We looked the tree over good when we picked it and couldn't see a thing wrong."

"Slim said it was a lousy tree soon as he saw it."

"He did? They say he was a hell of a good man. Been checking timber for B. and A. a good many years, hadn't he?" Sparkhill's voice was friendly.

"He knew his trees." Johnny watched Sparkhill, feeling the anger grow in him again. "Maybe you better get yourself a guy like that around here."

Sparkhill was still friendly. "You going straight through to town?"

"What's that to you?"

"I figured maybe you'd want to if it wasn't for the inquest. Likely we could fix it for you."

"You don't have to worry. I'll be there." Johnny's eyes were hard and narrow. He put his left hand forward to the counter. Sock him once, good and hard on the side of the jaw, and you'd be over there on top of him before he hit the ground. He's scared of that inquest, the son of a bitch. He knows something and you could spill it out of him like it was water, right here in front of the timekeeper.

Sparkhill shrugged his shoulders. "Suit yourself," he said. "It isn't necessary, but I guess you knew Crawford pretty well, so naturally you'd want to be there. I hadn't thought of it that way."

Johnny let his right fist unclench. He moved forward

a little and leaned his elbows on the counter, still watching Sparkhill. I never have hated the son of a bitch, he thought, and I don't hate him now. I still think he knows something, maybe I ought to have pasted him. Jesus, I don't know. He said sharply: "How come you canned Farne?"

"Farne?" Sparkhill was surprised. "The son of a bitch walked out on me. I couldn't talk him into staying on."

Jesus, Johnny thought, if I only knew for sure the bastard was lying. But maybe he isn't. You can't go and beat the can off a guy just because you think there's something phoney about him—not when you're married and got a kid and beginning to look ahead a bit. And if jumping him about Farne that way don't pull something out of him it's a cinch he's got a good alibi ready for anything else you want to ask.

"What did he quit for?" Johnny said.

Sparkhill shrugged his heavy shoulders again. "Don't ask me. They say that's the way he is."

"No, they don't. They say he quits when he's good and ready, not out on the job."

"Listen," Sparkhill said, "what are you getting at?"

"What I asked you. Why Farne went down the road."

"Go ahead and ask him. He's the only one that knows."

"Maybe I'll do that," Johnny said.

Going up the path towards the tent again, he thought: You soft fool, a guy like that can make a sucker out of you any time without half trying. If you can't sock somebody there isn't any goddamned sort of a thing you can do; you can't even talk big enough to run a bluff. There's something there: he wouldn't have been in such a hurry to check you out ahead of the inquest if there wasn't. Now you'll go look for Farne and if you find him he won't know anything; only you won't find him—Sparkhill's goddamn sure of that. Anyway, what good is it, any of it? Alec's dead and he's going to stay dead. That's what Julie says and she's right; and it isn't that she's soft either, or scared, or that she doesn't think Alec's as good as the rest of us think he is. It's her figuring, and if she does it it's straight figuring.

He looked up and saw that Julie was waiting in the doorway of the tent. She could be Alec standing there, he thought. And tonight, before she goes away, I'll talk it right out with her, just as if it was Alec. That way I'll know what I've got to do.

26

JULIE put young Alec down on the floor and watched him start off happily on rediscovery of the hotel room. It was a pleasant room, big and high-ceilinged, looking out through two wide windows. Johnny had told her to ask for it, a room on the same floor and the same side of the hotel as the one he and Alec had always taken when they came to town, but with a double bed instead of twin beds. The clerk at the desk had been friendly and glad to see her when she wrote her name and he had told her about the message that had been left for Johnny two or three weeks earlier. And they had been nice about the baby, finding a cot for him and wanting to warm his food; and several times the chambermaid had taken him away to some distant part of the hotel to look after him while Julie went out. They said he was a good baby because he didn't cry very often and they liked him because he looked like Johnny already.

He had found the wastebasket now and was happy with it, pulling out the paper lining and making it crackle in his fat hands. Julie said: "He's going to be here soon now and you've got to show him how pleased you are, baby. You're big enough to do that now." She got up and walked over in front of the long mirror, smoothing down her dress. It's wonderful to see yourself again, all of you at once instead of just a little bit at a time. And I look nice, much nicer than I thought. Even when I stood here with nothing on, the first night we got in, you couldn't tell I had had a baby; I'm all smooth again and flat and hard in the right places, not droopy or spread the least little bit. And now, with this dress and new shoes and good stockings, I look the way I want me to look. I think I look like a wife somehow, not just a girl any more, but the sort of wife somebody would keep on wanting hard. She saw her mouth in the mirror and smiled at it; like the sort of wife who would keep on wanting her husband hard too, she thought. That's the best thing there is, wanting him and having him want me. That's why it can't matter terribly what happens. But I don't want him to get into trouble; that could be bad trouble, either way. He could get so hard angry the way he does and hurt somebody, perhaps even kill somebody, or he could say things without enough reason for saying them and make bad trouble for himself that way. And if there's nothing he can do at all, nothing he can find except more talk like Bob Filling's, that might be almost as bad, because he will think he hasn't done what he should have for Alec. That's nearly worse than the other, it's the worst thing there is for us, making him feel badly about himself. That's why I want that message at the desk to really mean something, not to be just something we've missed because we weren't here in time. Two or three weeks, the man had said; that could mean it's too late already.

She went back across the room and sat down by the open window, listening to the noise of the city while little Alec tried to climb up to her lap. He should come soon, she thought, very soon now unless something has gone wrong. They could put him in jail if he did something very bad up there, like fighting right at the inquest or even outside it. But I don't really think he would, because he doesn't get mad that way, not blind stupid mad like some people do. He always knows what he means to do and does it the way he means to; being mad is something he uses the way he wants to, instead of letting it use him. He's so calm and easy-going most of the time you wouldn't ever think he could get mad the way he does, and I guess that's all part of it; because the getting mad grows out of being really calm and good-natured it's not mean or stupid.

Just the same, I'll be frightened till I see him because of the other thing, the way it can hurt him if he thinks he hasn't done enough. I know it isn't right to think that way, but Alec doesn't really matter any more. We're going to be sad because he's gone and we're going to be missing him almost without knowing it for years and years— Johnny will even more than I shall—but it doesn't really matter about him. It only matters about us, Johnny and me and little Alec. I know that's the truth, even if it is terrible to think it. And Alec would say it that way, straight out, in a cold-blooded way, making it sound worse on purpose.

She heard his footsteps through the open transom, coming along the passageway, and recognized them instantly in spite of the deadening carpet. She picked up little Alec, ran to the door and opened it. He looked up as the door opened and smiled at her, then smiled again at the baby and took him out of her arms: "Hello, youngster," he said. "How does it feel to be back in the big city?" He put his free arm about Julie's shoulders, guided her back into the room and shut the door. "God, Julie, I've missed you. I left the suitcase down below and told them we'd get it up later, because I wanted to see you quickly."

"I'm glad," Julie said. "Was it awful?"

"Kind of a long story. They got a whitewash verdict." He put the baby down on the cot, then went across the room and stood looking out the window.

"You didn't find Farne?"

He shook his head. "No, couldn't find a thing about him except the guy with the gas-boat thinks he headed east from Vancouver right away." He turned back into the room and sat down in a chair. "That's the first time since I was a kid I've ever felt really lonely. Gee, you look swell, honey. Come here."

She came across and he pulled her down to him. "I've missed you so much I want to hurt you," he said. "Where'd you get the dress?"

"At the old store. Marked down too. Like it?"

"It's the prettiest one you ever had, all fresh and cool-looking. What else have you done?"

"Not much. I saw Dolly and she took us out to her house. She's happy with Arthur—happier than I ever thought she'd be—but she cried hard about Alec. Most of the time little Alec and I just stayed here and wrote letters. Once we went out to the park. But we missed you too."

"I'm no good any more without you. I'm scared all the time. I think I did right up there, but I never was sure. I wanted you or Alec there to tell me."

"Talk about it now. There wasn't any trouble?"

She saw him frown and was afraid again. "No," he said slowly. "You never could tell about anything, whether people were lying or telling the truth, whether they were being just slow or really mean. Always before I've known, but this time I didn't. I felt sore at first, so I wanted to break the whole thing up. Then it didn't seem to matter so much. What mattered was saying everything I wanted to say and if they wouldn't let me do that I was going to break things up for fair."

"What did you say?"

"They asked me all the usual stuff about how it happened and then, when they said I could go, I told them the tree hadn't ever ought to have been rigged in the first place, and what Alec said. They took that all right, and I tried to tell about Farne and they didn't want to let me, but I said it anyway. And one guy asked if I thought the tree was no good why I started in to work at it. So I had to say I didn't think much about it when Alec said that, just that the tree didn't look so hot but likely it would get by. Then they let me go and called Bob up there."

"What did he say?"

"Not much, but more'n I thought he would. He said he didn't pay much attention to the tree, but he wouldn't anyway. Then a little dark guy on the jury asked him a whole lot of questions about Farne, and Bob said he didn't know much but he didn't figure Farne quit. And they said, why not? And Bob said it wasn't like him, and they all kind of laughed and let him go. That's the way it went all through, the little dark guy keeping asking questions and not getting anywhere with it."

"Didn't they want to know where Farne was?"

"The little guy kept asking that, but there wasn't anybody knew and they figured they'd leave it to the jury whether they wanted him found, seeing how hard it would be. The way they did it all there wasn't anything a guy could get sore at. It seemed fair and aboveboard as you could want so long as you were sure nobody was lying. And if anybody was lying it couldn't change the tree being no good and breaking and killing Alec; that was true and everybody knew it. That's what I meant when I said it didn't seem to matter so much once it was all going on."

"What else happened?"

"Well, at the end there Sparkhill got up and gave a talk about how more people would have been killed if I hadn't seen the tree break and called it right for them to get under the cars in time. I came closest to getting real sore when he was saying all that, but the way he said it put a guy in the wrong all the time so he couldn't get sore and not seem crazy. When he was through we all went out and had to wait pretty near three hours before they called us back in to hear the verdict. They said it was accidental, but from now on the management ought to make a more careful check on what trees they rigged. They said sometimes a conky tree could fool even a real expert man, so that there couldn't be any blame on anybody. Then on top of that they said that all juries on logging inquests ought to be made up of guys that know logging."

"What made them say that?"

"Seems the little dark guy made all the trouble that kept them so long, and he hadn't ever been around logging. He wanted to make them wait and get hold of

Farne. And they didn't like the way he kept asking questions. I was talking to him afterwards. Kind of a bullheaded little guy, bitter as hell. He had blue eyes that looked at you so hard you don't remember much else about him, and he said he figured the thing was phoney all through, but it was no use to buck it too hard because there wasn't anything you could really get your teeth in. But he said that was okay, we had done fine and it all added up in the long run. Seemed real interested in Alec. Said he had heard about him somewhere."

"I think you did fine," Julie said. "It was just the way he would have wanted you to do."

Johnny pushed her away a little and looked at her. "Is that the truth? You really mean you don't think Alec would have thought of something better if he had been there?"

Julie nodded. "I don't think he would even have done so much. He would have said there wasn't enough to go on, so it wasn't the time. I think you did a lot of good."

"I couldn't ever have felt good about it if it hadn't been for talking with the little dark guy," Johnny said. "But he seemed to have a lot the same ideas as Alec and he's more hardboiled with them than Alec ever was."

"Did they give you the message down at the desk?"

"About going up to the B. and A. office? Sure, but I guess it's too late now. They said Chris Eldridge left it, but that must be because they don't know he's quit."

"No," Julie said. "I asked them. He came in himself."

"He did? He must have got fixed up down south."

"You'll go up there, won't you? Right away."

"I hadn't figured to. I thought we'd try and hire out

at Alberni or Comox or some place where there's a road out of camp instead of like it is up there. It would be better for you and young Alec."

Julie shook her head. "I don't care. I like it up north. We were always happy there and if they want you back now it must be for something good. I don't think people can get ahead always changing."

"It might be all right, with Chris back. And maybe it still wouldn't be so easy to get on any place else—I don't know. Won't do any harm to go up there and see, anyway."

"Do that," she said. "And come right back. I'm going to be worrying."

The girl in the outer office remembered him and smiled her pretty, efficient smile. "Hello, Mr. Holt," she said. "Mr. Eldridge is going to be glad to see you. He's in right now."

Waiting, Johnny thought: She's still cute. I used to be kind of scared of her, but I'm not now; I guess that's because of Julie. She came back and showed him into Chris Eldridge's office. Chris came from behind the desk, his hand out.

"Glad to see you again, Johnny. You're sure a hard guy to chase up these days."

Johnny smiled slowly. Chris is all right, he thought; if you like a man, you like him, that's all. Just the same, I don't see why he should get by with that. "It isn't so long ago since I got the idea this outfit didn't give a damn if it never did find me again."

Chris laughed easily. "Sit down," he said. "That

wasn't between you and me. We've shaped things up a bit different around here since then."

"And now you're looking for a loader? Seems as though there ought to be more of them around than me."

"No. We're looking for more than that. But before we go any farther, is that right in the papers this morning? About Slim Crawford, I mean."

"I guess so. We killed him up there at Yellow River. Last Wednesday."

"Jesus, that's terrible. How did it happen? The paper said a tree broke."

Johnny told the bare outline of the story and Chris shook his head. "That kid was going places," he said. "Soon as he settled down. I've been trying to hunt him up for the last month, same as I have you. And I guess there's the same story back of his going up to Yellow River—figured he couldn't get on any place else."

"What is it you want me for?"

"I want you down at Camp Five first, running the skidder side. Things are in a bit of a jackpot up there and it needs a good side-push to straighten it out. And when you do get that sorted out we'll be shopping for a foreman at Camp Four. We aren't running there now, but we will be as soon as Camp Five is really logging. How about it?"

"I'm kind of changed," Johnny said. "I'm not the way I used to be."

"Because of Slim, you mean?"

"That's it mostly, I guess. The rest of it too, that trouble we had last year about the union. The way that was handled don't sit so good."

"Maybe you've got a right to be sore about all that. Somebody made some mighty big mistakes that time."

"Did anybody do anything about straightening them up? Where's Eric Denton working now? If he is working."

Chris laughed. "Eric's right back in the cab of the Two Spot. I got hold of him soon as I hit town again. They had been running two locomotives up there ever since he quit and even then the guy on the Climax had to let her get away on the grade above camp and dump herself and fifteen loads of logs into the lake. So Eric's back till things straighten up and I let Dad Hutchins quit on the mainline. Tom Davidson's back on the job too."

Johnny nodded. "That's what I meant." He hesitated, then went on. "If the rest of the old gang is satisfied to go back, I guess there's no reason for me to hold out. But I'd like to be damn good and sure they can't pull the same trick again—on me or anybody else."

"You mean you want to organize a union of some sort?"

"No." Johnny felt clear and sure of himself as he always did talking to Chris. "But I'd want to be darn good and sure nobody interfered with the boys trying to organize."

Chris nodded. "I know what you mean," he said. "It's not easy. But look; if you go up there, you go to get logs out. And if the logs are coming out you don't have to worry about me bothering you any."

"You mean you'd stand for them organizing a proper union? You won't expect me to try to break it up for you or stand back and let you people down here break it up?"

"Sure. Why not? It's got to come sooner or later. It's

come every place else long ago. I've thought often enough the whole thing would work out better with decent unions."

Johnny looked at him. "Hell, Chris. I never figured you out much of a liar. You mean that?"

"I mean I'll try it out. I'm general manager here now and there's only the stockholders to fire me. You run your camp the way she looks to you, and if you're getting the logs out I won't have any kick coming. If you're not getting them, chances are somebody bigger than me will kick soon enough."

Johnny thought of Chris Eldridge standing on the stern of the tug as it pulled out of the Cove after Charlie Davies was killed, and heard his voice as it had been then, challenging, almost threatening: "Twenty? Couldn't be pushing the boys any, could it?" He pulled out his tobacco pouch and papers. "Hell, Chris, I believe you mean that. I believe you were wise to this before I ever was."

Chris laughed. "I wouldn't say it's all new to me. But I wouldn't say I've done much about it except wait. That's all I'm going to do now. It's not my job to organize a union."

Johnny stood up. "I'll phone you in about an hour," he said.

"No hurry. Take your time. Think it all right through. Take till the end of next week if you want."

"No," Johnny said. "I'll know inside an hour."

Walking along Hastings, then up Granville towards the hotel, Johnny thought: That's what Alec said would happen. But he couldn't ever have known it would come that clear and straight. It isn't clear and straight really;

it's the way Chris says, a man will have to just wait for them, maybe help a little some way, but not much. Maybe he could do more working from the bottom right in there with them, but I don't think so, not my kind of guy. That little dark guy at the inquest, he's got what it takes; Alec had too in lots of ways, but I haven't. I know now what they need and what they ought to have and I can run a good camp; those two things ought to add up to something.

He climbed the stairs and walked along the passage towards the room. Julie was waiting for him. "Don't talk loud," she said. "He's sleeping. What happened?"

"It was Chris all right. He wants me to go side-push up at Camp Five and after that maybe running Camp Four."

"You told him you'd do it."

"No, I said I'd let him know."

Julie came out into the passage, closing the door behind her. "Listen, Johnny Holt," she said. "If you want to help men you'd better take your chance and run a camp. I love men, all different kinds of men; so did Alec and so do you for that matter. But playing around with something you're not fit for isn't going to help them. You get in there and run a decent camp where spar trees don't break and men don't get killed for no reason, or fired and blacklisted for no reason, and you'll be doing something big. You're made to be a logger and I married you for a logger and you're going to be one."

Johnny shook his head. "It wasn't any of that," he said. "I talked all that right out with Chris."

"What was it then?" She spoke softly, but her voice

was urgent, impatient, and she was trying to read his face in the dim light of the passage.

"It was going up there again, where Alec was so much. Won't it make you unhappy, remembering him there in so many places, doing so many things?"

Julie came close to him so that he saw her eyes shining and her head held very straight. "Darling," she said, "I want us to remember him."

GLOSSARY

BALDWIN. A straight-connected rod locomotive, generally large and used for fast hauling on the mainline, where the road-bed is good and grades are light.

BEACH. Headquarters camp, which is usually also the boom camp, where the logs are dumped from the trains into the salt water, is for this reason likely to be referred to as "the Beach."

BOOMSTICK. A log cut 60—80 feet long instead of the usual 32—40. Coupled by chains passed through holes bored at each end, these hold together rafts of logs to be towed to the mills.

BUCKER. A man who follows the fallers, cutting the trees they fell into log lengths.

BULLCOOK. This man sweeps out the bunkhouses, makes the beds, packs in wood and water and generally helps out around camp. From this a locomotive switching and straightening around cars is said to be "bullcooking."

BUNK. A heavy steel cross-piece set a few feet from either end of a skeleton car or flat car. The first layer of a load of logs rests or bunks directly on these.

BUNK LOAD. Bottom layer of a load of logs, logs resting directly on the steel bunks (above).

CATTY. A man who is catty is quick on his feet and good on the job. This is about the ultimate expression of admiration.

CAULKS, CAULKED SHOES. Short spikes of hard steel, set into hand-hammered, hemlock-tanned soles, give the logger his foothold on slippery or sloping logs. The logger is careful to keep his caulks in good shape and buys a new pair of boots, at about $16.50, every six months or so. Quitting the woods for good a logger is likely to talk about "hanging up his caulks" or "throwing his caulked boots in the stove."

CHASER. He unhooks the chokers from the logs when they have been hauled or yarded up to the track by the donkey engine.

CHEESE BLOCKS. Wedge-shaped, movable blocks of steel set up on the bunks of the cars to hold the logs in place.

Glossary

CHERRY-PICKER. A small donkey engine loaded on to a skeleton car or flat car and taken out along the track to pick up logs or loads dropped from cars on the way down to the Beach.

CHOKER. A short length of heavy cable coupled to the main cable (sky line or mainline) and having a hook attached at the free end. This hook is passed under the log and brought round to hook back on to its cable, thus making a running noose which is drawn tight by the mainline when the engineer starts to bring in the turn.

CHUCK or "salt chuck." Tidal water. The destination of all good logs.

CLIMAX. A powerful type of locomotive. The smaller sizes, 35 tons and up, are used for the same kind of work as the Shays. Engineers and loggers generally regard them with a good deal of affectionate admiration. Climbing a steep grade they are reputed to say: "I guess I can, I guess I can." Once over the hump this breaks into a triumphant: "I can, I can, I can." Every so often you will hear in a camp: "Remember the old 80-ton Climax down at the Lake? Every time Joe started her too sudden she'd pull a car in half."

COLD-DECK. Donkeys are often put out in the woods to haul logs to a pile within reach of another donkey or skidder at the track. This pile is the cold-deck—logs stacked to beat the expense of running in a switchback or spur line. Poker terms are almost as common as railroad terms in the woods.

CRUISER. A man who goes out in the woods to estimate the volume of timber standing on a given acreage. He does a good deal more than this and submits his work in the form of a map divided into 40-acre squares and showing the contours and general physical features of the country as well as the volume and type of timber. Loggers like to call cruisers "guesstimators," but good cruisers do very accurate work.

CRUMMY (see also "Gut Wagon" or "Mulligan Wagon"; all three are in common use). A box car or an old caboose converted to passenger carrying by the addition of a few wooden benches, and used to carry the men to and from work.

DUMP. A log dump, or "the dump," is commonly a trestle built out over water. Generally an apron of piles slopes down from it and the logs roll down this when they are dumped from the cars. There are several methods of dumping. Perhaps the most usual is the "parbuckle"—cheese blocks are knocked out on the water side, cables are passed under the loads and hooked to the cross-log at

Glossary 405

the brow of the apron. The boom donkey tightens on the cables and slides the whole load over and down.

ENGINEER. Used of any man who is running a steam-boiler—thus for yarding and loading and rigging levermen as well as for locomotive engineers. Also for any man who works on the survey crew, regardless of whether he is actually a civil engineer or merely a transit man or chain man.

EYESPLICE. In wire rope, as in hemp, an eye formed by bending the end of the rope back and splicing it into itself. Uses are manifold and fairly obvious.

FALLER. The man who cuts the trees down. Fallers work in sets of two, head and second fallers, with one or more buckers following them. Most fallers are contract or "bushel" workers—paid at a rate of so much per thousand board feet of timber felled.

FARMER. A green man or one who is slow or clumsy on the job is likely to be called a "farmer" or "hayseed."

FRICTION. A term used to denote braking power applied to donkey-engine drums as these are revolving to let out line. A free-running drum would spin and snarl the lines, so the speed of revolution must be controlled by the leverman.

GOAT or "rigging goat." Term applied to a small, general-purpose donkey engine, especially the one used by the "rigging up crew" to raise spar trees and rig them with the necessary guy lines and blocks.

GRADERS. Pick-and-shovel men who dig and blast out the railroad grades.

GUT WAGON. See "Crummy."

HAULBACK. A lighter line, coupled to the mainline which hauls the logs in from the woods, operated from a second drum on the donkey through an arrangement of blocks. Its function is to draw the mainline and chokers back out to the woods to pick up a fresh "turn" of logs.

HAYWIRE. An allusion to the farm practice of repairing machinery with the light wire used to bale hay and straw. Any piece of equipment not up to the peak of operation efficiency is haywire to a logger. (See "Farmer.")

HOOKTENDER or "hooker." Is in charge of the chokermen and the whole operation of hauling logs from the woods to the railroad track. He is sometimes called the "side-push," implying that he is sub-foreman in charge of the whole operation of one "side" of a multiple-operation camp.

LANDING. An area of ground directly around the base of a spar tree, where logs are piled to be loaded on cars.

LEVERMAN, LOADING. Operates the levers which control the loading tongs.

LEVERMAN, YARDING or SKIDDER. Operates the levers which control the yarding or skidding of logs from the woods to the track.

LOADER. Loads logs from the landing on to the cars. Normally a crew of one head and two second loaders, working to a close routine, keeps pace with the logs brought in by one yarding machine. When yarding from a cold-deck pile at the rate of forty to sixty loads a day two crews are used, each consisting of one head and one second loader. These alternate through the day, spelling each other off. Loggers generally regard loading as the most dangerous and physically exacting job in the woods.

LOCATION. This refers to the final location of a proposed railroad, as set by the engineer's or surveyor's stakes. (See "Preliminary Line.")

MAINLINE. Used, in its ordinary sense, of the important stretch of railroad connecting up with the Beach and fed by spur lines and subsidiary tracks. Also of the heavy cable which hauls the logs from the woods to the landing. (See also "Haulback," "Sky line.")

MULLIGAN WAGON. See "Crummy."

PILING. Logs used as piles—driven into the ground to form the support of a trestle or wharf.

PRELIMINARY LINE. A line run off by the engineers along the approximate location of a proposed railroad. From the data obtained in running this line the ultimate location of the railroad grade is decided.

PUSH. A word used for the camp foreman and occasionally for lesser foremen. (See "Hooktender.")

RAINTEST. A stiff, heavy material from which the Coast logger's winter coat and pants are usually made. To some extent, and for a limited time only, water-repellent. Some loggers use a dressing of parawax to increase this tendency.

RIGGER. "The rigger" is the high or head rigger or high climber, all terms for one and the same job. He has a crew consisting of a second rigger, several "extra riggers" and his engineer. He and

Glossary 407

his second rigger do the spectacular job of climbing and topping the spar trees and, in the case of a skidder, the back trees. What is a good deal more important, they are responsible for the proper rigging of a tree, its support with guy lines, the way the blocks are set and how the lines run out in the woods.

RIGGING MAN. This term is applied more or less indiscriminately to all loggers who work around the machines, distinguishing them from trainmen, fallers and buckers, graders and trackmen. A rigging man is quite likely to insist that only men of his particular calling are really entitled to the title "loggers"—that the others, including even the fallers and buckers, are not loggers at all.

RUN-AROUND. A length of passing track, switching back into the main track at each end. Usually long enough so that a whole train of loads or empties can be left standing on it while the main track is clear.

SETTING. The whole of the area logged from a single spar tree.

SHACKLE. A U-shaped piece of steel, closed by a threaded pin passing through holes at either end, one of which is also threaded. Used, for instance, to couple the eyesplice at the end of a cable back on to the cable itself, thus making a noose.

SHAY. A geared locomotive, slow but powerful and adapted to heavy hauling. Shays of about 70 tons are commonly used in hauling logs from the landing to the mainline. Occasionally, when grades are bad, larger Shays are used on the mainline itself.

SIDE ONE, TWO, etc. Most large logging camps run two or more sides—that is, two or more entirely separate operations, each on its own spur of track, having its own facilities for rigging trees, yarding logs and loading. The full operation of a two-side camp, including grading, track laying and maintenance, falling and bucking, rigging, yarding, loading, hauling calls for the employment of about 250 men with the cookhouse and camp staff.

SKELETON CAR. A railroad car made up of two sets of four wheels joined by a heavy timber across which the steel bunks are set to carry the logs. A car to serve the same purpose is made by simply setting bunks on the deck of a flat car, but the skeleton car is more common.

SKIDDER. A yarding machine with a tight sky line, and for this reason able to haul from greater distances than the ordinary yarder with its endless slack sky line. Really big skidders bring logs from distances up to 5,000 feet from the track, but these machines are only economical in operation under the most favorable conditions. The reach of a skidder of normal size is 1,200 feet on the square lead, 1,600 on the corners of the setting. (See "Sky line.")

Skid Road. Like many logging terms, this is a survival of horse- and bull-logging days, when roads were built with greased cross skids and the logs hauled directly over these by the teams. Now applied to the line along which logs are hauled to the track from any given setting of blocks and rigging. Thus a spar tree, looked down on from the air, is the hub of a complete wheel of skid road "spokes."

Sky Line. In the case of a skidder, a heavy cable stretched from the spar tree out to a "back tree" at the far edge of the setting. A wheeled "bicycle" or carriage runs along this, bringing the logs from the woods when drawn by the skidding line, carrying the chokers back out to the waiting chokermen when drawn by the "receding line," which corresponds to the "haulback" of the yarder. In the case of a yarder the sky line is the same as the mainline, going from the spar tree through a block attached to a tree stump at the back of the setting, and is itself coupled directly to the haulback line.

Spar Tree. This may be a standing tree, topped and rigged, or a tree brought in from elsewhere and raised for the purpose. A good spar tree is clean and sound, four feet or more in diameter at the butt and varying in height from 90 feet to 200 or more, depending on the lay of the country and the type of machine used. Most spar trees are about 120 feet high. The advantage of hauling through a block set high above ground this way is easily understood. There is always a lift on the forward end of the log, holding the nose from plowing into the ground, tending to slide it around or over stumps or other obstructions.

Spot Fire. Sparks and burning embers of a forest fire, caught by its up-draft and driven by the following wind, set small fires far ahead of the main fire. These are the fire fighter's main concern once he has a good fire trail built.

Spotting Line. A line used by the loading leverman to "spot" empty cars under the loading tongs. Cars may be let down-grade by slacking the friction on the spotting-line drum or hauled against grade by applying steam.

Glossary 409

SQUARE LEAD. This is the setting of blocks and rigging on which logs are hauled to the tree along a road directly at right angles to the track. "Diamond lead" is the haul from the corners of the "setting."

STRAW LINE. The lightest size of steel cable commonly used in the woods. Also called "tenas" from the chinook word meaning "little." It is dragged out by riggers, passed through blocks and brought back to the drums of the donkey. Then the heavier cable is attached, the straw line wound on to the drum and the heavy cable thus drawn into place.

SURVEY CREW. Used by loggers alternatively with "engineers" for the crew that works with the civil engineer, laying out railroad, surveying logged areas, future camp sites and other such necessities.

TIMBER. Being the title of this book, the word should have its definition. "Timber!" is the traditional warning cry of fallers from coast to coast. Without the exclamation point the statement is somewhat calmer, but rather more comprehensive. Timber is the logger's word for standing trees, the untouched resource. Finally it is the word of the sawmill men for their most spectacular product—the great squared "timbers" cut for bridge and other construction purposes. I believe a Washington mill once squared out a Douglas fir timber 6 feet by 6 feet and 175 feet long.

TONGS. The tongs used for loading are scissors type, much like iceman's tongs but a good deal larger. Ordinary loading tongs weigh about 75 lbs. per pair, but for big timber larger ones, up to 125 lbs., are used. With the weight of the cable this makes a formidable drag on the loader, who has to work fast and surely. But his own dexterity, with the assistance of a good leverman handling the drums, can do much to reduce it.

TRACKMEN. Applied to the steel men, who lay ties and steel, and the track-maintenance gangs. Like the graders in British Columbia, these are often northern Italians.

TURN. Another bull-logging term that has survived. Originally used to mean a single trip and return made by one team hauling logs. So, one trip of the chokers hauling logs to the landing and their return to the woods. Now generally used to refer simply to the drag of logs coming in in the chokers.

TWO SPOT, etc. Logging-camp locomotives are numbered and each usually carries its number in large figures on the front of the boiler and the side of the cab. They are nearly always referred to by these numbers, much as a ship is referred to by name. "Remember the old Two Spot at Camp Four?" "Boy, do I!"

WHISTLEPUNK or "signalman." Goes out with the chokermen and relays the hooktender's shouted signals by electric whistle to the donkey. The job is usually given to boys starting in the woods—given a quick-tempered hooker, some of them end right there too—but sometimes to loggers too old or too crippled to do other work.

Y. A fork in a railroad track. In a two-side camp "the Y" will be the junction of the two spur lines.

YARDER. The donkey engine that hauls logs from the woods to the track. A yarder may be a single-purpose donkey or it may be a "duplex" machine, having loading drums as well as mainline and haulback drums fed their steam from the same boiler. In comparison with a skidder, a yarder operates at greatest efficiency up to six or eight hundred feet from the track on the square lead, up to one thousand or so on the diamond lead. Provided railroading difficulties are not great and the terrain is suitable, yarders (or high lead machines, as they are often called) are probably still the most efficient and economical means of logging.